A MIKE CONNOL

ELECTRIC
Beach

A NOVEL BY

JOE HILLEY

RIVEROAK®

Good News in Fiction

COOK COMMUNICATIONS MINISTRIES
Colorado Springs, Colorado • Paris, Ontario
KINGSWAY COMMUNICATIONS LTD
Eastbourne, England

RiverOak® is an imprint of
Cook Communications Ministries, Colorado Springs, CO 80918
Cook Communications, Paris, Ontario
Kingsway Communications, Eastbourne, England

ELECTRIC BEACH
© 2006 by Joe Hilley

This story is a work of fiction. All characters and events are the prod-
uct of the author's imagination. Any resemblance to any person, living
or dead, is coincidental.

The Web site addresses recommended throughout this book are offered
as a resource to you. These Web sites are not intended in any way to
be or imply an endorsement on the part of Cook Communications
Ministries, nor do we vouch for their content.

Cover Design: Two Moore Designs/Ray Moore
Cover Photo: Photospin

First Printing, 2006
Printed in the United States of America

3 4 5 6 7 8 9 10 11 Printing/Year 11 10 09 08 07 06

Library of Congress Cataloging-in-Publication Data

Hilley, Joseph H.
Electric beach / Joe Hilley.
p. cm.
ISBN-13: 978-1-58919-075-7
ISBN-10: 1-58919-075-0
  1. Connolly, Mike (Fictitious character)--Fiction. 2. Trials (Murder)--
Fiction. I. Title.

PS3608.I439E44 2006
813'.6--dc22

2005033523

For Raisa

I've been locked up way too long
In this crazy world
How far is heaven?

"Heaven"
Los Lonely Boys

Prologue

Sunlight streamed through Camille Braxton's dining-room windows and reflected off the mahogany table, casting a glare across her pale, colorless face. Around the table were twelve matching Chippendale chairs with silk cushions that accented the color of the walls and highlighted the rich, dark luster of the tabletop. Camille sat with her chair turned to one side. Her left elbow rested on the table. Her legs were crossed.

She wore a white tennis outfit with green piping on the sleeves of the shirt and the hem of the skirt. Her white leather tennis shoes were spotless. Small round tufts on the back of her socks were perfectly positioned against the tendons behind each ankle. On her left wrist was a Yurman watch with a silver band. On the right, a diamond tennis bracelet. In her left hand she held a cordless telephone.

In her lap, dark brown splotches soaked through the front of her skirt. Drops of coffee dribbled a trail across the table to a cream-colored saucer with a cup tilted at a precarious angle against the handle of a sterling silver spoon that rested there. Coffee filled the saucer to the rim.

A voice called from the phone.

"Camille! Camille! You there?"

Camille's mouth was open, but her lips were silent. Her eyes were fixed in a blank stare.

Bessie Lawson entered the room through the butler's pantry.

"Miss Camille?"

There was no response. She tried again.

"Miss Camille?"

Bessie moved around the table.

"You all right?"

She took the phone from Camille's hand and switched it off. Camille let her hand drop to the table and laid her head on her arm.

"He did it again."

Bessie set the phone on the table. A frown wrinkled her forehead.

"Who you talking about?"

"Perry."

Bessie looked concerned.

"Something happen to Mister Perry?"

Camille did not respond. Bessie picked up the cup and saucer.

"You made a mess with your coffee. Let me get a rag and wipe that up."

Camille raised her head.

"That son of a—"

Bessie cut her off.

"Miss Camille." Her voice had a parental tone. "Don't talk like that."

Camille wiped her eyes with her fingers and sat up. She glanced at the splotches on her skirt. Her face went cold with anger. She slapped the table and shouted.

"How could he do this to me?!"

Bessie jumped at the sound of her voice. The coffee cup rattled against the saucer.

Without warning, Camille flung her arm in a backhand swipe that struck the telephone and sent it sailing across the room. It bounced off the wall at the end of the table and fell to the floor.

Bessie's eyes were wide. Her mouth gaped open.

"Miss Camille! What is wrong with you?"

Camille pushed herself away from the dining table.

"Come on."

She started across the room toward the front hall. Bessie hesitated. Camille glared at her from the doorway.

"Don't just stand there. Set that cup down and come on."

Bessie set the cup and saucer on the table and followed her out of the dining room. They moved down the hall to the staircase. Camille started upstairs. Once again, Bessie hesitated.

"What's wrong, Miss Camille? You ain't acting like yourself."

Camille was already halfway up the steps.

"That was Mitzi. She saw Perry last night." She looked down at Bessie from the stairs. "He was coming out of one of those tanning salons on Airline Highway."

Bessie frowned at her.

"A tanning salon? What's wrong with that? Maybe he's just working on his tan."

Camille gave her a sarcastic look.

"It's a whorehouse, Bessie."

Bessie looked perplexed.

"A whorehouse?"

"A whorehouse. Hookers. Prostitutes. Sex." Camille turned away and continued up the steps. "And who knows what else. Come on."

Camille reached the top of the stairs and turned right. She called to Bessie as she disappeared down the hall.

"Come on, Bessie. I need your help."

Bessie sighed and started up the steps.

The master bedroom was located on the left side of the hall, facing the back of the house. Camille strode across the room to the dresser and jerked open the top drawer. She stretched her arms wide apart, grabbed the drawer on either side, and slid it from the dresser frame. Holding it against her chest, she wheeled around and started toward the door.

Bessie stepped aside to let her pass. Camille scowled at her as she moved into the hall.

"Don't just stand there. Grab the next one and come on."

Perry's study was across the hall on the front side of the house. His desk sat opposite the door. Behind it, two large windows afforded a view of the front yard below. Camille carried the drawer into the study and set it on the desktop. She moved around the desk to the first window and raised it as high as it would go. Bessie entered the room with the second drawer as the window banged against the top of the frame.

"Just set it there." Camille nodded toward the desk. "Go get the next one."

She steadied herself against the window frame and kicked the screen with her foot. Bessie gasped as the screen ripped loose on one side.

"Miss Camille!"

Camille kicked again. The screen tore free. She leaned out the window and watched as it fluttered to the ground below. A smile spread across her face as she took the drawer from Bessie.

"Go get the other one."

In one quick motion, she turned aside and tossed the drawer out the open window. It crashed to the ground outside and splintered into pieces. She lifted the other drawer from the desktop and shoved it out the window. Bessie leaned around her and watched as it landed on the growing pile in the yard below.

Camille nudged her aside.

"Get the other drawer, now. Hurry up."

Bessie turned away and started back to the bedroom.

When the last of the dresser drawers was gone, they took all of Perry's clothes from the closet. Shoes, suits, whatever belonged to him went out the window. Swept up by the relief of finally doing something, of taking control, of hitting back, they tore the mirror from the dresser and threw it out. Somehow, they managed to push the dresser frame out with it. Then they turned to the study.

When they were finished, Perry Braxton's belongings lay in a heap on the front lawn. As the last of it went out the window, his dark gray Suburban turned into the driveway. Camille rested her hands on the windowsill and watched.

The Suburban moved a few feet up the driveway, then stopped. From the second floor, she could see him behind the steering wheel, staring at the mess, then looking up at her, his eyes wide with amazement and disbelief. In a defiant gesture, she thrust her fist out the second-story window and pointed with her index finger toward the street. A moment later the truck backed away.

One

Mike Connolly turned off the television and trudged down the hall toward the bedroom. At fifty-seven, he no longer cared for long days, and this one had been way too long. Mired in a robbery trial that had dragged on all week, he was tired to the bone. Through the door at the end of the hall he could see the bed. Light from a lamp on the night-stand gave the room a soft glow. The bed looked warm and inviting. A few more steps and he'd be there.

Connolly lived alone in the guest quarters behind the Pleiades, a four-story mansion built in 1901 by Elijah Huntley, a broker who made a fortune importing bananas from Costa Rica. Located on Tuttle Street in the better part of midtown Mobile, the house had been an architec-tural marvel in its day, with elevators, electric lights, and a crude form of air-conditioning. Now owned by Huntley's great-great-granddaugh-ter, Lois Crump, the house and grounds still evoked wonder and awe, but it was not a practical residence. By the time it passed to Lois, she was living in Birmingham and had little time or money for mainte-nance. To make the place more affordable, she rented out the guesthouse. Connolly was the latest in a succession of tenants.

When he reached the end of the hall, he slipped off his house shoes, turned out the light, and fell into bed. There had been a time when he wouldn't have given a day like this a second thought, but now all he wanted was to close his eyes and think of nothing. He rested his head on the pillow and pulled the cover over his shoulders. Just as he drifted off to sleep, the telephone in the living room rang.

"Go away," he moaned.

He rolled over, pulled the cover over his head, and buried his face in the pillow. Five rings later the telephone fell silent. He gave a sigh of relief and moved the sheet from over his face. A moment later, the cell phone on the nightstand began to ring. He rolled to one side and took it from the stand. The green glow from the screen illuminated the number. He recognized it immediately. Someone was calling from the police station. He pressed a button to accept the call.

"Hello."

"Mike, this is Perry Braxton."

Connolly rubbed his eyes and wished he hadn't answered the phone.

Perry Braxton was the son of Hylton and Charlotte Braxton, who operated a dozen discount shoe stores. Braxton had grown up knowing the good life in Mobile but had chosen to forgo the family business. Instead, he tried his hand at real estate development, investing his father's money in waterfront condos. Most of the legal work on the real estate deals went to Hagar, Litton, and Lynch, a large firm in the Tidewater Bank Building. He came to Connolly with DUIs and traffic tickets.

"Yeah," Connolly sighed. "What's up?"

"I'm down here at the police. They're talking to me about Camille. I need you to help me."

Connolly glanced at his watch on the nightstand but couldn't read the numbers.

"Now?"

"Yeah."

"Who's asking the questions?"

"Some guy named Hammond, mostly."

Connolly turned on the lamp and picked up the watch.

Ten thirty.

"All right. I'll be there in a few minutes. Tell them I'm on my way."

"Okay."

"And don't answer any more questions until I get there."

Connolly switched off the phone and tossed it on the pillow. Growling and grumbling, he shuffled across the room to the closet and slipped on the pants to a dark gray suit. He found the shirt he'd worn that day and put it on without a tie. He slid his bare feet in a pair of cordovan loafers, threw on his jacket, and started down the hall toward the door.

Outside, the night air was cool and damp. He paused a moment and looked toward the sky. A few stars twinkled through the hazy glare of the city lights. Behind him, a half-moon was rising.

In front of him was his car, a 1959 Chrysler Imperial he had acquired years ago from a lady on Japonica Street who had hired him to settle her husband's estate. There wasn't much left after they paid all the bills. She offered him the car for his fee. It had turned out to be a pretty good deal.

He climbed in the car and started the engine.

Police headquarters was located in a three-story building on Government Street that once had been the offices of an insurance company. Only a mile or two from midtown, it took Connolly five minutes to reach it from the guesthouse. He arrived there shortly before eleven.

The receptionist's desk in the lobby was empty. He walked past it to the stairs and made his way to the second floor. At the top of the stairs he entered a large room filled with desks that sat along the walls and in two rows down the center of the room. In between the desks were filing cabinets with papers stacked on top. Anthony Hammond's desk sat near the stairs. He glanced up as Connolly entered.

"He's in there."

Hammond nodded toward an interrogation room to the right of the stairway. Connolly opened the door and stepped inside.

The room was stark and bare with white walls and a tile floor. A plain metal table sat in the middle of the room beneath a fluorescent light. Braxton sat in a chair on the far side of the table.

"What's this all about?"

"Camille is missing," Braxton replied.

"Since when?"

"Day before yesterday."

"Tuesday?"

"Yeah."

"What happened?"

"I don't know."

"You don't know? You didn't report it?"

Braxton glanced away.

"I'm not living there now."

Connolly frowned.

"What—"

Braxton interrupted him.

"She threw me out."

"When?"

"Couple of weeks ago."

"Where are you living?"

"In an apartment on Louiselle Street."

Connolly found a chair across the room and brought it to the table. He took a seat across from Braxton.

"She got a lawyer?"

"Yeah." Braxton smiled. "Bob Dorsey."

Connolly smiled too. Dorsey was an attorney who did one thing

very well. Most of his clients were women. He had a reputation for making unfaithful husbands pay.

"Who's representing you?"

"On the divorce?"

"Yeah."

"Nobody. Yet."

"So, who reported her missing?"

"Bessie. Our maid. Bessie Lawson. Camille left the house Tuesday
morning. Supposed to be back by lunch."

"Never came back?"

Braxton shook his head. Connolly continued.

"Where was she going?"

"I don't know."

"They find her?"

"Not yet."

"Do they think you had something to do with it?"

"I guess. They keep asking me where I was. What I was doing. Who
I was with."

"What did you tell them?"

"The truth."

"Which is?"

"I went fishing Tuesday. Gone most of the day."

"Where?"

"Horn Island."

"What time did you leave?"

"Not too early. I think I was at the marina around nine."

"What marina?"

"Klinefelter's. In Pascagoula."

"Pascagoula? Isn't it closer to go from Dauphin Island?"

"Not really. I don't like to put in down there anyway."

"Anybody with you?"

"No."

"Buy anything that morning? Get some money from the ATM?"

"Bought some gas at the marina."

"Got a receipt?"

"Probably. Not with me. Might be one at the house."

"What time did you get back?"

"Around dark."

"All right." Connolly stood. "Sit tight. Let me talk to Hammond."

Connolly left the room and closed the door. Hammond was still
seated at his desk.

"You got anything more than a hunch?"

Hammond gave him a sullen look.

"She threw him out. Hired a lawyer. Filed for divorce. He couldn't stand the thought of losing all that money. That's more than a hunch."

"Losing what money?"

"Her money."

"Camille's money?"

Hammond rested his arms on the desktop and hunched forward.

"She's one rich lady." He gave Connolly a knowing smile. "Your man loves that money."

Connolly had no idea what Hammond was talking about. But that didn't really matter. He was sure Hammond didn't know much, either.

"Is he under arrest?"

Hammond sat up straight.

"I'm not sure."

"Is he free to go?"

"Not right now."

"Then, he's under arrest?"

"Technically." Hammond shrugged. "Maybe."

Connolly stood with both hands on the desk and leaned forward.

"Look, Anthony, the man says he was fishing. Put in at Pascagoula around nine and spent the day at Horn Island. I'll get you a receipt where he filled up with gas. You got anything to show he wasn't where he says he was?"

Hammond gave a heavy sigh.

"No."

"I didn't think so." Connolly backed away. "We're going now."

He walked to the interview room and opened the door. Braxton looked up. Connolly nodded.

"Let's go."

Braxton rose and stepped through the door. Connolly turned to Hammond.

"You have any more questions, give me a call."

Hammond leaned back in the chair and folded his arms behind his head. Connolly turned away and guided Braxton down the stairs.

Two

---

*I*n spite of the long night with Braxton, Connolly awoke the following morning before sunrise. Less than an hour later, he had showered, dressed, and headed downtown.

Government Street was all but deserted in the gray, predawn light. He lowered the window and let the cool, damp air swirl through the car. At Royal Street, he turned right and made his way behind the courthouse to St. Pachomius Church.

One of the oldest structures in the city, St. Pachomius sat behind the courthouse obscured by the thick foliage of the oaks that sprawled above it and the shadows of the glass and steel buildings that surrounded it. Steps led up from the sidewalk at the street to a portico supported by large, round columns that stood like sentries guarding access to the sanctuary inside. Beyond those columns were huge doors standing fifteen feet tall. Connolly parked the car in front and walked up the steps. At the top, he moved past the columns and pushed against one of the doors. The door swung open.

Inside, the sanctuary was cool and dark. He closed the door behind him and glanced around. Walls to the left and right were lined with stained-glass windows depicting scenes from the life of Christ. The early morning light illuminated the vivid colors and made the images come to life. Down front, a railing separated the nave from the chancel steps. An opening in the railing allowed access to marble steps that rose from the sanctuary floor to the chancel.

The floor of the chancel was marble as well. Near the front, lecterns stood on either side facing the nave. Toward the back, pews were arranged on either side for a split chancel choir. Beyond the choir was the altar behind still another railing near the rear wall of the church.

Connolly took a seat in a pew near the back and let his eyes move slowly around the room. It looked old and smelled old but its age gave it a regal aura. The building was alive with mystery and wonder.

Before long, others began to arrive for morning prayers. They moved quietly down the aisle past him. In a few minutes, Father Scott entered the nave and climbed the steps to the chancel.

When the service ended, Connolly slipped from the pew and walked out the back of the church. He made his way down the steps to the Chrysler and got in behind the wheel. He arrived at the office a little before eight.

His office was located on the third floor of the Warren Building, a 1920s-era structure on Dauphin Street across from Bienville Square. Once a prestigious address, it was now occupied by private detectives, sleazy lawyers, and Connolly. Mrs. Gordon, his secretary, sat at her desk near the door as he entered. Now seventy-five, she had been his secretary since the day he became a lawyer. She scowled at him as he came through the door.

"What are you doing here?"

"It's my office," Connolly quipped. "I work here."

"Don't you have something going on over at the courthouse?"

Connolly stopped in his tracks. Panic gripped his chest. He glanced at his watch.

"I forgot all about it."

Mrs. Gordon stood.

"The file's right here." She stepped around the desk to a chair and retrieved a thick manila folder. "Nothing left but closing argument. I'm sure you can think of something to say between here and the courthouse."

Connolly ran his hand through his hair.

"I can't believe I forgot about a trial."

"Oversleep?"

"No. Perry Braxton called me last night. I had to go down to the police station." Connolly took the file from Mrs. Gordon. "He's supposed to come by here this morning. Ask him if we can meet this afternoon."

"You better get moving. Judge Cahill will be looking for you."

Connolly turned away and opened the door. As he stepped out, he glanced back at Mrs. Gordon with a smile.

"Thanks."

She waved him off with the back of her hand and moved to her chair behind the desk. The door banged closed. He ran down the corridor toward the elevator.

Connolly reached the courthouse before anyone noticed he was missing. Closing arguments took an hour and a half. The jury deliberated forty-five minutes before convicting his client. He was back at the office before lunch.

Braxton arrived at two. Mrs. Gordon ushered him down the hall to Connolly's office. Connolly stood as he entered.

"Sorry I couldn't see you this morning."

They shook hands. Mrs. Gordon retreated from the room and closed the door.

"No problem," Braxton replied.

Connolly pointed to a chair in front of the desk. Braxton took a seat and leaned against the armrest. Connolly settled into his chair behind the desk. Braxton took a piece of paper from the pocket of his jacket and handed it to Connolly.

"Here's the receipt from the marina."

Connolly glanced at it and laid it on the desk.

"Good. I'll check into it." He took a legal pad from a desk drawer and picked up a pen. "Let's begin at the beginning. Who was she?"

Braxton looked puzzled.

"Who was who?"

"The woman you were seeing. Who was she?"

"What woman?"

Connolly propped his elbows on the desk and leaned forward. He gave Braxton a stern look, eye to eye.

"First thing you have to understand. You tell me whatever I want to know. You hold out on me, you're on your own. Got it?"

Braxton looked uncomfortable.

"Yeah." He shifted positions in the chair. "Sure."

Connolly leaned back, rested his head against the wall, and folded his hands in his lap.

"Now. Who was she?"

"Not anybody you'd know."

Connolly stood. Braxton raised his hand, gesturing for him to stop.

"She wasn't anybody. Really."

Connolly moved around the desk and opened the office door. Braxton continued to protest.

"She was just a girl. Sit down."

Connolly stared at him. Braxton gestured with both hands.

"Sit down. She was just a girl. I don't know her name."

Connolly gave him a skeptical look. Braxton grinned.

"Honest. I don't know her name."

Connolly closed the door and returned to his chair.

"That was the problem." Braxton continued. "I didn't know her name, or any of the others'."

"This wasn't the first time?"

"No. It wasn't the first time."

"You're telling me this was a sexual encounter, not an affair?"

"Yeah. That's right. It was sex. That's all. Just sex."

More like dynamite, Connolly thought.

"All right. Camille found out you were frequenting hookers. When did she throw you out?"

Braxton turned sideways in the chair again.

"I don't know. Four or five weeks ago."

"You said she filed for divorce."

"Yeah."

"Serve you with papers yet?"

"Yeah. Served me Monday."

Connolly frowned.

"Monday?"

"Yeah."

Connolly sat up straight.

"You were served with divorce papers on Monday. She disappeared on Tuesday."

Braxton nodded.

"Doesn't look so good, does it?"

"No." Connolly picked up a newspaper from the corner of the desk and tossed it onto Braxton's lap. "Neither does this."

Braxton stared at the paper. Headlines across the top read, HUSBAND QUESTIONED IN WIFE'S DISAPPEARANCE.

"Article says you spent the day fishing at Horn Island. Did you talk to reporters?"

"No."

"How'd they know about your alibi?"

"I don't know." Braxton scanned the article. "I guess Hammond told them."

"I doubt it." Connolly watched Braxton's eyes. "He seems to think your wife is wealthy."

Braxton laid the paper on the desk and looked at him.

"She is wealthy."

"How wealthy?"

"She's a Tonsmeyer."

Connolly gave him a blank look.

"And that means something?"

"Tonsmeyer." Braxton repeated the name as if Connolly should recognize it. "Tonsmeyer Trust. Owns Edgewood Mall. Timber. Half a dozen buildings down here in town. Bunch of warehouses on the waterfront. You've never heard of them?"

"I don't know. So, she's wealthy?"

"Yeah. She's wealthy. They think I killed her for her money?"

"Who knows what they think. They're looking for a suspect with a motive."

"And I'm it?"

"You're it." Connolly nodded. "Who manages the Trust?"

"Tidewater Bank. Ford Defuniak looks after it. You know him?"

"Name sounds familiar. You ever have any dealings with him?"

Braxton looked away.

"No. Not really." He crossed his legs. "If you want to know about the Trust, there's an attic full of records over at the house."

"The house where you and Camille live?"

"Yes."

"Whose house is it?"

"Ours."

"Your name on the deed?"

"Yes."

"If your wife ends up dead, how much do you get?"

Braxton looked disturbed by the question.

"You think I killed her?"

Connolly was undeterred.

"I want to know where all the land mines are. If she's dead, what do you get out of it?"

Braxton glared at him.

"I get the house and a devastated twelve-year-old daughter."

Connolly ignored his look.

"She have anything outside the Trust?"

"Yes."

"Who would get that?"

"I would. You think I killed her?"

Connolly leaned over the desk toward him.

"Listen. I'm not asking you anything the DA isn't going to ask. I just want to know what your answer's going to be before he asks you on the witness stand. And before I spend a month building a defense that gets blown away by a couple of simple questions."

Braxton gave him a sober look.

"I'd get something. I don't know exactly how much."

Connolly leaned back in his chair. Braxton took a deep breath.

"You're assuming she's dead."

Connolly shrugged.

"I hope she's alive. But Hammond's not waiting. You can't, either."

The room grew quiet. Braxton leaned his head back against the top of the chair. Connolly dropped his pen on the desk and folded his hands together.

"Now. One more thing."

"What's that?"

"The fee."

Braxton gave him a smile.

"It always comes down to money."

Connolly ignored the comment.

"If they file charges against you and this case goes to trial, you're looking at a preliminary hearing. Then about ten or eleven months after that your case will come up for trial."

"So, that means this thing will drag on for a year?"

"At least. If they charge you. But you don't want to wait for them to charge you before you get to work on this. We need to track down witnesses, talk to everybody now. Get them committed to a version of the facts before the police get to them."

"You think they haven't talked to everyone already?"

"Hammond is good, but he's like every other detective I know. Once he finds a suspect, he stops looking at the big picture."

Braxton nodded.

"So, what's this going to cost?"

"I'm not sure. Give me a retainer. I'll bill against it, and we'll see where this goes. If they charge you with something, I'll have a little better idea by then of what the total cost will be. How about five thousand dollars to start?"

"I'll have to get you a check."

Braxton stood. Connolly came from behind the desk.

"That'll be fine." He opened the office door. "In the meantime, anybody comes around asking questions, trying to talk to you about this, you send them to me. Understand?"

Braxton nodded.

"Yeah. I understand."

Connolly guided him toward the door.

"I don't want to see any more alibis or theories about our defense in the newspaper. Got it?"

Braxton nodded once more. Connolly walked with him up the hall.

Three

All weekend Connolly kept replaying the conversation with Braxton in his mind. Each time, he felt that same gnawing in his stomach. The sensation he got when he was sure he was being manipulated. He thought about it while he watched a baseball game on television. And he thought about it when he went for a run late Saturday afternoon.

By the time he awoke on Monday morning, he had decided to stop worrying and start working. He talked it over with himself as he stared at the mirror in the bathroom.

"If anyone knows what happened, it'll be the maid."

He stroked the razor across his face.

"Bessie. Bessie …"

He rinsed the razor in the sink and made another stroke.

"I can't remember her last name." He lifted his chin to shave along his jaw. "But she'll know what this tale is all about."

He finished shaving and wiped his face.

"She'll give me a straight answer."

The Braxton residence was located on Turnin Lane in Spring Hill, an affluent neighborhood on the western edge of the city. Large, but not imposing, the house sat fifty yards off the street, surrounded by azaleas and oaks. A narrow driveway ran from the street past the end of the house to a three-car garage in back. Connolly turned off the street and brought the Chrysler to a stop in front of the garage. He got out of the car and walked to the back door. A middle-aged black woman dressed in a white uniform and white sneakers met him there. They spoke through the screened door.

"May I help you?"

"My name is Mike Connolly. I'm a lawyer. I represent Perry Braxton."

She nodded and waited for him to continue.

"You must be Bessie."

"Yes. I am."

"I was wondering if I could talk with you for a few minutes."

"Well, I suppose so."

She unlatched the screen door and held it open for him as he entered. Connolly stepped inside and followed her to the kitchen. Spacious counters lined the walls to the left. A commercial oven sat along the wall to the right, across from the door. In the center of the room was a table with four chairs. Bessie pointed to the table.

"Have a seat. You want some coffee?"

"No, thank you."

Connolly took a seat. Bessie poured herself a cup of coffee and sat across from him. Her voice was soft and quiet.

"I sure do hate it."

"I know this is difficult for you to talk about."

"I worry about Sarah. She's just a girl." She glanced at Connolly. "Mrs. Braxton ain't coming back."

Connolly nodded thoughtfully. Bessie shook her head slowly and took a sip of coffee.

"I sure do hate it."

"Tell me about Monday."

"You mean Tuesday." She looked at him over the coffee cup. "That's the day she went missing."

"We'll get to Tuesday. Let's back up to Monday. What happened on Monday?"

"Well ... let's see ... I think Monday was just a regular day. Sarah left for school about seven twenty."

"How does she get to school?"

"They swap out. The mothers swap days."

"Car pool?"

She nodded.

"Yes. Car pool."

"All right. Sarah left for school. Then what?"

"Mrs. Braxton spent the morning at the dining-room table. Going over some papers." Bessie glanced up. "You know, she and Mr. Braxton were getting a divorce."

"Yes."

She took a sip of coffee.

"She was in the dining room, looking at those papers. Phone rang a couple of times. I'm not sure who all it was that called. We had lunch. Then she left that afternoon. Got back right about the time Sarah got home from school."

"Any idea where she went?"

"No. I don't have no idea. She pulled herself together before she left, but she wasn't made up like she was going out any place special."

"What about that night?"

"I fixed supper. Put it on the table. They was eating when I left."

"What time do you leave?"

"Soon as supper's ready."

"She didn't tell you about anything unusual happening that day?"

"No. Not that I can remember."

"Okay. What about Tuesday? What time did you arrive for work?"

"I always get here at six thirty."

"What happened?"

"Sarah went to school. Then we was in the kitchen. She was giving this big luncheon Thursday. Something to do with the ballet. Sarah takes lessons there. I don't know what it was all about, but she was all excited. Bunch of ladies coming over, you know."

She took another sip of coffee and looked away.

"Middle of the morning she said she was going up to Tootsie Trehern's shop to see about some flowers." She looked at him. "Tootsie's is up on Old Shell Road. You know where it is?"

"Yes."

"I was glad she was going because it got her out of the way so I could get some work done. She wasn't much help with things like that."

"What time did she leave?"

"About ten." She took another sip of coffee. "That's the last time I saw her." She glanced toward the door. "I can see her now, going right out that door."

"Was that the only place she was going? Up to Tootsie's?"

"Well, she was going there, and then she was going to stop by Pollman's Bakery and get us some bread to go with our lunch. She liked their bread."

"The police say you reported her missing."

Bessie nodded.

"When did you do that?"

"I called them about supper time. I called Mr. Braxton first, but he wasn't too worried. I told him I had a bad feeling about it. He said she was probably just out shopping someplace. I didn't think so. When she goes shopping, she gets all made up and dressed and everything. That morning she just ran a comb through her hair, grabbed her car keys, and headed out. She wasn't going shopping." Bessie shook her head. "No, sir. She was going to that one place for that particular thing and then coming home. She knew Tootsie. She wasn't worried about how she looked."

"You called Mr. Braxton. Then you called the police?"

"Yes. I told them she was missing. They took down some information over the phone, but they didn't seem too concerned either, at the time."

"Did they send someone out to talk to you?"

"The next day they did. I stayed with Sarah that night. Had to call my sister to take care of my kids, but I wasn't going to call Mr. Braxton back after what he said the first time. I just took care of her myself. Next morning, Camille still wasn't back. I got Sarah off to school, and I called my brother. He works for the city. Knows a lot of those policemen. In a little while a detective called me. Anthony somebody."

"Hammond. Anthony Hammond."

She nodded.

"That's him."

"Did he come talk to you?"

"No. But wasn't long till a patrol car showed up. Policeman asked some questions. Took some information about her. I gave him a picture of her."

"At some point they called Mr. Braxton in for questioning. Any idea why they did that?"

"I don't know. I guess they thought maybe he knew something."

"Do you know anything that would have made them suspicious of him?"

"Nothing ... I mean ..."

"What?"

"Well, you know, people talk."

"About what?"

"People are wondering if it had something to do with their divorce. You know, it just don't look right. She files for divorce and then turns up missing like that. That's all."

"Do you think that had something to do with it?"

"I don't know." She sighed. "I just don't know."

"Did you talk to Mr. Braxton about this?"

"Not really. He came by to check on Sarah that night. Wednesday night. Her grandmother came and stayed with her."

"Which one?"

"Mrs. Stabler. Camille's mother."

Connolly frowned.

"Stabler? I thought Camille was a Tonsmeyer?"

"She is. Sort of. Tonsmeyer was Mrs. Stabler's maiden name."

"Oh." Connolly thought for a moment. "What kind of car does Camille drive?"

"Mercedes. Old car. Used to be her daddy's."

"Could you give me a picture of her?"

"Sure."

Bessie set the coffee cup aside and rose from the chair. She disappeared through the dining room. In a minute or two she returned and handed him a photograph. Connolly glanced at it. The picture was one of Perry and Camille together.

"That one has both of them. Took that one day last year. They was going to a party with Sarah."

Connolly studied the photograph a moment, then slipped it in the pocket of his jacket.

"Do you know which way she would have gone when she went to Tootsie's?"

Bessie picked up the coffee cup from the table and walked to the sink.

"Well, I reckon she would have gone the same way she always goes. Out Turnin, swing around on Wimbledon to Hillwood, then up to Old Shell Road." She rinsed out the cup, opened the dishwasher, and placed it inside. "That's the way she likes to go. Keep from getting out on McGregor Avenue. Hard to get out there at that intersection." She closed the dishwasher and leaned against the counter. "But now that's if she was just going right up there. Sometime she start out one place and then end up going to two or three others."

"But you said you thought she wasn't going shopping."

"That's right. I felt like that when I talked to Mr. Braxton, and I feel like that now. She didn't leave here to go shopping around. She was going to Tootsie's and then to Pollman's and then coming home."

Connolly stood.

"I appreciate your time."

He started toward the door.

"I hope I helped." She moved from the counter to follow him out. "And I hope you find her alive." She took a deep breath. "But I don't think you will."

He grasped the doorknob.

"Out Turnin, down Wimbledon to Hillwood, and up to Old Shell?"

"That's the way she usually goes."

"All right." He stepped out the door. "Thanks for your help."

She latched the door closed behind him. He got into the Chrysler, turned it around, and drove down the driveway.

Four

*C*onnolly left the Braxtons' house and drove up Turnin Lane. A little way up the street he came to Wimbledon Drive. There, he turned right, went a short distance to the intersection with Hillwood Road, and turned left. He drove slowly, trying to see what Camille might have seen as she went that way on Tuesday. That is, if she went that way.

A mile or so down Hillwood he came to Old Shell Road and turned right. Tootsie Trehern's shop was a quarter of a mile down the road. He parked the Chrysler near the door and got out. Through the window he could see Tootsie inside glaring at him from behind the counter near the cash register.

Tootsie Trehern was an icon in Spring Hill. Her shop sold flowers and assorted gift items, but most of her business came from coordinating events. Mardi Gras parties, prom nights, weddings—whatever the occasion, she was the one to see. A party managed by Tootsie was a hit before it happened. Leave her out, and it was a flop before the invitations were mailed. She was the gatekeeper to local society. If she liked you, you were in everywhere. If she didn't, you'd be left out with no hope of ever being accepted.

Connolly had known her since he first dated Barbara. Tootsie did their wedding. She did their daughter's sixteenth birthday party. But in many and various ways she had made it clear she didn't like him. When he and Barbara divorced, her dislike for him turned bitter.

A bell jingled as he opened the door to the shop. He stepped inside and made his way around three oversized flowerpots. Tootsie was waiting for him at the counter.

"Hello, Mike."

The tone of her voice made the greeting sound like an obligation. The sound of it made him smile.

"Tootsie."

She wasn't amused.

"You just happened to be in the neighborhood?"

"I need to ask you about Camille Braxton."

She gave him a cold look, as though he had touched a sore subject.

"What about her?"

"She left her house last Tuesday morning. Her maid said she was coming to your shop. Did she make it?"

Tootsie lit a cigarette and took a long drag on it.

"That was almost a week ago. You know how many people have been in here since then?"

"And you know every one of them. Was she in here?"

Tootsie exhaled the smoke. She had a solemn look on her face.

"No." She shook her head. "She didn't come in. I wish she had. I haven't seen her in two or three weeks." She stared at him a moment. "You representing Perry? I read about him in the paper."

"Have you seen him recently?"

"No," she scoffed. "I'm not his type."

"Have you heard anyone mention seeing Camille?"

"No." She took another drag from the cigarette and exhaled the smoke. "I mean, everyone who talks about her mentions the last time they saw her, but I haven't heard anyone say they've seen her since sometime the week before she ... disappeared."

Connolly nodded.

"Okay. Thanks for your help."

He turned toward the door.

"You have a royal pain for a client, you know."

Connolly glanced at her over his shoulder as he opened the door.

"Most of my clients are."

He heard her chuckle as he stepped outside.

From Tootsie's shop, Connolly drove downtown to the office. Mrs. Gordon was in the copier room as he entered. He stopped in the hall and spoke to her from the doorway.

"Have you seen Hollis recently?"

She stood at the copier, her back to him.

"No. Why?"

"I need him to help me with this Perry Braxton case."

A copy came from the machine. She checked it, raised the cover, and placed another document for copying.

"I still think you ought to hire a reputable investigator."

"Hollis is reputable."

She gave him a look over her shoulder.

"Not hardly."

Connolly took his cell phone from his pocket and punched in a number. He listened as the call rolled over to voice mail. He pressed a button to end the call. The phone beeped. Mrs. Gordon glanced at him, then turned back to the copier.

Connolly sighed.

"Gave him a cell phone so I could reach him, and he never turns it on."

"Probably doesn't know where it is."

Connolly chuckled.

"You may be right."

Hollis Toombs lived in a shack on a bayou in the coastal savanna marsh south of Mobile near Fowl River, a few miles east of Bayou La Batre. When he was nineteen, he joined the Marine Corps. After three tours in Vietnam he returned home to find he had inherited the shack and a few hundred acres of marsh from his uncle, a fact that rankled several of his cousins. They contested the will, which is how Hollis and Connolly became acquainted. Connolly won the case. Hollis got to keep the shack and the marsh, but he didn't have any money to pay Connolly's fee. He agreed to work off what he owed by helping with some of Connolly's cases. When he finished working out the debt, Connolly hired him as his investigator. Connolly liked him, in spite of his eccentric disposition, and he had a stomach for doing things most private detectives would turn down, which made him handy to have around.

Connolly slipped the cell phone into his pocket and started down the hall. As he reached the door to his office, the cell phone rang. He took it from his pocket and checked to see who was calling. He smiled when he saw the number.

"Where are you?"

"Mile or two south of Sprinkle's Store," Hollis replied.

"I have something I need you to do."

"What is it?"

"I'll tell you when you get here."

"Who said I was coming up there?"

"Come by the office this afternoon."

"Buy me lunch at that place up the street."

"All right."

"I'll be there in thirty minutes."

Hollis ended the call before Connolly could reply. Mrs. Gordon appeared at the door.

"I guess he didn't drop it in the bayou after all."

"I guess not."

Connolly moved around the desk and took a seat. He leaned the chair back and rested his head against the wall.

"Wake me in half an hour."

"You ought to sleep at night."

"I do." He adjusted his head to a comfortable position and closed his eyes. "The nights just aren't long enough."

Half an hour later Connolly walked up the street to the Port City Diner. Hollis's pickup was parked at the curb near the corner. Connolly found him waiting inside. They sat at a table in back. Connolly had a turkey club. Hollis ordered a muffuletta.

"What sort of case you got this time?"

His voice had a sarcastic tone. Connolly ignored it and swallowed a bite of sandwich.

"Missing wife."

"A missing wife?"

"Yeah."

"You want me to find somebody's wife?" Hollis took a bite of his sandwich. "Maybe she don't want to be found."

"Maybe so." Connolly nodded. "That's what we need to find out."

"You think she run off?"

"I think anything's possible."

"Where do I start?"

"She lives in Spring Hill. Left her house last Tuesday going to a little shop on Old Shell Road. Maid was there when she left. That's the last time anyone has seen her. I checked at the shop. She never made it."

"You got an address?"

"Yeah. I'll give you the details. What I want you to do first is to start with the house next to hers and go door-to-door all the way from her house to the shop and find out if anybody saw her that day."

"How far we talking about?"

"Not far. There aren't that many houses."

When they finished eating, they walked outside to Hollis's pickup. Connolly took a city map from the inside pocket of his jacket and opened it on the hood of the truck.

"This is where she lived." He pointed to the map. "Twenty-three thirty-four Turnin Lane. The maid said she would have gone out Turnin to Wimbledon Drive." He traced the route on the map with his finger. "Go down to Hillwood Road. Up to Old Shell. The shop she was going to was to the right on Old Shell. The Pink Flamingo. Tootsie Trehern runs it."

"Got a picture?"

Connolly looked puzzled.

"Picture?"

"Of the lady."

"Oh. Yeah."

Connolly took the photograph Bessie had given him from his pocket and handed it to Hollis.

"Her name is Camille Braxton. Man in the picture with her is her husband, Perry Braxton. He's our client."

"They think he's involved?"

"Hammond had him in for questioning Thursday night. I reckon they think he did something."

Connolly folded the map and handed it to Hollis.

"Got any questions?"

Hollis glanced at the map as he thought for a moment.

"Paying me in cash?"

"Of course."

"Want me to get started today?"

"Yes."

Hollis opened the door to the pickup.

"I better get moving." He got in behind the steering wheel and closed the door. He smiled at Connolly through the open window. "Thanks for lunch."

Connolly nodded in response. Hollis started the truck and drove away from the curb.

Five

As Hollis drove away, Connolly crossed the street and made his way through Bienville Square. On the opposite side of the square he continued down St. Joseph Street to the YMCA. Once a place for wayward travelers to find a cheap room, the Downtown Y had been transformed into a state-of-the-art fitness club. It was a popular noontime gathering place for many who worked in the surrounding buildings. Connolly was certain he would find Bob Dorsey on one of the handball courts.

The walk took ten minutes. He was sweating when he reached the Y. The cool air felt good as he opened the door and stepped inside. He moved past the receptionist's desk and followed the hallway by the elevators to the handball courts on the far side of the ground floor. The end walls of the courts were made of thick Lexan glass that afforded a view from the hall. Dorsey was playing on the last court. Connolly watched through the glass.

In a little while the game ended. Dorsey and his opponent congratulated each other and stepped from the room. Dorsey turned to Connolly.

"Change your clothes and let's play a game."

Connolly shook his head.

"Wouldn't last five minutes."

Dorsey wiped his face with a towel.

"It's not too bad once you get used to it."

Connolly smiled.

"I'll take your word for it. You got a minute?"

"Yeah. Let's walk over to the snack bar. I need something to drink."

They walked down the hall in the opposite direction from which Connolly had come. Around the corner they came to a small snack bar near the locker room. A cooler sat near the counter. Dorsey opened it and took a bottle of water.

"You want something?"

Connolly took a bottle of juice. Dorsey caught the attendant's eye and gestured for him to put both drinks on his tab. They found a seat at a table. Dorsey twisted the cap off the bottled water and took a drink.

"Well, I assume you're here to talk about Camille and Perry Braxton."

Connolly took a sip of juice.

"Yeah."

"Newspaper said you're representing Perry."

Connolly shook his head as he swallowed.

"Not on the divorce."

Dorsey grinned.

"You don't do them anymore?"

"Not if I can help it."

"They tell me having one of your own leaves a rather unpleasant taste in your mouth."

"It gives you a different perspective."

"How's Barbara these days?"

"She's all right."

"See much of her?"

"Yeah. I see her now and then."

The grin on Dorsey's face grew wider.

"Still got a thing for her, don't you?"

Connolly looked away. Dorsey kept going.

"Maybe one day you'll convince her to take you back."

Connolly took a drink of juice. He was ready to change the subject.

"I talked to their maid this morning."

Dorsey nodded.

"Bessie's a good lady."

"She said Camille was out of the house all afternoon on Monday. Left right after lunch, got home just before her daughter came in from school. Did she come see you?"

"No. But I got a pretty good idea where she was." Dorsey took a sip from the bottle of water. "Your client was spending a lot of time over at Panama Tan."

Connolly frowned. Dorsey smiled.

"It's a tanning salon on Airline Highway. From what I hear, the women over there know how to make five minutes last all day." He gestured with the bottle in his hand. "You know the guy who's running the place."

"Who's that?"

"Manny Fernandez."

Connolly rolled his eyes.

"I thought he was in prison."

"He's out." Dorsey chuckled and took another sip of water. "Camille found out Braxton was going over there. I got a hunch that's where she was Monday afternoon."

"You think she went over there?"

"Yeah. She called me. All excited. Said she had something good. Didn't want to talk about it on the phone. She was supposed to come see me Tuesday afternoon. Obviously, she never made it." Dorsey raised his eyebrows. "I'm not a criminal lawyer, but it looks to me like Braxton's in bad shape on this. Anybody tell you about the wills?"

Connolly did his best to hide his surprise.

"What about them?"

"They changed them a few months ago. Buie Hayford did it for them. You know Buie?"

"Yeah."

"He's the lawyer for the Trust. You know about the Trust?"

"Yeah. What did they change in their wills?"

"Biggest thing was the conservator for their daughter. Changed it from her mother to Braxton."

Connolly shrugged.

"Nothing too strange about that."

"No. Except by the terms of the Trust, if Camille dies, the daughter gets whatever Camille would have taken from the Trust. We're talking about a lot of money. Making Braxton the conservator would have given him control over all of that money while the daughter was a minor. He could have done just about anything short of giving it away."

"*Would* have given him control?"

Dorsey gave him a cheesy smile.

"I asked about her will at our first meeting. We changed it that day."

"Did Braxton know she changed it?"

"I don't know. I didn't tell him. Only thing I sent him was the complaint for divorce."

They sat quietly for a moment. Connolly took a sip of juice.

"Did you have anyone following him?"

Dorsey shook his head.

"Didn't get to it. I would have. But we hadn't gotten that far when she disappeared."

Connolly nodded.

"She hasn't just gone off someplace where she doesn't want to be found, has she?"

"If she did, she didn't tell me about it."

Connolly took another drink of juice. Dorsey tossed the water bottle in a trash can near the cooler.

"Well, I've got to get dressed and get back to the office."

He stood. They shook hands.

"Hope you find her alive."

Connolly nodded in response. Dorsey moved past him toward the locker room.

Connolly left the gym and started toward the office. As he walked, his mind drifted to the conversation he had with Bessie earlier that day. He could see Camille hurrying around the kitchen, getting her daughter off to school. The smiles on their faces. The frantic rush to get ready on time. Then, a few casual words.

"I'm going up to Tootsie's. I'll be back in a few minutes."

With that, she slipped out the door and was gone.

Loneliness washed over him, as if he'd lost something himself, something he'd never thought was important until the moment it was gone, only to realize too late it was the most important thing of all. It seemed odd to feel that way about her. He'd known Camille for years, but only because he'd represented Braxton. He'd only seen her maybe five or six times. Still, the sadness wouldn't go away. He slowed as he passed the fountain in the center of the square. Water gurgled in the background but he was lost in thought. Suddenly, he stopped. His mouth fell open.

The kitchen he'd seen in his mind was Camille's, and the morning had been just as Bessie had described, but the face he'd seen wasn't Camille's. It was Barbara's.

Memories of Barbara raced through his mind. He rubbed his forehead with the heel of his hand and shook his head, trying to make them go away. But still they came. Finally, he gave in. The memories carried him away. A smile came to his face.

They met at a fraternity party when they were both in college. He remembered the moment as clearly as if it were happening right then. The way the corners of her mouth turned up when she smiled. Her hair falling just above her shoulders. The sparkle in her eyes. And her beautiful legs. She was with a football player, a second-string guard from Dothan who was more interested in himself than her. Connolly asked her to dance. They were married the following summer.

Connolly attended law school. Barbara took a job as a teacher to support them. When he graduated, they moved home to Mobile. He opened an office, hired Mrs. Gordon as his secretary, and earned a modest but steady income. They bought a house, had a daughter, led a normal life. Then, he discovered the taste of gin. By the time their daughter graduated from high school, he was up to a quart a day just to function. Barbara had endured it as long as she could. They divorced.

Just then, someone nudged him. He glanced to the left. A man stood beside him dressed in wrinkled khaki pants and a dirty T-shirt. His hair was dirty and greasy and lay flat against his head. He was unshaven and filthy.

"Got any spare change?"

The stench of his breath jarred Connolly away from the world that filled his mind.

"Excuse me?"

"Got any spare change?"

Connolly slipped his hand in his pocket and took out a few coins. He dropped them in the man's hand. The man glanced at them and walked away without reply. Connolly looked around. He stood alone in front of the fountain. The midday crowd had dwindled. He checked his watch and started toward Dauphin Street and the office building.

Six

*C*onnolly spent most of the following day at the courthouse. When he returned to the office that afternoon, he found Hollis sitting in a chair near Mrs. Gordon's desk.

"Finished already?"

"Sort of. I've knocked on every door. Half of them aren't home."

"Anybody see anything?"

"A lady on Hillwood. She knows the Braxtons. Said Camille's car broke down in front of her house one day last week. Thinks it was Tuesday or Wednesday."

"Camille's car?"

"Yeah."

"Did she say what happened to her?"

"Somebody stopped and picked her up. She didn't get a good look at the driver. I checked the house across the street, but nobody was at home. Nobody else around there saw anything. You want me to go back?"

Connolly ran his hand over his cheek as he thought.

"No," he said, slowly. "Let me talk to the lady you found. What's her name?"

"Kathleen Cathcart. Older lady. Lives by herself." Hollis dug a piece of paper from his pocket and handed it to Connolly. "I wrote down the address."

Connolly glanced at the paper.

"All right. I'll talk to her this afternoon." Connolly turned away and started down the hall. "Come on back here."

Hollis followed him. Connolly tossed his jacket across the chair by the door to his office and moved behind the desk. He opened the top drawer and took out an envelope filled with cash. He counted out some money and handed it to Hollis.

"That enough?"

Hollis counted the bills and nodded.

"It'll do."

Connolly returned the envelope to the drawer and pushed it closed.

"I have something else you can do on this case."

"What is it?"

Connolly took a seat in the chair behind his desk.

"You ever hear of a place called Panama Tan?"

"Panama Tan?" Hollis gave Connolly an odd look. "What's that?"

"A tanning salon."

"Can't say that I have." He shoved both hands in his pants pockets and leaned against the doorframe. "But then, I'm not really much for an electric beach."

Connolly grinned.

"Electric beach?"

"Yeah. Stand in one of them stalls in front of a bunch of lightbulbs?" Hollis shook his head. "I'd rather have the real thing. Sand. Waves. Sunshine."

Connolly chuckled.

"It's out on Airline Highway."

"What's going on out there?"

"The Braxtons were getting a divorce when she went missing. I talked to her lawyer. He says Panama Tan is really a front for a prostitution ring and that Perry Braxton was a frequent customer."

Hollis grinned.

"A whorehouse?"

"Yeah."

"That why they was splitting up?"

"Looks like it." Connolly leaned back in his chair. "I need you to find out what's happening over there."

Hollis grinned again.

"At this ... Panama Tan?"

"Yes."

Hollis ran his fingers through his hair and smiled.

"You want me to hire a prostitute?"

Connolly chuckled.

"No. I want you to watch. Listen. See who comes and goes. Find out what's happening."

Hollis raised one eyebrow. An amused smile spread across his face. Connolly shook his head.

"That's not what I meant. I have a pretty good idea what happens inside."

Hollis began to laugh.

"You know what I mean," Connolly quipped.

"I'll check it out." The grin on his face grew wider. "This may take a while." He started laughing again. "I'll have to ... get a feel for the place."

Connolly threw a pencil at him. Hollis tried to stop laughing.

"I'll find out what they're doing."

He turned toward the door to leave. Connolly sat up straight in his chair.

"You still have that picture I gave you?"

Hollis stopped laughing long enough to answer.

"Yeah."

"Better let me have it. I might need it."

Hollis took the photograph from his pocket and handed it to Connolly, then turned back to the door.

"I'll get back with you in a few days."

Connolly heard him laughing as he disappeared up the hall toward Mrs. Gordon's desk.

Kathleen Cathcart lived in a one-story brick house on Hillwood Road. Pine trees towered above the yard and covered the azaleas and camellias in thick brown straw. Dead limbs were scattered about the lawn, and a thick mat of straw lay on the roof. Connolly turned the Chrysler into the driveway and parked near a cobblestone sidewalk that led to the front door. He got out and made his way to the house.

As he passed the front window, the curtain moved to one side. A woman peeked out. He smiled and gave her a friendly wave. She closed the curtain. A few seconds later, he heard her unlock the door. She pulled it open a little way and spoke to him from inside.

"Yes?"

"My name is Mike Connolly. I'm an attorney. Are you Kathleen Cathcart?"

"Yes, I am."

Through the doorway he could see she was an elderly woman. Her thin white hair was combed back from her face but in no particular order. She wore a cotton print housedress and fuzzy slippers, and though she had on no makeup, her complexion was smooth and clear. Her eyes were alert and watched him intently. Connolly smiled at her.

"I was wondering if I could talk to you a few minutes."

"Do you have a card?"

"Excuse me?"

"A card. Do you have a business card?"

"Yes, ma'am."

Connolly took a business card from his pocket and handed it to her. She glanced at it and opened the door a little wider.

"What do you want to talk about?"

"I think you spoke to my investigator earlier."

She looked puzzled.

"Your investigator?"

"Yes, ma'am. Hollis Toombs."

"Oh, Mr. Toombs."

"Yes, ma'am."

"Very nice man. He brought me the newspaper."

"I'm glad to know he was kind to you."

She scowled at him.

"He wasn't kind." Her voice took an imperious tone. "He was a gentleman. He was just being a neighbor."

"Yes, ma'am. He asked you a few questions about Camille Braxton. I was wondering if we could talk about her a little bit."

"I told him everything I know."

"Yes, ma'am. What did you see?"

"Like I told Mr. Toombs, she had car trouble one day last week. Might have been Tuesday. I'm not sure. It was in the morning. She stopped right out there." She pointed across the street. Connolly turned to look as she continued. "Almost blocked Mr. Turner's driveway. I suggested Mr. Toombs talk to Mr. Turner, but he's not home right now. Went to see his sister in Pensacola. Probably won't be back for a few days."

"Do you know what happened to the car?"

"Tony's came and got it."

"Tony's?"

"Tony's Chevron. They're on Old Shell Road."

"They came and got the car?"

"Yes. Sent a tow truck for it that morning. Not long after she left."

"She left?"

"Someone stopped and picked her up."

"Did you see who it was?"

"No. I started to go out and see if she needed some help, but she had her phone. One of those cell phones. I saw her dialing a number. Then somebody stopped to help her. So I didn't bother to go out there. I don't walk too well anymore. Takes me a while to get around. She would have been gone before I could get out there."

"What were they driving?"

"Who?"

"The person who picked her up."

"One of those big things ... sort of like a station wagon."

"An SUV?"

"Yes. An SUV. I'm not sure what kind it was."

"What color was it?"

"Rather dark. Looked black to me."

"You're sure the woman you saw was Camille Braxton?"

"Yes."

"Did you know her?"

"Yes. I know her. I've known her since the day she was born. My husband and I were in a Mardi Gras society with her parents. Knights of Mirth. I held her the day she came home from the hospital." She smiled. "Such a beautiful baby."

"Yes, ma'am. You think Mr. Turner saw her?"

"Oh, no. He didn't live here then. That was forty years ago."

"No. I mean that morning. When she had car trouble."

"Oh, I'm sure he did, if he was home. He goes up to the gym at Spring Hill College in the mornings to exercise. Usually gets home around nine thirty or ten. But he's not home right now."

"Yes, ma'am." Connolly smiled. "Well, Mrs. Cathcart, I appreciate your time. Thank you for talking to me."

"I hope I was able to help."

"Yes, ma'am. You were a big help."

Connolly stepped away and turned toward the Chrysler. He heard her lock the door behind him.

Seven

onnolly backed the Chrysler down Mrs. Cathcart's driveway and into the street. From her house he drove up Hillwood to Old Shell Road. Tony's Chevron sat on the corner to the left. He parked the Chrysler in front of the first service bay. A mechanic working on a car inside turned and stared as the Chrysler came to a stop. He wiped his hands on a rag and stepped toward the car. Connolly opened the door and climbed out.

"Man, that's a pretty car."

"Thanks," Connolly replied.

"Fifty-nine Imperial. Don't see many of them anymore."

"No. You don't."

The mechanic looked it over once more, then glanced at Connolly.

"What do you need today?"

"One of your tow trucks picked up a car on Hillwood last week. I wanted to ask some questions about it."

The mechanic wiped his hands on the rag once more.

"You'll need to see Tony about that."

An office was located along the front of the station on the far side of the service bays. The mechanic turned in that direction.

"Hey, Tony! Somebody here to see you."

Tony appeared at the office door, dressed in dark blue uniform pants and matching shirt. His name was emblazoned with white letters above the pocket, but two pencils, a pen, and a tire pressure gauge blocked most of it from view. Connolly moved across the garage to the office. Tony backed away from the door to let him enter.

Large plate glass windows along the front and the far side afforded a view of the gas pumps in front and the area at the opposite end of the building. A counter ran beneath the windows. A desk sat in the far corner. Tony leaned against the counter and folded his arms across his chest.

"Yes, sir. What could I do for you?"

"You sent a tow truck out to pick up Camille Braxton's car last week."

Tony turned to a computer terminal on the counter behind him and punched several keys. Information appeared on the monitor screen.

"Braxton?"

"Yes."

Tony studied the screen.

"Sent the truck out Tuesday, at ten twenty-nine." He turned around to face Connolly. "Logged back in with the car at five minutes after eleven."

"Where is the car now?"

"We have it."

Connolly's eyes grew wide in surprise.

"You have it?"

"Yeah. It's out back." Tony turned around to check the screen. "Yeah." He turned back to Connolly. "Nineteen sixty-seven Mercedes 200-D. Work on it all the time."

"May I look at it?"

"Sure." Tony opened a drawer under the counter and took out a set of keys. "Come on."

Connolly followed him out the door and around the station to a lot in back.

"That's it over there." Tony pointed to a gray Mercedes parked by the fence behind the building. "Belonged to her daddy. Good car, but pretty old. I told her she needed to get rid of it, but she didn't want to. We keep it running for her."

They walked across the lot to the car. Connolly looked through the driver's window. A purse sat on the front seat.

"Is it locked?"

"Should be."

Tony moved toward the door, key in hand. Connolly grabbed the handle and pulled. The driver's door came open. Tony backed away.

"I guess not."

Connolly swung the door open wide and leaned inside to look around.

"What's wrong with it?"

"Needs a new fuel pump. I called the house the day after we picked it up. Left a message. She hasn't called back. I'm sure she wants it fixed. I just like to check with the customer to make sure before I start working on them. What's up? She talk to you about buying it or something?"

Connolly leaned across the front seat and took a pen from the pocket of his jacket. The top of the purse was open. He used the pen to push the sides farther apart. Tony watched from the corner of the car through the front windshield.

"I don't think you should mess with her stuff. I didn't know that purse was out here. We need to lock it in the safe."

The corner of a white envelope stuck out the top of the purse. Connolly took it by the corner between his fingers and gently lifted it out. He dropped it on the seat. It landed facedown. The envelope had been opened. The folded edge of a letter was visible beneath the flap. He slid the pen under the envelope and turned it over. It was addressed to Camille. Buie Hayford's return address was in the upper left corner. Connolly pinched the corner of the envelope between his fingers and shook it. The letter fell out on the seat. Using the pen, he unfolded the paper.

What he found was a copy of a letter Hayford had sent to Ford Defuniak, the officer at Tidewater Bank who handled the Tonsmeyer Trust. In it, Hayford asked for an inventory of the Trust assets and for information about Camille's personal investments. When Connolly finished reading the letter, he folded it and slipped it back inside the envelope. He dropped the envelope in the purse and backed away. As he moved out of the car, Tony nudged past him.

"Let me get that out of there." He sounded irritated. "We need to put it in the safe."

Connolly grabbed him by the shoulder to stop him.

"Leave it. We have to call the police."

"The police?" Tony looked startled. "What for? I ain't done nothing wrong."

"Camille Braxton is missing."

"Missing?"

"Hasn't been seen since Tuesday morning, about the time your tow truck picked up this car. Who drove the truck?"

"Gerry. That was him you were talking to before."

Connolly took his cell phone from his pocket and punched in a number. A moment later, he was talking to Anthony Hammond.

"I found Camille Braxton's car."

"Where?"

"Tony's Chevron on Old Shell Road. You know where that is?"

"Yeah. You sure it's hers?"

"Yes. They towed it in here Tuesday morning."

"Tuesday?"

"Yeah."

"How'd you find it?"

"We can talk about it when you get here."

Connolly pressed a button to end the call. He tucked the phone in his pocket and turned to Tony.

"I need to talk to your tow truck driver before the police get here."

Connolly closed the car door. He followed Tony back to the building and around the corner to the service bay. Tony shouted across the garage.

"Gerry!"

The mechanic Connolly had seen before came from behind a car in the bay.

"Yeah."

"This guy needs to talk to you about that Mercedes you towed last week." Tony turned to Connolly. "He towed the car."

Gerry turned to Connolly.

"What you need to know?"

"Do you remember towing the car?"

"Yeah. Sure."

"Was anyone there with the car when you arrived?"

"No."

"Mrs. Braxton wasn't there?"

"No."

"A neighbor? Anybody?"

"No. Just the car."

"Did you see anything?"

"Like what?"

"Like ... I don't know. Like anything."

Tony interrupted.

"Mrs. Braxton is missing."

Gerry looked startled.

"Missing? They think I had something to do with it?"

"No," Connolly replied. "But you were there right about the time she was last seen. Did you notice anything out of the ordinary? Did anything catch your eye? Something on the ground. A scratch. A smudge."

Gerry shook his head.

"No. Not that I can recall."

"Was the hood up?"

He thought for a moment.

"No. When I got there, nobody was there, but I knew the car. Keys was in it. I've towed it before. Call came in. Tony told me to go get her car. Told me where it was down on Hillwood. I found it. Towed it in. She's a regular customer."

"You didn't see anything strange or ... anything?"

"No."

"Okay." Connolly turned away. "Thanks."

He walked from the service bay past the gas pumps to a soft drink machine in front of the office. He put in three quarters and pressed a button. A can of Coca-Cola rattled through the machine and dropped into the dispenser bin. He opened it and took a drink.

As he sipped on the Coke, an unmarked police car turned into the parking lot and came to a stop along the end of the building. Connolly walked around the corner. Anthony Hammond stepped from the car.

"Where is it?"

"Around back."

Connolly led him around the building to the Mercedes.

"Is it open?"

"Yeah."

"You been inside it?"

"Took a look."

"Touch anything?"

"Her purse is on the front seat."

"Her purse?"

"Yeah."

"You looked through it?"

"There's a letter sticking out the top. I looked at the letter."

Hammond gave him an aggravated frown.

They reached the car. Hammond looked through the window, then opened the driver's door and leaned inside.

"What about the trunk?"

"I don't know," Connolly replied. "I didn't look in there. Might have if I'd thought about it."

Hammond stood and took a small radio from his pocket. He pressed a button. The radio beeped. A dispatcher answered his call. He stepped away from the car as he talked, his back to Connolly. In a few minutes he slipped the radio into his pocket and turned to Connolly.

"We'll have some people out here in a little while to process the car."

Connolly gave him a serious look.

"You should have found this, Anthony."

"What?"

"You should have found this car. It wasn't difficult. Been right here since Tuesday."

"You know how many cases I'm working? I don't have time to track down every wife that skips out on her husband."

"That's not what this is about."

"Yeah? Well, just what do you think this is about?"

"You don't think she skipped out. You think she's dead and you've already decided her husband killed her. You aren't interested in investigating this to find out what happened. You're only interested in making a case against my client."

Hammond glared at him.

"They got the keys in there?"

"Yes."

"We'll need them to open the trunk."

He turned away and started toward the building.

Eight

Connolly waited at the service station as evidence technicians processed Camille's car. While he watched, he telephoned Buie Hayford, the lawyer whose name was on the letter he'd found in Camille's purse. They arranged to meet at Hayford's office later that afternoon.

By five thirty the police were finished with the car. Photographs had been taken from every possible angle. Fibers had been vacuumed from the seats. The car had been dusted for fingerprints. Finally, the technicians loaded it on a rollback and packed their gear to leave. Connolly walked to the Chrysler.

As he opened the car door, he glanced across the lot outside the service station. The afternoon light had turned. It was late in the day. About the time he would have enjoyed a Tom Collins. Something sweet to soothe away the tension, mellow into the evening.

He growled at himself to chase away the thought.

"And then you'd guzzle the whole bottle."

He got in behind the steering wheel and started the car.

From the service station he drove down Old Shell Road toward town. At Tuthill Lane he turned left and drove over to Spring Hill Avenue. Hayford's office was located two blocks down the avenue in a three-story nineteenth-century house across the street from Temple Beth El.

Once the home of Claudia Payden, a wealthy Mobile socialite, the house had been left to the Mobile General Hospital Foundation, which she helped establish. The foundation sold it to a group of doctors who planned to tear it down and replace it with an office building. When neighbors heard about it they organized a committee to stop the project. One of the committee members was Charlie Hayford, Buie's brother. Charlie's wife had a brother who happened to be the mayor of Mobile. The doctors saw the handwriting on the wall and quietly sold the house to Buie.

Like Connolly, Hayford graduated from law school at the University of Alabama, but there the similarities ended. While Connolly grew up the hard way in Bayou La Batre, Hayford enjoyed a much easier life in Mobile. He graduated from St. Anthony High School and Duke University before attending law school. He was captain of the football team, president of his fraternity, and the 1969 Mardi Gras king, facts attested to by numerous plaques and photos on the walls of his office. When he graduated from law school, he used family contacts to establish a practice that catered to the business and investment needs of wealthy members of Mobile society. Connolly wasn't surprised when he learned Camille Braxton and the Tonsmeyer Family Trust were his clients.

Connolly turned the Chrysler off Spring Hill Avenue into the driveway that ran alongside Hayford's office. He parked in back and went inside. It was almost six when he arrived. All of the assistants were gone. The office was quiet.

A voice called from down the hall as he closed the door.

"That you, Mike?"

"Yeah," Connolly answered.

Hayford poked his head from around a corner.

"Come on in."

Connolly walked down the hall. Hayford waited at the door to his office.

"Have a seat." He pointed to a chair in front of his desk. "Want something to drink?"

"No, thanks."

"We've got plenty of ginger ale. Boylan's. Buy it by the case from New Jersey."

His eyes twinkled playfully.

"Okay." Connolly smiled. "I'll have some ginger ale."

Hayford disappeared down the hall. He returned a few minutes later carrying two tumblers filled with ice and two bottles of ginger ale. He set a glass and bottle in front of Connolly.

"This stuff is great. Somebody at our AA meeting told me about it."

The bottle was green and had a dark blue cap. The word "Boylan's" was written across the cap in white letters. Connolly twisted it off and poured the ginger ale in the glass. As he emptied the bottle, a young man leaned through the doorway. He was dressed in a dark suit with a white shirt and muted red tie.

"I'm leaving now."

Hayford smiled and nodded.

"Okay, John. See you tomorrow."

The young man disappeared. Hayford took a sip of ginger ale and nodded toward the door.

"You know him?"

Connolly shook his head.

"I don't think so."

"That's Billy Glover's boy. John."

Connolly recognized the name.

"Didn't he go to law school?"

"Yeah. Had a little trouble with the bar exam. Billy's one of my clients. Asked me to help him out. I gave him a job."

"Not an easy exam."

Hayford nodded and took other sip. He smiled as he swallowed.

"He's taking it again in December. I know a couple of people I can put the squeeze on. Get them to give me the questions ahead of time."

Connolly took a sip from his glass.

"This is good."

"Yes, it is. I'll get you the address. Nothing like good ginger ale." Hayford sipped again. "So, you're defending the infamous Perry Braxton."

"Yeah."

"Think they'll ever find Camille?"

"Hard to say. Longer it goes, less chance they'll find her alive."

Hayford nodded.

"Perry is an interesting guy." He lifted his gaze and looked away toward some unspecified place behind Connolly. "Kind of arrogant sometimes. But very smart."

"Ever have much contact with him?"

"A little. He and Camille developed some property down at Dauphin Island. I helped her with it. He tried to get the Trust involved in a deal over in Gulf Shores last year, but I told her she ought not do it. Defuniak agreed." Hayford paused to take a sip from his glass. "Do you know Ford Defuniak?"

Connolly shook his head.

"Know who he is. That's about it."

"He's in the trust department at Tidewater Bank. They manage the Trust. He looks after most of it. I think he's a vice president or something." He took another sip. "They have so many vice presidents down there ... I think even the secretaries are vice presidents."

Connolly smiled.

"I guess that didn't set well with Braxton."

Hayford gave a look in Connolly's direction and shook his head.

"Perry didn't like it, but we had to do what was best for everyone."

"He got mad?"

"Yeah."

"When was that?"

"Last year sometime." Hayford took another sip from his glass. "Finding out much about what happened to her? I haven't heard anything except what's in the news."

"I found her car."

Hayford looked surprised. He set the glass on a blotter that covered the desktop in front of him.

"You did?"

"Yes."

"Where was it?"

"Tony's Chevron."

Hayford frowned.

"And the police didn't know about it?"

"No."

Hayford shook his head. His eyes darted away.

"Amazing."

Connolly looked across the desk for a place to set his glass. Hayford took a coaster from a small container near the telephone and tossed it to him. Connolly set the glass on it.

"They would have found it if they'd been looking. It wasn't difficult to locate."

"Anything in it?"

"Her purse was sitting on the front seat."

"It was still in the car?"

"Yeah. I guess no one noticed it when they towed it in. She had car trouble and called Tony's. They sent a truck to get it. Before the truck got there, somebody stopped and picked her up."

Hayford looked intrigued.

"How'd you find out all of this?"

Connolly gave him a satisfied smile.

"Ask enough questions, you can find out anything. There was a letter in her purse. From you to Defuniak. Something about an inventory of her assets."

Hayford leaned back in his seat.

"You read it?"

"Seemed like the thing to do."

Hayford turned toward the window. He took another sip of ginger ale and stared out the window.

"I don't suppose it hurts to discuss this," he mused. "You're probably the only one out there really looking for her."

Connolly picked up his glass and sipped the ginger ale. He waited for Hayford to continue.

"She wanted to make a gift. A large gift. To Spring Hill College." Hayford glanced at Connolly. "You need to keep this quiet until we know for sure what's happened to her."

Connolly nodded. Hayford continued.

"They're building a new library. She wanted to make a gift for it. We needed to know what was hers, and we wanted to know what was in the Trust. That's all that was about. We were going to see if the other beneficiaries of the Trust would go along with donating something from the Trust. Maybe pay for the whole thing. But before we approached them, we wanted to know how much she could give and how much trouble it would be for the Trust to make a gift. That sort of thing." Hayford turned to face Connolly. He rested his elbows on the desk. "Somebody picked her up?"

"Yes."

"That means there's someone out there who knows more about this."

Connolly nodded. Hayford looked uneasy.

"I don't like the sound of that."

"Neither do I." They sat in silence a moment, staring at each other. Connolly set his glass on the desk. "I understand they changed their wills."

Hayford leaned back in his chair again.

"Yes."

"Why'd they change them?"

"They had a little trouble before. This most recent thing about him and all wasn't the first time they separated. But they always reconciled. Sometime last year they went through one of these ... reconciliations, and she wanted to make a couple of changes as a gesture to him."

"What did they change?"

"Made him custodian of their daughter's property. Named him as her executor."

"He hadn't been executor before?"

"No."

"Who was?"

"Her cousin, Scott Bourdreaux. I got the feeling from talking to them that it was mostly Perry's idea. But she went along with it."

"I talked to Bob Dorsey. He had her execute another will when she came to him for the divorce. Did he tell you about it?"

"Yes." Hayford nodded. "Didn't surprise me. And, I must say, I was a little relieved."

"Relieved?"

He looked Connolly in the eye.

"I never trusted Perry."

"Think he knew about the new will?"

"I don't know. I didn't tell him. I doubt Dorsey did. If Camille didn't tell him, he probably didn't know about it."

"What's the likelihood she told him?"

"I couldn't tell you." Hayford gently rocked his chair. "But your case might just turn on that one fact."

Nine

*C*onnolly glanced at his watch as he stepped out of Hayford's office. It was seven fifteen. He walked across the parking lot to the Chrysler, got in behind the steering wheel, and backed the car away from the building. At the street he brought the car to a stop and waited for traffic to pass. As he waited he remembered Hayford's last comment about Braxton.

I never trusted him.

That phrase echoed through his mind. Before the traffic cleared, he thought of his earlier conversation with Bob Dorsey. *Camille. Panama Tan.* One thought tumbled into the next. *Prostitutes. Manny Fernandez.* The tumbling thoughts screeched to a halt. Manny Fernandez.

Connolly first became acquainted with him five or six years earlier when Fernandez was swept up in a prostitution raid at the old Johnson House Motel on Government Street. Fernandez was indicted on fifteen counts. But Connolly was able to get most of the charges dismissed. Fernandez pled guilty to two counts of solicitation. He served a year in Kilby Prison.

Fernandez was an interesting guy, but he had lived a troubled life. He was born in Puerto Rico. His father worked as an engineer for a radio station. In 1978, the elder Fernandez witnessed the death of two young political activists in what became known as the Cerro Maravilla incident. The murders sparked an extensive investigation. Fernandez's father supplied critical information that led to the ouster of several top government officials. Death threats against him and his family forced the FBI to relocate them. They settled first in New York, then Pensacola.

Already a troubled kid, Fernandez found it hard to adjust to his new life. At fifteen, he dropped out of school and ran away to Mobile. Young, impressionable, and looking for acceptance, he eventually came under the tutelage of Pete Rizutto, a man known to every pimp and hooker from New Orleans to Jacksonville. Under Rizutto's wing, Fernandez found the companionship for which he'd been looking. Remembering it left Connolly with a sense of heaviness. Fernandez was a likable guy, but with Rizutto calling the shots, the boy had no chance at a different life. He'd been in and out of prison most of his life. Connolly wasn't surprised to hear he was back to doing the same thing again.

Traffic moved by. Connolly eased the Chrysler out of the drive and turned right.

A mile or two down Spring Hill Avenue he turned left onto Florida Street. Several blocks later he came to Airline Highway. There, he turned right and drove west past Edgewood Mall. Evening traffic was heavy. He had to wait through several traffic lights.

Beyond the mall, the highway was lined with shopping centers and commercial buildings. A service road ran along either side to give access to the shops. Not far from the mall was a gas station off the service road to the right. Just past it the purple and pink sign for Panama Tan glowed in the gathering darkness. Connolly slowed the Chrysler.

Panama Tan occupied a commercial building that once had been home to a movie theater. Now painted purple, it sat back from the road farther than most of the surrounding shops. A parking lot stretched from the street to the building. That lot was all but empty. A sign at the corner of the building directed customers around the side to a smaller lot in back. From the street Connolly could see several cars parked back there.

He turned the Chrysler off Airline Highway onto the service road and drove past the building. Beyond it was a row of shops that faced the highway. Three doors down was an alley that led between the stores. Connolly turned the Chrysler into the alley and drove around back.

Behind the shops, cardboard boxes were piled near the corner. A large Dumpster sat at the opposite end of the building. Connolly turned the corner and switched off the headlights. He brought the car to a stop at the Dumpster. He watched a moment, then switched off the engine.

A streetlight glowed behind Panama Tan, illuminating the parking lot. He heard the muffled sound of cars zipping past on the highway out front. But there in the Chrysler the night was quiet, still, and dark.

Before long the air inside the car became stuffy and hot. Connolly's skin grew tacky and damp with sweat. He turned the ignition key one click to the right and pressed a button on the armrest to lower the window. With the window down he rested his head against the ledge of the door. The damp night air felt cool on his face. His eyelids began to droop. In a few minutes he was asleep.

Sometime later he was awakened by the sound of a car door slamming. He jerked his head from the ledge and glanced around. Across the way, a dark-colored Suburban was parked behind Panama Tan. A man walked from it to the building and opened the door. Three women came from the building and entered the Suburban. The man got in the front. Moments later, they drove away. As the Suburban came from behind the building, a gray BMW sedan followed behind it.

Connolly watched until they passed the end of the building. Then he started the Chrysler. With the lights still off, he backed away from the Dumpster, turned the car around, and drove toward the parking lot in front. He placed his foot lightly on the brake pedal as he neared the front corner. To the left he saw the Suburban turn onto Airline Highway. The BMW followed. The two vehicles blended into traffic as they moved away into the night.

Connolly was certain Fernandez was the man in the Suburban but wasn't sure he wanted to find out where they were going. He lifted his foot from the brake, hesitated for a moment, then switched on the headlights, and pressed the gas pedal. The Chrysler rolled across the parking lot. He waited for oncoming traffic, then turned left. The car surged ahead. In no time at all he had the BMW in sight. The Suburban was half a block ahead.

At Montlimar Drive the Suburban turned right. The BMW followed. Connolly slowed the Chrysler and let them move away, then made the turn. They wound past a cluster of office buildings and made their way to Highway 90. The Suburban paused at the intersection and turned right. Once again, the BMW followed. Connolly let the Chrysler fade behind, waiting until they made the turn and moved away before making the turn himself.

Traffic was light now. Connolly slipped farther behind but kept them in sight. They continued west on Highway 90. In a mile or two they came to an area dotted with tired, worn-out motels, remnants from a time in the 1950s when the highway had been the main thoroughfare between Mobile and New Orleans. To the right was the Norton Motel, followed by the Carson and the American. Across the highway were the Newman, the Bailey, and the Traveler's. All of them were single-story buildings arranged in a U around a pool in the middle with an office near the highway. Vacancy lights blinked beneath billboard signs that still advertised air-conditioning and telephones in every room.

A hundred yards beyond the Traveler's Motel was the Shady Acres Motor Court. A relic from an even earlier era, Shady Acres was a cluster of small cabins along a winding gravel driveway that meandered from the highway in a loop beneath a grove of sprawling oak trees.

The Suburban slowed and moved to the left lane. The BMW changed lanes behind it. Connolly turned into the parking lot at the American Motel. He watched as the Suburban and the BMW turned left into the drive at Shady Acres. Connolly waited until they were out of sight, then drove across the highway.

Gravel crunched beneath the tires as the Chrysler rolled off the pavement and came to a stop beside the first cabin. Connolly switched off the engine and headlights, then opened the door, and got out. At the far end of the drive, headlights from the Suburban glowed in the dark. He pushed the door closed and slipped around the back of the cabin.

Stooping out of sight beneath the windows, he ducked from cabin to cabin and worked his way toward the Suburban. At the far end of the drive, he crouched beside a cabin wall and watched.

The Suburban was parked in front of a cabin twenty yards away. The BMW came to a stop on the opposite side. Fernandez stepped from the Suburban. A slender man with short, dark hair, he opened the rear door and motioned with his hand for the occupants to get out. The jerk of his hand and the tilt of his head left little doubt the gesture was an order.

A woman's foot thrust through the open door wearing a red spike-heeled pump. The foot was followed by a slender female leg, bare to the top of the thigh. Seconds later, the woman's head appeared as she ducked through the doorway and stood. She straightened a very short skirt and ran her fingers through her hair. A second woman climbed from the car. The door on the opposite side opened and a third stepped out. At the same time, the front door of the BMW popped open. A muscular young man jumped out and opened the rear door.

A man in a dark suit climbed from the car. He had a large round belly that bulged against the buttons of his shirt and thick arms that pulled his jacket tight across the shoulders. The collar of his shirt was open, spread wide by his fat neck. He was older and heavier than Connolly remembered, but he recognized him immediately. He was Pete Rizutto.

The driver closed the car door.

Fernandez guided the women into the cabin. Rizutto followed them. The driver leaned against the BMW and lit a cigarette.

With the cabin door open, Connolly could see inside. Klieg lights sat on a stand in the corner of the room. Between the lights and the door, a video camera rested on a tripod. The women shuffled inside, followed by Fernandez and Rizutto. Someone closed the door.

Connolly moved away from the corner of the cabin and worked his way back to the Chrysler. He took his time and did his best to keep quiet and out of sight. Ten minutes later, he moved around the last cabin in front. The Chrysler was parked a few feet away. He stepped toward the car and reached for the door handle on the driver's side. As his fingers slid around it, a hand grabbed his shoulder. He wheeled around. Fernandez stood behind him.

"What are you doing here?"

Connolly gave him a tight smile.

"Manny Fernandez. Imagine meeting you here."

"You won't think it's so funny if Pete finds out you're here."

"Still hanging with your old pal Rizutto?"

"What are you doing?"

"You and Rizutto in the porn business now?"

"You shouldn't have followed us." A scowl wrinkled Fernandez's forehead. He glanced toward the Chrysler. "Not in that land yacht you drive. I made you when we turned off Airline. You better hope Victor didn't see you."

"Victor?"

"Pete's driver."

"What happened to Sonny?"

"Sonny's gone."

"Gone?"

"It ain't like it used to be. Things have changed. Lot of new people. It's a whole new ball game." Fernandez opened the car door and pushed Connolly toward the front seat. "These people don't fool around. They find out you were here, they'll slit your mother's throat and make you watch."

Connolly took a seat behind the steering wheel. Fernandez glanced around, checking.

"You gotta leave before somebody finds out you're here."

He closed the door. The window was down. Connolly spoke to him from inside the car.

"What do they have on you, Manny?"

"What you mean?"

"What have they got on you that makes you do stuff like this?"

"They ain't got nothing on me. These are my people. Now get outta here."

Fernandez moved away and disappeared in the shadows behind the cabin. Connolly started the engine and backed the Chrysler away.

A mile down the road he passed the Hungry Fisherman, a lounge across from the Norton Motel. Cars filled the parking spaces in front of the building. From the highway he could see a neon vodka logo glowing in the window. He knew the place well. He knew every place. The ones he'd visited and the ones he'd only imagined. His nostrils flared at the memory of the way they smelled, a combination of stale cigarette smoke and beer. The cool rush of the air conditioner. The hushed conversation of serious drinkers.

He lifted his foot from the gas pedal. The Chrysler's engine rumbled as it slowed. Red brake lights shone in the mirror as he moved his foot to the brake pedal. A pang of loneliness stabbed deep in his soul. His foot slid from the brake to the gas pedal.

"Not tonight," he whispered.

The Chrysler picked up speed.

Ten

Connolly awoke the next morning before six. He showered, dressed, and walked down the hall to the kitchen. There, he poured himself a cup of coffee and took a muffin from the bread box on the counter. He stood at the sink and ate the muffin as he drank the coffee. When he finished, he grabbed his jacket and started out the door.

As he stepped outside, he found Hollis Toombs leaning against the front fender of the Chrysler, his arms folded across his chest. Hollis's pickup truck was parked nearby. Connolly gave him a cautious smile.

"What's up?"

Hollis's jaw jutted forward.

"What were you doing at Shady Oaks last night?"

"I got curious."

Hollis moved in front of Connolly, their faces inches apart.

"Your curiosity could get somebody killed." His voice was low and tense. He jabbed Connolly in the chest with his finger as he spoke. "Don't ever do that again."

Connolly took a step back. Hollis continued.

"You're lucky Fernandez didn't shoot you on the spot."

Connolly retreated another step, rubbing his chest where Hollis had jabbed him.

"Fernandez used to be my client. He isn't going to do anything." He continued to rub his chest. "Your finger hurts."

"Listen to me. They catch you messing with their business, they'll do more than thump you in the chest. They're not in this for fun and games. This is their business."

"What exactly is their business?"

"You were right about Fernandez. Runs that tanning salon as a front for prostitution. Works for a guy named Pete Rizutto. He was the guy in the BMW last night. Heavy connections to the mob in New Orleans. Big-time mob. Not just some hoods from Biloxi. But there's more to it than that. I ain't figured it out yet."

"I know Rizutto. What about the women?"

"I'm not sure about the girls. Look like foreigners to me."

"Foreigners?"

"Yeah. Nobody seems to know anything much about them, and those that might aren't saying."

"What about last night? I saw a video camera in that cabin they were in."

Hollis gave him a disgusted look.

"They're making movies."

"Porn films?"

"Yeah. Porn films."

"What about Braxton?"

"I don't know. I haven't had time to find out about him yet. I haven't seen him there." Hollis moved toward the pickup truck. As he stepped inside, he turned to Connolly. "Just stay out of the way. This is some serious stuff. Lot of strange people involved. I'll let you know what I find out." He slammed the door and started the truck. As he backed away, he leaned out the window. "Just stay out of the way."

He turned the truck around and started down the driveway.

Connolly spent the morning at the office. At noon, he walked up Dauphin Street to Wintzell's Oyster House, a popular restaurant two blocks beyond St. Alban Cathedral. He met Braxton there for lunch. They sat at a table near the back. Connolly had a bowl of gumbo and a salad. Braxton had a plate of raw oysters.

"So," Braxton began, "what have you learned so far? I heard they found Camille's car."

"I found it."

Braxton looked surprised.

"You found it?"

"Yeah."

"How'd you do that?"

"Ask the right questions, you can find out most anything."

Braxton slurped a raw oyster from its shell.

"Who told you where it was?"

He wiped juice from the oyster off his chin with his napkin. Connolly took a spoonful of gumbo.

"She had car trouble. Service station on Old Shell Road towed it in for her."

"Tuesday?"

"Yes."

"Anything in the car?"

Connolly glanced at Braxton.

"Her purse."

A look of something flashed across Braxton's eyes. Connolly wasn't sure if it was anger or surprise, but he didn't like what he saw.

"Huh." Braxton reached for a bottle of hot sauce. "Seems odd. Anything else?"

Connolly took a bite of salad.

"Police spent most of the afternoon going through the car. I don't know what they found. They don't have to tell us yet."

Braxton looked puzzled.

"Yet?"

"You haven't been charged with anything. They don't have to disclose what they have until we get to court."

Braxton looked perplexed.

"Get to court? What would they charge me with?"

"I don't know." Connolly shrugged. His voice had a sarcastic tone. "Murder?"

Braxton gave him a dismissive look.

"They don't have a body."

"Don't need one."

Braxton chuckled.

"Yeah. Right."

"It's been done before."

"Hammond still thinks I had something to do with it?"

"Yeah." Connolly paused to take a sip of iced tea. "I talked to Buie Hayford. He said you tried to get the Trust involved in some sort of real estate deal."

Braxton's look turned sober.

"Yeah. He and Defuniak pretty much torpedoed it. You talk to Defuniak?"

"Not yet. Why did they balk on the deal?"

"Said they didn't like the location. It was down at Gulf Shores. Pretty far out toward Fort Morgan Point."

"Did you get it done anyway?"

"No." His voice dropped off. "My credit isn't that great."

Connolly lifted the napkin from his lap and wiped the corners of his mouth. He took another sip of tea and tried a new subject.

"I understand you and Camille changed your wills not too long ago."

"That was her idea."

"You didn't ask her to do it?"

"No." Braxton was still shaking his head as he slurped another

oyster from its shell. "How long do you have to wait before you probate the will?"

Connolly was unnerved by the question. For a man whose wife was
missing, Braxton seemed curiously detached from the subject of her
death. He took another sip of tea and set the glass on the table.

"It's not time for that. Do you have the wills?"

"They're in the safe-deposit box at the bank."

Connolly watched Braxton closely.

"Did you know she changed hers?"

"Yeah." Braxton looked oblivious. "I thought that's what we're talking
about."

"No. I mean after she went to see Bob Dorsey. He prepared a new
will for her. She signed it the first day she went to see him."

Braxton stopped chewing. His eyes looked intense. Muscles along
his jaw flexed. Connolly continued.

"You didn't know about that?"

"No." Braxton wiped his fingers on his napkin. "I didn't." He took a
drink of tea. "Doesn't surprise me, though."

They ate in silence for a moment. Connolly changed the subject
again.

"Just how large is this Tonsmeyer Family Trust?"

"Huge."

"You said you had some records for it."

Braxton ate another oyster, dropped the shell on the plate, and
pushed it aside.

"Records?"

"For the Trust."

"Yeah." Braxton took a sip of tea. "Attic at the house is full of them."
He looked Connolly in the eye for the first time. "Why?"

"Mind if I take a look at them?"

"You think there's something in them that will get the police off my
back?"

Connolly shrugged.

"Maybe. Who knows?"

"I don't see the point."

Connolly persisted.

"When Hammond had you in for questioning, he talked about the
Trust. When I found the car, there was a letter in it about the Trust.
When I talked to Bob Dorsey, he talked about the Trust. Same thing with
Buie Hayford. Every time I get a lead, it takes me to someone who talks
about the Trust. I'd like to see the records and find out a little about it
for myself."

Braxton wiped his hands on his napkin and laid it on the table.

"Help yourself." He glanced at his watch. "I need to go. I have a meeting in fifteen minutes."

He stood. Connolly stood as well. They shook hands. Braxton turned to leave.

"Let me know if you find out anything else."

He walked away without waiting for a reply. Connolly watched as he made his way to the front of the restaurant.

Eleven

Connolly spent the next morning playing phone tag with Ford Defuniak. On the fourth call he managed to get Defuniak's cell phone number from his assistant. Early that afternoon they finally connected. Defuniak was in his car.

"Hey, Mike. You caught me." His voice sounded as if they'd known each other for life. "It's a gorgeous afternoon. I'm on my way to the golf course. What could I do for you?"

"I wanted to talk to you about Camille Braxton."

There was silence on the phone.

"You still there?"

"Yeah," Defuniak replied. "Just had to make a turn. Buie said you're representing Perry."

"Yes."

"Well, I don't know what I can tell you. I mean, it might be better if we met with Buie too."

Connolly was unwilling to give in.

"I'm just interested in tracking down a few details about where she was, what she did, that sort of thing."

Defuniak sighed.

"If you want to talk today, I can see you after my golf game. Otherwise, you can call my assistant and set something up. I'll tell her to give you a time."

"Let's do it today."

"Okay. Meet me at the clubhouse around four."

"Which clubhouse?"

"Mobile Country Club."

A tingle ran down the back of Connolly's neck. Defuniak was driving to the Mobile Country Club. The clubhouse was only a few blocks from Kathleen Cathcart's house. He would drive right by her house on his way there.

"All right. See you at four."

He let the receiver slip from his fingers to the cradle on the desk.

At three thirty, Connolly left the office and drove up Dauphin Street away from downtown. The golf course at Mobile Country Club lay along the banks of Eslava Creek in Spring Hill, between Airline Highway and Old Shell Road. Twenty minutes later, he passed Mrs. Cathcart's house and made the turn into the club.

Near the street, the drive was lined with azaleas and large oaks. A little farther, the road turned left into the open and followed a fairway. Past the tee box for the fourteenth hole it veered to the right and passed through a stand of tall pine trees. It emerged from the trees at the tennis courts. Ahead, the drive circled in front of the main clubhouse, a white two-story structure with elegant columns and a staircase that swept from the ground to a balcony on the second floor. A putting green lay to the left. Rows of golf carts sat to the right near the bag drop.

Just past the carts, Connolly turned right and parked in a lot behind the building. He entered through the pro shop. A clerk at the cash register greeted him.

"Yes, sir. What could we do for you today?"

"I'm supposed to meet Ford Defuniak. Have you seen him?"

"Yeah. He's in the Nineteenth Hole."

"The Nineteenth Hole?"

"The lounge." The clerk called across the room. "Robert."

A man appeared from around the corner, dressed in green trousers and a khaki shirt with the club logo above the pocket.

"Yes, sir."

"Show this gentleman to the lounge."

Robert nodded for Connolly to follow. They walked across the shop to a door that led to a wide hallway. Ahead, Connolly could see the entrance to the locker room. Halfway there, Robert turned through a door to the right and into the lounge. He gestured toward a man sitting at a table by the window. Connolly gave Robert a smile, slipped a couple of dollars in his palm, and started across the room. Defuniak saw him coming and stood.

"Mike Connolly?"

"Yes."

The two men shook hands.

"Now that I see you, I think I've met you. You were at a reception for Judge Agostino a few years ago."

Connolly nodded.

"That seems like a long time ago."

Defuniak pointed to a chair across the table.

"Have a seat."

Both men sat. Defuniak looked away and raised his hand for a waiter's attention. A woman dressed in green pants and khaki shirt came to the table. Defuniak turned to Connolly.

"You want anything?"

Connolly glanced at his watch.

"A Coke would be good, thanks."

Defuniak tilted his head.

"Sure you don't want something else? They make a wonderful martini."

Connolly shook his head. Defuniak persisted.

"Feels good going down."

Connolly gave him a tight smile.

"Better not."

Defuniak glanced at the waitress and pointed to his glass.

"Give me another one of these."

She nodded.

"Whisky sour?"

"Yes, ma'am."

The waitress moved away from the table. Defuniak turned to Connolly.

"So. Camille Braxton."

"Yes."

Defuniak had a pained look on his face.

"Terrible situation. I hate it. Camille's a good woman. High maintenance, but a good woman."

"I talked to Buie Hayford yesterday. He mentioned you were handling her business for the bank."

Defuniak nodded.

"I work in the trust department. We manage the Tonsmeyer Family Trust. Private banking department has her personal assets. I end up working with both, but I'm just a vice president." He smiled at Connolly as he took the last sip of his drink. "We have three other vice presidents in our department. I'm just a little fish."

The waitress appeared with their drinks. She set them on the table and moved away. Connolly took a sip of Coke.

"I located Camille's car."

"I heard about that. Found it at a service station."

"Tony's. Up here on Old Shell."

"Get anything out of it?"

"Her purse was sitting on the front seat."

"Her purse? They didn't lock it up?"

"Overlooked it, I guess."

"Find anything in there to help you?"

"A letter from Buie to you about an accounting they wanted."

Defuniak lifted an eyebrow, then let it relax. He took a sip from his drink.

"I guess Buie sent her a copy."

"Looks like it."

"Did he tell you what it was about?"

"Said she wanted to make a donation. They were trying to figure out how to do it."

"She wanted to give a bunch of money to Spring Hill College."

"You talked to her about it?"

"Yes."

"When?"

His eyes darted away. He looked out the window.

"Monday."

"Monday?"

"Yeah."

"She disappeared on Tuesday."

"I know."

"Did you see her Tuesday?"

"No. I was out ... out of town that day. Had to go up to Hattiesburg."

"Did she come to your office?"

"When?"

"Monday. When you talked to her about the letter."

"Yes. Wasn't there very long. She had a question or two about some property she thought the Trust owned."

"What property?"

"A piece out in the country."

Defuniak checked his watch. Connolly continued.

"What about it?"

"Uhh ... the Trust owns a lot of property. Most of it came from Camille's grand ... great-great-grandfather. I think. Anyway, he owned a lot of property. Some of it went to the Trust. Some of it went to various family members. So, it's all kind of cut up. A little confusing. She wanted to know about one of those pieces of property." He checked his watch again. "Look, I hate to rush, but I'm supposed to meet my wife for dinner, and I still have to get home and take a shower."

He took a sip from his drink and stood.

"Come on. I'll walk you to your car. You park in back?"

"Yeah."

Connolly stood and followed him out of the lounge. They walked up the hall to the pro shop. Defuniak led him toward the door on the opposite side.

"They have some good stuff in here."

Defuniak stopped at a display of golf clubs. He took one from the rack and held it as if preparing to swing.

"Do you play?"

"No," Connolly replied. He took a club from the display. "I never took up golf."

"I buy all my stuff here."

Connolly tried to grip the club, but it felt wrong in his hand and the club face opened to the right. He was sure that was the wrong way. Defuniak grinned at him.

"It's a left-handed club."

Connolly gave him a puzzled look.

"Left-handed?"

"Yeah." Defuniak took the club from him and gripped it. "It's designed for someone who's left-handed." He gave the club a halfhearted swing. "Try it with the other hand and it works just fine."

He returned the club to the display rack and stepped toward the door.

"I buy all my clubs here. Not always easy to find good left-handed clubs."

He pushed open the door and stepped outside. Connolly followed him across the parking lot. Past the first row of cars, Defuniak stopped and turned to him.

"Well, I better get going." He extended his hand toward Connolly. "Wife will be upset if I'm late."

They shook hands.

Defuniak turned away and continued across the lot. Connolly opened the door to the Chrysler and watched. Four cars over he saw Defuniak get into a dark blue Chevrolet Suburban.

Twelve

*T*he following afternoon Connolly drove to the Braxtons' house. Like before, he parked in back and knocked on the kitchen door. Bessie greeted him.

"Good afternoon, Mr. Connolly. You're back again?"

"Perry said there were some records in the attic. Financial records. I'd like to take a look at them, if it's not too much trouble."

"Sure." She opened the door and held it for him as he stepped inside. "If Mr. Braxton says it's all right, it's no trouble to me." When Connolly was inside she closed the door and locked it. "Kind of hot up there, though. Specially this time of day."

Connolly followed her across the kitchen and through the dining room. In the hallway they made their way up the stairs. On the second floor they turned right and walked to a door at the end of the hall. Beyond it, a narrow staircase led to the attic. A single lightbulb dangled from the ceiling about a third of the way up the steps. Bessie flipped a switch on the wall by the door. The light came on.

"Watch your step. These stairs are kind of steep."

Connolly followed her. She paused when she reached the top and took a deep breath.

"There they are."

She pointed across the attic to a jumble of cardboard boxes. They were stacked four boxes high and four boxes wide.

"Camille been spending a lot of time up here lately. Some days she'd be up here almost all day."

Sweat appeared on Connolly's forehead. He wiped it away with the back of his hand. Bessie turned to start down the stairs.

"You be careful up here. Don't get too hot, now. I'll bring you some tea in a minute."

Connolly stared at the boxes as the sound of Bessie's footsteps faded away downstairs. He sighed and unbuttoned his shirt collar. Talking to witnesses was enjoyable. He liked finding them, listening to their stories, sorting fact from fiction. But documents, especially financial documents, left him bewildered. He slipped off his jacket, laid it across a dusty chair, and flipped open one of the boxes.

Inside he found pages and pages of records, neatly sorted and placed in order by date. The box he had opened began with 1999 and ran back to 1995. He leafed through the documents without taking them from the box. Dust tickled his nose. He turned aside and sneezed.

A few minutes later, Bessie returned with a glass of iced tea. She handed it to him and smiled.

"I heard that sneeze. Lot of dust up here."

Connolly took the glass from her.

"Thanks." It felt cold in his hand. He turned it up and took a long drink. "Lot of everything up here." He crunched a piece of ice between his teeth. "Camille come up here often?"

"Yes." Bessie stepped to the far side of the boxes. "Most of the time, I'd see her over there." She moved around the stack. "Here." She pointed. "Right here." She glanced back at Connolly. "This is what she was looking at right here."

Connolly came around the stack. Out of sight behind the boxes was a chair. In front of the chair was an open box. A stack of papers lay on the floor beside it.

"I don't know what all that is." She gestured again to the boxes and papers. "But that's right where she was sitting last time she was up here."

Connolly moved around her and took a seat in the chair. He set the glass of tea on the floor and picked up the papers.

"These are letters." He scanned through them. "This one's from 1922. From a lawyer." He shuffled the papers. "Oliver Gilmore, out at Grand Bay. It's addressed to someone named Pierre Tonsmeyer."

"Mr. Pierre."

"You knew him?"

"No. But my mother used to speak of him. He died before I was born."

"Who was he?"

"I'm not sure. I think he would have been Camille's grandfather, maybe."

Connolly read the letter and was soon lost in thought. When he looked up, Bessie was gone. He moved the letter aside and read the next.

The letters were addressed to Pierre about a conservatorship for his father, a man named Theron Tonsmeyer. Connolly could not tell from the letters what had created the need for the conservatorship, but it was clear Theron was no longer capable of making sound business decisions.

Connolly looked through the remaining letters in the stack and laid them aside, then turned his attention to the box in front of the chair.

Inside were maps, folded and crammed in with reams of reports from an engineering firm. From what he could tell, the documents were geological reports. He glanced through them, then took out one of the maps. It was large and unwieldy. He unfolded it across the stack of boxes and turned it around to orient it in front of him. His fingers traced along the lines of the map as he read off the place-names.

"Grand Batture Islands." His voice was a low whisper. "Bayou Caddie." He paused. "This is a map of the swamp south of Grand Bay." He ran his finger along the coastline. "Sandy Bay. Point of Pines."

Places he'd known all his life. They rolled through his mind, transporting him from the attic to a time forty years earlier and memories he'd tried to forget.

It was a hot Saturday afternoon in July. He sat on the back steps with his father listening to a baseball game on the radio. The Mobile Bears were playing Birmingham at Hartwell Field. He'd wanted to go to the game, but Rick, his younger brother, had the measles. Instead, they stayed home. He spent the morning playing catch with his father. After lunch, they took the radio to the porch. They sat in the shade on the top step and listened. Early in the fourth inning, his father groaned an awful, hollow sound. He clutched his chest and collapsed on the porch. He was dead before the ambulance arrived.

Unable to cope with the loss of her husband, Connolly's mother turned to alcohol to escape the worries of raising two children alone. Often in a drunken haze, she was frequently gone for days at a time, leaving Connolly and Rick to fend for themselves. Then, she met a man at a truck stop in Loxley and left altogether.

On their own for good, the two boys crammed what they could in a pillowcase and hitchhiked to Bayou La Batre, a rough-and-tumble fishing village on the coast, deep in the heart of the low country south of Mobile. They arrived there unannounced at the home of their uncle, Guy Poiroux.

Uncle Guy was captain of a shrimp boat. When he wasn't doing that, he worked an oyster skiff in the bays and inlets along the coast. As a teenager, Connolly spent summers working for him. The places on the map in the attic weren't just places. They were his childhood. Even now, the memories touched a pain deep in his soul. His eyes grew moist. He folded the map and returned it to the box.

By then, the sun was beginning to fade. The attic had grown dim. Ice in the glass of tea had melted. He took a sip, then turned aside and picked up his jacket. At the bottom of the stairs he switched off the light and started down the hall.

When he reached the kitchen, he found a young girl sitting at the kitchen table. She looked to be about ten or twelve years old. Bessie stood at the sink, preparing supper. She glanced at him over her shoulder.

"Find what you were looking for?"

"I'm not sure."

The young girl smiled at him. He smiled back.

"You must be Sarah."

"Yes, sir," she replied. "Have you been in our attic?"

"Yes."

"It's hot up there."

"Yes, it is. Do you like to play up there?"

"No. I'm not allowed. But Mama lets me go up there with her sometimes. Do you know where my mother is?"

He gave her a tender smile. Behind her, Bessie caught his eye. She shook her head. Connolly took a chair from the table and sat.

"No, I don't. But a lot of people are looking for her." A schoolbook lay on the table. He turned it around and opened it. "What subject is this?"

"Reading."

He turned a few pages in the book.

"Literature. *The Old Man and the Sea*. What's that about?"

"It's about a man who catches a big fish. But sharks eat most of it before he can get it to shore."

"I remember that story. He has a friend. A young boy."

"Yes."

Connolly glanced at the page.

"Ernest Hemingway."

Sarah nodded in reply. Connolly closed the book. He stood to leave.

"Bessie, you said you knew about Pierre Tonsmeyer. Have you ever heard of Oliver Gilmore?"

Before she could answer, the front door opened and someone entered the house. Footsteps echoed across the hardwood floor in the dining room. Connolly turned to see a woman standing in the doorway. In her late seventies, she was dressed in a white suit with a pink blouse. Her gray hair was tucked neatly in place.

Sarah slid from her chair at the table and darted toward the woman.

"Ma-ga." She wrapped her arms around the woman. "Ma-ga, are you going to stay with me tonight?"

"No, dear." The woman replied warmly. "You're going to stay with me." She looked down at Sarah. "I'm taking you to my house."

The woman glanced up at Connolly.

"I'm Sarah's grandmother. Jessica Stabler."

She offered her hand. He shook it politely.

"Yes, ma'am. I'm Mike Connolly."

She let her hand slip from his. Her face held the same pleasant smile as before, but her eyebrows lifted. The muscles in her neck tensed.

"You represent my son-in-law."

"Yes, ma'am."

Bessie interrupted them.

"Mr. Connolly was just asking about Oliver Gilmore."

Mrs. Stabler ushered Sarah back to the kitchen table.

"Mr. Gilmore?" She helped Sarah into her chair. "What did you want to know about him?"

"From what I can tell, he was the lawyer who set up the Tonsmeyer Trust."

"Yes. He and my grandfather were good friends. He lived out at Grand Bay. But that was years ago. He's dead now."

"Any idea what happened to his practice?"

"No." She shook her head. "I have no way of knowing."

"Maybe I can find someone out there who knows something about it."

She nodded thoughtfully.

"Perhaps you may."

He stepped to the door. As he opened it, he turned back to Sarah.

"It was good to meet you."

Sarah gave him a timid smile.

"Nice to meet you."

He pulled the door open. Mrs. Stabler called to him.

"Mr. Connolly."

He turned to face her.

"If you're going to be available this weekend, I'm having a party at my home Saturday night. You might like to attend. Several of my cousins will be there. They might be able to answer some of your questions."

"I wouldn't want to intrude."

"Oh, it's no intrusion. I have a party every year when my night blooming cactus opens. It'll be in full bloom Saturday night. Come over around seven. I'll make sure they're there."

Connolly nodded.

"Yes, ma'am."

He stepped outside. Bessie came behind him and closed the door.

Thirteen

By Friday afternoon Connolly had talked himself out of going to Mrs. Stabler's house. The Stablers gave this same party every year to celebrate a flower that only bloomed at night, but that was just an excuse. The point was to have an early summer party while they could still do it outdoors, before the weather turned too hot.

It was just like the party they held in December to celebrate Christmas and the one they held in February to celebrate Mardi Gras. All the women would stand around talking about where they shopped, and what they bought, and when they last went to the spa. The men would talk about the fish they caught last week or the ski trip they took to Colorado last winter. Connolly had been to these events before, and he always had a difficult time hiding his frustration with the mundane nature of the conversation. Besides which, the possibility that someone there would give him helpful information seemed remote. There was simply no point in going.

That was the way he felt most of Friday, but by Saturday afternoon he'd come around to going. It would be boring, but what did he care? The trail in this case led to the records in the attic. The records led to the Trust and Oliver Gilmore. Questions about Gilmore took him to Jessica Stabler, and she had invited him to the party. Perhaps he should go. He really should. Besides, Barbara would be there ... maybe. He'd heard she was back on everyone's list since she divorced him. It would be good to see her.

The Stablers' house sat on a five-acre lot surrounded by a high wall covered with ivy. A circular drive wound from the street past overgrown camellias to the front of their home. From there, it curved back to the street at the opposite side of the property. The drive was lined with cars by the time Connolly arrived. A teenager dressed in black pants and a white shirt came from the front steps as he approached. When the Chrysler stopped, the young man opened the door.

"I'll get the car for you."

He handed Connolly a ticket. Connolly got out. The boy got in.

"Be careful with it."

"Yes, sir."

The boy closed the door. Connolly started toward the house. The car rolled quietly down the drive. As he reached the top step, the front door opened. A man in a white waiter's jacket greeted him.

"Good evening, sir."

"Good evening."

"Welcome to the Stabler residence. Everyone is out by the pool."

Connolly stepped inside and made his way down the hall toward the back of the house. Near the dining room a woman dressed in a maid's uniform came from the kitchen.

"They're out here."

She guided him through the den to a door that led to the terrace around the swimming pool. Connolly stepped outside. Mrs. Stabler emerged from the crowd and moved toward him.

"Mr. Connolly." She had a pasted-on smile. "You made it."

Connolly smiled and nodded.

"Wouldn't miss a party at your house."

He glanced around hoping to catch a glimpse of Barbara. Mrs. Stabler took his arm and led him through the crowd.

"Well, I imagine you know *some* of these people."

The tone in her voice was both gracious and condescending. He knew full well she thought it all but impossible they knew any of the same people. But he stuck a smile on his face and followed along. A moment later, they approached a couple standing near the diving board.

"Mr. Connolly, I'd like you to meet Buffy and Tift Baldwin."

Connolly nodded politely.

"Tift."

Tift gave him a big smile.

"Mike Connolly. I haven't seen you in a long time. How have you been?"

"Well as can be expected."

Mrs. Stabler stood near Buffy.

"Mr. Connolly is representing Perry."

Buffy laid her hand on Mrs. Stabler's arm.

"Jessica, you are such a dear for going ahead with this party. I'd be a wreck if my daughter was missing."

Mrs. Stabler smiled at her.

"Well, it's what Camille would have wanted, I'm sure. Besides, I think it's important for Sarah. Just my way of telling her there's hope."

Tift caught Connolly's eye.

"You think he did it?"

Buffy jabbed him in the ribs with her elbow. The drink in his hand sloshed onto the sleeve of his jacket. Connolly glanced at Mrs. Stabler, then back to Tift.

"You still have that hunting camp up on the Tennsaw River?"

Tift shifted his drink to the other hand.

"Yeah. Went up there last weekend. Deer all over the place. Of course, it's six months until hunting season. By then they'll all be so far into the Delta we'll never find them."

Buffy smiled at Connolly.

"What's Rachel up to these days?"

"She has her hands full with her daughter."

"Someone told me she had a baby. How old is she?"

"She's two."

"My, seems like only yesterday Rachel was two."

"Yes, doesn't it?"

Mrs. Stabler took his arm.

"Come on, Mr. Connolly. There are a few people over here I want you to meet." She glanced at Tift. "You'll excuse us, won't you?"

"Certainly." He nodded to Connolly. "Good to see you, Mike."

Connolly followed Mrs. Stabler. Behind him he heard Buffy's coarse whisper as she lit into Tift.

Mrs. Stabler led him past the pool and down a path to the garden. Plants of every variety lined the way, but Connolly had no idea what they were.

"Your garden looks nice."

She glanced at him over her shoulder. A scowl wrinkled her face.

"Cut the crap." Her voice was cold and biting. "You don't have any idea what's in my garden."

The night blooming cactus sat on a table near a sea of day lilies. Mrs. Stabler gestured toward the table as they moved past.

"This is the reason for the occasion. It'll open after the sun goes down."

He followed her to the far side of the garden where fifteen or twenty people had gathered around a wrought-iron table and chairs. Everyone stood as Mrs. Stabler approached. She addressed them as a group.

"I'd like you all to meet Mike Connolly. Some of you may know him. He's an attorney. Perry called him the other night when the police had him down for questioning. He's interested in finding out what you might know about Camille and her disappearance. I think he's particularly interested in hearing about Oliver Gilmore, though I have no earthly idea why.

I'd appreciate it if you all would talk to him."

She turned to Connolly, her voice low, her tone restrained. "These are all Camille's cousins." She glanced at the group. "Well, some of them are cousins, and some of them are spouses. They'll introduce themselves. I've asked them to talk with you." Her face went cold. She moved closer. "I invited you here because I think you'll have a better chance finding out what happened to my daughter than the police will. Don't think for a minute I care one bit about my son-in-law." She turned to the group and flashed a smile. "We'll eat in about an hour."

They nodded to her. She turned back to Connolly.

"I don't suppose you'll be staying."

Connolly shook his head.

"No, ma'am."

She moved up the path and disappeared into the crowd around the pool. Connolly turned to face the cousins. Several brushed past him and followed Mrs. Stabler. A man stepped forward and thrust out his hand.

"I'm Hokie Tonsmeyer. Camille is my cousin."

Connolly shook his hand.

"Glad to meet you."

"You want to know about Oliver Gilmore?"

"Yes."

"They tell me he used to live out at Grand Bay. My daddy knew him. I think he was dead by the time I was born."

A woman slinked past him.

"I have nothing to say to you. Perry Braxton can rot in prison for all I care."

Hokie smiled.

"Don't pay any attention to her. She's drunk. And jealous. She's been after Perry since the first time he and Camille went out."

A second man stepped forward. Older than the others, he was about the age of Mrs. Stabler.

"I think most of Mr. Gilmore's relatives moved away. He had a brother and two sisters. The brother lived down there near him, but I think the sisters lived up around Chattanooga somewhere. I can't imagine any of them being alive now."

Connolly nodded.

"I didn't catch your name."

"John Watts. My wife is Camille's first cousin."

"Did he have any children?"

"Who? Oliver?"

"Well ... yes. Him or the brother."

"Oliver didn't have any children. His brother had a daughter and a son, I think. They might still be alive, but I don't know where they are."

A woman standing a few feet away chimed in. She spoke in a slow, slurred drawl.

"That son was killed in Vietnam."

Watts glanced at her.

"No. Couldn't have been. He'd have been too old for Vietnam."

She took a sip from the glass in her hand.

"Well, it was one of those places over there. He's dead."

Hokie nodded to Connolly.

"She might be right."

Watts drifted away. Another woman moved closer. She smiled at him as she approached. Connolly recognized her immediately.

"Hello, Linda."

The woman squeezed his arm and bussed him on the cheek.

"Hello, Mike. Haven't seen you in a long time."

"It's been a while."

"You taking care of yourself these days?"

"Doing the best I can."

"You look good. I heard you got straightened out."

"I am today."

She leaned on his arm.

"That's good. You look good."

Connolly smiled.

"Thank you. You look nice yourself."

She guided him away from the rest of the group.

"You still living in Lois Crump's guesthouse?"

"Yes."

"Ever see her?"

"Not much. She lives up in Birmingham now."

"That's right." She led him a few steps farther. "Listen, most of these people have no idea who Oliver Gilmore is. They just met with you because Aunt Jessica asked them to and because she always throws a good party."

"Do you know anything about him?"

"Not really. He died before most of us were born. John knows a little something about him because he's into family history. Keeps track of all that."

"John?"

"John Watts. The man you were talking to with Hokie."

"Oh."

"I used to be good friends with a girl named Ann Gilmore. She and I were in glee club together in high school."

"Was she related to him?"

"Yes. But I don't know how. What's so important about Mr. Gilmore?"

"I'm looking for the files from his law practice."

"Oh. I see. Well, I don't know if she knows anything about that, but last I heard she was still living out there at Grand Bay. Married a guy named David Sessions. His family owns a lumber business."

Connolly slipped his arm from hers.

"Thanks. I'll check it out."

He glanced behind him. The cousins were gone. Linda gave him a look. Her fingers touched the back of his hand.

"Ever get lonely in that guesthouse?"

Connolly moved away.

"Linda, I appreciate your help. It's always good to see you." He gestured toward the garden path. "We better get back to the party. People will wonder what's happened to us."

She gave him that look again.

"They'll know what happened to us. The real question is, will they care?"

Connolly nodded.

"You're probably right."

He waited for her to move past, then followed her up the path toward the swimming pool.

Fourteen

Connolly left the party and started toward midtown feeling tense and restless. As he drove down Spring Hill Avenue, he lowered the window and let the night air in the car, but it did little to ease his growing sense of frustration. Over and over Mrs. Stabler's voice kept playing in his mind. The condescending tone. Her backhanded way of giving him a compliment and ridiculing him at the same time.

And Buffy. The look on her face when she asked about Rachel. From what he'd heard, Buffy had her own problems to worry about.

The car rolled quietly down the street. Houses and shadows blended together on either side like a seamless dark wall. The night enveloped him like a soft, comfortable shirt.

But in his mind the voices continued.

"They never liked you. Didn't like you from the beginning. And for no good reason. You went to college. Did anyone notice? No. All they noticed was how old your car was or the kind of clothes you wore. You went to law school. Did it make a difference? No. All they remembered was where you grew up."

Restless tension grew to frustration. He mumbled to himself.

"Always looking at me like I was some kind of second-class citizen."

"And Barbara. Where was she?"

He thought sure she would be there. He missed her now more than ever.

"Did someone tell her I was going to be there? Did she not come because of me?"

The questions sounded ridiculous, but the more he tried to push them aside, the more they kept coming. Before long, frustration gave way to anger.

"They're idiots. The whole crowd. Mrs. Stabler. Buffy. Tift. And Linda. She came on to me like she was a friend, like she was concerned, but it was just pity."

He didn't need her pity. She could find some other project. He wasn't interested. His voice took a mocking tone.

"Are you still living in Lois Crump's guesthouse?"

He banged his fist against the car door.

"Lying sack of ..."

His voice trailed away.

At Sage Avenue he turned right and cut across to Dauphin Street. The traffic light was red at the intersection. He brought the Chrysler to a stop and glanced to the left to check for traffic. The A-1 Package Store sat on the corner. Lights in the parking lot forced him to squint. There wasn't a car in sight. He thought of running the light.

As he waited, his eye wandered back to the store window. Inside, rows and rows of bottles lined the shelves, labels turned out, facing him. Even from a distance he recognized each one. Seeing them was like seeing an old friend. He let his eyes move down the shelves. In his mind he heard the name of each brand. He looked away.

The light was still red. He glanced over his shoulder and checked for traffic. Headlights flashed in the mirror. A moment later, the lights disappeared as the car turned onto a side street. Behind him there was only empty darkness.

He looked to the left once more. Bottles on the shelves seemed to dance and spin. By then, he could taste the contents of each one.

Finally, he could stand it no more. He put the car in reverse and backed up the street, then turned the steering wheel to the left, and steered across the oncoming lane to the parking lot at the package store. He stopped in a space beside the building and opened the car door.

"I'll just go in and look," he told himself.

He stepped from the car and walked to the front entrance. A buzzer sounded as he opened the door. The clerk smiled at him from behind the register, then averted her eyes.

Connolly felt a rush of energy. His face was flush. His skin tingled. The palms of his hands were tacky and damp.

Instead of browsing, he walked straight to a shelf of gin along the back wall. He took down a bottle and returned to the counter. The clerk punched the keys on the register. Connolly felt the veins in his neck throb. The sound of his heart pounded in his ears.

The clerk slipped the bottle in a brown paper bag and said something. Her lips moved and he heard words coming from her mouth, but he couldn't understand what she was saying. He shoved his hand in his pocket and took out a twenty. She set the bag on the counter and gave him a smile. He handed the money to her and did his best to look calm. She punched more keys on the register. The drawer opened. She gave him change.

Relief washed over him as he took the change and shoved it in his pocket, but his movements felt jerky and out of control. He grabbed the bottle and bag from the counter and turned toward the door.

Outside, he ducked his head as he hurried along the front of the building to the Chrysler.

He opened the car door, tossed the bottle on the seat, and slid in behind the steering wheel. The engine came to life. He backed the car away from the building and steered it to the street and across the intersection.

Voices in his head began to shout.

Are you stupid?! Throw it out the window.

"It's just a drink."

There's no such thing as "just a drink."

"I can handle it."

No, you can't.

"I deserve it. I need something to calm me down."

You need a cold shower.

"These people. They think they're so good. So much better than me. I don't need them. I don't need anyone. Not Jessica Stabler or Tootsie Trehern or Linda or Barbara. Not any of them."

The voices fell silent. Minutes later he turned off Tuttle Street into the driveway at the Pleiades. He parked the car beside the guesthouse and went inside.

In the kitchen, he set the bottle on the counter and looked at it a moment, then backed away to the opposite side of the room. Sweat trickled down his back. He leaned forward, resting his hands on his knees, and stared at it. As he watched, the red and silver label seemed to glow. A man on the label turned his head toward him. Their eyes met. The man smiled.

Connolly rubbed his hands over his face and looked again.

Letters across the top of the label jumped from one side to the other, rearranged themselves in gibberish, then sorted themselves out again. Time stood still. The present seemed unimportant. The past was irrelevant. The future never crossed his mind.

He opened a cabinet by the sink, took out a glass, and set it next to the bottle. The man on the label looked at him and winked. Connolly twisted off the cap.

The sharp, sweet smell of gin wafted up his nose and drifted through his sinus cavities. Taste buds on his tongue came to attention. Already his throat burned. He picked up the bottle to pour a drink. His hand trembled. The bottle neck clinked against the rim of the glass. He hesitated and tipped the bottle away.

An image of Barbara crossed his mind. She glared at him, arms folded at her chest, a stern scowl on her face. He saw Mrs. Stabler gliding through the crowd at the party. Heard the sound of Buffy's voice. Linda's pity.

He shoved the glass aside, raised the bottle to his lips, and took a sip.

Sometime later Connolly opened his eyes and found himself lying on the couch looking up at the ceiling. Sunlight flooded the room through the picture window on the opposite wall. He raised his head and glanced around. The living room looked the same. The television was still in the corner. But on the coffee table he saw the gin bottle was empty a third of the way down.

Pain pounded his head from both sides. He fell back on the couch.

After a moment, he rolled to a sitting position and grabbed the bottle by the neck. Without giving himself time to think, he jumped from the sofa and ran to the kitchen. He shoved the neck of the bottle down the sink and watched as the contents gurgled down the drain. When it was gone, he tossed the bottle in the trash can.

The smell of gin tickled his nose. Even from the trash can, the face on the bottle label seemed to call to him. He picked up the trash can and carried it out the door.

Behind the guesthouse, he flipped off the lid of a large, green garbage can and took out a plastic bag filled with kitchen waste he'd thrown out several days before. He set the bag on the ground, dumped in the contents from the kitchen can, and covered the gin bottle with a newspaper. Then, he tossed the bag of kitchen waste on top of it and replaced the lid.

Back inside, he washed his hands at the kitchen sink. As the water ran, he poured dish soap down the drain and watched it bubble up. When he was sure all traces of gin were gone, he turned off the water and dried his hands on a towel, then smelled the towel. It smelled like gin.

He walked down the hall to the washing machine and tossed in the towel. Then he noticed the smell from his shirt. He peeled it off, followed by his pants, then his underwear, and shoved all of it in the washing machine. He covered it with detergent and turned on the machine. Water filled the tub.

The agitator began to swish back and forth as he stood there, naked, watching the clothes move around in the soapy water. Tears streamed down his face. He pounded the washing machine with his fist.

Fifteen

When Connolly arrived at the office Monday morning, Mrs. Gordon was already seated at her desk near the door. Seeing her sent pangs of guilt through his riddled soul. She handed him a stack of phone messages as he walked by.

"These were from Friday."

His eyes met hers for an instant, then darted away. He took the messages from her and flipped through them as he moved down the hall. Halfway to his office he stopped and turned in her direction.

"I need an address for someone in Grand Bay."

His head was down, his eyes focused on the messages. When he did not hear her respond, he glanced up, expecting to see her knowing look. Instead, she had turned to face the computer behind her desk.

"Think you can find it?"

Her eyes focused on the monitor screen.

"Who is it?"

"Somebody named David Sessions. Owns a timber business."

"In Grand Bay?"

"Yes."

Mrs. Gordon gave him a smirk.

"What's happened now?"

Another pang of guilt shot through him.

"Nothing." He ambled up the hall in her direction, still looking through the phone messages. He glanced up at her again. "There used to be a lawyer down there named Oliver Gilmore. He's dead now. I need to track down his files."

"What for?"

"Perry Braxton."

"Perry Braxton." She made no attempt to hide the disdain in her voice. "You're spending a lot of time on him."

"Did he send us a check?"

"Yes. But you've just about billed all of it out."

"Good. Send him a notice and tell him to make another payment."
She turned to her desk and scribbled a note.

"Doesn't the bar association handle that sort of thing?"

Connolly gave her a puzzled look.

"What? The fee?"

"No." She looked irritated. "Files for deceased attorneys."

He let his hand with the phone messages drop to his side and focused his attention on the conversation.

"They do now, I guess. This guy probably died around 1930. Something like that. Back then, I don't know what they did. Wouldn't surprise me if they were thrown away."

Mrs. Gordon turned to her desk again and picked up the telephone. Connolly listened as she placed a call to the local bar association. After a brief conversation she hung up the phone.

"They don't know what the procedure was back then. She thinks the presiding judge might have handled it. Sounds like no one's going to know where they are."

"Well, I have to find them. See if you can find that guy's address. David Sessions."

Connolly walked down the hall to his office. He returned a couple of phone calls, then began working on a file. In a few minutes Mrs. Gordon appeared in the doorway. He glanced up from the desk.

"Yes?"

She gave him a satisfied smile.

"David Sessions." She stepped to the desk and handed him a piece of paper. "He owns Alabama Lumber. Highway 90, west of Grand Bay."

Connolly glanced at the piece of paper to see the address and phone number.

"Where'd you find this?"

"The Internet."

A frown wrinkled his brow.

"The Internet? We have the Internet?"

"Comes with the phone service."

Connolly looked puzzled.

"When did we get that?"

"Two or three years ago."

"I don't remember getting that."

Mrs. Gordon turned away.

"I don't doubt it."

She took a few steps past the door, then came back.

"Are you all right?"

He moved the file on his desk aside, as if looking for something, and avoided her gaze.

"Yes. Why?"

"You just seem a little ... different. Did anything happen over the weekend?"

"No." Connolly looked up at her and smiled. "I'm all right."

She looked at him for a moment, then disappeared up the hall. When she was gone, he closed his eyes and rested his head on the desktop.

Grand Bay was a small town deep in the low country south of Mobile. Concealed beneath the lush foliage of acres and acres of pecan trees, its distinction lay not in the beauty of its verdant landscape but in the unique disposition of its people. Opinionated but not cantankerous, they were old-school Southerners with a dash of Creole ambiguity. Grandmother's china next to a pickle jar full of gumbo. A church bazaar with Jack Daniels in the trunk of the car. It was a peculiar little place.

Connolly found Alabama Lumber without any trouble. Located on the west side of town, the lumberyard covered a lot along Highway 90. A chain-link fence twelve feet high surrounded the facility with three strands of barbed wire across the top for good measure. Large, heavy gates stood open at the entrance. A lock the size of Connolly's fist dangled from a chain on the gate to the left.

He steered the Chrysler into the lot and made his way past stacks of fresh-cut lumber to a weathered wooden building near the center of the property. A sign identified it as the office. He parked near the end of the building and stepped from the car. As he did, the front door of the building opened, and a man stepped out.

Dressed in gray work clothes, he was tall and slender and wore a cap the color of his shirt and pants. The cap had a long, dirty bill that hid most of his thinning hair. His skin was tanned and leathery, and he had a rawboned look about him, like a man who had worked hard all his life with nothing to help him but his own grit and determination. He turned in Connolly's direction.

"Can I help you?"

His voice was rough and gravelly. Connolly came around the car toward him.

"I'm looking for David Sessions."

"You've found him. But I'm not interested in talking to any salesmen today. I've got more to do than I can get done."

"I'm not a salesman. I'm a lawyer."

"I've got less time for lawyers than I do for salesmen."

"I need to ask you a few questions."

David stared at him a moment.

"I'll give you five minutes." He turned back to the building and opened the door. "Come on inside. We can talk in here."

Connolly followed him.

Inside, a counter ran the length of the room from left to right opposite the door. Behind it were two desks. A computer terminal sat on each, surrounded by stacks of papers. Two clerks sat at the desks busily shuffling papers and working the computers. David guided Connolly through a doorway to the left at the end of the counter.

Beyond the door was an office. A plain metal desk sat to the right. A metal chair sat in front of it. David closed the door and pointed to the chair as he moved behind the desk.

"Have a seat."

Connolly took a seat in the chair. David leaned against the corner of the desk.

"What could I help you with?"

"There used to be a lawyer who practiced here named Oliver Gilmore. Somebody said your wife might have been related to him."

David nodded in response.

"Had an office upstairs over the bank. Used to be the bank. Then it became the post office. Now it's empty."

"Did you know him?"

"No. He died a long time before I was born. Why are you interested in him?"

"I'm trying to locate the files from his legal practice."

David folded his arms across his chest.

"Now I don't know about that. Why are you interested in his files? Whatever he had would be a little out of date by now, wouldn't it?"

"I think there might be something useful in one or two of them."

The look on David's face indicated he was waiting for Connolly to continue.

"Apparently Mr. Gilmore prepared some documents for a trust. I'd like to see his file on it."

David smiled.

"You talking about the Tonsmeyer Trust?"

Connolly was surprised by his answer.

"You've heard of it?"

"Tonsmeyer Trust owns half the buildings in town. Lots of farmland. Owns a huge tract of swampland down here south of town. Runs from the state line halfway to Bayou La Batre." He chuckled. "Everybody knows about the Trust."

"Tonsmeyer must have been quite a businessman."

"The old man was. His son wasn't much of anything. The old man started working for a guy named Otto Sommers during the Civil War. Sommers had a wharf down at the bay. Down there where the Trust owns all that land. Tonsmeyer was just a kid. When the Yankees blockaded Mobile, Sommers went to smuggling. Tonsmeyer worked for him. They say he was a genius. Kept track of everything in his head. When the war ended, he knew more about Sommers' business than Sommers did. After Sommers died, he left everything to Tonsmeyer." David paused for effect, then continued. "That old man owned all the swamp around the wharf clean up to the high ground and a big chunk of stock in the railroad. That's where Tonsmeyer got his start."

"Interesting man."

"Yeah."

"Does Mr. Gilmore have any relatives around here?"

David glanced down at the floor.

"Most of his people moved away years ago. Got a few living in New York. Some out in Colorado."

"Think your wife knows anything about his files?"

David shook his head.

"Nah. I doubt it." He pushed himself away from the desk and stood. "They have a couple of cousins here." He unfolded his arms from across his chest and leaned against the wall. "Is this going to get all tied up in some big lawsuit?"

"I don't think so."

"He has one cousin around here that might be able to help you." A smile crossed David's face. "Actually, she's Gilmore's cousin and she's my cousin, too. She married my cousin and I married one of hers."

Connolly smiled.

"She's your cousin by marriage."

"Marriage. Blood. It don't make much difference. Family is family. She's a widow now. Getting old. Lives by herself. I wouldn't want to send you to her if she's going to get tangled up in a big mess."

"I just want to see the files."

David looked away.

"Her name is Gladys Newman." He sighed. "She lives down on the Potter Tract."

Connolly frowned.

"The Potter Tract?"

"Yeah." David seemed to notice the look on his face. "It's a long story. Potter was a Yankee speculator. Came down here around 1910. You don't have time for the whole story today, and neither do I. Just go down Main Street through town. Keep going. That'll take you south toward the swamp. When the road ends, turn right. You'll be on a dirt road. Go down that a mile or two. You'll come to a house that sits right next to the road. That's her house."

Connolly stood.

"I appreciate your help."

David stood away from the wall. The two men shook hands.

"You be careful when you go down there." There was a hint of laughter in his voice as he guided Connolly toward the door. "She wouldn't be afraid to shoot you if she thought you were up to no good."

Connolly smiled.

"I'll be careful."

David opened the office door. Connolly followed him outside.

Sixteen

Connolly left Alabama Lumber and drove to the center of town. At Main Street, he turned right. Two blocks later he passed the building where Gilmore's office had been. A few blocks farther, he was out of town. Shops and stores gave way to pecan orchards, tung orchards, and groves of satsuma trees.

Before long, he reached the end of the pavement. Ahead, the land dropped off into the swamp. To the right was a dirt road that ran through a pecan orchard, the branches locked together in a thick green mat that covered the ground with cool, dark shadow. Connolly turned the Chrysler off the pavement. The road was dry. He pressed his foot against the gas pedal. The car surged forward. Dust rose behind him in a cloud that rolled through the trees on either side.

A mile down the road he came to a small wood-frame house with white siding. From a distance, it seemed the house sat in the middle of the road. As he approached, he could see the road ran directly at the house. Then, twenty yards from the side window, it turned sharply left and curved around the house and a weathered barn that sat in front of it. Beyond the barn, the road turned back to its previous course and continued into the distance on the opposite side.

"This must be the place."

He slipped his foot from the gas pedal and pressed the brake. The car slowed. Dust that had been behind him now rolled over the car, enveloping it in a gritty red haze. The car came to a stop beneath a pecan tree a few yards off the road near the house. He opened the door to step out, but before he could get both feet on the ground, the front door of the house flew open. A woman's voice called to him.

"Who are you and what do you want?"

Connolly took his jacket from the front seat and stepped from the car. He turned toward the house to see who called.

A large, robust woman wearing a loosely fitting cotton dress came from the house. She took a few steps toward him, then stopped. Her thin white hair was combed straight back from her forehead and tucked behind her ears. A strand of pearls hung around her neck, and on her feet she wore a pair of pink rubber flip-flops. But in her hands she gripped a double-barreled shotgun.

She glared at him, as if waiting for an answer.

Connolly raised both hands.

"Don't shoot." He was amused at the sight of her. A grin spread across his face. "I didn't come to start any trouble. David Sessions suggested I come to see you."

She lowered the shotgun.

"David called a while ago. I just wanted to make sure it was you. You want to see Oliver's files?"

"Yes, ma'am." He slipped on his jacket and stepped around the back of the car. "If this is a bad time, I can come back another day."

She leaned the shotgun by the door and started across the yard toward the barn.

"Now's as good a time as any. The files are out here in the barn."

Connolly followed her.

The barn was made of heart pine lumber and had a tin roof. Once painted red, most of the color was faded from the boards, leaving them grayed with only a hint of paint remaining in a few places. The roof was rusted dark brown.

They walked across the grass beneath the pecan trees to a set of double doors at the end of the barn. A padlock kept the doors closed tightly together, but Connolly was certain anyone who wanted in could find a way. Boards were missing from the sides in several places. Overhead, the doorway to the loft was open.

Gladys took a key from the pocket of her dress and poked it in the lock. She gave it a twist. The lock came open. She slipped it out of the way.

As she moved the lock, the doors fell open toward them. The one on the left swung on its own and came to rest against an anthill to one side. She caught the one on the right as it came toward her and pushed it out of the way. Light spread across the floor of the darkened barn. Connolly stepped inside.

A tired and worn tractor sat to one side. On its yellow frame was a large black M. Between patches of rust he could see the name Minneapolis-Moline. Gladys noticed the tractor caught his attention.

"That tractor belonged to my grandfather. It's older than you are." She stepped past him. "What you're looking for is over here."

She moved to the right onto a raised wooden floor. He followed her past a basket of canning jars and a stack of worn plow parts. In the far corner, she reached over her head and grasped a small white cord that dangled from the rafters above. Connolly glanced up to see the cord was attached to a light socket holding a single bulb. A twisted strand of electrical wire ran from the socket to a white porcelain insulator attached to a timber above them. The wire looked to be as old as the tractor parked near the door.

Gladys pulled the cord. The light came on.

Along the wall was a stack of boxes, browned and crumbling from age and the ravages of heat and humidity.

"That's them." She pointed to the boxes. "Not sure what you're looking for. They aren't in any particular order."

Connolly stepped past her and opened the first box. A roach ran out as he moved the lid.

Inside were papers and files that had been created before he was born. The pages were dried and made a crinkly sound as he shuffled through them. Staples and paper clips had rusted, leaving stains on the corners. Some had rusted completely away. The file folders were dotted with mildew and remains of dead silverfish. He turned his head and sneezed.

Gladys backed away and picked up a five-gallon bucket. She turned it upside down and took a seat on it.

"What are you looking for, anyway?"

"Files on the Tonsmeyer Trust."

"You and everybody else."

Connolly glanced at her over his shoulder.

"Somebody else has been looking for them?"

"Two or three fellows from Texas came out here last year."

He turned to face her. She gestured toward the boxes.

"Spent half a day digging around in that stuff. Another fellow came out here a few months ago, but he didn't stay very long."

Connolly turned back to the boxes and continued to sort through the files.

"Who were they?"

"The first bunch were from some oil company. I don't know which one. The last fellow, I don't think he ever said who he was. Young guy."

Connolly took a file from the box and looked through it. Gladys kept talking.

"Citadel man."

Connolly gave her a puzzled look.

"Excuse me?"

"A Citadel man. That last guy who came out here was a Citadel man."

Connolly turned back to the boxes. Gladys shifted positions on the bucket.

"Citadel Bulldogs. Good school. Pitiful football team." She chuckled to herself. "But, when your biggest rival is Furman, what can you say?"

Connolly talked as he looked through the boxes.

"He told you he attended the Citadel?"

"He didn't say much of anything. But he had a tag on the front of his car. One of those foreign things. Bright red. And right there in the front was a baby blue tag with white letters. 'Bulldogs.' Didn't have to ask. I knew what it was."

"You watch a lot of football?"

She chuckled again.

"Look around. Not much else to do out here. I have a satellite dish on the other side of the barn. Get a hundred and fifty channels. There's a game on right now. Replay of Harvard and Yale from last year, not that anybody cares."

Connolly reached the end of the first box without finding anything about the Trust. He closed the box and set it aside, then opened another. Gladys continued to talk to him about football. In the third box he found the Trust files.

"Here we go."

He took out a file folder and held it in the light to read. Gladys rose from her seat on the bucket and stood beside him.

"Find what you were looking for?" She leaned over his shoulder as he scanned the document. "I probably should have given those files to someone."

Connolly nodded as he continued to read. She backed away and returned to her seat on the bucket.

The original Trust document bore stamps and numbers that had been affixed to it when it was recorded in probate court. The document had been signed on November 15, 1922. It was recorded on November 24 of that same year. As he looked at the signatures, he noticed it had been signed by Theron Tonsmeyer as grantor and by Pierre, his son, as conservator.

Connolly stared blankly as he thought.

Pierre was his father's conservator.

He calculated the dates in his mind. If Tonsmeyer was twelve during the Civil War, he would have been born sometime around 1850. That would make him ... about seventy-two in 1922.

He laid the document aside and turned to the box again.

"Now, you can look at anything you want to." Gladys's voice had the tone of a schoolteacher. "But you can't take any of it with you."

Connolly turned toward her.

"I need copies of some of this."

"That's fine. Just figure out what you want and give them to me. I'll make copies for you. But I'm not letting any of that stuff out of my sight."

Connolly slipped off his jacket. He found a nail on the wall and hung the jacket on it. He loosened the cuffs of his shirt and rolled up his sleeves, then turned back to the box. Gladys sat on the bucket and watched. As the afternoon wore on, Connolly heard her snoring. He chuckled at the sight of her sitting on the bucket, her chin resting against her chest.

Finally, late that afternoon, he finished with the last box. He dusted his hands against each other and looked around.

"You sure this is all of it?"

He spoke loud enough to rouse her but avoided looking in her direction. Gladys jerked awake.

"Did you say something?"

He smiled at her.

"Are you sure this is all the files you have?"

"Far as I know. Something missing?"

"I don't know. Maybe."

Gladys rubbed her eyes and stood. Connolly handed her several documents.

"I need to get copies of these."

She took them in one hand and clutched her hip with the other, rubbing it.

"Sat too long in one place. Should have walked around a little."

Connolly straightened his shirtsleeves, buttoned the cuffs, and slipped on his jacket.

Gladys moved with slow, halting steps toward the cord for the light. Connolly started toward the doorway. As she reached for the light, he noticed two boxes sitting beside the door. He moved the lid off one as Gladys clicked off the light.

Inside, he found more files and papers. He took out a file and leaned through the doorway for enough light to read it. Gladys moved across the room toward him.

"What did you find?"

"Turn the light on, please."

She moved closer and peered over his shoulder.

"Is that some more of Oliver's papers?"

"Yes. Turn the light on."

Gladys waddled across the room and clicked on the light.

Connolly knelt on one knee and flipped through the pages in the first box. The box contained records regarding Tonsmeyer's financial transactions. Near the back of the box were medical records and reports from a number of physicians, all of whom appeared to agree that Theron Tonsmeyer was senile. He opened the second box. It contained copies of pleadings that had been filed in court. Among them was an order appointing Theron's son, Pierre, as his conservator. The date on the order was August 6, 1919, more than three years before the family trust was created. Connolly turned to Gladys.

"I need to take these boxes with me."

Gladys shook her head.

"Can't let you do that."

"These boxes are very important. Has anyone looked at them?"

"I don't think so."

"Those other people you were telling me about. They didn't look at these?"

"Not that I know of. I'm not even sure how those got there."

"We have to get these to a safe place. Someplace where I can spend time going through them."

"Why? They've been right here for seventy-five or eighty years. What's so important about them?"

Connolly took out the file with the order granting the conservatorship.

"Look." He held the file for her to see. "This is an order appointing a conservator for Theron Tonsmeyer."

Gladys glanced at the document.

"Okay."

He handed her the file and took the papers she was holding in her other hand. He shuffled through them and found the trust document.

"This document created a trust that's now known as the Tonsmeyer Family Trust. It was signed by Theron Tonsmeyer on November 15, 1922." Connolly pointed to the conservatorship order. "This order appointed a conservatorship for him in August 1919. More than three years earlier."

Gladys gave him a blank look.

"And?"

"The conservatorship was granted because Mr. Tonsmeyer was incapable of handling his own affairs."

"What are you saying?"

"These two documents right here raise a serious question about whether the Trust was properly created." He looked through the papers and held another document for her to see. "Look at this. This is a deed transferring property to the Trust." He turned to the signature page. "It was signed by Theron Tonsmeyer, that's all, just him, after he'd been found incompetent."

"Is that a problem?"

"Yes."

"It's been a long time. You think it makes any difference? You think anyone's interested in that now?"

He gave her a look.

"There's a lot of money involved. I'm sure everyone is interested."

She glanced at the boxes.

"What would you do with them?"

"I'd like to take these two boxes to my office."

"Is this going to look bad for Oliver?"

"I don't know."

"He was a good man."

"I'm sure he was. Look, I'm not interested in what happens to the Trust or the property or anything. I'm not trying to litigate any of this. I'm defending a murder case."

She looked startled.

"A murder case? What's all this got to do with a murder case?"

"Right now, I have no idea. But, as much as I'd like to avoid it, I think I need to find out what this is all about."

Gladys looked away for a moment.

"Well, David seems to think you're all right. You'll take care of them and bring them back when you're through?"

"Yes, ma'am."

She started through the doorway.

"You'll have to carry them. I'm not able to tote much anymore." She walked on ahead of him, holding the documents he'd given her from the other boxes. A few steps out the door, she called to him over her shoulder. "But just those two. Leave the other boxes where they are." She gestured with the papers in her hand. "I'll get you copies of these other things."

Seventeen

*C*onnolly returned from Gladys Newman's barn early that evening. Twilight had passed. Darkness cloaked the city, broken only by the amber glow of streetlights and the harsh glare of headlights from passing automobiles. As the Chrysler rolled down Government Street, his mind began to wander.

Staring through the windshield, the hood of the Chrysler became a bar made of burnished wood. He knew a place that had one like it. On the bar was a glass. A good, heavy glass. The kind that made a clinking sound when ice hit the bottom, then rolled around and dinged against the sides.

He fought to keep the images from his mind, but the comfortable feeling they brought made them difficult to resist. The sound of gin, gurgling from the bottle, splashing on the ice. The feel of the glass in his hand, solid, cool. The bite against his tongue as the drink slid toward his throat.

There was a little place on Dauphin Island Parkway where he used to go. Nobody bothered anyone. You could sit in the back and ...

Thoughts of Saturday at the guesthouse came crashing in. Waves of guilt poured over him. The voices returned.

"You blew it. You really blew it. They were right. You'll never amount to anything. You'll always be a drunk. A nobody. You might as well ..."

Suddenly, his cell phone rang. He fumbled through his pocket to find the phone, then flipped it open. The call was from Perry Braxton.

"Get over here," Braxton demanded.

Connolly didn't like the tone of his voice.

"Over where?"

"My apartment."

Connolly lifted his foot from the gas pedal. The engine in the Chrysler slowed to an idle. The car coasted. He glanced ahead. Already he could see the light at Houston Street. Tuttle was just a few blocks beyond that. He listened, but his mind was on the guesthouse.

"What's going on?"

"The police are here." Braxton's voice fell to a low whisper. "They have a warrant."

Connolly focused on the moment.

"A warrant? For what? For you?"

"They're going through everything. They've already hauled a truckload of stuff out of here."

Connolly checked the mirror and changed lanes.

"Have they asked you any questions?"

"No. Not many."

"Well, don't answer them. I'll be there in a minute."

"All right."

"Just don't talk to them."

Connolly closed the cover on the phone and dropped it on the seat beside him. He was almost to Houston Street by the time he finished the call. At the traffic light, he moved into the turn lane and stopped to wait on traffic. While he waited, his mind returned to the glass on the bar. He rubbed his hand over his face and thought of a hot shower instead. After an afternoon in Gladys Newman's barn, he had been looking forward to relaxing.

"A glass of gin ... ger ale would be nice too."

He smiled at himself. It felt good to make a joke out of what he'd done Saturday night. Better than the condemnation he'd wallowed in all weekend.

Traffic cleared. He turned left.

Braxton's apartment was located on Louiselle Street. As he made the turn off Old Shell, he could see the street ahead was crowded with police cars and vans. Officers milled about on the grass between the street and the building. He brought the Chrysler to a stop behind a police car and stepped out. One of the officers approached the car.

"This area is closed right now, sir."

Connolly took a business card from the pocket of his jacket and offered it to the officer.

"I'm Mr. Braxton's attorney."

The expression on the officer's face didn't change.

"I'm sorry, sir. We can't let you in right now."

"Can't let me in?"

"No, sir. No one's allowed in the building while we're conducting a search."

"Where's Mr. Braxton?"

"He's in a patrol car."

"Which one?"

The officer glanced around, searching.

"That one right there."

He pointed to a patrol car a little way up the street.

Connolly started toward it.

The officer stepped in his way.

"You'll have to wait."

"Wait?"

"Yes, sir."

"He called me about five minutes ago and asked to see me. Is he under arrest?"

"He's in the car."

"Is he free to go?"

"I can't answer that."

"But he's in a police car and the only way he can get out is if you open the door?"

"I'd say that's about right."

"Then, you're telling me he's under arrest, but he can't have access to his attorney?"

The officer took a breath as if about to answer. Before he could respond, a voice called from the shadows near the building.

"It's okay."

They both turned to see who spoke. Anthony Hammond came from the building toward them.

"It's all right. I'll take care of it."

The officer moved away. Hammond came across the lawn.

"You want to talk to Perry?"

"Yes," Connolly replied. "What's going on?"

"Executing a search warrant."

"For what?"

"Evidence."

"Evidence of what?'

"Murder."

"Murder?"

"Capital murder, to be exact." The corners of Hammond's mouth turned up. He did his best to suppress a smile. "Couple of fishermen found Mrs. Braxton's body this morning." He paused. The smile he'd tried to suppress became a wide, knowing grin. "You'll never guess where."

"Surprise me."

"Horn Island."

Connolly felt like he'd been kicked in the stomach.

"Right where your man said he was fishing."

"Where's the body now?"

"Federal government owns the island. Some kind of national seashore. Park rangers had to come out and retrieve the body. They took it to a facility in Bay St. Louis. Did an initial identification on it. Once they found out who it was, they called us. Ted Morgan sent some of his people over there to get it this afternoon. He'll do an autopsy on her."

"What kind of shape was she in?"

"Pretty good, from what I hear. Preliminary report says there were two blows to her head, but she was still intact."

"Blows to the head?"

"Yeah. Morgan will have all that in a few days. You want to talk to your client?"

"Yeah."

Connolly followed Hammond to the police car. Hammond opened the rear door. Braxton stuck his foot out as if to stand.

"No," Hammond ordered. "Stay in the car."

Braxton gave him an angry look.

"I can't get out?"

"You do your talking from in there."

Connolly stepped to the door and glanced inside. Braxton sat on the rear seat leaning slightly forward, his hands handcuffed behind his back. Connolly gestured to him through the door.

"Move over."

Braxton slid to the opposite side of the car. Connolly sat on the seat beside him, the door open, one foot on the ground outside. Hammond moved away and stood behind the car.

"They're taking me in?"

"Yeah," Connolly replied. "They tell you about the body?"

"Yeah." Braxton nodded. "Can I make bail?"

"I don't know."

Braxton looked worried.

"I can't make bail?"

"Not immediately. They'll take you to the jail, process you in. It'll take a while."

Braxton looked puzzled.

Connolly did his best to explain.

"They have to get your fingerprints. Get your age, weight, that kind of thing. You can answer those questions, but don't talk about anything else. I doubt they'll try to interrogate you, but if they do, just tell them you aren't talking without your lawyer being present." He caught Braxton's eye. "Understand?"

"Yeah. Why can't I make bail?"

"Capital murder."

"How long before I can get out?"

"Listen, bail in capital cases is ... rare."

"You mean I'll have to spend the night in there?"

With a question like that, there wasn't much point in explaining things further. He'd find out soon enough what the system was like. Connolly nodded.

"Yes. You'll have to spend the night."

Braxton sighed and turned toward the window.

"That's not right."

Connolly turned toward the car door.

"I'll be down to see you in the morning."

He stepped out. Hammond came from behind the car and closed the door.

Eighteen

*E*vidence technicians finished with Braxton's apartment around eight that night. A tow truck arrived as they came from the apartment. Connolly turned to Hammond.

"What's that for?"

"Taking his Suburban."

"Suburban?"

"Yeah. Easier to examine it at the impound yard. We'll get it back to him when we're finished." He smiled at Connolly. "But I don't think he'll be needing it." He chuckled. "Might need to sell it to pay your fee."

The tow truck stopped in front of the apartment building. A patrolman waved the driver toward the Suburban parked down the street. Connolly leaned against the Chrysler and watched them load it. As the tow truck clattered down the street with the Suburban, Hammond and the patrolmen got in their cars. When the taillights of the last police van turned the corner, Connolly moved around the car and up the sidewalk toward the building.

Braxton's apartment was in a complex of four buildings set at right angles to each other forming a square. In the middle of the square was a courtyard with a swimming pool. A breezeway ran through the center of the building, facing Louiselle Street. Braxton's apartment was on the first floor, facing the pool. The front door of the apartment was located on the left side of the breezeway near the far end. Connolly grasped the doorknob and gave it a twist. The door was locked.

He walked out of the breezeway and around the corner. A sliding glass door along the back led from the apartment to the courtyard. Connolly gave the handle a tug. The door slid open. He stepped inside.

The only light in the apartment came through the open door. Connolly moved around a sofa, felt along the wall for the light switch, and flipped it on. The harsh glare of the light made him squint.

The area by the door was arranged as the living room with a sofa, an armchair, and a television. Beyond it was the kitchen. A small table sat in the corner to the left, separated from the kitchen by a counter. To the right, between the living room and kitchen, was a hallway. Connolly glanced around the living-room area.

The sofa sat opposite the sliding door. In front of it was a coffee table. Magazines lay on the table, neatly arranged in two stacks. The remote control for the television sat atop one of the stacks.

Chairs were tucked against the dining table. The kitchen counter was clean. Nothing seemed out of place.

He sniffed the air. There was a hint of grease and cigarettes, but nothing foul or acrid. He crossed the room and moved into the hallway. The door to the bathroom was on the left. Across from the bathroom was the apartment's only bedroom. He stepped to the bathroom door and flipped on the light.

A shower made of clear glass stood along the back wall. Inside it, the walls and door were clean and dry. To the left was the toilet. A rack above it held a stack of neatly folded towels. The sink sat along the wall to the right with a medicine cabinet above it. Connolly opened the cabinet. Inside, he found a razor, shaving cream, and a bottle of aspirin. All of it appeared to have gone untouched. He closed the cabinet and crossed the hall to the bedroom.

From the doorway he reached inside the room and turned on the light. On the left wall was a closet with the doors standing open. The closet was bare. Clothes lay in a pile on the floor between the closet and a bed that sat to the right. The bed had been stripped. Linens lay on the floor beyond the clothes from the closet. The mattress had been moved and rested at a precarious angle on the box springs. Beyond the bed was a dresser against the far wall. Its drawers were half open with clothes sticking out.

"Clothes," he whispered to himself. "They were looking for his clothes."

Relief swept over him. He had entered the apartment worried that the police had found a murder scene, but the condition of the rooms told him otherwise. Typical techniques for gathering fingerprints left smudges everywhere. Chemicals used in forensic imaging had an acrid odor that lingered for days. Yet there were no smudges on the objects in the apartment. No telltale dust residue on the floor. No smell of chemicals in the air. Nothing had been disturbed except the contents of the bedroom.

Connolly surveyed the room once more, then switched off the light, and retreated to the hallway. He turned off the light in the bathroom and the one in the hall, retracing his steps to the living room. There, he locked the sliding door. He crossed the room to the front door, turned off the light, and stepped outside to the breezeway.

The heels of his shoes clicked against the concrete as he walked toward the street. The noise echoed off the walls. As he walked, the relief he'd felt in the apartment faded, giving way to a sense of loneliness. Like the day in the park after he'd talked to Bob Dorsey, he felt as though something important had been carelessly discarded, wasted, only to realize its value when it was too late. By the time he reached the Chrysler, he was in a funk. He opened the door and dropped onto the front seat.

His own life had been a wreck. His wife gave up on him. His daughter cut him out of her life. Only in the past two years had things begun to moderate between them. Then he remembered Saturday, outside the liquor store, the bottle on the counter, the taste of gin against the back of his tongue.

Streetlights reflected off the gauges on the dashboard.

What would they think if they knew the truth?

Guilt fell across his shoulders like a heavy weight, pressing him down in the seat, pushing him past the car through the pavement. Sinking to the depths of his soul. Now he not only felt guilty about what he'd done, he felt compelled to talk about it, to tell her what he'd done. But he knew the consequences of that, and the thought of never seeing her again was more than he could bear.

Old thoughts surfaced.

She's lost. You've lost her for good now. She'll find out. She always did.

He sighed and leaned his head against the back of the seat.

You need a drink. A good, strong drink. Drive over there. Tell her what happened. Let her tell you what a loser you are, and then have a drink. You can take just one. That's all. Just one to cut the edge off the day.

Then a voice came crashing through his mind, so clear it was all but audible.

You don't have to tell her anything.

His eyes popped open. He lifted his head and whispered the thought out loud.

"I don't have to tell her."

The dark thoughts seized the moment.

Yeah. Just lie.

He took the key from his pocket.

"I don't have to lie. But I don't have to tell her either. I'm under no obligation to disclose anything to anyone." For some reason, the guilt seemed lighter. "I'm a lawyer. I can hold my own actions in confidence with myself."

He laughed at it and took the key from his pocket.

"I don't have to tell her anything."

He smiled.

"All I have to do is remember not to do it today." He inserted the key in the ignition and started the car. "And get up in the morning and remember it one more day."

With the steering wheel turned hard to the left, he made a U-turn from the curb. At the corner, he turned left onto Old Shell Road and drove toward town. He lowered the window and propped his elbow on the ledge. The smile he'd had before became a grin.

At Ann Street, he made a right. Two blocks beyond Government Street, he came to Barbara's house. He brought the car to a stop at the curb and got out. He pushed the door closed without making a sound and stood by the car, staring at the house.

A two-story white frame, it had dormer windows across the front. A walkway ran from the street to steps that led to the porch. Seeing the sidewalk reminded him of Rachel as a little girl, playing in the yard. He caught a whiff of steaks cooking on a charcoal grill. He could see that old grill sitting at the end of the driveway. Saw himself standing by it, with Barbara watching through the kitchen window.

From down the street a dog barked, jerking Connolly's mind from the past. He glanced around awkwardly, shoved both hands in his pockets, and wandered up the sidewalk toward the house.

When he reached the porch he paused, unsure whether to ring the doorbell or turn away.

Outside Braxton's apartment, coming to see Barbara had seemed like a good idea. Now, he felt out of place. He backed away.

"Too many memories," he whispered.

Still, he couldn't bring himself to leave. Their divorce had been acrimonious, but then Rachel had given birth to Elizabeth, their only grandchild. He stopped drinking. Barbara stopped dating. Without a bottle of gin to separate them, things had warmed between them.

He took a seat on the steps.

A few moments later, he heard the sound of someone unlocking the front door. The door opened. Someone stepped out. He knew by the sound of the footsteps it was Barbara.

"Mike?" Her voice had a note of concern. "What's the matter? Are you all right?"

He turned his head to one side and tossed a look over his shoulder in her direction.

"I'm fine."

She stood behind him. By the rustle of her dress he knew she'd folded her arms across her chest. He could see the look on her face without turning around.

"Have you been drinking?"

The tone of her voice was stern, demanding. He ignored the urge to defend himself.

"Not today."

She nudged his shoulder with her foot.

"Move over."

He slid to one side. She took a seat to his right on the step above him. Her feet rested beside him. Connolly felt her shoe against his arm.

"We used to sit out here a lot." His voice sounded far away. "Watch Rachel play. Riding her bicycle up and down the sidewalk. Seems like a long time ago."

"It was a long time ago."

"Sometimes it seems like yesterday too."

"What's the matter?"

"You hear about Camille Braxton?"

"Read about it in the newspaper." Her hand rubbed lightly across his shoulder. "Mentioned your name in the article."

"They found her body."

Her hand moved away.

"I guess everyone knew that would happen."

"They arrested Perry tonight."

"I guess everyone knew that was going to happen, too."

Connolly propped his elbows on the step behind him and leaned against them.

"You ever think about how fragile life is?"

"Ye ... s." The question seemed to catch her off guard. "I guess."

Connolly leaned forward, his hands in front, gesturing as he spoke.

"I mean, one day she was here. And then, she was gone. She hadn't planned to die. It wasn't something she knew was coming. She was just ... going on an errand. Supposed to be back by lunch ... never came home."

He paused. Barbara did not respond. He continued.

"I wonder what she would have said if she had known she was going to die." He propped an elbow on his knee and rested his chin against his hand. "What would she have said to her daughter that morning when she sent her off to school, if she knew she'd never see her again? If she knew that moment was the last moment they had?" He glanced over his shoulder toward Barbara. "What would she have said to the maid? To her husband?"

"Somebody said they were getting a divorce."

"But, if she'd known she was going to die, would it have made a difference? If she had known that day was the only day she had, would it have made a difference?"

"I don't know. Would it make a difference for you?"

"What?"

"If you knew this was the only moment you had?"

He fell silent for a moment.

"Yeah," he said, finally. "It would."

"What would you say?"

Connolly knew what he would say.

"I'd say ..." He stood. "I'd say it's late." He moved to the bottom of the steps, then stopped and turned to face her. "There are a lot of things I'd say. But I don't think any of it could erase what's happened."

She looked puzzled.

"What's happened?"

"I was drunk for ten years. I missed my life." His voice grew more intense as he spoke. "Our daughter's life. Our life. I missed it, and it's never coming back." He shoved his hands in his pockets and sighed. His voice dropped. "And nothing I say could ever bring it back. You don't get a do-over."

An amused smile spread across her face.

"A do-over?"

"Yeah. You know. When you were a kid playing a game in the yard and something didn't go right, you'd yell, 'Do-over,' and you got to take your turn again and get it right." He shook his head. "You don't get a do-over with life."

"No. But you can learn. You can pick up where you are and move on."

"Maybe so."

He turned away and started down the sidewalk. A few steps later, he turned back to her.

"Sorry to bother you. I should have called first."

Even in the dark he could see her smile.

At the Chrysler he turned toward the house in time to see Barbara move up the steps to the front door. He watched as she went inside. When she was gone, he climbed inside the car and drove away.

Nineteen

*B*y the time Connolly reached Government Street, he knew he never would get to sleep. Instead of turning left toward Tuttle Street and the guesthouse, he turned right and drove downtown. At Claiborne Street, he turned left. Two blocks later, he passed in front of St. Alban Cathedral. Beyond the cathedral he made a right on Dauphin Street and drove toward Bienville Square. He brought the car to a stop at the curb in front of the office and reached for the key to turn off the engine. From his seat behind the steering wheel, he glanced up at the third floor. The building looked dark and forbidding.

"I don't want to be in there, either."

He moved his hand from the key, put the car in gear, and continued down the street. A block and a half beyond the office he came to Royal Street. The Essex Hotel sat on the corner to the left. Lights along the second floor lit up the front of the hotel, but the street was deserted and quiet. The traffic light was red. He rested his foot on the brake pedal, checked the street once more, and idled slowly around the corner to the right.

A few blocks down Royal he turned right onto Church Street. Up ahead, St. Pachomius loomed in the night. He brought the Chrysler to a stop in front of the steps and switched off the engine. Shadows danced across the front of the church as a breeze rustled through the oaks that towered above the roof. He sat there in the dark, staring at the church from the front seat of the car, thinking of Barbara.

From somewhere deep in a dreamless slumber a tapping sound drummed in Connolly's head. *Tap, tap, tap.* The sound grew louder. His eyes popped open and darted around in disoriented confusion. A police officer stood beside the car. He had a nightstick in his hand.

"Get out of the car."

Connolly stepped out.

"I'm not drunk."

The officer gave him a skeptical smirk.

"Yeah. Sure."

He turned Connolly toward the car and patted him down. When he was finished, Connolly turned to face him.

"Look." He extended both arms wide apart, closed his eyes, and touched first one hand, then the other to his nose. He opened his eyes and smiled at the officer. "Watch this." He moved around the officer to a parking stripe on the pavement. He placed his feet on the stripe, extended his arms, and walked heel to toe down the stripe. When he reached the end, he turned and smiled again. "I'm not drunk. I just fell asleep."

"What are you doing down here?"

"I was out. It was late. I wanted to think. I parked here and fell asleep."

The officer slipped the nightstick in his utility belt.

"Find somewhere else to do your thinking."

He turned away and started toward a patrol car parked in the street behind them.

Connolly climbed into the Chrysler. The officer waited while Connolly steered away from the curb.

From St. Pachomius, he drove to Dauphin Street and parked in front of the office building. He made his way to the third floor and spent the rest of the night asleep in his chair behind the desk.

A few hours later the sun was up. Connolly took the elevator to the lobby and walked up the street to the Port City Diner for a doughnut and a cup of coffee. Thirty minutes later, he walked over to the courthouse and made his way to Judge Cahill's courtroom. He arrived almost an hour before the first docket was scheduled. He crossed the empty courtroom and moved past the bailiff's desk to the door behind the judge's bench. Beyond it was a reception area that led to the judge's chambers.

Connolly heard Cahill's voice coming from his office. He peeked inside. Cahill sat at his desk talking on the telephone. He motioned for Connolly to enter as he finished the call and hung up.

"Good morning, Mike."

"Your Honor."

"You have a case on the docket this morning?"

"Yes, sir. Thirey."

Cahill gave him a blank stare.

"It's a robbery," Connolly explained.

Cahill shrugged.

"Too many cases to remember by name."

A stack of files sat on the left side of the desk. Another stack sat in the center. He reached for a file from the stack in front of him. While he talked, he opened the file and began scribbling inside.

"You need something? DA's office gets upset if I do anything on their cases without notifying them first. Henry will be up in a little while."

"I don't have anything on that case."

Cahill finished with the file and laid it to the right. He took another and opened it.

"I hear they arrested Perry Braxton last night."

He glanced at Connolly, then scribbled something in the next file. Connolly stood a few feet away.

"Yes, sir. Did they assign his case to you?"

Cahill closed the file in front of him, laid it to the right with the others, and picked up another.

"It's a capital case." He glanced at Connolly. "I get all the capital cases. Clerk's office is making up a file on it right now." His eyes brightened as if he recognized a look on Connolly's face. He cocked his head forward. A resolute expression appeared on his face. The file he'd picked up was still in his hand, suspended in air before him. "You can ask for it, but I'll deny it."

Connolly had a nervous smile.

"What?"

"I know that look." Cahill laid the file in his hand on the desk and opened it. "You came in here to tell me you're going to ask me to set a bond for Perry Braxton. And since we're having this *ex parte* conversation anyway, I'll just go ahead and give you an answer." He looked Connolly in the eye. "It's a capital case, Mike. The man's accused of murdering his own wife. I'm not setting a bond."

Connolly sighed. He folded his arms across his chest as he thought about what to say. Cahill glanced at the file on his desk, scribbled something in it, then looked up at Connolly.

"Now, if you need to file your motion, then by all means, file it. I don't mind. But I'm telling you right now. I'm not setting a bond." He glanced at the file on the desk once more, then closed it. "There are five wise men on the court of appeals in Montgomery. They might have a different opinion. But I've never been reversed on a question of bond, and I doubt I will be on this one."

Walter, the bailiff, appeared at the door beside Connolly.

"Judge, you got the files for this first docket?"

"Yes, Walter." Cahill tapped a stack on the front edge of the desk with his finger. "Right here."

Walter brushed past Connolly and moved across the office toward the desk. He picked up the files, then started for the door. He nodded at Connolly as he passed.

"Morning, Mr. Connolly." He didn't wait for a response. "Your man on this docket ... Thirey. He was out on bond on a case in Judge Pulliam's courtroom when he picked up that robbery we had set for this morning." Walter looked at Cahill. "We going to transfer our case?"

"Yeah," Cahill replied. He looked at Connolly. "Pulliam can handle both of them. He's going to revoke the bond on the other case anyway. Makes it easier to do it all at once."

Connolly nodded and turned to follow Walter out of the office. Cahill called after him.

"Mike?"

Connolly turned back.

"File your motion if you want to." Cahill's voice took a paternal tone. "I'll hear whatever you have on it."

"Thanks, Your Honor."

Twenty

Connolly left the courthouse and drove across town to the county jail. Ten stories high, it was located near the end of Water Street, across from the banana wharfs that lined the Mobile River. Built of dark brown brick, it had a hulking, formidable appearance. Steel bars, rusted from the salt air that drifted in from the bay, covered the windows and added a garish element to the building's imposing character.

Built in the 1950s and never remodeled, it was dirty, worn, and cramped. Filing cabinets lined every inch of the walls around the entrance lobby and down the hallways. Wedged between the cabinets was a metal detector for visitors, the building's lone public acknowledgment of modern technology. Beyond the metal detector was a large steel door that led to the booking area.

A guard sat at a desk near the door. She looked up as Connolly approached.

"May I help you?"

"I'm here to see a prisoner. Perry Braxton. He's my client."

The guard checked a list for Braxton's name, then pointed to a basket on the desk.

"Empty your pockets and step through the metal detector."

Connolly laid his car keys in the basket and walked through the detector. The guard handed him his keys and banged on the steel door with her fist. She shouted loud enough to be heard outside.

"Visitor!"

The door swung open. Connolly stepped inside and made his way past the booking area to the elevator near the rear of the building. Braxton was waiting for him in the interview room on the eighth floor. He looked brash and cocky.

"You going to get me out of here?"

"Not today."

"That's what you said yesterday."

Connolly didn't like the tone in his voice.

"That's what I'm going to say every day."

Braxton looked puzzled.

"What do you mean?"

"I talked to Judge Cahill. He's not going to set a bond."

Braxton frowned.

"So, how long will I be in here?"

"At least until the preliminary hearing."

Braxton gave him an angry look.

"Till the hearing? When will that be?"

"I don't know. They haven't set a date for it yet. Probably three or four weeks."

Braxton sighed.

"Any chance we could get another judge to hear it?"

"No. Cahill gets the capital cases."

Braxton looked away for a moment, then turned to Connolly.

"This isn't right."

"It's a capital case."

"I have an alibi. I gave you that receipt. There's no way I could be in Pascagoula and in Mobile at the time they say she disappeared."

"Maybe so. But we don't need to put that into evidence until the preliminary hearing."

"They already know it. I told Hammond about it the other night. I told him that's where I was. You have the receipt. Show it to him and get me out of here."

"You're not going to be able to talk your way out of this. They've arrested you because they're convinced you did it. The person you have to convince is Judge Cahill, and the best time to do that is at the preliminary hearing."

Braxton shook his head.

"Tell me something. How many capital cases does the state win?"

"Most."

Braxton sighed once more and turned away. Connolly continued.

"They win most of the cases regardless of the charge."

"So, the odds are against me?"

"The probabilities are against you."

"Whatever that means." Braxton looked resolute. "You find out anything new?"

"What do you know about the Trust?"

"What do you want to know?"

"The original trust document was prepared by a lawyer named Oliver Gilmore. You know anything about that?"

Braxton had a blank look on his face.

"Not really."

"Any reason why an oil company from Texas would be asking questions about the Trust?"

"What's that got to do with my case?"

"Don't know yet. Maybe nothing."

"Did you look at the records in the attic?"

"Yes."

"Anything in there?"

"Some geological reports. A few maps. Did you ever hear anyone mention anything about how this trust was formed?"

"Just the standard Tonsmeyer story. Wanted to fight in the Civil War. His mama wouldn't let him. Worked for a smuggler."

"Ever hear anything else? Something nobody wanted to talk about?"

"No." Braxton grinned. "Is there?"

"I don't know for sure."

"Interesting."

Connolly folded his hands on the table and leaned closer.

"We have to talk about Panama Tan."

Braxton leaned away.

Connolly continued.

"Bob Dorsey thinks it's a front for prostitution."

Braxton smiled.

Connolly pressed the issue.

"He thinks you were a frequent customer."

The smile on Braxton's face became a grin.

"That's what he thinks?"

"That's what he thinks."

"People always say that about places like that."

Connolly gave him a serious look.

"Perry, you have to tell me about it. I know about Manny Fernandez."

Braxton's grin faded. Connolly watched his eyes.

"I know about Pete Rizutto."

Braxton's gaze dropped to the table.

Connolly became impatient.

"You have to tell me what's going on. You are charged with capital murder. Your life is on the line. I'm not going to court on this and get blown away when they start talking about Shady Acres and porn films and who knows what."

Braxton looked pale but didn't respond. Connolly was insistent.

"You have to tell me."

Braxton glanced at him.

"I can't."

"You can't?"

"If I tell you about all of that, I'll be a dead man."

"If you don't tell me about it, you'll be a dead man anyway."

Braxton looked away, as if thinking. He took a deep breath, then shook his head and stood.

"Not in here."

He crossed the room and banged on the door with his fist for the guard to let him out.

Twenty-one

From the jail, Connolly drove south toward Fowl River. Noon had passed by the time he reached Mary's Place, a Creole restaurant located a few hundred yards from the banks of the river. His stomach told him it was time to eat, but he resisted the temptation to stop.

The Chrysler rumbled over the wooden-plank bridge that spanned the river. Across the bridge, he turned right onto a narrow paved road. A mile farther, he left the pavement and turned onto a freshly graded dirt road. Red dust rolled through the air behind the car as it glided deeper and deeper into the brown sea of marsh grass known to the locals as Mon Louis Island.

Two miles down the road he slowed the car and turned again, this time onto a muddy two-rut trail. The car rocked from side to side as it wallowed through the mud, sliding past the pines and cypress that dotted the marsh. Connolly drove with one foot on the accelerator and one on the brake, alternately pressing the car for more momentum and fighting to avoid slamming into the trees while at the same time keeping the front wheels ahead of the rear.

Finally, the trail reached the high ground along Garon's Bayou, a narrow inlet that meandered through the marsh and into the river. The muddy trail became hard and firm. Connolly relaxed his grip on the steering wheel and slipped his foot off the brake pedal. Ahead, a tar-paper shack came into view. Nestled in a clump of scrub oaks and pines, it sat only a few yards from the bayou. A rickety pier led from the back of the cabin to the water. Hollis's pickup truck was parked out front. Connolly parked the Chrysler beside it and stepped out.

The smell of grilled fish filled the air. He slipped off his jacket and laid it across the seat of the car, then walked around the corner of the shack. Hollis was sitting on a wooden stool beside a propane grill between the shack and the bayou. An ice chest sat beside him. On the grill were three fish.

"You eating, or just passing through?"

"Eating," Connolly replied.

Hollis opened the ice chest, took out two pieces of fish, and laid them on the grill.

"I got fish and light bread."

"Sounds good."

Connolly stepped closer. Hollis lifted the edge of one of the fish with his fingers, checked the underneath side, then flipped it over.

"Isn't that a little hot?"

"Nah." Hollis lifted the edge of a second fish. "Pull up a chair."

An empty milk crate lay nearby. Connolly moved it near the ice chest, turned it upside down, and used it for a seat.

"What have you found out about the tanning salon?"

"Not enough."

"You can't give me anything?"

"Haven't got it all pieced together yet. I'm still working on it."

Connolly gave him a look.

"I'll let you know in a few days," Hollis replied. "I don't want to tell you half the story and have you dive in on top of me again. Just sit tight." He nudged the fish around the grill with his finger. "How's your missing lady?"

"They found her."

"Alive?"

"Dead."

"Now it's a murder case?"

"Yeah."

"They arrest your client?"

"Yeah."

"That what you come to tell me?"

"Part of it."

"What's the other part?"

"I need to go out to Horn Island."

A frown wrinkled Hollis's forehead.

"What for? Fishing ain't as good out there as everybody says."

"That's where they found her body."

A paper plate lay on the ground by the grill. Hollis picked it up, laid a piece of fish from the grill on it, and handed it to Connolly.

"Bread's in the ice chest."

Connolly took the paper plate and set it on the ground beside the milk crate. He opened the ice chest, took out a loaf of bread, and removed two slices from the wrapper.

"You think you could set it up?"

Hollis stood and stepped toward the shack.

"Yeah," he called over his shoulder.

He disappeared inside. A moment later, he returned carrying more paper plates, two forks, and a roll of paper towels. He handed Connolly a fork.

"When you want to go?"

"How long will it take to set it up?"

"Not long. We'll have to rent a boat. Leave from Dauphin Island."

"Weekend's better for me."

"Weekends are big days for charter boats. Get one cheaper during the week."

Connolly took a bite of fish. "All right. Pick a day."

"Friday."

Connolly nodded.

"Get us a boat."

Twenty-two

*T*he drive up from Fowl River left Connolly hot and sleepy. The back of his shirt was damp with sweat, and his eyelids sagged at the corners. At Tuttle Street, he had to fight to avoid going to the guesthouse for a nap. Files on his desk at the office needed his attention. Mrs. Gordon would have a stack of phone messages waiting for him. If he bailed on the remainder of the day, he'd hear about it tomorrow. Reluctantly, he continued down Government Street.

At Claiborne Street, he moved to the left lane and put on the turn signal. The office was two blocks away on Dauphin. Whether he wanted to or not, he owed a duty to his clients to return their calls and work their cases. He lifted his foot from the gas pedal. The engine rumbled to an idle. The Chrysler slowed.

Then, at the last moment, he hesitated. A part of him resented being tied to the office. He did a good job for his clients. In spite of the time he'd spent with Braxton, none of his cases had suffered for it. His foot slid from the brake to the floor. The car rolled past the turn.

"Oops." He grinned at himself. "Missed that one."

Jackson Street would take him to the same place. It was only a block away. He touched his foot against the gas pedal. The car moved toward the corner, then slowed for the turn. Once again, he hesitated. In his mind he saw Mrs. Gordon scowling at him, the corners of her mouth turned up with that condescending look only she could give.

He heard her growling at him.

"Where were you yesterday?"

But Mrs. Gordon wasn't in charge. He watched out the window with satisfaction as he moved past that street as well. Behind him, a car horn sounded. In the mirror he saw an irritated driver gesture with his hand. Connolly gave a wave out the window, then glanced ahead.

Joachim Street was his last chance. If he missed that turn, he'd have to go all the way to Royal Street. The car from behind him came around to the right and shot past in a hurry. It sped down the street and disappeared through the entrance to Bankhead Tunnel. While he watched, Joachim Street came and went. Connolly let his arm dangle out the window and tapped a rhythm on the door with his fingers. The Chrysler tooled along at an idle.

Royal Street was a block beyond the courthouse. From there, he could turn left and go two blocks to Dauphin Street. In five minutes he'd be in front of the office. In ten, he'd be seated at his desk. He checked his watch.

"Nothing there I can't do tomorrow."

He glanced over the seat and checked for traffic, then moved the car to the lane by the curb. At the corner, he turned right and made his way behind the courthouse. A little way up Church Street he found an empty parking space across from St. Pachomius. He brought the car to a stop there and got out.

A breeze rustled through the oaks that sprawled across the roof of the church. Dark shade covered the front of the building and spilled across the steps that led up from the sidewalk. Connolly slung his jacket over his shoulder as he crossed the street. The breeze danced across his damp shirt. A refreshing shiver ran down his spine. At the top of the steps, he moved past the columns under the portico and pushed on one of the doors.

Inside, the sanctuary was cool and quiet. Sunlight through the stained-glass windows gave the room a soft glow. He let his eye roam across the images in the windows, and in his heart he knew why he'd been reluctant to go anywhere else. Behind him, the door banged closed. He made his way down the aisle to a pew near the front.

At the end of the pew he paused and glanced at the altar sitting near the wall beyond the chancel. As a boy, he'd been taught to genuflect before sitting, a practice he always forgot. This time, he remembered. He steadied himself with one hand on the pew and touched his knee to the floor. He held that position long enough to make the sign of a cross on his chest, then stood.

Suddenly nervous and self-conscious, he looked around to see if anyone noticed how awkward he felt. The sanctuary was empty. He took a seat.

For a long time he just sat there, drinking the silence like a glass of cool water. After a while, he took a Prayer Book from the rack on the back of the pew in front of him and opened it to the Psalter. He began to read. The words sank deep into his spirit.

When he had read for a while, he closed the book and turned the kneeler down. He slid off the pew to his knees and rested his arms across the back of the pew in front of him. With his eyes closed, his mind began to wander, and he found it hard to concentrate. Over and over he saw the clerk at the liquor store. The bottle as she put it in the bag. The next morning when he awoke on the sofa in the guesthouse.

Without warning, someone nudged him. He glanced up to find Father Scott standing beside him.

"Move over."

Connolly rose from the kneeler and scooted to the left. Father Scott took a seat beside him.

"Haven't seen you in morning prayers lately."

Connolly looked away.

"I've been ... working on a case. It's taken me in a different direction the past few weeks."

"What kind of case?"

"Murder. I think."

Father Scott raised an eyebrow.

"Would be good to know if it is or isn't, wouldn't it?"

"Yeah."

"You don't look yourself."

"Well ... I don't feel myself."

"I feel that way sometimes. Like a soldier, dropped from a helicopter into the jungle. Easy to tell where you are from above. But once you're in the thick of it, it's not so clear."

Connolly nodded. They sat quietly for a moment. Then, Father Scott stood.

"Wait here."

He left the pew and walked down the aisle, then turned across the front of the sanctuary along the railing that separated the nave from the chancel steps. On the far side, he opened a door and disappeared inside the sacristy. Connolly heard him opening cabinets and moving things around.

Moments later, he emerged from a door beyond the railing, vested in his alb with a stole draped around his neck. He started up the steps to the chancel and made his way to the altar. In one hand he carried a silver chalice. In the other, a silver paten. On it Connolly saw a large chunk of bread.

When he reached the altar, Father Scott bowed, his arms outstretched, then moved around the altar to face the nave. He set the chalice and paten on the altar and gestured with both hands toward Connolly.

"Come."

His voice rolled across the chancel and rumbled through the church like thunder. Connolly rose and moved to the bottom of the steps. He paused. Father Scott spoke again.

"'Come unto me, all of you who labor and are heavy laden, and I will give you rest.'" He gestured with his hand. "Come on."

Connolly lifted his foot to the first step. Tears filled his eyes as he made his way to the chancel and moved past the rows of pews for the choir. At the altar rail he knelt and bowed his head. Father Scott waited a moment, then began to pray.

"These elements of bread and wine which we have laid upon your altar, O Lord, are some of those same elements consecrated to you in the service this morning and which we reserved for ministry this day. We offer them to you afresh and anew, that they may be a holy sacrifice, the body and blood of Christ, worthy to set before you. Amen."

Father Scott took the chalice and plate and brought them to the altar rail.

"Mike Connolly, this is the body of Christ." He offered Connolly bread from the plate. "Take and eat in remembrance that Christ died for you."

Connolly pinched off a small piece of the bread and held it in his hands. Father Scott held the chalice in front of him. It was half full of red wine. "This is the blood of Christ, which was shed for you."

Connolly dipped the bread into the chalice, soaking a corner of it in the wine. His hand trembled as he raised the bread to his lips. Father Scott returned the chalice and plate to the altar, then turned to stand in front of Connolly once more.

"O Lord, pour out your Spirit on Mike as he kneels here in your presence." He laid his hands on Connolly's head as he prayed. His voice echoed through the sanctuary. "Drive out all evil spirits from his life. Lift the veil of confusion that surrounds him. Fill him with your presence, with the power of your Holy Spirit. Restore his life. Renew his life. Fill him with your peace. In the name of the Father, and of the Son, and of the Holy Spirit. Amen."

Father Scott lingered there, his hands atop Connolly's head. Connolly glanced up at him and stood. Father Scott came from behind the altar rail and took him by the elbow.

"The Lord of all creation is with you."

Without another word between them, he ushered Connolly through the chancel to the nave and up the aisle to the door. When they reached the door, Father Scott paused and looked him in the eye.

"Go in peace to love and serve the Lord."

He pushed open the door.

Connolly stepped outside.

Twenty-three

*T*wo days later, Hollis called the office.

"Meet me at Grant's Pass Marina."

"Where?"

"Dauphin Island. First marina on the left after you come off the bridge."

"Now?"

"Friday morning. Six o'clock."

"What for?"

"I thought you wanted to go out to Horn Island."

"I do."

"We're going Friday. Be there at six."

"Six? In the morning?"

"That too late?"

"No." Connolly sighed. "I'll be there."

He heard Hollis laughing as he hung up the phone.

The only early mornings Connolly ever enjoyed were the ones that came at the end of a long night. Rolling out of bed before sunrise was never one of his strengths. When the alarm clock sounded Friday morning, he struggled to reach the nightstand and hit the snooze button. Five minutes later, the alarm sounded again. He raised his head from the pillow and squinted toward the numbers on the clock.

"Three fifteen."

He groaned as he threw back the covers and stumbled down the hall to the shower.

From the guesthouse, Connolly drove south. Dauphin Island lay at the mouth of Mobile Bay, six miles below Cedar Point. The route from Mobile took him down the west side of the bay. With no traffic, the drive was uneventful. A little before five, he stopped for coffee at Sprinkle's Store south of Bailey's Crossroads on Mon Louis Island, not far from

Hollis's cabin. At five thirty, he turned onto the Dauphin Island Bridge, a two-lane span that ran from Cedar Point across Grant's Pass to the north side of the island.

The bridge was deserted. He pressed the gas pedal. The Chrysler picked up speed. Expansion joints in the concrete roadway slapped against the tires. The car rocked gently in time with the sound. Before long, Connolly grew drowsy. He rubbed his eyes, sipped the last of the coffee from Sprinkle's, and did his best to stay awake. When that didn't work, he lowered the window and leaned his head out into the salt air.

By the time he reached the island, the sun was peeking over the horizon. He lifted his foot from the gas pedal and let the car coast down the grade from the bridge to the road. Fifty yards farther, he turned off the pavement onto the parking lot at the marina and brought the car to a stop in front of a large dry-dock warehouse. He switched off the engine and slid low in the seat.

Sometime later, he was awakened by the crunch of tires on the oyster shells that paved the parking lot. From the corner of his eye he saw Hollis's pickup come to a stop to the right. He sat up in the seat, ran his hands through his hair, and opened the car door.

Hollis called to him.

"I see you made it."

Connolly climbed from the car. He folded his arms for a pillow on the car top and rested his head.

"Wake me when we get back."

Hollis stepped from the truck.

"I brought you something."

Connolly opened his eyes and lifted his head to see. Hollis held a green and white box in one hand and a cup of coffee in the other.

"Anything left in that box?"

Hollis had a playful grin.

"Come find out."

Connolly pushed himself away from the car and stepped around the rear bumper. Hollis met him there and handed him the box.

Connolly glanced inside and smiled.

"Nothing like a Krispy Kreme in the morning."

Hollis thrust the cup of coffee toward him.

"Here."

Connolly set the box on the trunk of the Chrysler and took the coffee. With his free hand, he took out a doughnut.

"You want one?"

"Nah," Hollis replied. "I had some in the truck."

Connolly took a bite of the doughnut and chased it with a sip of coffee.

"What's the name of our boat?"

"Kingfisher."

"Who's taking us out?"

"Taylor Harper."

Connolly swallowed a bite of doughnut and took another sip of coffee.

"Never heard of him."

"Not likely you would. Says he's my cousin. Tried to explain it to me two or three times. I never understood what he was talking about."

"He know how to get us where we're going?"

"Goes there all the time."

In a few minutes, a blue Ford pickup turned off the road and into the parking lot. Hollis nodded.

"That's him."

The truck came to a stop a hundred yards away, near a wooden pier on the opposite side of the parking lot. Hollis drank the last of his coffee and tossed the empty cup in the back of his truck.

"Let's go."

Connolly grabbed the box of doughnuts and followed him across the parking lot.

The pier jutted three hundred feet out in the water. Boats filled the slips along either side. Connolly glanced at them as they walked past. Ripples on the water made a sloshing, gurgling sound against the hulls as they bobbed in the slips. Every few steps, he caught a whiff of dead fish. A wave of nausea swept through his stomach.

"Lot of boats in here."

Hollis nodded.

"Lot of maintenance."

The Kingfisher was a thirty-four-foot Crusader. It was moored in a slip near the end. Taylor was already on board, stowing gear and preparing to get under way. The boat's engine ran at an idle. Exhaust swirled around the stern. Connolly felt his stomach roll over as he followed Hollis aboard.

Taylor opened a locker near the cabin door and took out a red life jacket.

"Here."

He handed it to Connolly. Connolly set the coffee and the doughnut box on a small white table bolted to the rear deck. The boat rocked to one side as he reached for the jacket. Taylor waited as Connolly steadied himself against the table. He retrieved a second one from the locker and offered it to Hollis.

Hollis shook his head.

"I can swim."

Taylor thrust the jacket at him.

"We don't leave the dock until everyone has one on."

Reluctantly, Hollis took the jacket and slipped it on. The front gapped open. Straps dangled at his side. Taylor tugged one of the straps.

"Hook it up."

Hollis fastened the straps in place. Taylor took a life jacket from a rack behind the cabin and slipped it on himself, then turned to Connolly.

"I'm Taylor Harper."

They shook hands.

"You ever been out before?"

"Not in a long time."

"I didn't think so." Taylor took a small bottle from his pants pocket. "Hold out your hand."

Connolly opened his palm. Taylor twisted the cap off the bottle and dropped two tiny tablets in Connolly's hand.

"Take these."

"What is it?"

"Motion pills."

"Motion pills?"

Taylor grinned.

"Bonine. Keep you from hurling."

Connolly glanced at Hollis, then swallowed the tablets. Taylor slipped the bottle in his pocket and stepped around the cabin toward the front of the boat. He untied the bow line, then climbed back to the rear deck.

He nodded at Connolly.

"You can sit here." He patted the back of a chair that was bolted to the deck next to the small white table. "If it gets too rough, you can go inside." He tilted his head back and scanned the morning sky. "Looks pretty good. I don't think we'll have any trouble."

He took the coffee cup from the table and dumped the contents over the side of the boat. With a flick of his wrist, he tossed the empty cup in a plastic bucket that sat in the corner near the transom. He pointed to an ice chest near the cabin door.

"There's some Cokes in that chest. Get one and sip on it while we ride. It'll help your stomach."

He moved past Hollis to a ladder on the opposite side of the cabin and started up to the bridge on the deck above.

"Lay off the doughnuts for a while. They'll fizz with the Coke in your stomach." A few minutes later, he shouted down from his perch at the wheel.

"Hollis, untie those stern lines."

Hollis stepped to the back of the boat and untied the lines from the cleats on the dock. Connolly took a seat in the chair facing the stern.

Hollis sat in a chair across the table from him.

The boat lurched as the transmission engaged. They started forward, away from the dock.

Moving at idle speed, they slowly made their way out of the marina. As they passed the last red and white buoy, the engine noise grew louder. Their speed increased. The bow rose. The stern slid low in the water as the boat climbed its own wake, then leveled out. Moments later, they skimmed across the water.

Hollis caught Connolly's eye and shouted at him over the engine noise.

"You okay?"

Connolly nodded.

Hollis turned in his chair and opened the ice chest. He took a can of Coca-Cola from the box, opened it, and handed it to Connolly. Connolly smiled and took a sip.

From the marina on the north side of the island, they went east around Fort Gaines, a series of brick-and-mortar ramparts built to defend the mouth of Mobile Bay during the 1800s. Past the fort, they turned west. Wind whipped around the cabin. The boat bounced against the waves, giving Connolly a jolt every few seconds as the bow rose and fell in time with the crest of the waves. He took another sip of Coke and watched as the island faded in the distance behind them. Hollis pulled his cap over his eyes and dozed.

A mile past Dauphin Island a drilling platform appeared off Connolly's side of the boat. Not quite a quarter of a mile away, it looked huge and imposing with its steel columns rising out of the water and its tangled superstructure towering overhead. Connolly turned to look at it. Coke sloshed from the can onto his shirt. He brushed it away and leaned around the cabin into the wind to see what else lay in front of them. Ahead, a line of rigs stretched across the blue Gulf water toward the horizon. He stared at them for a moment, then settled back in the chair.

After a while, an island appeared to Connolly's left. He yelled at Hollis over the engine noise.

"That it?"

Hollis lifted his hat and glanced around, then shook his head.

"That's Petit Bois."

He pulled the cap back over his eyes and slid low in the seat. Connolly leaned to one side and let his hand dangle in the spray from the boat's wake. He took a sip of Coke and thought of nothing at all.

In a little while, the engine began to slow. Hollis opened his eyes and sat up straight. Connolly glanced around the corner of the cabin. Ahead of them was a small island. Hollis called to him over the noise of the wind and the engine.

"This is it."

The engine slowed further. The bow dropped. The stern sank low in the water. Behind them, the boat's wake rushed toward the transom. Just before it splashed over the edge, the stern rode up the wake and settled in the water. They trolled at an idle.

Hollis pointed.

"There's Horn Island."

Connolly turned to look.

Fifteen miles long, the island began as a shank of sand on the east end and gradually rose from the water to a height of five or six feet above sea level. Half a mile down, the sand was covered with sea oats. Farther to the west was a stand of tall, spindly pine trees.

Taylor leaned over the railing on the top deck and called down to them.

"There's a dock around here." He gestured with his thumb over his shoulder. "We can tie up there for a few minutes if you want to get off and look around. This island is protected. A ranger's usually out here. I don't think they'll mind."

Connolly nodded.

Taylor guided the boat to the dock a quarter of a mile down the island. He held it close with the engine while Hollis tied the bow line. Connolly wrapped a stern line around one of the pilings; then Taylor turned off the engine. The sudden quiet was a welcome relief from the noise of the trip.

Taylor leaned over the railing.

"Have a look around." He smiled down at them. "I'll be right here."

Connolly and Hollis climbed from the boat and made their way down the dock. When they reached the end, Hollis paused and glanced around.

"You know where you're going?"

"Hammond said they found her on the east end." Connolly pointed to the left. "I saw some crime scene tape down here as we were coming in."

They hiked back to the beach at the east end of the island.

Yellow tape marked off an area twenty feet wide and forty feet long at the water's edge where the sand rose a little higher and was covered with sea oats. Connolly stood there trying to imagine what it looked like when they found her. Hollis scanned the area.

"Think this is the place?"

"Yeah," Connolly replied. "I doubt they have more than one crime scene out here."

His eyes wandered from the beach to the water. A sandbar glistened in the sun fifty yards from shore. He glanced at Hollis.

"What do you think?"

They spoke in hushed tones.

"Not much to say. She washed up. Somebody found her."

Connolly pointed toward the water.

"I wonder what the current's like out there."

Hollis shrugged.

"I don't know. Why?"

"You see that sandbar out there?"

"Yeah."

Connolly turned to the right, tracing with his finger as he moved.

"That sandbar runs all the way down to the tip of the island." By then, he faced east. "To get here, the body had to wash over the sandbar at high tide. Or it had to drift all the way around the end over to here." He turned to Hollis. "Think that's how it happened?"

"I don't know. Waves sort of run from east to west. I guess it could happen." He smiled at Connolly. "You thinking somebody just dumped her here where she'd be found?"

"There's no way she washed in here."

Hollis shrugged again.

"The ocean is an amazing place. Anything's possible."

Connolly took a disposable camera from his pocket and snapped a couple of pictures. When he was finished, they returned to the boat.

Taylor was asleep in the captain's chair behind the wheel on the top deck. At the sound of their footsteps on the dock, he lowered his feet to the deck and sat up.

"Ready?"

Hollis nodded.

"We're ready."

Taylor pressed a button on the console in front of him. The engine came to life. Connolly climbed aboard and untied the stern line. Hollis untied the bow line and jumped aboard in front. The boat backed away from the dock. Connolly called up to Taylor.

"Can we go all the way around the island?"

Taylor nodded and pushed a lever on the console. The boat jerked as the transmission slipped into a forward gear.

They rode west a hundred yards offshore and made their way around the island. As they rounded the far end, Connolly again noticed the drilling platforms all in a row extending east toward Dauphin Island.

"I never knew there were so many rigs out here."

"You wouldn't."

"What do you mean?"

"Can't see them from shore. Drop over the curve of the earth about ten miles out. If you were on shore, those rigs would be just below the horizon."

Connolly nodded. He hadn't thought of that.

"Must be a lot of oil out here."

Hollis shook his head.

"Natural gas. But there's no telling where they're getting it."

Connolly looked puzzled.

"What do you mean?"

"They guide those drilling bits anywhere they want to." Hollis pointed to a platform. "They might be working a bit from there that runs way off somewhere."

Connolly was skeptical.

"You mean, they can put the bit in the ground in one place, and after it gets in the ground, they can turn it and make it go somewhere else?"

"They do it all the time."

"How far are we talking about?"

"Miles."

Connolly was astounded.

"Miles?"

"Record's ten miles, I think."

Hollis turned away and caught Taylor's eye. He waggled his finger at him. Taylor nodded. The engine noise grew louder. The bow climbed on top of the water. They skimmed east, across the Gulf toward Dauphin Island.

Twenty-four

*C*onnolly arrived at the office Monday morning looking refreshed and relaxed. Mrs. Gordon looked up from her desk by the door as he entered.

"A boat ride with Hollis couldn't have been that much fun."

Connolly chuckled.

"Good morning, Mrs. Gordon."

She thrust a stack of phone messages toward him as he moved past. "Here."

Connolly took the messages. The one on top was from Henry McNamara, the assistant district attorney who handled cases in Judge Cahill's courtroom.

"Henry called?"

"Yes."

"Did he say what he wanted?"

"No. Just wanted you to call him back."

Connolly walked down the hall to his office. He hung his jacket on the coatrack by the door and took a seat in the chair behind his desk. He picked up the phone and called McNamara. They arranged to meet later that morning.

Connolly left the office shortly before ten and made his way to the courthouse on Government Street. There, he crossed the lobby to the elevator. On the fourth floor, the doors opened to a reception area outside the district attorney's office. A desk sat opposite the elevator, partially hidden behind a counter that stood chest high. Juanita, the receptionist, glared at him over the countertop.

"May I help you?"

Her skin was smooth as porcelain, and she had a certain air of dignity about the way she carried herself that always left Connolly wondering whether her gruff disposition was merely an act. Beyond the tone of her voice, however, there was little emotion about her. No frown.

No scowl. Only that voice, and eyes that rolled up as she looked over the top of reading glasses perched in the middle of her nose.

Connolly stepped to the counter.

"I have a meeting with Henry."

"What about?"

The tone in her voice put him on the defensive.

"A case."

"Whose court?"

"Judge Cahill."

She lifted the telephone receiver and began punching in a number. She stared at him as she waited for McNamara to answer the phone.

"I'll see if he has time to meet with you."

Connolly moved away. There was a water fountain on the wall near the elevator. He started toward it. Before he took a drink, she called to him.

"Henry will be out in a minute." Her voice was loud and flat. "Have a seat."

Connolly took a drink, then found a seat in a chair as far from her as possible.

In a few minutes, a door opened near Juanita's desk. McNamara appeared. Almost six feet tall, he had broad shoulders and an athletic physique. He had been in the DA's office almost three years, but his innocent, round face and boyish manner made him seem much younger than he was.

"Come on in, Mr. Connolly."

Connolly rose from his seat and crossed the lobby. McNamara led him through a labyrinth of offices and cubicles to a small conference room on the far side of the building. Sparsely furnished, the room held only a plain folding table and four chairs. The walls were bare and windowless. A fluorescent light in the ceiling above the table made the room seem even more stark. McNamara's file lay at the far end of the table.

"Have a seat."

He closed the door and pulled a chair from the end of the table. Connolly took a seat nearby. McNamara folded his hands in his lap. He had a somber look on his face.

"I understand you represent Perry Braxton."

"Yes."

"We conducted a search of his apartment the day he was arrested. Anthony said you were there."

"Yeah."

"I made copies of the arrest and incident reports for you." He slid the copies across the table to Connolly as he continued looking through the file. "I have a copy of the return on the search warrant in here somewhere."

He flipped through several pages in the file. When he found what he was looking for, he laid it on the table.

Connolly studied the list.

"This all you took?"

"Yes. Clothes, and his Suburban."

"Where is it now?"

"The clothes are at the lab. The vehicle is impounded."

"Find anything in the Suburban?"

"Don't know yet. The evidence people vacuum up everything. You know, try to get as much as they can. They're going through it. I don't know what they found. They haven't sent me a report on it."

"How long before you hear from the lab on the clothes?"

"A few days."

Connolly laid the list on the table and leaned away.

"Have they finished the autopsy?"

"It's finished. I don't have a report on it, either." McNamara closed his file and slid it aside. He rested his hands on the table and leaned forward. "Listen, I'll give you all the reports as I get them, and I'll call Hammond and tell him to let you see the physical evidence. You can have it tested by your expert if you want to. I don't care about all of that. I want to talk about something else." He slipped his hand inside the pocket of his jacket and took out a picture. "This is a man named Pete Rizutto." He laid it on the table. "We'd like to know what your client knows about him."

Connolly glanced at the photograph.

"You offering us a deal?"

"Maybe. But first I want to know if your client is willing to talk about this man." McNamara tapped the photo with his finger. "Pete Rizutto."

"You have to give him a reason."

McNamara shrugged.

"Your man's looking at the death penalty. That ought to be reason enough."

Connolly found it impossible to suppress a smile.

"Henry, he's not going to talk just to spend the rest of his life in prison."

McNamara leaned away.

"You see if he's willing to talk. About Rizutto. Then we'll discuss a deal."

* * *

Connolly left the district attorney's office and rode the elevator to the lobby. From there, he retraced his steps across Government Street and up the alley to the service door behind the office building. He crossed the lobby to the main entrance and stepped outside to Dauphin Street. The Chrysler was parked up the street near the Port City Diner. He opened the door and got in behind the steering wheel.

He arrived at the jail a few minutes later. Braxton was standing in the interview room when he reached the eighth floor.

"Judge change his mind about the bond?"

Connolly pointed to the stainless steel table in the center of the room.

"Take a seat."

They stepped over the bench and sat opposite each other across the table.

"We have to talk about Rizutto."

Braxton leaned over the table toward Connolly.

"I told you before," he whispered. "I'm not talking about him."

"The DA's asking about him."

Braxton leaned away. A frown wrinkled his brow.

"About Rizutto?"

Connolly nodded in response.

"How do they know about him?"

"I tried to tell you before, you can't manage this case. You can't steer your way around this stuff."

Braxton lowered his head for a moment, then looked at Connolly.

"I'm not talking."

"They're willing to make a deal."

"What kind of deal?"

"They haven't said. They want to know if you're interested."

"Isn't that like admitting to a crime or something?"

"Saying you're interested?"

"No. Talking."

"Not exactly. We'd come up with an agreement. A written agreement. You'd agree to talk. We'll prepare a written statement. It's called a proffer. Actually, the way it works is you tell me what you know. Then, I prepare a document that says what I think you could testify to truthfully about whatever it is they're interested in. They'll take what you say and try to verify it. If your story checks out, they'll let you plead out to whatever it is we've agreed to."

"And what if they aren't satisfied?"

"Then we go to trial and they can't use what you tell them."

"You sure?"

"Yeah."

Braxton turned away, his face clouded with thought. When he spoke, his voice sounded far away.

"I'll talk, but they have to drop the charges."

Connolly shook his head.

"I ... don't think they'll do that."

Braxton turned to face him.

"You tell them I'll talk, but they have to drop the charges and relocate me." He stood to leave. "If they want Rizutto, they'll do it."

He banged on the door and motioned for the guard to let him out.

"There's one thing you have to know."

"What's that?"

"If they're interested in Rizutto, they're probably going to want you to testify."

"In court?"

"Yes."

The guard unlocked the door. Braxton glanced over his shoulder at Connolly.

"Find out what they say."

The guard swung the door open. Braxton stepped out of the room and started toward the cellblock.

Twenty-five

At noon, Connolly walked up the street and ate lunch at the Port City Diner. He lingered there as long as his conscience would allow, then sauntered down the sidewalk toward the office. The afternoon was sunny and warm. A stack of files awaited him at his desk. He was in no hurry to return to them.

Mrs. Gordon was out when he arrived. He passed her desk and moved down the hall. In his office, he slipped off his jacket, hung it on the coatrack by the door, and stepped to the chair behind the desk. The files that required his attention were stacked to the left, each of them begging to be opened. He flopped into the chair and leaned back, resting his head against the wall. A moment later, he propped his feet on the desk, folded his arms in his lap, and closed his eyes. Almost instantly, he was asleep.

From somewhere in a deep slumber he heard a voice calling to him. Then, something struck him on the forehead. Pain shot through the bridge of his nose. He jerked his feet from the desk and leaned forward, clutching his face. As he did, a small box of ink pens fell from his lap. He picked up the box and lifted his head. Mrs. Gordon stood at the door.

"You hit me!"

Her arms were folded across her chest. She gave him a smirk.

"You were snoring."

He rubbed his fingers over his nose and checked to see if he was bleeding.

"You threw a box of pens at me?"

"Be glad I wasn't holding a cup in my hand." She turned away. "Get busy on those files. They aren't going to take care of themselves."

Still rubbing his nose, he reached for the file on top of the stack. It was a car wreck case he'd been handling for a lady in Citronelle. Medical records he'd subpoenaed had arrived. He looked through them, scribbled a note to Mrs. Gordon to schedule the doctor's deposition, then moved the file to the opposite side of the desk.

The pain in his nose subsided. He reached for another file.

Sometime later, Mrs. Gordon appeared at the door again. In her hand she held a large manila envelope. Connolly glared at her.

"Don't throw it."

She stepped into the room.

"Don't tempt me."

"What is it?"

"I don't know. Someone named Gladys Newman left it for you."

Connolly pushed away from the desk to stand.

"Is she still here?"

"No."

"When did she come by?"

"About a half hour ago."

"Why didn't you tell me?"

"You were finally working on those files. I was busy. She didn't seem interested in hanging around."

She stepped to the desk. Connolly took the envelope from her.

"Here." He handed her the files he'd finished. "Take care of these."

She took them and disappeared up the hall.

Connolly tore open the envelope. Inside, he found copies of the documents he'd wanted from the first few boxes of Oliver Gilmore's files, the Tonsmeyer Trust Agreement and one of the deeds conveying property to the Trust. He glanced through them and laid them on the desk.

As he lifted his gaze from the desktop, his eyes fell on two crumpled cardboard boxes sitting on the office floor beneath the window. He'd brought them back from Gladys's barn intending to go through them in detail, but then Braxton had been arrested, and Camille's body had been found, and everything seemed to come at him in a hurry. Sorting through documents wasn't something he enjoyed, either. The boxes had sat there, undisturbed, since he unloaded them from the Chrysler. Now, he was curious about what they contained.

He moved from the chair to the window and picked up the first box. He sat it on the desk and stood there, flipping through the pages. What he found were records of early transfers of stocks, financial assets, and various parcels of real estate to the Trust. All of the documents bore Theron Tonsmeyer's signature accompanied by that of his son, Pierre, who signed as his conservator.

In a little while, Mrs. Gordon appeared at the door.

"Do you have any more of those files for me?"

He looked up, startled by her voice.

"Files?"

She moved around him to the far side of the desk.

"These." She tapped the top of the stack. "You're supposed to be working on these."

"I needed a break."

"It's four o'clock."

"Oh." Connolly glanced at his watch. "I didn't realize it was that late."

She peered over his shoulder.

"What's that you're looking at?"

"Oliver Gilmore's files."

She moved around him for a closer look. As she leaned over the box, her nose wrinkled and her eyes grew watery. She turned away and sneezed. Connolly grinned.

"Kind of moldy."

"What in the world are you doing with them?"

"I'm not sure."

She moved across the room and retreated up the hall.

When he finished with the first box, he set it on the floor and picked up the second. Afternoon faded into twilight. Shadows stretched across the room. The office grew dark as sunset came and went. He switched on the overhead light and continued to work.

Late that night, he came to the last file in the box. Unusually thin, it contained only three pieces of paper. He took it out and opened it. Inside, he found a letter addressed to Oliver Gilmore from Porter Reeves, an attorney in Mobile. The letter was dated June 6, 1934. Reeves represented a number of disgruntled Tonsmeyer relatives. From the tone of the letter, both Theron and Pierre were dead. Cousins were fighting over their estates. Reeves was preparing to file a petition in court in an attempt to set aside conveyance of mineral rights from Theron to Pierre for the tract at Grand Bay. With the letter was a page of notes scrawled in almost illegible handwriting and a letter from someone named Mary Adams replying to Reeves and informing him that Oliver Gilmore had died.

Mineral rights. He'd come across them in the attic at the Braxtons' house. The geology reports. The maps. At Gladys Newman's barn he learned lawyers from an oil company had been out there looking at Gilmore's records. When he and Hollis rode out to Horn Island they passed a long line of oil rigs. Minerals. Mineral rights. Here it was again.

He laid the file folder aside and picked up the copy of the deed Gladys delivered that afternoon. It was the deed from Theron Tonsmeyer conveying the property along the water in Grand Bay to the Trust. Thirty sections were listed in the description. He shook his head in amazement.

"Thirty square miles."

Beneath the description, two exceptions were noted. One for taxes for the current year, the other for mineral rights that Theron had reserved for himself. His signature appeared on the last page, but unlike the other documents this one was not accompanied by a signature from Pierre.

Connolly whispered to himself.

"Without the conservator's signature, there would always be a cloud hanging over these transactions. Why would anyone create a trust like this, with property like this, and leave open the question of whether it had been legitimately funded?"

He rubbed his eyes and checked his watch. It was twelve thirty. He was sure Reeves had found what he'd noticed that day in Gladys's barn. Yet the Trust had survived. His mouth opened wide with a yawn. He laid the papers on the desk and turned to the coatrack. Whatever had happened, it would have to wait until morning. And it would require a trip to probate court.

"Just what I need." Connolly sighed. "More documents to read."

He took his jacket from the coatrack, turned off the light, and started up the hall.

Twenty-six

*T*hough most court offices had moved to the new building up the street, probate court was still housed in the old one, a bland government building constructed in 1940 at the corner of Government and Royal. Over the years, it had been expanded and remodeled and now covered the entire block. Connolly entered the building from Royal Street and walked down the steps to the records room in the basement.

At the bottom of the steps, he turned right and made his way to the recording clerk's office. Desks and workstations used by court personnel sat behind a counter that stood just inside the door. To the left, a doorway led to the records room that filled the remainder of the basement. From where he stood, he could see rows of index books in there waiting for him.

Something inside him shriveled at the thought.

Behind the books were shelves and cabinets crammed with plat books, maps, burial records, birth records, records long forgotten, and records not even the court employees could remember. Ignored and shunned by everyone except a few real estate attorneys and a cadre of title abstractors, it was an archaic world with its own customs and procedures. And it was a treasure trove of information, a diary recording the heart of the county from the original land grants in 1690 all the way to the present.

Connolly stopped at the counter. A clerk came from her desk.

"May I help you?"

Connolly gave her a smile.

"I need to ramble through your records."

She gave him a disapproving look.

"Ramble?"

"Ramble. Plunder." From the look on her face he wasn't sure she understood what he meant. "Troll around. See what I can find."

A thin, officious smile appeared on her face.

"Sir, this is probate court. In here we refer to it as research."

Connolly grinned.

"Yes. Research. That's exactly what I need to do. Is it all right if I have a look?"

"Help yourself."

She turned away and stepped toward her desk. Connolly moved past the counter and through the doorway to the records room.

Transactions recorded after 1980 were indexed in a computer database. Terminals for searching those records were located in the back of the room at a counter along the wall behind the rows of oversized index books. Transactions recorded prior to 1980 were indexed in the books.

Connolly hesitated as he passed the books. The size of the task he'd undertaken suddenly struck him. The Trust was huge. There would be hundreds of transactions, spread over many years. He didn't know where to begin or what he was looking for. His finger ran along the top of the nearest book, a leather-bound, oversized volume for the year 1949 with the title *Reverse Index* on the spine. A sense of heaviness fell over him. He sighed.

A voice from behind him broke the silence of the room.

"That's a heavy sigh."

He glanced around to see a woman standing behind him. He gave her a puzzled look.

"Don't know where to begin."

"What are you looking for?"

"A conveyance of mineral rights."

"What year?"

"Well ... that's the question."

"You need a year. Have to have a place to begin."

He nodded thoughtfully.

"Sometime between 1922 and 1935."

"Well, you could begin with 1922 and work your way through each year. But sometimes you can take a shortcut."

She moved to a computer terminal along the back wall and pressed a few keys. A search page appeared on the monitor.

"Sometimes you can find a deed or something in here that gives a reference to the earlier transaction you're looking for. Takes a few minutes to do a search, but if you get a hit, you can cut out half a day of looking through those index books."

Connolly grinned.

"I like that idea."

She moved aside. He stepped to the computer.

"Might as well do the easy part first."

With a few key strokes, he entered Theron Tonsmeyer's name in the computer. Moments later, a message appeared on the screen indicating there were no records available under that name. He did the same for Pierre, with the same result. Next, he entered the name of the Trust.

A list of documents appeared on the screen with names of the parties, a brief description of the location of the property, and a number indicating the type of transaction involved. He scrolled down the list through entries for deeds and mortgages, none of which struck him as out of the ordinary. At the bottom of the screen, he clicked an icon for the next page. Three pages later, he came to a transaction with a code he didn't recognize.

The woman who helped him earlier stood at a terminal down the counter. He caught her eye.

"What's the code 601 mean?"

"Mineral lease," she replied. "It's either 600 or 601. It's supposed to be 601, but sometimes they put it in as 600 like a regular lease."

The entry he'd found was a lease from the Trust to Pavilion Oil Company in 1989. He noted the book and page number for the location of the actual document, then continued down the list. Most of the entries were either deeds or mortgages, but on the fifth page he found another mineral lease. This one was to Zapato Rojo Oil Company dated in January of the current year. He noted the book and page number, checked the last page of entries on the screen, and walked to the front of the room. The clerk he'd seen before was at her desk. He handed her a slip of paper with the numbers for the documents he wanted.

"I need to see these."

She glanced at the numbers on the paper, then crossed the room and disappeared down a row of shelves. In a few minutes, she returned with two strips of microfilm. She placed the first one in a reader and found the correct page for the lease to Pavilion. Connolly took a seat at the reader and scanned down the document. The property involved in the transaction was located in the northern end of the county. He moved quickly through the document to the signature page. The lease had been signed on behalf of the Trust by someone from the bank named Kurt Eldredge. He read a few paragraphs, then turned to the clerk.

"Do you have the other one?"

She leaned over him and changed the microfilm in the reader, then located the first page for the lease to Zapato Rojo.

"It's rather long."

Connolly scanned through the pages of the document. The lease granted Zapato Rojo the right to exploit minerals on a piece of property described in an attachment. There, he found a list of thirty section numbers. He was certain they were the same ones he'd seen on the deed from Tonsmeyer to the Trust for the property along the water at Grand Bay.

The clerk hovered nearby. Connolly turned to her.

"I need a copy of this."

She stepped closer and leaned over his shoulder.

"Just that page?"

"No. The entire document."

She frowned.

"We charge a dollar per page."

Connolly turned back to the document on the screen.

"Okay. I need all the pages. Including the attachments."

He moved from the description in the attachment to the signature page of the lease and scanned to the bottom of the page. The clerk nudged him.

"I need to get there to print that out."

Connolly heard the sound of her voice, but his mind was carried away by what he saw on the screen before him. The document had been signed by someone from the oil company and Ford Defuniak on behalf of the Trust. A note at the bottom of the page indicated it had been prepared by a law firm in Houston. Images from that day in Gladys Newman's barn ran through his mind. It had taken him a week to find her.

How did someone from Houston know where to look?

The clerk nudged him again.

"Do you still want a copy?"

Connolly heard her this time.

"Yes." He scooted the chair away from the reader and stood. "Sorry. I was thinking about something else."

She ignored him and took a seat at the reader. In a moment, pages slid from the machine to a paper tray on the side. Connolly leaned against a desk nearby and folded his arms across his chest.

"Where would I find court records from the 1930s and '40s?"

She glanced at him over her shoulders.

"Which court? Circuit court? Probate court?"

"Circuit court. I guess. A petition to set aside a deed ... a conveyance."

"Circuit court. If they still have the files, they're in the warehouse over on Conti Street. A lot of the old ones were destroyed when they put them on microfilm. Some of the older cases never had a court file."

"Isn't there a record of the orders from them somewhere?"

"If a judgment was entered, it might be recorded here in our records. But that's up to the parties. We don't do it automatically. Most of the judgments we have are recorded in the real property books. A few are in the personal property books." She gathered the pages from the paper tray and stood. "Your best bet would be to check the circuit court minutes."

Connolly gave her a puzzled look.

"The minutes?"

"Minutes of the court. Court orders used to be 'spread upon the minutes of the court.' Noted in the minutes." She handed him the copies. "What year are you looking for?"

"Nineteen thirty-four. Maybe thirty-five."

Connolly reached inside his jacket for his wallet. She sloughed him off with a wave of her hand as she moved toward her desk.

"Don't worry about it. Just take them."

He slipped his wallet back in his pocket.

"Thanks."

She took a seat at her desk. Connolly continued the conversation.

"Where are the minutes?"

"The ones we have are in the back. At the end of the real property books." She looked at him with a sarcastic smile. "You'll have to ramble around in them. They aren't indexed."

Connolly grinned.

"Research."

"Yes." She turned to the work on her desk. "Dusty, moldy research."

Connolly returned to the records room and disappeared down a long row of dimly lit shelves. In a little while, he found four oversized books bound in dark green leather sitting on a shelf near the back of the basement. On the spine of each were the words "Circuit Court Minutes" emblazoned in gold lettering. From the dust along the top of the books, it had been years since anyone moved them. He took the books from the shelf, carried them to a table in the corner along the basement wall, and began searching for a record of the petition Porter Reeves had said he was going to file almost seventy years ago.

Two hours later, he found the entry in the third book. Dated March 14, 1935, the order stated simply, "Petitioners request for relief is hereby granted. The conveyance of mineral rights from Theron Tonsmeyer to Pierre Tonsmeyer dated December 26, 1922, and recorded in Book 465, Page 408 of the records of probate court of Mobile, Alabama, is hereby rendered null and void and of no effect."

Holding the book open to the correct page, Connolly lifted it from the table and started toward the clerk's desk.

Twenty-seven

*I*t was noon when Connolly left the records room. He climbed the stairs from the basement to the courthouse lobby and walked outside. As he reached the corner at Government Street, he saw Henry McNamara coming toward him. McNamara gestured for him to wait as he caught up.

"Did you get a chance to talk to Braxton?"

"Yeah."

"And?"

"He says if he talks, you'll have to drop the charges and relocate him."

He expected to see McNamara scowl, or laugh, but McNamara was unfazed.

"I'm not sure we can drop a capital murder." He looked away. "And I'm not sure we can relocate anyone. We're not the FBI. I think we've done it once or twice, maybe. I'll have to see what we can do." He turned back to Connolly. "But he's willing to talk?"

"Under those conditions."

"Okay." McNamara turned to leave. "I'll call you. It may take a day or two."

McNamara disappeared down Government Street.

Connolly walked up Royal Street. When he turned the corner onto Dauphin, he saw Hollis's pickup truck parked in front of the office building. He entered the lobby and took the elevator to the third floor. Mrs. Gordon was sitting at her desk as he stepped through the doorway.

"Is Hollis here?"

She rolled her eyes and nodded toward his office. Connolly made his way past her desk to the hall. Hollis sat in a chair in front of his desk. He glanced over his shoulder.

"You had lunch yet?"

"No." Connolly glanced at his watch. "I didn't realize it was lunchtime."

"My stomach won't let me forget. Regular as any clock."

Connolly slipped off his jacket and took a seat behind the desk.

"I hope you're here to tell all about Manny Fernandez and the tanning business."

"Yeah." Hollis rose partway out of his chair and reached behind him for the door. He pushed it closed with a bang and settled in his seat. "Those women they got came here from one of those small European countries of no consequence but are always causing trouble. Bosnia, Croatia ... someplace like that."

"So, they're immigrants."

"From what I hear, they're illegal. Fernandez has them living in a warehouse."

Connolly frowned.

"A warehouse?"

"Yeah. One of those buildings over by the old banana wharfs."

"In a warehouse?"

Hollis nodded. Connolly ran his fingers through his hair.

"How many women?"

Hollis gave him a sarcastic look.

"I don't know. I didn't do a head count."

"Four? Five?"

"I'd say eight or ten. Not more than a dozen."

Connolly shook his head. Hollis shifted positions in the chair.

"It may not be as bad as it sounds. I hear they can fix those places up pretty nice these days. Buddy of mine from Atlanta told me they do it up there all the time."

Connolly sighed and looked away, his voice a low whisper.

"A warehouse?"

Hollis crossed his legs.

"Fernandez hauls them down to the tanning store every day. Has them down there by ten in the morning. They're there till one or two at night, then he carts them back to the warehouse. Some nights, he takes a couple of them over to that motel. Shady Acres. You saw what they're doing over there."

"Who owns Shady Acres?"

"I don't know. Hard to tell. Looks like it's changed hands several times. I don't think they have any connection to Fernandez."

"What about Rizutto? The guy in the BMW."

Hollis nodded.

"He doesn't have anything to do with the daily business. I mean, he's not running the cash register or greeting customers. But it's his operation."

Connolly leaned back in his chair.

"I met him once or twice. Paid my fee when I defended Fernandez a few years ago."

Hollis nodded.

"Then you know what he's like. Works out of Biloxi, but everybody thinks he's tied in with a guy named Morella from New Orleans. If he is, he's pretty well connected. Morella has businesses up and down the Gulf Coast. Biloxi, Pascagoula, Mobile, Pensacola, Panama City."

Connolly nodded thoughtfully.

"You don't think he owns Shady Acres?"

"He could. But most of what he has are bars, restaurants, that sort of place."

"And tanning salons."

"Yeah. He owns a few of those."

"How many?"

"I don't know. But if this is any indication, he probably has a bunch."

Connolly leaned forward in his chair.

"Anything else?"

Hollis had a pained look on his face.

"I got a bad feeling about this one, Mike. I mean, Rizutto ..." He shook his head. "That's the mob. And women from some foreign country ... that's pretty serious. I think you should just deal with Braxton and leave the rest of this alone. I mean, we can't bust something like this up, and right now, we haven't ruffled any feathers. Far as anyone knows, you're just checking to see what the story is. That's it. Just deal with Braxton and let the rest of this go."

Connolly was silent for a moment. Then, he looked Hollis in the eye and whispered.

"They're living in a warehouse."

Hollis nodded. Connolly leaned back in his chair.

"Anything else?"

"Not really." Hollis stood. The tone of his voice lightened. "Just lunch."

"Lunch?"

"Yeah. Lunch." He opened the door and gestured for Connolly to follow. "You're buying."

Connolly rose from his chair and came around the desk. He retrieved his jacket from the coatrack and followed Hollis toward Mrs. Gordon's desk.

Twenty-eight

*F*rom the office, Connolly and Hollis walked up Dauphin Street to the Port City Diner. Most of the noontime crowd was gone when they arrived. They sat at the end of the counter in the back and ate while watching the kitchen crew through the service window. Connolly had half a Reuben sandwich and a bowl of gumbo. Hollis had a muffuletta. Neither found small talk easy. They ate in silence.

When they finished, they walked outside and down the street to the pickup. Hollis opened the truck door.

"Thanks for lunch."

"You like those muffulettas?"

"Yeah." Hollis smiled. "But you can't get them just anywhere." He nodded toward the kitchen. "That guy in there makes a good one."

"I've never had one."

Hollis climbed into the truck and closed the door. He propped his elbow on the window ledge and spoke to Connolly through the open window.

"Call me if you need anything else."

Connolly stepped closer to the truck.

"You know where this warehouse is?"

Hollis looked away.

"You don't want to—"

Connolly interrupted him.

"You know where it is?"

Hollis sighed.

"Yeah. I know where it is."

"You got time to take me down there?"

"Get in."

Connolly walked around the truck and climbed inside. Hollis started the engine and steered the truck into traffic.

They drove up Dauphin Street to the cathedral and turned left. Two blocks later, they turned left onto Government. At Water Street, they turned left again and rode past the docks along Mobile River. The traffic light at Beauregard Street was red. They came to a stop. Across the street on the corner was the GM&O railroad station. Once a beautiful passenger depot, it was now abandoned and crumbling in disrepair.

Connolly glanced at it through the windshield.

"They ought to fix that."

Hollis looked across the seat at him.

"Fix what?"

Connolly pointed to the depot.

"That train station. There aren't many like it anymore."

The traffic light changed to green. They turned onto Beauregard and drove toward the river. Beyond the GM&O terminal were rows and rows of single-story warehouses. Hollis turned left past the third row. Connolly looked around.

"What street is this?"

"Streets in here don't have a name. You go by that number."

He pointed to a number on a sign on the side of a building as they drove past. Connolly noted the number and the broken beer bottles in the gutter. The buildings looked empty. Weeds grew through cracks in the pavement.

At the end of the street, they turned left again. A faded blue sign identified it as Morgan Street. Warehouses on the right were three and four stories high. When they reached the next corner, Hollis turned right. He slowed the truck as they came to a cross street. A concrete signpost identified it as Conception Street Road. He pointed to the building on the corner.

"That's it."

Made of red brick, the building was three stories high. Rows of windows lined the top two floors, but they had been painted gray. A single door faced Conception Street Road. It had been painted the same color as the windows. Connolly watched as they moved past the end of the building.

On the opposite side he could see more windows lined the second and third floors on the back of the building. A door was located midway down the back wall. Beyond it was a loading dock for trucks with a concrete parking area around it. An eight-foot chain-link fence lined the rear of the property.

"You're sure they live in there?"

"I saw Fernandez bring them down here. Took them in through the front door."

"Why would they film their movies at the Shady Acres, when they could do it right here?"

"I don't know. Maybe they never thought of it. Maybe they didn't want to attract too much attention to this place. Four or five cars parked down here would be a big crowd."

"Maybe."

Connolly stared out the window. A moment later, the building disappeared behind the next warehouse. He turned forward in the seat, his face clouded, his mind deep in thought.

Hollis glanced across at him.

"What?"

"Huh?"

"What are you thinking about?"

"I'm imagining what it would be like to live like that."

"It's probably got running water. I mean, for the business they're in, Fernandez would want them to shower and all that."

Connolly glared at him until he caught Hollis's eye.

"You mean it's all right to be herded from one place to another. Locked up. Fed. Brought out to have their bodies exploited? Every day? Multiple times each day?"

Hollis didn't reply. Connolly turned away.

"Can you imagine what it must be like to have some sweaty guy wallowing all over you? Seeing you ... naked. Seeing him naked. Touching you. Groping you. Running his hands over your ..."

Hollis waved his hand in the air.

"Okay. Okay. I get the picture. I wasn't even talking about that. I just meant, the place might not be as institutional as it looks." He downshifted. The truck picked up speed. "Give me a break."

Connolly grinned.

"Institutional. That's a good word. That's the longest word I've ever heard you say."

"I like short ones. Like 'Pay me.'"

Connolly laughed. Hollis gave him a look.

"No. I mean it. You owe me for what I've done."

Connolly took out his wallet. He counted out several bills and laid them on the seat. Hollis picked them up and counted them as he drove. Satisfied, he slipped them into his pocket. Connolly glanced across at him.

"What are you doing tonight?"

"Nothing. Why?"

"I want to take a closer look at that warehouse."

Hollis jammed his foot on the brake pedal. The nose of the truck dropped. Connolly slid forward against the dash.

"What are you doing?"

Hollis whipped the steering wheel to the right and brought the truck to a stop on the shoulder of the road. He turned in the seat and stared at Connolly. His eyes were wide. His look, intense.

"You want to go in there?"

"Yeah."

"What for?"

"I want to see what's inside."

"I thought this was a murder case."

"It is."

"Well then, what does this have to do with that?"

Connolly didn't reply. Hollis continued.

"Look, I talked to the missing lady's neighbors. That's fine. I found somebody who saw her. Great." His voice grew louder as he talked. "You think her husband liked to hang out at a tanning salon. I'm glad to check it out. But this is different. Going into that warehouse is a side trip. It's got nothing to do with a dead lady who washed up on Horn Island."

"Maybe. Right now, I don't know. I don't know much of anything. But I know this. She was a wealthy lady and she was about to divorce her husband. They were getting a divorce because of those women." Now Connolly's voice grew louder. "Women you say live in that warehouse. If we found them, the district attorney can find them. I want to talk to them now, before I see them on a witness stand in a capital murder trial where my client's life is at risk."

Hollis leaned away and took a breath.

"Look, I've been glad to help you in the past." His voice was calm but firm. "I took a job with a lawn service so you could find out what that judge's wife was doing. I went with you when you wanted in that dead rich fellow's house over in Point Clear. That was all right 'cause the only risk there was jail time. But this is different. These people find us in there, they'll kill us."

Connolly glanced at him.

"Are you saying you won't go?"

Hollis didn't respond. Connolly persisted.

"Is that what you're saying? You don't think you can get in there and get out without getting caught?" There was a twinkle in his eye. "Huh?"

Hollis gave him a quick look. His face was stern and serious, but as he turned away a smile flickered across his face.

"No." He sighed. "I ain't saying that."

"Then what are you saying?"

Hollis stared ahead out the windshield. A broad grin spread across his face.

"It'll have to be really late."

Twenty-nine

*H*ollis brought the truck to a stop at the curb in front of the office building. Connolly opened the door and stepped to the sidewalk. He turned toward Hollis and spoke to him through the open door.

"I'll see you in the morning."

Hollis put the truck in gear.

"Don't oversleep."

Connolly closed the door. Hollis drove away.

Instead of returning to the office, Connolly crossed the street and walked through Bienville Square. Oaks draped in Spanish moss covered the ground with thick, cool shade, a welcome relief from the sweltering heat. Connolly slipped off his jacket as he passed the fountain in the center. On the far side of the square he turned right and made his way down St. Francis Street to Ken's Barber Shop in the middle of the next block.

Though small and cramped, the shop was a fixture of downtown business life. Most men who worked in the offices around Bienville Square visited it at least once a month. Stories about it appeared in local magazines and newspapers, and since 1920 every winning candidate in the mayor's race had given a campaign press conference while seated in one of its barber chairs.

The shop had been started by Ken Mainwaring who moved to Mobile from Pittsburgh in 1910 on a friend's promise of a job as a sponge diver. When diving proved more difficult than he'd imagined, he bought a pair of scissors at a secondhand store and began telling everyone he was a barber. He rented the shop on St. Francis from Gus Mayer, the friend from Pittsburgh who promised him the sponge-diving job. Ken lived in a back room, which meant he was always available. Businessmen downtown soon caught on and started coming in for a shave and a trim on the way to the office. He continued the service even after he married and moved to midtown.

When Ken died, his son Johnny took over. Now an old man, he still opened the shop each morning at six thirty. Usually, someone was waiting at the door when he arrived, looking for a shave and a trim before an important meeting. Johnny shared the business with Will, his grandson.

Connolly pushed open the door and stepped inside.

Two barber chairs sat side by side near the center of the room. Behind them was a narrow counter that stood chest high and ran the length of the room along the wall to the left of the door. Above the counter was a large mirror. To the right of the door, office chairs with plastic bottoms on a metal frame lined the wall. Hair from the day's work littered the floor.

Connolly glanced around. Both barber chairs were full, but no one was waiting. He took a seat near Johnny's chair.

"Slow day?"

The old man focused on the head of the man in the chair.

"Not too bad for June." He drew the man's hair away from his head with a comb and ran the clippers across it. "I've seen worse."

Connolly smiled and picked up a magazine. A few moments later, the door opened. Buie Hayford entered. Johnny nodded at him and continued to work on the man in the chair.

"Have a seat, Mr. Hayford. We'll get to you in a minute."

Hayford took a seat beside Connolly. He picked up a magazine from the chair next to him and flipped through it. He spoke to Connolly as he turned the pages.

"You making any progress with Perry Braxton?"

"A little."

"Anything I need to know about?"

"Maybe."

Will finished with the man in his chair. As the man stepped down, Connolly nodded to Hayford.

"Go ahead."

Hayford laid the magazine aside and stood.

"You sure?"

"I'm waiting for Johnny."

Hayford slipped off his jacket and hung it on a coatrack in the corner. He stepped to the barber chair and took a seat. Will draped an apron over Hayford's chest and fastened it behind his neck.

Johnny finished with the man in his chair and gestured to Connolly. Connolly took a seat. Hayford glanced at him.

"Come by the office this afternoon. Let's talk."

Connolly nodded. Johnny fastened an apron behind his neck. Seconds later, the buzz of the clippers lulled him to sleep.

Late that afternoon, Connolly drove to Hayford's office. He parked in back and entered through the rear door. As he started down the hall,

Hayford came from the break room with a bottle of ginger ale in each hand. He gestured with a nod.

"Come on. I just took them out of the refrigerator."

Connolly caught up with him as they stepped into the office. Hayford handed him a bottle and took a seat behind his desk.

"This is good ginger ale."

He took a sip. Connolly took a seat in a chair in front of the desk. Hayford smiled at him.

"So, anything I need to know about your client?"

Connolly shrugged.

"I don't suppose. Something in particular you're concerned about?"

Hayford took another sip of ginger ale.

"Since Camille's body has turned up, we now have to think about her estate. At least one of us does. We're preparing a petition for probate court to get things rolling. Does Perry know the will was changed?"

"Yes."

"Is he going to cause trouble?"

"I don't know. I haven't talked to him about it."

"Think you could nail that down for me?"

"I can ask him." Connolly took a sip from the bottle. "Are you sure you want me to bring this up? I mean, it might just stir things up to ask."

Hayford shook his head.

"Ask him."

"All right." Connolly took another sip of ginger ale. "I read Oliver Gilmore's files on the Trust the other day."

Hayford looked puzzled.

"Gilmore's files?"

"Found them in a barn at his cousin's house in Grand Bay. I think I told you about this before."

A frown cut deep furrows in Hayford's brow.

"No, you didn't. Why are you interested in those files?"

"Every time I turn around, I'm running into the Trust. So, I just decided to dive in and see what it was all about."

"I could tell you what you need to know about it. All you have to do is ask."

"The way I understand it, the Trust was created by Theron Tonsmeyer."

"That's correct."

"Did you know his son had been appointed conservator for him?"

"Yeah."

"Before he transferred property to the Trust?"

Hayford set the ginger ale bottle on the desktop and leaned forward as they talked. His voice became deeper and more somber in tone.

"That isn't a problem. Conservator can grant property. That's what he's there for."

"You ever look at the deeds?"

"Most of them. Trust was ... thirty, forty years old by the time I saw it."

"Tonsmeyer signed the Trust Agreement and all of the documents transferring property to the Trust. His son signed as conservator on everything except the Trust Agreement and the deed for the property at Grand Bay. And, when they conveyed that tract to the Trust, Theron, the father, conveyed the mineral rights to his son."

Hayford nodded.

"You've been to probate court."

Connolly nodded.

"I spent a few hours in the records room."

Hayford picked up the bottle of ginger ale and leaned back in his chair.

"The way it was told to me, the old man loved that land down there and didn't want it disturbed. He and Gilmore were afraid if they just put some kind of restriction on it in the Trust, someone would find a way to manipulate it around so they could get at any oil that might be under the land." He glanced at Connolly. "There's reason to believe they knew there was a lot of oil under it."

Connolly took a sip of ginger ale and listened.

"They tangled the thing up pretty good. Made a mess out of the title. Didn't have much confidence in any one document, so they just confused the whole thing."

"But somebody decided to challenge it."

Hayford nodded and took another sip.

"Not everyone was included as beneficiaries of the Trust. After the son died, some of the cousins who'd been left out found out about the mineral rights and the rumors about oil and they filed a petition to set aside conveyance of the mineral rights."

"Which they did."

"Yes. They did. But what happened after that is not recorded at the courthouse."

Connolly smiled and nodded for him to continue.

"The conveyance was set aside, but there was still a big question about what happened to the rights. The old man's will was about as obscure as this conversation. But before anyone had time to sort it all out, the bank stepped in on behalf of the Trust and offered to buy out the cousins."

"Did it work?"

"Yeah. They settled."

"That's recorded someplace?"

Hayford shook his head and smiled.

"Nope." He turned his chair sideways and propped his feet on the trash can. "They decided since Tonsmeyer had made such a mess of it, they would add some confusion of their own. The settlement documents are in my safe."

Hayford took a sip of ginger ale. Connolly felt confused.

"So, how did Zapato Rojo agree to the oil lease?"

Hayford gagged. He bolted upright in his chair. Ginger ale spewed from his mouth across the desktop. He leaned forward, coughing and choking. Connolly watched, helpless.

"Are you all right?"

Hayford coughed.

"Yeah."

He wiped his chin with his hand and brushed drops of drink from his shirt.

"Tastes good when you swallow it." He took a handkerchief from his hip pocket. "Not a good idea to snort it."

Connolly smiled. Hayford wiped his hands and leaned back in the chair.

"What were you saying?"

"If ownership of the mineral rights is in such a mess, how did Zapato Rojo agree to the oil lease?"

"Where'd you see that?"

"It's recorded in probate court. Ford Defuniak signed it for the Trust."

Hayford responded with an acknowledging look.

"You think that has something to do with Camille's death?"

"I don't know. But everywhere I look, I run into it. Hammond asked about the Trust two or three times. I talked to Bob Dorsey, he mentioned the Trust. I found Camille's car, there was a letter in it about the Trust. I came to see you, you talk about the Trust."

Hayford stood.

"Well, it's a big trust. Lots of money. Everybody likes money." He moved toward the door. "Come on. I'll let you out. I need to get moving."

Connolly was caught off guard by the abrupt end to their conversation. He sat there a moment, trying to collect himself. Hayford called from down the hall.

"Don't worry about the bottle. The maid will get it."

Connolly rose from the chair, took a last sip from the bottle of ginger ale, and started toward the door.

Thirty

*C*onnolly arrived home at the guesthouse around six that evening, still wrestling with his conversation with Hayford. He kicked off his shoes and collapsed on the couch. With his feet propped on the coffee table, he flipped on the television to watch the local news. As he watched, his thoughts moved from Hayford to what he and Hollis planned to do later that night. A sinking feeling stabbed him in the stomach.

Since the day Bob Dorsey first mentioned Panama Tan, Connolly had wanted to talk to the women who worked there. But getting to them had posed a problem. He couldn't just show up like a client. Manny Fernandez knew him. He would know he wasn't there for the normal reasons. When Hollis drove him by the warehouse, going there seemed like the thing to do. Now he wasn't so sure it was a good idea.

The newscast moved to the weather. Connolly's eyes grew heavy. He rested his head on the back of the couch. As the newscast turned to sports, he drifted off to sleep.

Suddenly, headlights washed across the room. Connolly bolted upright and glanced at his watch. It was three in the morning.

"Hollis."

He dug his shoes from underneath the coffee table and slipped them on, then started toward the door. As he grabbed the doorknob, he remembered his jacket and darted back to the couch for it. Hollis was waiting for him when he reached the truck.

"You wearing a suit for this?"

Connolly looked down at what he was wearing.

"Uh ... oh."

He walked back to the guesthouse and disappeared inside. Five minutes later he returned dressed in jeans and a T-shirt. He opened the truck door. The dome light came on inside. Hollis grinned at him.

"Slept in your clothes?"

Connolly climbed inside and closed the door. Hollis backed the truck away from the house and turned it around.

"You sure you want to—"

Connolly cut him off.

"I'm awake. I'm awake."

They drove down Government Street in silence. With no traffic in sight, it seemed as if they had the city to themselves. Connolly rolled down the window. The damp night air blew against his face. It felt good but did little to awaken him.

At Water Street, they turned left. Streetlights cast a glare over the pavement and illuminated a narrow corridor through the darkness. Beyond the curb, buildings along the docks disappeared in dark, murky shadows.

In a few minutes, they reached Beauregard Street. Hollis slowed the pickup and made the turn in front of the train station.

"Keep your eyes open."

Connolly yawned.

"For what?"

"Anything. A car parked behind a building. The street sweeper. Anything." Hollis glanced at him. "Don't go to sleep."

Connolly leaned his head against the door and watched.

"You just drive."

As he looked out the window, the doubts he'd felt before about what they were doing returned. He was a lawyer, not a detective. Maybe Hollis was right. Maybe he shouldn't worry about all the details. It wasn't his job to uncover the truth. All he had to do was represent Braxton. Make sure he got a fair trial.

The truck hit a pothole. His head bounced against the door. He looked over at Hollis, trying to gather the courage to tell him they should turn around. Before he could speak, the truck slowed and turned in front of the warehouse.

A mercury light hung from a telephone pole near the door in front. Its blue glow magnified the foreboding nature of the building. Connolly glanced around.

"Where are we going to park?"

Hollis looked alert, focused.

"You just now thinking about that?"

Beyond the alley that ran beside the warehouse was a vacant lot, overgrown with weeds and littered with trash. Next to the lot was a two-story building. Smaller than the warehouse on the corner and less imposing, it once housed a vending machine distributor. Three or four discarded machines sat between the street and the front of the building.

The glare of the mercury light reflected off broken glass on the front of the machines.

Connolly felt a chill run over him.

An alley ran from the street up the far side of the building. Hollis turned the truck into it. As they rounded the corner, the headlights fell on a stack of rusted vending machines half hidden in the weeds behind the building. Next to them was the frame of a four-wheel wagon twice the size of Hollis's truck. Broken boards and painted canvas were piled on top.

A frown wrinkled Connolly's brow.

"That looks like it used to be a Mardi Gras float."

Hollis switched off the headlights.

"It was. This is where most of them are made. Guy that owns the place used to have a vending business. Made a bunch of money. Retired to Costa Rica or someplace like that. Lets his nephew use the building. Sammy somebody. I can't remember his name."

"Sammy Bowles?"

"Yeah."

"I thought he was a big-time designer."

The truck coasted to a stop alongside the building. Hollis switched off the engine.

"He is. But that don't mean he spends a lot keeping up the place." He opened the door. "Come on. Let's go."

Hollis slipped out of the truck and started around the back of the building. Connolly got out and followed. They worked their way behind the building to the opposite corner. There, Hollis crouched behind an empty drum. Connolly knelt beside him.

The vacant lot lay between them and the warehouse. Beyond the lot was an alley beside the warehouse and the fence around the loading dock in back.

Hollis pointed across the lot.

"We got to get past that fence."

"How?" The tone in Connolly's voice reflected his second thoughts. "Maybe we should ..."

Hollis had a broad grin on his face. He opened the front of his jacket to reveal the handles of a bolt cutter protruding from the waistband of his blue jeans. He pulled it out and handed it to Connolly.

"Hold this a minute."

Connolly took the cutter. Hollis tightened his belt, then grabbed the handles of the cutter.

"Follow me."

They scurried from the shadow of the building across the vacant lot to the gate across the alley. A thick chain with a heavy lock held it closed. Hollis worked the chain around to a point opposite the lock, put a link in the jaws of the cutter, and squeezed the handles. The chain snapped in two. Chain and lock fell to the ground.

Hollis pushed open the gate and nodded for Connolly to enter, then followed him inside. He closed the gate from the other side and replaced the chain with the lock dangling in front. Anyone passing on the street would think it was secure.

From the gate, they made their way to the loading dock. Four roll-up doors led from the platform around the dock inside the warehouse. Connolly watched as Hollis scrambled up to the platform and checked the doors. The doors rattled as he pulled on the handles. He turned to Connolly and shook his head.

Farther up the building was another door. They moved along the wall and made their way toward it. Halfway there, the door suddenly opened toward them.

A woman's head and shoulders appeared from behind the door as she craned her neck to see around it. Hollis and Connolly stood motionless, watching, waiting to see what would happen. The woman stepped outside. As she turned to close the door, she looked directly at them. Even in the dim light, Connolly could see a look of panic on her face.

"It's okay." He placed his finger over his lips, gesturing for her to keep quiet, as he stepped toward her. "We just want to talk."

"Who are you?"

She spoke with an accent so thick and heavy he could barely understand her.

"I'm an attorney."

He took a business card from his pocket and offered it to her, a gesture as awkward and out of place as the moment felt.

She took it from him and glanced at it as if she could read it in the faint light.

"What are you doing here?"

"We just want to talk."

"You must leave."

Connolly pointed with his thumb toward the building.

"How many women does Manny Fernandez have in there?"

Panic returned to her face.

"I'm sorry. I can't talk to you."

She turned to go inside. Connolly grabbed the door.

"Please. You must leave."

Connolly brushed past her and stepped inside. She followed after him. Hollis trailed behind and pulled the door closed.

Beyond the door was a narrow hallway. A bare bulb in the ceiling provided the only light. Connolly moved down the hall toward the interior of the building. To his right, a stairway rose toward the second floor. At the end of the hall was a door. He glanced at the woman.

"Is this where he keeps you?"

He pulled the door open and took a step inside. The room was completely dark. From the echo of his footsteps he was certain the floor was empty. He backed out of the room, closed the door, and started up to the second floor.

The woman hurried after him.

"Don't go up there," she pleaded.

"Why not?"

He moved up the stairs to the second-floor landing and another door. He pushed it open and looked inside. Light shone faintly from the streetlight outside through the painted windows. He felt along the wall for a switch. Hollis grabbed his hand.

"Don't." Hollis nodded toward the windows. "Turn on a light in here and anyone watching outside will see it. We don't need the attention."

Connolly closed the door and continued up the steps. The woman and Hollis followed. At the top of the stairs, Connolly opened a door to the third floor.

Unlike the others, this floor was well lit. To the left was a makeshift wall of unpainted plywood. To the right were twelve cots arranged in rows across the room. Beyond them was a table. Along the wall behind the table was a counter with a sink and a microwave oven. A small refrigerator stood at the end of the counter. Several women sat around the table. Two or three lay in bed. A large fan in the corner kept the air moving, but the room was hot and stuffy and smelled of cigarette smoke.

Connolly took a few steps into the room. The woman followed after him. Hollis lingered near the door.

"How long have you lived in here?"

"Six months," she replied. "Maybe a little longer."

Connolly counted the beds.

"There are twelve of you?"

"Yes. Now."

"Now?"

"We were three at first. Please. It is not good for you to be here."

Connolly glanced at her.

"What are you afraid of? Manny Fernandez?" He turned away, still surveying the room. "Where are you from?"

"Why do you care?"

Connolly glanced at her.

"Your accent. I just noticed your accent. That's all. You don't sound like you're from anywhere around here."

A glimmer of a smile flickered across her face.

"Bosnia. I am from Bosnia."

He turned toward her again.

"How do twelve women from Bosnia wind up in a warehouse in Mobile, Alabama?"

"It is a long trip."

Connolly moved farther into the room.

"Please," she insisted. "You must leave. If anyone finds you here, it will only be bad for us all."

Just then, a door opened to the right. Connolly jumped. A woman emerged through the doorway, drying her hair with a towel. Her naked body was thin, almost gaunt, and she had a hollow look in her eyes. She glanced in their direction but paid no attention as she made her way across the room.

"What ..." Connolly lost his train of thought as his eyes followed her across the room. Finally, he turned to the woman beside him. "What's your name?"

"Raisa."

Connolly took a photograph of Camille from his pocket and handed it to her.

"Have you ever seen this woman?"

Raisa glanced at the picture. Her eyebrows lifted ever so slightly, and her mouth dropped open just enough to be noticeable.

"No." She handed him the picture and turned away. "I've never seen her."

Connolly took the photo from her. He looked at Hollis as he slipped it in his pocket. Hollis gave him a nod. Connolly smiled at Raisa.

"I'm sorry to bother you so late at night."

He started toward the door. Hollis held it open as he approached. As he reached the doorway, Connolly heard Raisa talking to another woman. He glanced at them over his shoulder. He couldn't understand what they said, but the woman with Raisa had a worried look on her face. Raisa ushered her toward the far side of the room. Connolly stepped through the door. Hollis pulled it closed and followed him down the steps.

Without a word between them, they retraced the path along the back of the warehouse, through the gates, and across the vacant lot to the building next door. Connolly crawled inside the truck and pulled the door closed. He glanced across the seat at Hollis.

"She's lying."

Hollis started the engine.

"I know."

"That means Camille really was at Panama Tan."

"Yeah."

"That means Manny or Rizutto could have seen her."

"Yeah."

Hollis backed the truck down the alley and into the street. Connolly slumped against the door and closed his eyes.

Thirty-one

The sun was up by the time they reached the guesthouse. Connolly crawled out of the truck and stumbled inside. He collapsed across the bed, fully clothed, and slept until noon.

When he awoke, he showered, changed clothes, and drove to Mobile General, the county hospital. A huge stone and masonry building, it sat at the edge of Broad Street not far from Connolly's office. Wide steps swept up two floors to a portico with a roof five floors above.

Connolly steered the Chrysler to the back of the building. He parked near the emergency entrance and went inside. Notepad in hand, he crossed the waiting area by the door and walked past the receptionist's desk to a corridor that led toward the interior of the building. A little way down the corridor he turned right and made his way to the morgue at the end of the hall. Large double doors separated the morgue from the remainder of the hospital. He pushed open one of the doors and stepped inside.

An empty gurney sat in the hallway. Bloodstained linens lay in a bundle on the floor beside it. Directly across from the doors was the county's single autopsy suite. From the hallway, Connolly could see the stainless steel table in the middle of the room. A light above it shone down on a cadaver that lay on the table. The chest of the body had been opened. The tile floor around it showed splatters of blood. Ted Morgan, the county coroner, glanced up from his work.

"You looking for me?"

"Yeah." Connolly turned away. "But it can wait."

Morgan stepped away from the table.

"Hold on." He stripped off the rubber gloves from his hands as he started across the room toward the door. "I need a break."

Connolly moved up the hall a little way to a point from which he could no longer see in the room. When Morgan reached the door, he tossed the rubber gloves in a waste bin.

"Make you sick?"

Connolly gave him a sheepish grin.

"Doesn't help much."

Morgan chuckled.

"Let me guess. You're here about a dead person."

Connolly smiled. They had been friends a long time.

"Anthony Hammond says you did an autopsy on Camille Braxton."

"Yeah."

Morgan retreated into the autopsy suite and disappeared to the left. Connolly heard the sound of water running from inside the room.

"Finished it a couple of days ago," Morgan called. "I don't think we have all the lab work yet."

He appeared in the doorway, drying his hands on a paper towel. After a wipe or two of his hands, he wadded the towel and tossed it in the trash bin by the door, then started up the hall. Connolly followed him to his office.

"What did you find?"

Morgan crossed the office. A stack of files and papers lay in a wire basket at the corner of the desktop. He shuffled through the basket, took out a file, and glanced at several of the pages inside, then tossed it on the desk.

"Report will be ready in a few days. You can read it for yourself."

Connolly leaned against the doorframe, smiling. He knew Morgan was teasing.

"Can't wait that long."

Morgan moved behind the desk and dropped into a chair. He gave a slow, tired sigh. Dark circles ringed his eyes. Connolly moved away from the door and took a seat in front of the desk. Morgan leaned back in his chair and folded his hands behind his head.

"You never read my reports anyway."

Connolly crossed his legs and laid the notepad on his lap.

"I prefer to hear it from you, firsthand. I always find out something that's not in the report."

Morgan smiled.

"She died from asphyxiation."

"She drowned?"

"No." Morgan frowned at him. "She suffocated. She was dead before she hit the water."

"I thought she had a blow to the head."

"She did. Two of them. But that isn't what killed her."

"How do you know?"

Morgan gave him a sarcastic look.

"I'm the coroner."

"I know that. But what told you she suffocated?"

Morgan leaned forward and took the file from the desk. He opened it and scanned through the pages as he spoke.

"She had two blows to the head. One in the back. A blunt object. Near as we can tell it was a five iron. Had another one to the right side of her face. On the jaw."

"Wait a minute." Connolly gestured with his hand for Morgan to stop. "You think she was hit in the head with a five iron?"

Morgan gave him a matter-of-fact look.

"Yeah."

"How do you know it was a golf club, much less a five iron?"

Morgan took out a photograph from the file and dropped it on the desk. He moved his feet to the floor and leaned over the picture. The photograph showed the back of Camille's head.

"This is a digitally enhanced photo of the wound."

"Digitally enhanced?"

"Yeah. Sharpens it up. Takes out the distortions from time. Enhances the bruising around the edges. Look right here." He pointed to an area along one side of the wound. "This is a bruise. Look at it with the naked eye, it's just a bruise. Take a picture of it and run it through this program, you see it's a long, slender bruise made by an object about the width of my finger." He glance up at Connolly. "You see that?"

"Yeah," Connolly replied.

"All right." Morgan took a second photo from the file. "This is a regular photograph of the wound."

Connolly glanced at it.

"Ordinary trauma to the back of the head. Right?"

Connolly nodded.

"Right."

"Enhance it and you get this." Morgan pointed to the first picture. "Angular. Triangular, actually." He dropped the photographs and leaned away. "Now, ask yourself: What makes an imprint like that? Triangle with a long, straight something out the top."

Connolly shrugged.

"I guess you figure it was a golf club."

"Not just any golf club. An iron. Five iron, in my opinion. The lady was struck in the back of the head with the heel of a five iron."

Connolly glanced at the picture. He wasn't sure he saw the resemblance between the shape of the wound and the heel of an iron, but it didn't really matter. Morgan had made up his mind, and that was what he would say in court, if anyone bothered to ask.

"What about the blow to the face?"

"Can't say for sure. Looks like a fist to me." Morgan made a gesture with his fist against his jaw.

"On the right side of her jaw?" Connolly wanted to make sure he understood. "Her right?"

Morgan nodded. Connolly felt a frown wrinkle his forehead as he thought about it.

"Her right. That would be from someone's left fist?"

"Probably. If they were standing in front of her. Facing her."

"But you could say it was a left-handed person."

"You would." Morgan shrugged. "I wouldn't. But I would say it is consistent with a blow from the left hand. But I can't say for certain that's what it was."

"Strong enough to knock her out?"

Morgan turned to another page in the file, a thoughtful look on his face.

"Yeah. It could have. The bone wasn't broken, but there was considerable bruising. It could have rendered her unconscious. She was unconscious after the blow to the back of the head, that's for certain."

"All right. She was unconscious, but then she suffocated. Why do you think she suffocated?"

"Well ..." He turned to a page in the file. "She had petechial hemorrhages. We did a blood gas analysis that showed—"

Connolly interrupted him.

"Petech what?"

"Petechiae. Small purple and red spots. Tiny hemorrhages just under the skin."

Connolly tried to picture it in his mind.

Morgan smiled.

"Like broken blood vessels behind an older woman's knees."

"Only these are somewhere else?"

"Yes. Around the eyes. Back of the hands."

"We're talking suffocation? She wasn't strangled?"

Morgan nodded.

"That's correct. She wasn't strangled. No compression injuries about the neck. Thyroid bone was intact. She wasn't strangled."

"And she didn't drown."

"No seawater in the lungs. No algae in her stomach. She died somewhere else and then ended up in the water."

"Anything suggesting how she got to where she was found?"

"Not that I could see."

"How long had she been dead?"

He turned to another page in the file.

"No maceration. Body was intact. Skin wasn't worn away. I'd say she hadn't been in the water more than two days."

"Not a week?"

"No." Morgan shook his head. "No way."

"What about a time of death?"

"Can't give you an exact time, but I'd say she hadn't been dead much longer than that, either. Two days."

"So, she died within a few days of when she was put in the water?"

"Yeah. Within a day or two. This body was in pretty good shape."

"She's been missing over two weeks."

Morgan smiled at him.

"Then, I'd say she didn't die immediately. We found something under her fingernails." Morgan looked through the pages in the file, then laid the file on the desk and sorted through the basket. "Here it is." He took out a piece of paper. "Just came back from the lab." He studied it a moment. "Huh. ASB."

Connolly gave him a puzzled look.

"ASB?"

"Acrylonitrile styrene butadiene."

The frown on Connolly's forehead deepened.

"I never liked chemistry that much."

"Plastic."

"Plastic?"

Morgan put the report in the file.

"Yeah. Like the lining of a refrigerator. A freezer."

Their eyes met.

"A refrigerator." Connolly whispered. "She tried to claw her way out."

Morgan nodded.

"I've seen 'em claw the enamel off a bathtub before."

Connolly slouched in the chair. Morgan closed the file and laid it on the desk.

Thirty-two

Connolly left the hospital and drove out Government Street to police headquarters. He ignored the receptionist and walked upstairs to Anthony Hammond's office. Hammond was standing at the photocopier when he arrived.

"I thought all y'all did was eat doughnuts and drink coffee."

Hammond gave him a "drop dead" look.

"What do you want?"

"You."

"Me?"

"Yeah."

"I'm busy."

Hammond turned away from the copier and started toward his desk. Connolly followed him.

"Let's talk about Perry Braxton."

Hammond tossed the papers he was carrying on the desk.

"Let's not." He took his jacket from the back of his chair and slipped it on. "I gotta go."

Connolly sat in a chair in front of the desk. Hammond turned to leave.

"I know a lot of lawyers who wouldn't have called you about the car."

Hammond stopped and turned toward Connolly.

"What?"

"You'd have found out about it when they hit you with it on the witness stand."

Hammond stared at him. Connolly gestured toward the chair behind the desk.

"Take a seat. Let's talk."

Hammond glared at him.

"Are you crazy?"

"Some people think so."

"I ..."

Hammond looked frustrated. Connolly folded his hands in his lap and smiled. Hammond jerked off his jacket and threw it on top of the filing cabinet that separated his desk from the desk beside him.

"Okay." He made his way around the desk and dropped into the chair. "You want to talk, let's talk."

"What do you have on Perry Braxton?"

"Did you talk to McNamara?"

"McNamara won't tell me anything you don't tell him first. I thought I'd just get it straight from you this time."

An amused smile spread across Hammond's face.

"McNamara is going to be a great prosecutor."

Connolly nodded.

"He'll have to start shaving first."

Hammond laughed. He opened the desk drawer, took out a file, and flipped through the pages.

"Where do you want to start?"

"The beginning. You had him in here for questioning late one night."

"Yeah. Routine stuff. Maid called in a missing person report. She was a little upset with Braxton for not calling it in himself. Got him in here. Asked him some questions. Didn't like his answers."

"What next?"

"You showed up. Filed some reports. Not much else we could do."

"Then the car."

Hammond nodded.

"Then the car. Nothing in there but the purse." He glanced at Connolly over the top of the file. "You already know about that."

Connolly smiled and nodded. Hammond continued.

"Nothing much else until the body showed up." He flipped through the file while they talked. "Ted Morgan's doing an autopsy. He'll have a report in a few days."

"How'd you wind up searching his apartment?"

"After the body was found, we had a preliminary report. Looked like a homicide. We searched Braxton's apartment. And we seized his car. A Suburban. You were there when we towed it."

Connolly nodded. A pang stabbed his stomach. He'd forgotten about the Suburban.

"What did you find?"

"Not much in the apartment." He took a paper from the file and tossed it toward Connolly. "That's an inventory. I'll get you a copy. We took some clothes, things like that."

Connolly glanced at the inventory from the search, then laid it aside.

"What about the Suburban?"

"That's a little more interesting. Found a shoe under the front seat. Looks like the right size for the victim. We're working on that. And we found a blood smear on the passenger window. We've sent that off for some DNA tests."

"Anything else?"

"You talk to Morgan already?"

"Yeah."

"Then you know about his golf club theory."

"Yeah."

"Based on that, we went back to the apartment—"

"You searched his apartment again?"

"Yeah."

"A second time?"

"Yeah."

"Without telling me?"

Hammond closed the file and leaned forward.

"I don't have to tell you anything. You understand me? Nothing. I tell you to get out, and you're out. McNamara doesn't care whether I talk to you. Judge Cahill won't make me." He gestured over his shoulder. "Everyone in this room would love to cuff you and haul you out of here. You understand what I'm saying?"

They glared at each other across the desk. Finally, Connolly smiled.

"Sure, Anthony. I understand. You found a set of clubs in the apartment?"

Hammond glared at him a moment longer, then leaned back and opened the file once more.

"Yeah." He took a deep breath. "We sent them out for testing."

"Got the result yet?"

"No."

"What did they look like?"

"Look like?"

"Yeah. What did they look like? Dusty old rusted clubs in a moldy bag in the back of the closet and haven't seen a course in years, or new ones in the corner of the room that get played every week?"

"I don't know."

"Where'd you find them?"

"In the apartment."

"Where in the apartment?"

Hammond stared at the file. Connolly pressed the question.

"Where in the apartment?"

Hammond slapped the file closed and yanked the desk drawer open.

"They were in the bedroom closet." He threw the file in the drawer and slammed it shut. "I have to go."

"How many were there?"

"How many?"

"Yeah. How many?"

"I don't know. I have to go."

"Did you do an inventory?"

Hammond reached across the desk, pulled open the drawer, and took out the file. He opened it on the desktop, jerked out a piece of paper, and slapped it on the desk in front of Connolly.

"There. That's the inventory."

Connolly glanced at it.

"Says here there were nine irons, a wedge, a putter, and three woods."

"That's what it says?"

"Yeah."

"Then that's what was there."

"That's a full set."

"What?"

"That's a full set. Fourteen clubs. That's all you can have in your bag when you play."

"So."

"So? You think a guy decides to kill his wife. He chooses a club from the bag in the back of his closet. Gets her to go out somewhere with him, even though they're in the midst of a divorce. Whacks her in the head with a club. Brings her body out to Horn Island in a boat. Dumps her there. But brings the club all the way back and puts it back in the golf bag in his closet?"

Hammond shrugged.

"And then, when you ask where he's been, he tells you he was at Horn Island when it all happened?"

Hammond gave Connolly a blank look.

"I don't know about all of that. All I know is, we found blood in his vehicle. I'd bet good money it's hers. We found a shoe in there. I'm sure it's hers, too. The woman was killed. He had plenty of motive. And when that club comes back with her DNA on it, your man will be on his way to death row."

"The death penalty?"

"Yeah. This is a death penalty case if there ever was one."

Hammond took his jacket from the top of the file cabinet and started toward the stairs.

Thirty-three

Connolly left Hammond's office and drove downtown to the county jail. He met Braxton in the interview room on the eighth floor. They sat at the table and talked.

"What did they say about my response?"

"They won't dismiss the charge."

Braxton looked frustrated.

"If I'm going to prison, I'm not telling them about Rizutto. I'd be dead before they got me to a cell."

Connolly nodded.

"Hammond thinks this is a death penalty case."

"They want to execute me?"

"Right after they give you a fair trial."

Braxton gave him a sarcastic grin. Connolly continued.

"They processed your Suburban. Found blood on the passenger window."

Braxton looked away.

"Found a shoe they think belonged to Camille."

"What's it look like?"

"I don't know. I haven't seen it yet."

"Do they have the other one?"

"Other one?"

"You said they found a shoe. I assume you mean they found one shoe."

"Yeah. One. And no. I don't think they have the other one. At least that was my impression."

Braxton ran his hands over his face. He leaned back and stared at the ceiling as he tugged at handfuls of hair.

"You think I should take their deal?"

"I think if you did it, if you killed your wife, pleading guilty to manslaughter and going to prison for a while would be a lot better than the death penalty."

Braxton let out a heavy sigh.

"Without talking about Rizutto."

Connolly shook his head.

"They won't give you a deal on the plea unless you talk about him." Connolly paused a moment. "Tell me about Rizutto."

Braxton's gaze was fixed on the ceiling in the far corner of the room. Connolly waited. Braxton rubbed his hands over his face again and ran his fingers through his hair.

"Pete Rizutto is the number two man in the Morella family. You ever hear about them?"

Connolly knew about Morella from the time when he represented Fernandez, but he wanted to hear what Braxton had to say.

"The name is vaguely familiar."

"They're into organized crime. The mob. Morella's an old guy, lives in New Orleans. Rizutto's married to his oldest daughter. They live in Biloxi. He runs everything on the Gulf from New Orleans to Panama City." He paused. "Actually, I think the line is at Apalachicola."

"Kind of a strange place to put your dividing line."

"Not really. Quiet. Out of the way. It keeps the peace. When the guys in Jacksonville need to meet the guys from New Orleans on safe ground, they meet in Apalachicola."

Connolly nodded.

"All right. Rizutto is in the Mafia."

"Yeah."

"Keep going."

"He has your friend working for him. Manny Fernandez. Fernandez runs the tanning salon."

"Panama Tan."

"Yeah."

"And it's really a prostitution operation."

"Yeah."

"And Rizutto has you."

"Yeah." Braxton nodded. "Rizutto has me."

"How'd he get you?"

"Now that's a long story."

"I need to know it."

Braxton sighed.

"I guess it's not really that complicated. Just the usual stuff, really. Women. Money." He glanced away, shifted positions on the bench. "I started going down to the casinos in Biloxi. Met some women. Lost a lot of money. Had a good time. Before long, I owed more than I could pay, and they had pictures."

"And they had you."

"Told me I could play for free if I helped them out."

"Helped them out?"

"Yeah."

"What did they want?"

"They're always looking for money, connections."

"What about Manny?"

"What about him?"

"How'd they get him?"

"I don't know. I think he's been with them a long time. He and Rizutto are pretty tight."

"What about the porn films?"

Braxton looked almost embarrassed.

"How'd you find out about that?"

"Tell me about them."

"That came later. After we got the tanning salon going. Rizutto had the women, seemed like a way to get more out of them."

"We?"

Braxton looked puzzled.

"Excuse me?"

"We. You said, 'We got the salon going.' Who's the 'we'?"

"Uhh ... everybody that was involved."

"You were involved."

"Yeah. I already said that." He gave Connolly a strange look. "You understand, I'm telling you this only because you're my attorney. I'm not telling the DA unless they drop the charges."

Connolly nodded.

"What did you do?"

"What did I do?"

"Yeah. You said you helped Rizutto with the tanning salon. What did you do?"

Braxton took a deep breath.

"I'd rather not say right now."

Connolly wanted to slap him.

"We have to talk about your role in all of this. All of it. Not just about having sex with women in Biloxi and owing a lot of money. I want to know everything, and I don't want to hear about it for the first time when someone testifies about it in court. You understand me?"

"Yeah."

Connolly waited a moment, then continued.

"Tell me about the women."

"What women?"

"The women at the tanning salon."

"What about them?"

"Who are they?"

"I don't know their names, if that's what you mean."

"Where did you find them?"

"Rizutto had a connection."

"How'd he get them involved?"

"I don't know all the details. They're from Europe. Bosnia ... Croatia. Someplace like that."

"They go all the way to Bosnia to find prostitutes?"

Braxton nodded.

"Big business. Rizutto makes a lot of money at it. Gets them from some Syrian guy."

"I thought you said they come from Bosnia."

"They do. Someplace over there. But the guy he deals with is from Syria."

"How do you know he's from Syria?"

"That's what they call him. The Syrian. Rizutto gets low on women, he says, 'I got to call the Syrian. Get some more in here.'"

"Where does he live?"

"Who?"

"The Syrian?"

"Over there in Europe someplace."

"How do they get them to come over here?"

"I don't know. I guess they want to come to America and he helps them out."

Connolly frowned.

"Helps them out?"

"Yeah. Gives them a job. Place to live. That kind of thing."

Connolly leaned away, thinking. After a moment, he folded his hands on the table and looked Braxton in the eye.

"Tell me about the salon."

Braxton leaned away.

"Like I said. It's Rizutto's operation. Manny runs it."

"Who owns the building?"

Braxton sighed.

"The Trust."

"The Trust?"

"Yeah."

"Your wife's trust? The Tonsmeyer Family Trust?"

"One and the same."

Connolly stared at the tabletop, thinking. Braxton leaned away and rested his head against the wall.

"Throw you for a loop?"

Connolly's voice became a whisper.

"If the Trust owns the building ... then Defuniak knows about all of this."

Braxton raised himself away from the wall. He swung his leg over the bench and stood.

"And that's where this conversation ends."

Connolly looked up at him from the table.

"You have to tell me everything."

"I've already told you way more than you need to know." Braxton walked toward the door. "I've told you more than I've told anyone else." He reached the door and pounded on it for the guard, then turned toward Connolly. "I'm not talking unless they agree to drop the charges."

The door opened. The guard escorted him down the hall.

Thirty-four

Connolly left the jail that evening more determined than ever to find out what was going on with Braxton, Panama Tan, and the women in the warehouse. On the way back to the guesthouse he formed a plan in his mind for the next step. It would be risky, but he could think of no alternative. He had to talk to Raisa. And he had to do it alone.

The following morning, Connolly awoke well before sunrise. He stumbled to the bathroom, turned on the faucet at the sink, and ducked his head under the cold water. When he could stand it no longer, he raised his head from the sink and stared at his face in the mirror. He'd felt worse, but he couldn't remember when.

"At least I'm awake."

He turned off the faucet and smoothed his hair in place with his fingers. Water trickled down his face. He mopped it with a towel, then started up the hall.

In the bedroom, he dressed in faded jeans and a T-shirt. He found a pair of scuffed work boots in the back of the closet and put them on. They were much heavier than the wingtips he usually wore, but his feet felt refreshed at the change. He laced them tight against his ankles and walked down the hall to the kitchen for a cup of instant coffee.

The sky was still dark when he stepped out of the guesthouse and turned toward the Chrysler. As he opened the car door, doubt came crashing through his mind. He grumbled to himself.

"This is crazy." His hand grasped the door handle, then hesitated. "I ought to go back to bed."

An image of Raisa came to his mind, followed by the naked woman as she stepped from the shower. He pushed the thought out of his mind and opened the door.

Tired but alert, he made his way down Tuttle Street and turned right onto Government. With the window down, he turned the side vent toward himself. Cool morning air blew in his face as he cruised toward downtown. At Water Street, he turned left, then made a right in front of the train station. In a few minutes, he reached the warehouse. There was no turning back now.

He let the car idle past the building as he scanned the shadows, watching carefully to see if anyone was there. The car rolled by the warehouse, then the vacant lot, and finally the building next door. He turned into the alley beyond the building and parked in front of the torn and tattered Mardi Gras float.

With little effort, he made his way from the car along the back of the building. Ahead of him lay the vacant lot and beyond that, the warehouse. He paused at the far corner and scanned the area once more, then started across.

The lot was overgrown with weeds that stood waist high. Wet from the morning dew, they brushed against his pants. By the time he reached the gate across the alley beside the warehouse, his shoes were soaked. The legs of his jeans were wet. He brushed himself off and checked the gate. The chain Hollis cut before was still where they left it. He slid it aside, pushed the gate open, and stepped past.

On the other side, he closed it, replaced the chain, and started toward the back of the building. He crept past the loading dock and down to the door where he'd first seen Raisa. He grasped the knob and gave it a twist. The knob didn't budge.

"I knew it couldn't be that easy," he muttered.

But at that moment, something inside him changed. The nagging fear of being caught, the taunting thoughts inside his head telling him it was crazy to try, all vanished. The notion of getting inside was no longer just an idea. Now it was a challenge. Time ticked away. With each moment, dawn grew nearer. He had to move fast.

He retreated to the loading dock and climbed onto the platform in front of the roll-up doors. In the dark, he felt along the first door and found the handle. He grasped it and lifted. The door didn't move. He tried the second with the same result. To the right, he could see a window located about eight feet above the floor of the platform. Light from the street reflected in the glass.

"If I could ..."

He scurried down from the loading dock to the ground and searched the area behind the building. In a few minutes, he found a fifty-five-gallon drum in a clump of weeds beyond the pavement near the fence. He gave it a shove with his foot. The drum fell over with a bang.

"Good," he said to himself. "It's empty."

He rolled it across the parking lot to the loading dock. Stretching his arms out wide, he grasped both ends of the drum. It rolled against his chest as he lifted it from the ground and heaved it onto the platform. His hands were wet and dirty. The front of his shirt was brown with rust from the drum, but there was no time to waste. He scurried up to the platform and rolled the drum to the wall underneath the window.

With the drum sitting upright against the wall, he climbed on top of it and squeezed his fingertips under the corners of the window frame at the bottom. Working carefully, he managed to slip his fingers in far enough to pull against the frame. The window swung toward him out of the way. He poked his head inside and looked around.

By now, the sky in the east was gray. Dawn was approaching. Sunrise wasn't far behind. Whatever he was going to do, he'd have to do it quickly.

The room beneath the window was empty. A door to the left stood open. Beyond it, Connolly could see the first floor was pitch dark. He grasped the window ledge and pulled himself into the opening. Halfway through, he realized he was going to drop into the room headfirst, but by then it was too late to stop. He kicked his feet and squirmed his way through, holding onto the ledge as long as possible. As his feet flailed the air, one shoe caught the rim of the drum. It tipped over and banged against the floor with a loud crash.

With one more frantic squirm, he slid past the tipping point. His hands slipped free as he plunged toward the floor below. His shoulder landed first, followed by his head, then his legs and feet. A loud groan escaped him as the force of the collision drove the air from his lungs. Pain shot through his shoulder.

Time seemed to stop as he lay on the floor gasping for breath. The pain in his shoulder, the panic of not being able to breathe, drove all other thoughts from his mind as he struggled to fill his lungs with air.

Finally, he caught his breath.

He rolled to a sitting position and rubbed his shoulder. After a moment, he stood. His hands were filthy. His jeans were a mess, but he was inside the building.

Focused again on the task at hand, he started toward the door. He peered around the corner into the blackness that filled the first floor. To the left, slivers of light slipped in around the edges of the roll-up doors, outlining them in the faint light of the approaching morning. To the right, there was nothing but darkness. He started down it, feeling his way with one hand against the wall to guide him. Before long, he was engulfed in the inky black space. Behind him, the outline of the doors at the loading dock was gone. The gray morning light that had filtered in from the room he'd climbed into was no longer visible. There was nothing but darkness.

Connolly's heart began to pound in his chest. He'd been afraid of the dark as a child and often slept with a lamp on all night. Now, that fear returned. A dizzying sense of disorientation swept over him. His mind did little to reassure him.

This time, there's a reason to be afraid.

He inched along, one foot in front of the other. Right hand on the wall, left hand in front of his face, just in case.

In a few minutes, he felt his right hand slip from the rough texture of the wall to something smooth. He stopped and felt with both hands, his head moving in the direction of his hands, though he couldn't see a thing. Then, his eyes dropped toward the floor. There, he saw a thin stream of light coming from under the place where he'd been feeling.

"A door."

He slipped his hands to the left, found the crack between the door and the doorframe, and felt his way down to the knob. He twisted and pulled. The door came open.

He stepped out to the hall that led from the back entrance to the stairway. The single bulb shining from the ceiling seemed to give all the light in the world. He blinked his eyes and squinted in the glare as he started up the steps.

At the third floor, he paused and listened through the door. From beyond it he could hear water running and the faint sound of voices. He turned the knob and opened the door and stepped inside.

He'd expected to see startled faces at his appearing, women clutching their robes, perhaps a gasp of surprise. Instead, no one paid him any attention. To the right, a woman lay on a bed, wearing nothing but a G-string. On the bed beside her another woman was drying her hair with a towel. Her bare body still glistened from the shower.

Connolly glanced around, trying not to stare. Then, a door to the right opened. Raisa entered dressed in a thick, heavy bathrobe. She started across the room toward him.

"What are you doing here?"

Connolly managed a smile.

"I had a few more questions."

She looked him over.

"You are a mess."

"Excuse me?"

Her thick accent made it difficult for him to understand. She pointed to his clothes.

"You are a mess. What have you been doing? Playing in the dirt?"

Connolly looked at himself. Dust and dirt from the warehouse had turned to mud against his wet clothes. There were dirty smudges along

the thighs of his pants where he'd slid across the window ledge. His shirt
was filthy.

"I guess I don't look so good."

He dusted himself off as he spoke. Raisa wiped his forehead with the
towel she'd been using to dry her hair.

"Your face."

She wiped along his chin. Dirt appeared on the towel. Though she
avoided looking directly at him, Connolly could see her eyes were dark,
intelligent, kind. She took his hands in hers.

"Look at your hands."

Taking him by the wrist, she led him across the room, past the rows
of cots to the sink along the far wall.

"Here." She handed him a bar of soap. "Wash your hands."

She turned on the water and scowled at him as he cleaned his
hands.

"What are you doing here?"

"I wanted to ask you a few more questions."

"Do you want to get yourself killed?"

"No."

"Manny Fernandez will be here to pick us up. They will kill you if
they find you here."

"I'm not worried about Manny Fernandez."

He finished washing his hands and turned off the water. Raisa
handed him the towel.

"What is so important that you would risk your life in coming here?"

He dried his hands and laid the towel on the counter.

"This." He took the photograph of Camille from his hip pocket and
handed it to her. "Tell me about her."

Raisa gestured with her hand in protest and turned away.

"I told you before, I don't know anything about her."

"Yes, you do. I could see it in your eyes."

She shook her head. Connolly thrust the picture toward her.

"Tell me what you saw."

"No." She shook her head. "I saw nothing. You must go."

"Well, if you won't tell me, I'll ask someone else."

He stepped away from the sink and called with a loud voice.

"Excuse me. Excuse me."

The women in the room turned to look at him. Most of them gave
him a blank stare. He held the picture for them to see.

"Have any of you seen this—"

Raisa grabbed his hand and jerked it to his side.

"Are you stupid?" She spoke in a whisper, but her voice was tense and angry. She snatched the photo from his hand, took him by the wrist once again, and led him toward the door.

Connolly pulled his hand free but followed her across the room.

"I want some answers."

She grabbed the doorknob and flung the door aside, then led him onto the landing at the top of the stairway. The door closed behind them.

"Okay. Ask your questions."

"Have you seen her?"

"Yes."

"Where?"

"She was at the salon."

"When?"

"I don't remember the day. It has been a few weeks."

"She came inside the salon?"

"No. She was outside."

"What was she doing?"

Raisa sighed. She looked uncomfortable.

"She was in his car."

"Whose car?"

"His."

She grabbed the picture and pointed to it. Her finger jabbed the image of Perry as he stood next to Camille in the photograph. Connolly glanced at the photograph.

"Do you know him?"

"He is a ... customer."

"What happened? What did you see?"

"It was the morning. Manny Fernandez brought us to the salon. We got out and started inside. Mr. Rizutto was there." She gestured toward Braxton in the photograph. "He came in his car. One of those ... SUVs. Like the one Manny Fernandez drives. He drove up very fast. Jumped out. He looked scared." She pointed to Camille in the photograph. "This lady was lying on the front seat. She didn't look too good. He got out. Very excited. He was talking to Mr. Rizutto. Mr. Rizutto said something to his driver. I don't know his name. The driver laughed. Got in the car. Drove away with her."

Connolly took the photograph from her hand.

"What happened after that?"

"Manny told us to get inside."

"Has anyone asked you about this?"

"No. They think we can't speak English so they think we don't know anything."

"They think you can't speak English?"

"They think I only know a few words."

"Can the others speak English?"

"No."

Connolly looked at the picture a moment. He knew he should leave, but something about her made him want to stay and talk.

"How did you get here?"

"Here? Manny Fernandez drives us here every night."

"No. To America. How did you get to America?"

A sad look came over her.

"They promised us a job."

"Doing this?"

"No. In entertainment. Movies. Modeling."

"Where are you from?"

"I am from Bosnia. Most of the others are from Croatia." She moved away toward the door. "You must go. They will be here soon."

Connolly was perplexed.

"How did you get here from Bosnia?"

The sadness in her eyes deepened.

"Please. I have to get ready."

Connolly persisted.

"How did you get from Bosnia to Mobile?"

She sighed. Her shoulders sagged.

"From Bosnia I went to Italy. I met several of the others there. We worked at a club in Turin. Then we were sent to Morocco and from there to Mexico City. Then we came here."

Connolly nodded.

"This is what you wanted to do?"

She scowled at him in anger.

"You think I want to spend my days having sex with strange men?"

Connolly grimaced at the thought of it.

"Why don't you leave?"

"We can't."

"Why not?"

"We owe them money."

Connolly was incredulous.

"For what?"

"Transportation. Housing. Clothes. Mr. Rizutto paid what we owed in Italy. That is how we were able to come here."

"You owed money in Italy?"

"Yes." She took another step toward the door. "I have to go."

"What did you owe money for in Italy?"

"Same thing. Transportation. Clothing. Housing. Only now we owe more."

Connolly frowned as he tried to grasp what she was telling him. He pointed down the stairs.

"You know, you can walk out the door and leave. You don't have to stay here. They can't make you do this."

She looked away.

"But we are ..."

Connolly realized what she was going to say.

"You're here illegally."

She gave him a worried look.

"They tell us if we leave, they will turn us over to immigration authorities and we will be sent to prison."

"For being here illegally?"

"Yes. And because we are prostitutes."

"What a crock."

"Excuse me?"

"It's an expression. They aren't telling you the truth."

She looked puzzled.

"The worst they would do is send you home. Deport you. Do you want to get away?"

"We want to live. And I'm sure you do as well. You must go now. They will be here for us soon."

She opened the door. Connolly glanced at his watch. It was almost nine. She smiled at him.

"Go now. Please. Before we all get into trouble."

She stepped inside and closed the door. Connolly turned away and started down the steps.

Thirty-five

*C*onnolly made his way down the stairs to the door on the first floor and stepped outside at the back of the warehouse. By then, the morning sun was bright. The air was thick and humid. He closed the door and hurried toward the loading dock. Sweat trickled down his back.

At the end of the building he scurried up to the platform, set the drum on its end, and climbed up to the window. He pushed it closed, then jumped down and rolled the drum to the edge of the loading dock. On the ground, he carried the drum across the parking lot to the place where he'd found it, then retraced his route through the gate and across the vacant lot to the building next door.

As he approached the Chrysler, he noticed something behind the stack of vending machines piled near the remains of the Mardi Gras float. White and rectangular, it was barely visible beneath a tangle of vines and canvas from the float.

His heart skipped a beat.

If what Raisa told him was correct, Camille was unconscious when she arrived at the salon in Braxton's SUV. Rizutto's driver had been dispatched to dispose of her. Morgan said she'd suffocated. Probably in a freezer.

"Or a refrigerator," Connolly whispered.

He made his way around the float.

From the other side he had a better view. What he'd seen beneath the vines and rubble was indeed a refrigerator, but it had been turned on its side, and he could see the door had been removed. He smiled at himself as he turned away and started toward the car.

From the warehouse, Connolly returned to Tuttle Street and the guesthouse. After a hot shower, he walked to the kitchen for a cup of coffee and a stale roll. He ate with his back leaning against the sink. His body screamed to get back in bed, but his mind refused.

That sinking feeling in his stomach had returned, the one he felt

when he was sure he was being manipulated. He'd spent weeks tracking down the details of Braxton's story. Now, with Raisa, any pretense of
an alibi Braxton might have had came tumbling to the ground.

He finished the roll and sipped the last of the coffee from the cup.

Kathleen Cathcart had told him Mr. Turner, the man across the
street, might have seen something the morning Camille disappeared.
He wanted to follow up on that and one other matter, and then he would
see Braxton one more time.

Finished in the kitchen, he changed to a suit and drove across town
to Spring Hill.

Connolly turned the Chrysler into the driveway at Turner's house
and got out. He walked to the door and rang the doorbell. Seconds later,
a man appeared from around the corner of the house.

"May I help you?"

Dressed in work clothes and pushing a wheelbarrow, Connolly
thought he was the gardener.

"I'm looking for Mr. Turner."

"Well, you've found him."

The man pushed the wheelbarrow to the sidewalk and set it down.
Connolly stepped away from the door.

"Sorry. I thought you were the yardman."

Turner smiled at him.

"I am the yardman. And the garbageman." He slipped off his work
gloves. "And the housekeeper. And Harold Turner."

Connolly came from the porch. They shook hands.

"My name is Mike Connolly. I wanted to ask you some questions."

"You're a lawyer?"

"Yes."

Turner nodded.

"Mrs. Cathcart told me you might come by."

"I spoke with her a few days ago."

"Something about a missing woman."

"Camille Braxton. Did you know her?"

Turner had a sober look.

"Nah." He pointed to two chairs on the porch. "Have a seat."

Turner stepped onto the porch and took a seat. Connolly sat in a
chair beside him. Turner took off his hat and wiped his forehead with
his hand.

"I didn't know her. Just what I read in the papers. I never met her.
I haven't lived here as long as Kathleen has."

"Do you remember the day we're talking about? It was a Tuesday.

Mrs. Cathcart said she had car trouble. Parked her car in front of your house."

Turner nodded.

"Yes. I remember it."

Connolly took the photograph from his pocket.

"The woman in this photograph is the woman we're talking about. Do you recognize her?"

He held the picture for Turner to see.

"Yeah." Turner nodded again. "That's her. That's the man who picked her up, too."

He pointed to Braxton standing beside Camille in the photograph. The gnawing feeling in Connolly's stomach grew more intense.

"You're sure?"

"Yeah. I'm sure. I saw her through that front window right there." He gestured over his shoulder toward the window behind them. "Stopped her car right at the end of my driveway." He nodded toward the street. "I thought she was going to block me in, but it rolled on by enough I could get out. I watched her, though. Never know what people are up to these days."

"So, you saw what happened?"

"Yeah. Like I say, I could see her pretty clear." He sighed and flopped his hat back on his head. "She had a cell phone. Made a call. Must have been someone she knew. She was smiling and waving her hand around like she was explaining her situation. Then about that time this gray SUV ... one of those big ones. Suburban or a Tahoe or ... I think it was a Suburban. It came up, going kind of slow. That guy there," he pointed to the picture again, "was looking at the car, like he recognized it."

"You saw him?"

"Yeah."

"I mean, you could see through the windows on the Suburban?"

"Yeah. I was looking right at him through the windshield. And then he opened the door, and I had a clear shot straight across there." He stretched his arm out and pointed across the front lawn. "I had a clear view."

Connolly nodded.

"What happened after that?"

"Like I say, he was looking over toward her like he knew her, or recognized the car, or like she was in the way. I don't know. He didn't look too pleasant. Like maybe he was mad or worried or something. I don't know. Anyhow, he pulled over and opened the passenger door. She got out of the car and walked up there where he'd parked. They said something to each other. I don't know what. I couldn't hear. But I could see. She didn't look too pleased, and from what I could tell he wasn't either. He was waving for her to get in and pointing and all. She finally got in and they drove off."

He took the picture from Connolly and looked at it again.

"That's them."

He handed the photograph to Connolly.

"See anything else happen?"

"No. I mean, the tow truck came a few minutes after they left. A guy from the Chevron station up on Old Shell Road. He hauled it off."

"Anything else you can remember?"

"No. I guess that's about it."

Connolly thought for a moment, then stood.

"Mr. Turner, I appreciate your time."

Turner stood. They shook hands.

"Sure thing. Hope I was some help."

Connolly stepped from the porch and made his way down the side-walk to the Chrysler. He gave Turner a grim smile.

"You were a big help."

He got in behind the steering wheel and backed the car into the street. As he turned to drive away, he glanced toward the house in time to see Turner disappear around the corner with the wheelbarrow.

Thirty-six

onnolly left Turner's house and drove down Hillwood to McGregor Avenue. From there, he continued south to Highway 90. At the highway he drove west, away from town through the suburban clutter that surrounded the city. As he passed through Irvington, he took the cell phone from his pocket and called Mrs. Gordon at the office.

"Anybody looking for me?"

"Not really. You coming into the office any time soon?"

"Not before lunch. Any messages?"

"Just the usual nonpaying clients."

"All right. I'll be back this afternoon."

He switched off the phone and laid it on the seat beside him.

Beyond Irvington, the highway narrowed to two lanes. He pressed the gas pedal. The engine responded with a surge of power. The Chrysler picked up speed. With the windows down, the warm air blew through the car making too much noise to listen to the radio. Instead, he let his mind roll through the things he knew about the case.

Braxton was lying. There was no way he could have been in Mobile and fishing off Horn Island at the same time. Turner had seen him. Raisa had seen him. The only loose end left to explain was the receipt from the marina in Pascagoula. He glanced at his watch. He'd have an answer to that question in less than an hour.

Having a client who lied to him wasn't a problem. Lots of clients lied to their attorneys. They didn't call it lying, most of the time. Usually, by the time they got to him they had thought through their situation so many times they didn't really remember much of what actually happened. Most of the time, the facts were so uncomfortable they had to come up with a story they could live with. Very quickly, their minds weeded out the conscious memory of things that contradicted what they wanted to believe about themselves. Which meant most of his time was spent uncovering the facts they failed to tell him and then reviving their memory of how things really happened. He'd grown accustomed to the process.

But Braxton was different.

For one thing, there was a good chance he was innocent, at least of murder. If Morgan was correct and Camille had suffocated inside a freezer, there was little chance she was dead when Raisa saw her in the Suburban that morning behind the salon. But why make up a story about the marina and going fishing at Horn Island?

Then there was the whole Panama Tan, tanning salon, women from Europe, prostitution, porn film thing. Braxton was reluctant to disclose any details of that, and what he did say came in piecemeal fashion, most of the time only acknowledging what Connolly had discovered on his own. He was facing a capital murder charge. There was no reason not to tell everything he knew.

Connolly let a long sigh escape. He glanced out the window and talked to himself.

"I don't see how what he knows and won't tell could be any worse than what he's already told me."

Lost in thought, he didn't notice when he crossed the state line. When he looked up, he was passing the Miss-Ala Lounge on the outskirts of Pascagoula. He lifted his foot from the gas pedal. The nose of the Chrysler dropped. The car slowed to the speed limit.

Connolly slid his hand into the pocket of his jacket and took out the receipt Braxton had given him from the marina. He glanced at it and noted the name across the top. Klinefelter's Marina. He was sure he'd been there before. It was somewhere on the west side of Pascagoula.

"On the river," he mumbled. "Below Clark's Seafood ... I think."

The traffic light at Market Street was red. He brought the Chrysler to a stop. Ahead, he could see the approach to the river bridge three blocks away. To the right, just beyond the intersection, a faded blue sign with white letters sat behind a clump of scrubby oaks and waist-high cogon grass. Streaks of blue from the sign's background dribbled across the white letters. Between tree branches Connolly could see the letters spelled the name Klinefelter's. An arrow along the bottom pointed to the right.

When the traffic light changed, he started forward. Past the blue sign he turned the Chrysler from the highway onto a narrow paved road to the right. The road wound through an oak thicket and emerged in a sea of brown marsh grass that lay along the river. Across the marsh, the road turned left, followed the river a few hundred yards, and came to an end beneath the highway bridge in a parking lot paved with oyster shells.

A small building made of concrete blocks stood to the right. A wooden dock stretched from the building over the river. The building was painted white, but rain had spattered red mud against the sides and left an orange stain three feet up the walls all the way around.

Connolly parked the car near the far end and got out.

The afternoon sky was cloudless and blue. Waves gently lapped the bank of the river. The putter of a boat motor drifted from up the way. Seagulls circled overhead, calling to each other. Their shrill sound pierced the constant rumbling of cars passing on the bridge overhead. Connolly stood a moment, listening, then moved across the parking lot and stepped inside the building.

From the doorway, a counter ran across the room to the opposite wall. Behind it was a row of shelves filled with cigarettes, snuff, and assorted items. To the left of the door was a rack with bags of potato chips and snack food. Past the rack was a live-bait tank. A teenage boy sat on a stool behind the counter reading a magazine. He laid the magazine aside and stood as Connolly entered.

"May I help you?"

Connolly took the receipt from his pocket.

"I was wondering if I could talk to someone about this receipt." He offered it to the boy. "I'm an attorney—"

The boy interrupted him, gesturing with both hands to refuse the receipt.

"Let me get my uncle."

"Sure." Connolly smiled. "Got a Coca-Cola?"

"Yeah."

The boy opened a drink box behind the counter and took out a bottle. He flipped off the top and handed it to Connolly.

"Seventy-five cents."

Connolly took three quarters from his pocket and handed them to him.

"Your uncle close by?"

"Yeah. I'll get him."

The boy came from behind the counter and stepped outside. Connolly sipped the Coca-Cola and waited.

In a few minutes a man about Connolly's age came through the door. The boy followed behind him and took his place on the stool behind the counter. The man approached Connolly and held out his hand.

"Richard Klinefelter."

Connolly shook his hand.

"Glad to meet you. I'm Mike Connolly."

"What can I do for you, Mike?"

"I represent a man who says he was down here about three weeks ago. He gave me this receipt." Connolly took the receipt from his pocket and handed it to Klinefelter. "Said he bought some gas for his boat. Put in here and went to Horn Island." Connolly took the photograph from his pocket. "This is him in this picture. With his wife."

Klinefelter held the receipt in one hand and took the photograph with the other. He glanced at the picture and handed it back to Connolly.

"I don't recall ever seeing that man before. But I'll tell you something else." He pointed to the receipt. "This receipt didn't come from here."

Connolly looked puzzled.

"It says Klinefelter's right across the top."

"I know." The man smiled. "But it didn't come from here." He held the receipt for Connolly to see. "You see this number right here?"

Klinefelter pointed to the receipt. Connolly nodded.

"Yeah."

"We own a convenience store up by the state line. You know where the Imperial Palace is?"

The Imperial Palace was a strip club located just across the line in Mississippi. It was a landmark and, until a few years ago, had been Connolly's second home.

"Know it well."

"Our store is half a mile this side of the Palace. My daughter runs it. They use our credit card account number. Same tax number. Same everything. The only difference is, we put this number on here so we can keep it straight. You know. So we can tell what came in here, and what came in there."

"So, this purchase was actually made at that store?"

"Yes. State Line Pick-A-Snack."

"And you're sure of it?"

"Yes, sir. Positive."

Connolly looked him in the eye.

"If you had to testify in court, under oath, what would you say?"

"About what?"

"About this receipt?"

"I'd say just what I told you."

Klinefelter handed him the receipt. Connolly tucked it in his pocket with the photograph. He took a last sip of Coca-Cola and tossed the empty bottle in a trash can near the door, then gave Klinefelter a smile.

"I appreciate your time."

"Sure thing." Klinefelter stepped behind the counter. "Glad I could help."

Connolly turned toward the door.

Thirty-seven

Connolly stepped out of the bait shop and walked across the parking lot to the Chrysler. He opened the door and sat on the front seat with his feet resting on the ground outside the car. He took the receipt from his pocket and looked at it once more.

Braxton had lied to him. Not just a story told from selective memory. Not just a defendant bending the facts to reconcile them with the conflicts in his mind. This was an outright fabrication. An alibi Braxton had concocted as a cover. A story he'd repeated not only to Connolly but also to Hammond and anyone else who asked. This was an intentional attempt to mislead everyone.

"But why?"

He bumped his fist against the steering wheel in frustration. The knot in his stomach boiled into anger. Muscles in his neck tightened. He stared at the receipt a moment or two, then swung his feet inside the car and put the key in the ignition. He stuck the receipt in his pocket and started the car.

From Klinefelter's he made his way back to Highway 90. There, he turned east and drove toward Mobile. Before long, the highway entered the savanna bog that formed the low country between Pascagoula and the state line, miles and miles of brown swamp grass and pine trees as far as he could see.

Connolly pressed the gas pedal closer to the floor. The Chrysler picked up speed. In spite of the noise from the wind blowing through the windows, he turned on the radio and cranked the volume as loud as it would go. He propped his elbow on the window ledge. The car flew over the pavement. The tension in his neck faded.

Near the state line, he passed Klinefelter's convenience store. He glanced at his watch and noted the time. Two fifteen. He scrawled it on the palm of his hand with a pen. Up ahead, the Imperial Palace came into view. The neon lights were already on. He thought of Marisa and the last time he saw her, sitting in her dressing room, finished for the night. In his mind, he heard her voice.

"You want to come over. It would be like old times."

She had a wonderful come-on smile and a deep, sultry voice when she was tired. The sound of it in his mind was like an echo from a past he wanted to forget, but even now his skin tingled at the thought of her. He followed the thought a moment longer and saw himself as he awakened from an afternoon nap. She lay beside him in bed, warm and soft and curled against him, her back pressed against his chest, his arm around her waist. He remembered the way she smelled, kind of musky in a way that made him pull her close and drape his leg across her thigh.

He slapped the steering wheel with his hand and shouted over the noise of the wind and blaring radio.

"It was poison!" It felt good to shout, so he did it again. "She was poison!" He raised his hand from the steering wheel and pointed out the window at the Imperial Palace as he passed.

"Poison," he whispered. "Sweet, deadly poison."

Beyond the state line, his mind moved from Marisa to the women in the warehouse. They were being kept like animals. Herded from the lot in the morning, put to work until late in the night, then herded back to the barn where they were watered and fed.

"Livestock. Nothing more than livestock."

They could walk out. Just go down the steps, open the back door, and leave. He'd wanted to do that the morning he talked to Raisa. Take her hand. Lead her to the car. Drive away with her. He could take her to the guesthouse. She could sleep in the extra room. No one would know she was there. He'd give her one of his shirts to sleep in. She would wake in the morning and glance around, disoriented, scared. Then she'd hear him and remember and come down the hall to ...

He ran his hand over his face and growled.

Before he realized it, he was driving down Government Street. He glanced at his watch. It was ten minutes to three. He checked the time he'd noted on his palm.

"Two fifteen. Two fifty. That's fifteen, twenty ... thirty-five minutes. Without trying. Perry could have made it in less time if he used the interstate."

Time wasn't a problem. Braxton could have driven to the state line, made a purchase, obtained the receipt, and been back to Mobile by the time Camille disappeared. But that assumed he'd planned the alibi.

"If he planned this as an alibi, he had to have known he was going to pick up Camille that morning."

And that seemed all but impossible. From what Bessie told him, the trip Camille took that morning came up on the spur of the moment. Even Raisa seemed to think Braxton was as surprised as anyone when he arrived at the salon with Camille slumped in the front seat. None of it could have been planned.

He stared out the window and mumbled to himself.

"The more I find out, the less I know."

When he reached Tuttle Street, he lifted his foot from the gas pedal and rested it on the brake. The Chrysler's engine rumbled as it slowed to an idle for the turn to the right and the guesthouse a few blocks away. At the last moment, he changed his mind. He moved his foot to the gas pedal. The Chrysler picked up speed again. In a few minutes, he arrived downtown. Past the entrance to Bankhead Tunnel, he checked the mirror and glanced out the window to the right, then changed lanes.

At Royal, he turned right and made his way to Church Street behind the courthouse. St. Pachomius sat in the middle of the next block. He parked at the curb in front of the building and climbed the steps toward the door. A breeze rustled through the trees above. Near the top, he stopped and looked around. The outside was as peaceful as the sanctuary. Instead of going inside, he took a seat on the steps and rested his elbows on his knees.

By then, it was almost four. Mrs. Gordon would be leaving the office in an hour. Not much point in rushing over to catch her before she left. Whatever there was could wait until tomorrow. He leaned back and propped against his elbows on the step behind him.

The jail was only a few blocks away. He had to talk to Braxton. They had plenty to discuss. He glanced at his watch again. There was a shift change at five, and for reasons that were never really clear to him, he'd always found it a bad time to visit prisoners. Braxton could wait.

Five o'clock came and went. Afternoon melted into twilight. Twilight faded to evening.

Sometime later he heard footsteps coming up the sidewalk on the far side of the church. A moment later, Father Scott appeared from the shadows. Connolly smiled at him.

"You're working late tonight."

"Had a meeting." Father Scott came up the steps and took a seat beside him. "A vestry meeting." He gave a heavy sigh. "I have lots of meetings."

Connolly nodded.

"You ever get out of here and do anything else?"

"I go fishing."

The answer struck Connolly as strange.

"Fishing?"

"Yeah. Great way to unwind."

"Yeah?"

"Yeah. Go a few miles out in the Gulf. Get away from everything. Cell phone won't work. Pager can't reach me. Relax. Smoke a cigar."

Connolly frowned.

"Smoke a cigar?"

"Sure."

"Isn't that like ... against the rules?"

Father Scott shrugged.

"I don't know. It's a habit I picked up in law school. I enjoy it."

"I forgot you used to be a lawyer."

Father Scott smiled.

"I have, too."

Connolly's eyes were fixed on the courthouse across the street, but his mind was far away.

"How do you know when to break the rules?"

Father Scott leaned back.

"I suppose you begin by deciding whether you want to pay the price."

Connolly lifted his eyebrows.

"Pay the price. I thought we weren't supposed to think of it that way."

"Well, not everything is illegal because it's wrong."

Connolly stared ahead as they talked.

"That's radical language coming from a priest."

"*Malum prohibitum*. Illegal just because there's a law against it."

"Like speed limits."

Father Scott smiled.

"I hate speed limits."

Connolly grinned.

"Traffic lights. I see no reason to sit at a traffic light at two in the morning when there's not a car in sight."

Father Scott glanced at him.

"I take it you've run a few?"

"Yeah. I've run a few."

Father Scott looked over at him.

"You thinking about breaking some rules?"

"Not really. I've got enough loose ends in my life, I can't afford to mess with the rules much." Connolly sighed. "But it's tempting."

"You've heard the old saying 'You can't get a little bit pregnant.'"

"The breaker of rules becomes a rule breaker."

"Something like that."

"Who makes the rules?"

Father Scott looked puzzled.

"What are you talking about?"

"Ahh ... nothing."

"You sure?"

"Nah. Just a client. You know how it is with clients. Can't live with them. Can't live without them." Connolly stood. "I need to get over to the jail."

He started down the steps. Father Scott followed him as far as the sidewalk.

They shook hands. Father Scott smiled at him.

"There are some bad rules, you know."

"Bad rules?"

"Some of them were made to be broken."

The answer intrigued Connolly.

"You may be right."

"You just have to be willing to take the consequences."

Connolly stepped away. Father Scott called over his shoulder as he started up the sidewalk.

"Call me if I can help."

Connolly grinned.

"You sure about that?"

Father Scott turned back to face him.

"Yeah. Call me. I'll help you in any way I can."

Connolly's face turned solemn.

"I just may do that."

He opened the door to the Chrysler and got in behind the wheel. Father Scott disappeared in the shadows around the corner.

Thirty-eight

Connolly arrived at the county jail around six thirty that evening. Except for the guard at the entrance, the lobby was empty. He passed the security desk without delay and took the elevator to the eighth floor. A guard on the cellblock directed him to the interview room. Braxton arrived moments later.

"What'd they say? Are they going to drop the charges?"

"I haven't talked to them yet."

Braxton looked aggravated.

"Why not?"

"We need to talk first."

"I thought we already talked."

"We did. But something's come up." Connolly pointed to the bench on the opposite side of the table. "Have a seat."

Braxton moved around the table, stepped over the bench, and took a seat. Connolly sat across from him.

"You told me you went to Horn Island the morning your wife disappeared."

"Yeah."

"Said you put in at Klinefelter's Marina in Pascagoula."

Braxton's eyes darted between the tabletop and somewhere over Connolly's shoulder.

"Yeah."

"Klinefelter's on the Pascagoula River."

Braxton nodded. Connolly continued.

"Under the bridge."

Braxton gave him a questioning look.

"What's this about?"

"You gave me a receipt showing you'd been there."

"Yeah."

"Said you bought some gas."

Braxton nodded. Connolly pulled the receipt from his pocket and showed it to him.

"This receipt."

Braxton glanced at it.

"Yeah. We've been through this before."

"You know where Hillwood Drive is?"

"Sure. Just up from the house."

"Bessie told me Camille goes that way when she goes to Tootsie Trehern's shop."

"Maybe. Sometimes she goes up Wimbledon."

"I had someone ask around on Hillwood."

Braxton dropped his gaze.

"Mike, I—"

Connolly interrupted.

"Let me finish. My guy went from house to house up and down Hillwood. We found two witnesses who say Camille had car trouble the morning she disappeared." He took the photograph from his pocket. "One of them identified you from this photograph."

Braxton stared at the tabletop. Connolly laid the picture in front of him.

"This afternoon I went to Klinefelter's. Showed them that picture. Showed them the receipt. That receipt didn't come from their marina. It came from a convenience store they run on the state line."

Braxton sighed. Connolly kept going.

"There's more."

"More witnesses?"

"Yeah."

Braxton leaned back and rested his head against the wall. Connolly let his eyes bore in on him.

"You came up Hillwood. Saw the car on the side of the road. Stopped and picked her up. Somewhere between the stop on Hillwood and Panama Tan, something happened to her."

The mention of the tanning salon seemed to startle Braxton. He shot a look at Connolly but kept quiet. Connolly continued.

"When you arrived there, Camille was already unconscious. The police have the SUV. They found blood on the passenger window. Her shoe was under the seat. Whatever happened, you panicked. Rizutto was at Panama Tan when you arrived. You told him what happened. He told his driver to take care of it. Based on the autopsy, I'd say he took her out someplace, whacked her in the head with something. Coroner thinks it was probably a five iron. He thought she was dead. Dumped her body somewhere. Looks like she was in a freezer or a refrigerator or something like that."

Braxton stared straight ahead.

"In a freezer? What makes you think that?"

"The coroner found residue under her fingernails."

"She wasn't dead?"

"Not then."

"What happened to her?"

"She suffocated."

Braxton looked surprised.

"Suffocated?"

Connolly nodded.

"Suffocated. When they did the autopsy, they found something under her fingernails. Lab says it's some kind of polymer. Plastic. Use it to make the lining in refrigerators and freezers."

"She wasn't dead before—"

"Before Rizutto's driver got in your car and took her away?" Braxton didn't reply, but the look on his face told Connolly enough. "But she was dead before she hit the water off Horn Island."

"How'd she end up there?"

"Someone moved the body. I'd say whoever did it read your alibi in the newspaper and moved the body to set you up."

Anger swept across Braxton's face. Connolly pressed the question.

"Know anyone who'd want to do something like that?"

"Maybe." Braxton took a deep breath, then slowly let it escape. "So, what do we do now?"

Connolly leaned over the table, his face inches from Braxton's.

"You have to tell me everything. And I mean everything." He gestured over his shoulder. "Or I'm walking out that door and withdrawing from this case."

"And then what? I tell you everything, and then what?"

"We worry about that after you talk to me."

"You want me to tell you about Rizutto?"

Connolly banged the tabletop with his fist.

"I want to know *everything!*"

Braxton looked away. Connolly threw up his hands in frustration.

"What's so bad that you don't want to talk about it? We've already talked about murder. About your wife. Whacked in the head. Stashed in a freezer. Last time we talked about prostitutes. Women brought here from foreign countries. Porn films."

Braxton shot a look at Connolly but said nothing.

"Is there anything worse?"

Braxton gave him another look. Connolly was impatient.

"What?"

Braxton stared past Connolly and whispered a reply.

"More bodies."

Connolly could barely hear him.

"Do what?"

Braxton cleared his throat and blinked. His eyes met Connolly's.

"There are more bodies."

Connolly drew back and braced himself.

"Start talking."

Thirty-nine

*T*he following morning, Connolly was already at his desk when Mrs. Gordon arrived at the office. At eight, he telephoned Henry McNamara and arranged to meet him at noon to discuss Braxton's case. He spent the rest of the morning catching up on cases he'd neglected over the past several days. At eleven forty-five he put on his jacket and walked up the hall. He paused as he reached Mrs. Gordon's desk.

"I'm going to see Henry. I'm not sure when I'll be back."

"Doesn't surprise me."

She sat with her back to him, working at her computer. She didn't bother to face him as she spoke. Connolly smiled at her anyway.

"I left some files on my desk. You can work on them while I'm gone."

Suddenly, she wheeled around in her chair. Her eyes blazed.

"Just exactly what is going on?"

Connolly was taken aback by her display of emotion. A frown wrinkled his forehead.

"What do you mean?"

"I mean, one day you drag in here in the middle of the afternoon. Look like you've been out all night. The next day, you don't bother to show up at all. Today, you're in here before the crack of dawn, work at your desk like a normal person, and now you're leaving and don't know when you'll be back."

Connolly pulled a chair up to the desk and took a seat.

"I can't tell you what's going on." He spoke in a low, even voice. "But I can tell you this. I'm not drinking. I have been out all night a couple of times, but it has nothing to do with partying, or Marisa, or any of those other things you still worry about."

She leaned away and folded her arms across her chest.

"I don't worry about you."

The look on her face made him smile. He moved the chair back and stood.

"I'm working on Perry Braxton's case. We're in a touchy spot right now. You'll just have to trust me." He turned away and opened the door, then glanced back at her one last time. "I'll be back."

She threw a paper clip at him. He laughed and stepped through the doorway to the corridor.

Connolly took the elevator to the lobby and left the building through the service door to the alley in back. Down the alley he came to Government Street in the middle of the block. He crossed the street to the courthouse and rode the elevator to the fourth floor.

When the elevator doors opened, he expected to see Juanita sitting at her desk looking gruff and irritated. Instead, he was greeted by a much younger woman with a pleasant smile and a friendly disposition.

"Good afternoon. May I help you?"

"I'm here to see Henry McNamara."

She punched a number into the telephone system.

"I'll check. I'm not sure he's back from court yet."

Connolly glanced around while he waited.

"Where's Juanita today?"

She switched off the phone.

"Juanita's gone to lunch. Henry doesn't answer his phone."

Connolly turned away to find a seat.

"I'll just—"

The elevator doors opened. McNamara stepped out and started toward him.

"Hello, Mr. Connolly." They shook hands. "Hope you haven't been waiting long."

"Just got here."

"Great. Come on back."

Connolly followed him past the receptionist's desk down a narrow hallway to an interview room. McNamara pushed open the door.

"Have a seat in here. I'll get the file."

Connolly stepped inside. All the interview rooms were the same. Bare walls, a cheap folding table in the center surrounded by four metal chairs. A fluorescent light hung overhead. He took a seat at the table and waited.

In a few minutes, McNamara returned with the file in one hand and an apple in the other. He closed the door and sat in a chair opposite Connolly.

"All right. You wanted to talk about a deal for Perry Braxton." He glanced at Connolly. "You want an apple?"

"No, thank you."

"Mind if I eat while we talk?"

"Go right ahead."

McNamara took a bite from the apple.

"So, talk."

"You want him to talk about Rizutto."

"Yes."

"In exchange for which you'll agree to let him plead to manslaughter."

"Right."

"What kind of time?"

"Two years."

Connolly leaned away, a pained look on his face.

"Two years?"

McNamara took another bite of the apple.

"Best I can do. That's the minimum on that charge. He'll do about eight months, and they'll let him out on parole." He took another bite. "Probably."

Connolly stared at him. McNamara glanced at the file.

"Better than an execution."

"Why are you so interested in Rizutto?"

"That's a sensitive matter."

Connolly leaned forward and rested his elbows on the table.

"Let's be honest, Henry. You're a good guy. You do a good job. But you prosecute cases in district court. You don't run your own investigations. Who wants to know about Rizutto?"

"Joint task force."

"Joint task force?"

"We have a joint task force with DEA; sometimes the FBI gets involved. Homeland Security. Depends on the case."

Connolly gave him a smirk.

"You want to work for the FBI?"

An embarrassed grin spread across McNamara's face.

"Task force is very interested in Rizutto. Your guy willing to talk?"

"He'll talk. But he needs something a lot better than two years at Holman Prison."

McNamara closed the file.

"Can't do it."

He pushed the chair away and started from the table.

Connolly waited until he was almost to the door.

"Prostitutes."

McNamara stopped short.

"What?"

"Prostitutes."

McNamara backed away from the door to look at Connolly.

"What about them?"

"Brought here from some small European country."

"Like?"

"Bosnia, perhaps."

"Bosnia? Isn't that in Asia?"

"Whatever," Connolly shrugged. "If he could talk about women being sold like cattle. Prostitutes. Porn films. Some of the most gross acts imaginable. Would you be interested in forgetting about prison?"

"Maybe. Is this going to be more of Perry Braxton's theories, like fishing at Horn Island, or you got something to back it up?"

"I have witnesses."

"Will they testify?"

"If you can guarantee their safety."

McNamara gave him a quizzical look.

"You're sure about this?"

Connolly grinned.

"You want to talk to one of them? Hear it for yourself?"

"Before we talk to Braxton?"

"Yes."

"When can you bring them in?"

Connolly shook his head.

"They aren't coming in. You're going to them."

"Where?"

Connolly stood.

"I'll have someone pick you up tonight. Two thirty. In front of Coyote's on Dauphin Street."

"Two thirty?" McNamara chuckled. "... a.m.?"

"Yeah."

McNamara shook his head.

"No way. I'm not going out on some wild chase in the middle of the night just to help your client."

"You want Rizutto?"

"I do."

"Two thirty. In front of Coyote's."

McNamara sighed.

"Let me call Hammond." He stepped away from the table. "I'll get back to you."

"I need to know in the next hour or two. I have to get things arranged."

McNamara glanced at Connolly as he reached the door.

"I'll see what I can do."

He disappeared down the hall. Connolly left the room and made his way to the elevator.

Forty

Connolly returned to the office before one. Mrs. Gordon was still at lunch when he arrived. A new stack of files sat on the corner of his desk. He resisted the urge to take a nap and, instead, took a seat behind the desk and opened one of the files.

Sometime later, Mrs. Gordon appeared at the door to his office.

"What are you doing?"

He was hunched over the files on his desk. He didn't bother looking up as he replied.

"Working."

"How was Henry?"

"Henry ... was Henry."

He closed the file he'd been working on and laid it aside, then picked up another. Mrs. Gordon lingered at the door a moment, then retreated up the hallway.

An hour later, Hammond called.

"McNamara said you wanted to talk."

"No. I've already talked. I told him I could produce a witness to verify what I told him."

"What did you tell him?"

Muscles in Connolly's neck twitched. A sense of frustration swept over him.

"I'm not going through this on the telephone. Henry knows what I said. You want to talk to the witness, or not?"

"He said something about meeting you at Coyote's."

"Yes. But you won't be meeting me. You'll be meeting a guy named Hollis Toombs."

"Hollis Toombs?"

Connolly could hear a smile in Hammond's voice.

"You know him?"

"Yeah. I know him. What time?"

"Two thirty."

"This afternoon? It's already a quarter till three."

"No. Tonight."

"Tonight? You mean you want me to meet you at two thirty in the morning?"

"Yeah."

"You're kidding."

"No. I'm not kidding."

There was silence on the phone.

"You there?"

"Yeah," Hammond growled. "I'm here."

"Are you part of this task force Henry was talking about?"

Hammond chuckled.

"Task force."

There was a scoffing tone to his voice.

"What's so funny?"

"Henry. He calls me up and tells me you have all this great information and that I should meet with you. He didn't say nothing about meeting any witnesses or some early morning rendezvous."

"Do you know what this is about?"

"Yeah."

"You gonna be there?"

Hammond let out a long sigh.

"Yeah. I'll be there."

When he finished talking to Hammond, Connolly called Hollis. This time, Hollis answered on the first ring. Connolly didn't bother with small talk.

"We're set. Come get me."

Hollis switched off the phone without saying a word.

Twenty minutes later, Connolly rose from his desk and walked up the hallway. Mrs. Gordon glanced at him as he opened the door.

"Gone for good this time?"

"Yes."

He stepped into the corridor and started toward the elevator.

Hollis was waiting out front when Connolly reached the lobby. He leaned against the front fender of the pickup truck, chewing on a plastic straw.

"You going in there dressed like that?"

Connolly glanced down at his jacket.

"No. I have some clothes in the car."

He walked up the street to the Chrysler, retrieved a gym bag from the backseat, and walked back to the pickup truck. Hollis was already sitting behind the steering wheel. Connolly opened the passenger door, threw the bag on the seat, and got inside.

Hollis steered the truck away from the curb and drove down Dauphin Street. Connolly kicked off his shoes and unfastened the galluses on the suspenders that held his pants.

"Did you bring a flashlight?"

Hollis reached under the seat with one hand and pulled out a long, stainless steel light.

"Will this do?"

Connolly took it and switched it on.

"This will do nicely."

He switched it off and laid it on the seat beside him.

When they reached Water Street, Hollis turned left. Connolly slid out of his pants, folded them on the seat, and took a pair of jeans from the gym bag. As they drove down Water Street, he slipped off his jacket and dress shirt and put on a T-shirt. The traffic light at the train station was red. While they waited for it to change he took out a pair of tennis shoes and slid his feet into them. He stuffed his suit and wingtips in the bag.

In a few minutes they were at the corner by the warehouse. They turned right and drove past it, then turned into the alley on the far side of the next building. The truck came to a stop near the junk pile and the tattered Mardi Gras float.

"You sure no one's here?"

Hollis gave him a look. Connolly asked again.

"You checked?"

"I checked."

Connolly opened the door and stepped out. He propped first one foot, then the other in the open doorway of the truck and laced up his tennis shoes. When he was finished, he stepped from the truck, took the flashlight from the seat, and closed the door. Hollis got out on the other side.

Together, they walked behind the building and across the vacant lot. Connolly glanced around, hoping no one was watching.

When they reached the warehouse, Hollis moved the chain on the gate out of the way and pushed it open. Connolly stepped past. Hollis pushed the gate closed and followed Connolly to the loading dock.

"That the window?"

Connolly glanced up at the wall on the far end of the platform.

"Yeah. That's it."

He climbed onto the platform in front of the roll-up doors. Hollis stood on the ground, still staring at the window.

"How'd you get in there?"

"Stood on a drum."

Connolly held out his hand to help Hollis. Hollis took it and pulled himself up.

"But how did you get through the window and inside without busting your head?"

"Fell on my shoulder."

Hollis shook his head.

"Come on. I'll give you a boost."

He moved down the platform and stood with his back against the wall below the window. Connolly shoved the flashlight into his hip pocket. Hollis squatted and laced the fingers of both hands together, forming a place for Connolly to put his foot. As Connolly stepped into Hollis's hands, Hollis heaved him up. Connolly rose high enough that his shoulders were level with the window ledge. He worked his fingers under the edge of the window frame.

"Hurry up," Hollis groaned.

Connolly squeezed his fingers farther under the edge, then pulled. The window swung open toward him. He ducked out of the way and pushed it over his head, then grabbed the ledge with both hands. As he hauled himself up, he felt his legs swing free. He locked his elbows over the ledge and hung there, dangling in the air as he worked to climb into the opening.

Hollis coached him from below.

"Swing a leg over."

"I can't."

Connolly felt the muscles in his arms shake from fatigue. He pressed hard against his elbows and pushed his toes against the wall. Finally, he worked enough of his body over the ledge to free his arms. He lay across the opening and rested there a moment.

Hollis called from below.

"You all right?"

"Yeah."

"Better get on through. Somebody's going to see us if we stay out here much longer."

Connolly pulled himself through the window opening. Just as before, when he crossed the tip-over point, his body began to plunge headfirst toward the floor. This time, he hung on with both hands on the right side, allowing him to bend his body through the opening. Then, as his feet slid through, he let go. He dropped to the floor, landing on his feet, out of breath. As he gasped for air, he glanced up at the window and called to Hollis outside.

"Hey, Hollis."

"Yeah."

"We got a problem."

"What's that?"

"The window's open."

"I'll take care of it."

Connolly heard Hollis's footsteps as he moved away. He took another deep breath or two, then took the flashlight from his hip pocket and started toward the door.

Sunlight lit the room he'd climbed into, but beyond it the warehouse was dark. He switched on the flashlight and peered around the corner of the doorway. The beam of light cut through the darkness like a knife. He flipped it around in front of him, unsure what he would find on the first floor. To his relief there was nothing but empty space, punctuated by rows of columns that supported the building. He crossed the first floor and found the door to the stairway. He opened it, switched off the flashlight, and started up the stairs.

At the next landing he opened the door and stepped onto the second floor. He flipped on the flashlight and shone it around the room. Like the first floor, the second was empty, but unlike the other floors this one had windows along the front, opposite the stairway door. Though painted gray, enough light filtered through that he was able to see. He switched off the flashlight, moved down the wall away from the door, and sat on the floor. He leaned his back against the wall and closed his eyes. The room was hot and stuffy. Beads of sweat formed on his forehead. Before long, he was asleep.

Forty-one

Sometime later, Connolly was awakened by the sound of footsteps coming up the stairs. Light in the room had grown faint while he slept. He blinked his eyes, trying to adjust to the darkness. The footsteps drew closer. With them came the sound of voices. Connolly felt his heartbeat quicken.

"How long has it been leaking?"

Defuniak. That voice was Ford Defuniak.

"I don't know. A day or two, maybe. Could have been longer. They just told me about it a couple of days ago."

Manny Fernandez.

Fernandez and Defuniak were coming up the steps. Connolly scooted farther from the door. As the footsteps came closer, he moved away from the wall and hid behind a column.

Defuniak continued to talk.

"I don't know why I ever let Perry talk me into this."

Fernandez laughed.

"Yes you do."

"Yeah," Defuniak replied. "I guess I do."

"But maybe we won't have to worry about him much longer."

"I hope not."

"Think you can convince Rizutto?"

"I don't know. But we gotta get these women out of here. Now that they found her body, the lawyers are talking about a hearing in probate court. Her lawyer's already been to see me about it."

"Does Rizutto know about that?"

"Not yet."

The footsteps stopped outside the door. Connolly's heart pounded against his chest. Someone grabbed the doorknob.

"You think it's leaked in here?"

The door came open. A shaft of light cut across the room. Connolly held his breath.

"No." Fernandez replied. "I don't think so."

The door opened wider. Someone stepped inside. The voices fell silent. Footsteps moved along the wall where Connolly had been sitting. He worked his way around to the opposite side of the column. A moment later, he heard Defuniak.

"I don't see anything."

Connolly's heart skipped a beat. Defuniak was only a few feet away. Drops of sweat ran down Connolly's forehead and trickled into his eyes. Defuniak moved farther along the wall to the corner, then backed away, checking the ceiling overhead. Connolly watched him out of the corner of his eye. One turn of his head and they would be face-to-face. Connolly's lungs screamed for a breath of air. Sweat burned his eyes, but he knew he couldn't move.

Finally, Defuniak stepped away.

"I don't see anything. Maybe it's not too bad."

He walked behind the column, less than an arm's length away. Then, the door slammed shut. The sound of their footsteps continued up the stairs.

Connolly relaxed and took a deep breath. He slumped to the floor by the column and wiped his face on his shirt. He could hear Defuniak and Fernandez talking in the stairwell.

"I don't think it's too bad yet," Fernandez suggested. "Who're you going to get to fix it this time?"

"You can't fix it?"

"Me? I don't know anything about plumbing."

"We're violating about a thousand code sections with this."

Connolly heard the door open on the third floor. Their voices trailed away. The door closed. He listened as footsteps moved across the floor above him.

With Defuniak and Fernandez upstairs, Connolly considered his options. He could slip out the door and down the steps to the first floor. That would allow him to hide in a place less likely for them to find him. But he ran the risk of being heard. The empty building was like an echo chamber. He stretched his legs out on the floor in front of him and folded his arms across his chest.

Better just sit right here.

After what seemed like an eternity, he heard the door open above him. Footsteps moved down the stairs. The sound grew closer, then faded as they passed the second-floor landing. A moment later, he heard the door open below as they moved out of the building.

Connolly sighed and whispered to himself.

"I hope Hollis closed that window."

With nothing to do but wait, time passed slowly. In the stuffy, humid air, Connolly's eyelids grew heavy. Before long, he dozed off to sleep.

Hours later, Connolly was once again awakened by the sound of footsteps coming up the stairs. This time, there were more feet climbing the steps, and the voices were louder. Noise from the stairs rumbled through the building, moving past the second floor and up to the third. The footsteps sounded heavy and weary, and the voices were in a language he couldn't understand.

Then he heard Fernandez.

"Come on. Let's go, ladies. We had a long day; let's not make this any longer than necessary."

From the sound of his voice, Fernandez was following behind the women. The door upstairs banged and bumped against the wall as they moved inside and across the floor. In a few minutes, he heard water running. Voices, bits of conversation, drifted down from above him. Then, he heard Fernandez once more.

"One, two, three, four ... nine, ten. Ten?" His voice grew louder, as if calling to someone. "Hey, didn't we ..." Then it trailed away. "Oh yeah. I forgot."

The door closed. Fernandez came from the third floor down to the landing on the second, then on to the first. The door opened below. Connolly listened. In a little while, a car started out front. Noise from the engine moved down the street and faded in the distance.

On the third floor, water was still running. From the sound of it, someone was taking a shower. A toilet flushed. Feet shuffled across the room. A bed squeaked. A cabinet closed. More water. Then, the noise began to subside. The water turned off. Less footsteps. And then, silence.

Connolly switched on the flashlight and made his way to the door. He eased it open just enough to peek out. Through the crack between the door and the frame he could see the stairway was empty. He opened the door and hurried up the steps to the third floor.

When he opened the door upstairs, most of the women were already in bed. A single light burned at the far side of the room near the sink by the refrigerator. Raisa sat at the table. She jerked around to look over her shoulder as he entered. Her face looked calm, but even from across the room he could see a startled look in her eyes. She rose and moved toward him, wearing only a cotton T-shirt and boxer shorts.

"What are you doing here?"

Her voice was low, almost a whisper.

The thin fabric of her shirt clung to her breasts. She was standing in front of him, only inches away. A woman used to being taken by strangers. Thoughts of her with a man, with him, ran through Connolly's mind. He smiled at her and did his best to focus on her face.

"I was looking for you."

"What do you want with me?"

"Can we talk?"

She glanced around, then gestured toward the door.

"Come out here."

They stepped out of the room to the landing at the top of the stairs. Connolly closed the door behind them and turned to face her. In the light of the stairway he could see she looked tired. Her eyes were weary and she was underweight. Skinny. Her shoulder bones protruded through the neck of the shirt. Her cheekbones were unusually prominent.

"I represent Perry Braxton. The man in the photograph I showed you before."

A frown wrinkled her forehead, as if she didn't understand.

"You said you saw the woman in his SUV, behind the salon."

She looked worried but nodded for him to continue.

"He has been charged with murdering her."

"Murdering her?"

"Yes."

"The police think he killed her?"

"Yes." Connolly hurried to explain. "He didn't. He didn't do what he should have done, but he didn't kill her."

She nodded again. Connolly continued.

"We are trying to work out an arrangement with the court."

"An ... arrangement?"

"A settlement. We are trying to settle the charges against him. We need your help."

"What does that mean?"

"It means, you would have to tell the police about what you are doing. About Manny Fernandez. Rizutto." He gestured with his hands at the building. "This place."

Raisa looked grim.

"They will kill us."

"Not if we get you out of here."

Her face looked grim.

"You can guarantee our safety?"

"I can guarantee you will be safer than you are right now."

She looked at him a moment, as if thinking. Connolly pressed the issue.

"Will you help?"

"Perhaps." She glanced around, a nervous look in her eye. "You came in here just now? Did they see you?"

Connolly shook his head.

"Don't worry about that. They didn't see me. Look, we don't have much time. I need you to talk to someone. Tell them what's going on here."

"Who would I talk to?"

"A detective with the police."

She shook her head.

"They will arrest me."

"No, they won't. Not tonight."

She looked startled.

"Tonight? You want me to talk to someone tonight?"

"Yes."

She looked frightened.

"Here? You want to bring a policeman in here?"

"No. I want you to go with me."

"Now?"

"Yes."

"I can't." She shook her head. "What if we get caught?"

"You've been out before. You were going out the first time I saw you."

"That was different. Liza was sick. I was going to find medicine for her."

"Well, tonight you can find freedom for her."

Raisa looked away. Sadness swept across her face.

"Not for Liza." She looked up at him. The sadness was gone as quickly as it came. "Where would we go? To talk to this detective?"

"Not far. I'll be with you the whole time. We'll walk out the back and across the lot behind this building. There's another street back there. They'll be waiting for us."

"You know these people?"

"Yes. The man who was with me before, and a police detective."

"And he won't arrest me?"

"No. He will ask you some questions. He will listen. That's all."

"And when do we get out of here? Tonight?"

"Not tonight. We'll have to arrange it so you don't leave before the police are ready. If you go tonight, Manny and everyone will know you talked. They'll hide. The police have to be ready to arrest them before we get you out."

Her face softened.

"Manny is not so bad. He tries to help us ... some. He's not so bad as Mr. Rizutto. And the guy who drives his car ..." She shook her head in disgust. "He is not good."

Connolly glanced at his watch.

"Get dressed. We need to go."

She hesitated, then opened the door and stepped inside. Connolly waited for her on the landing, straining to hear every sound in the building, hoping no one would come while they were out.

In a few minutes, Raisa returned wearing loose-fitting blue jeans, dingy white sneakers, and a denim jacket over the same cotton T-shirt. Together, they started down the steps and out the door behind the building.

Forty-two

At the bottom of the stairs, Raisa reached for the door. Connolly grabbed her wrist and shook his head. He took the knob and eased the door open just enough to see out through the crack between the door and the wall. Satisfied no one was there, he poked his head out and scanned the area behind the building in every direction. When he was sure it was safe, he took Raisa by the hand and led her out.

As he turned to close the door behind them, Raisa pulled away and grasped the doorknob. With her thumb, she pushed the bolt into the slot in the door. She took a bobby pin from her pocket and wedged it along-side the bolt, jamming it in an open position. She closed the door and slipped her hand in his. Together, they started toward the loading dock.

Raisa's smooth palm and slender fingers were buried in Connolly's grip. His hand felt as though it would wrap around hers twice. He liked the way it felt, holding her, protecting her. A few steps from the loading dock, she stumbled. She clutched his arm to steady herself. In the confusion, her breast brushed against his bicep. Thoughts he'd pushed aside before rushed back to his mind.

They moved past the loading dock and around the corner of the building to the gate across the alley between the warehouse and the vacant lot. Connolly let go of her hand and moved the chain aside. He pushed the gate open and nodded for her to go through. When she was past, he pushed it closed and replaced the chain with the lock showing in front.

He took her hand again and led her around the fence toward the back of the vacant lot. A rusted hulk of a truck was parked midway across the lot. Beyond it, cogon grass grew knee-deep around scrubby green bushes. Connolly took her as far as the truck.

"Wait here."

His voice was not quite a whisper. She nodded in response. He moved down the side of the truck and into the bushes. Moments later, he emerged at the next street one block behind the warehouse. He glanced in both directions. The street was empty. Hollis's pickup truck was nowhere in sight. A wave of panic washed over him.

No, he thought. *Hollis would never leave me out here. Even if Hammond didn't show, Hollis would be here.*

Then, headlights appeared around the corner down the street to the left. Connolly backed away from the curb into the bushes. He crouched low to the ground and waited. The headlights drew near.

Suddenly, a spotlight came on, shining from the passenger window. Connolly crawled deeper into the bushes, then ran for the truck where he'd left Raisa. He grabbed her hand as he raced past, dragging her with him around the end of the truck. He pulled her to the ground at the bumper. She looked terrified.

"What's the matter?"

"I don't know. Someone with a spotlight. Coming down the street."

"Who?"

"Police. Night watchman. I don't know."

"I thought you were taking me to the police."

"Not them."

She jumped to her feet. Connolly wrapped his arm around her waist.

"Wait."

With little effort, he dragged her back to the ground.

"It'll be all right."

She pushed her hair out of her eyes. The look on her face said she wasn't sure she should trust him.

Connolly peered around the corner of the truck. The spotlight went out. The car moved past. Through the bushes he saw it turn the corner to the right. He took his arm from around her.

"Wait here."

She nodded.

Connolly started from the truck and made his way back to the street. Minutes later, another set of headlights appeared to the left. This time there was no mistake. He ran back for Raisa.

"Come on. They're here."

She hesitated. He took her by the hand.

"It's okay. I'll be right there with you."

She came from behind the truck. They hurried toward the street.

Hollis's pickup came to a stop at the curb. Hammond sat on the passenger's side. The window was down. Hollis leaned around him.

"Get in. We'll have to talk while we ride."

Connolly led Raisa from the curb. Hammond opened the door and slid across the seat next to Hollis. Raisa stepped into the truck. Connolly pushed her toward Hammond and climbed in. The truck started forward as he banged the door closed.

Raisa sat on the edge of the seat, pressed between Connolly and Hammond. Connolly propped one arm out the window and leaned against the door. He draped his other arm along the back of the seat.

Hollis glanced at him from behind the steering wheel.

"There's a car keeps circling the area."

"We saw it. Who is it?"

"Goes down this street, up to the train station, back down, around in here."

Hammond glanced at Connolly.

"Night watchman."

Hollis frowned at him.

"That's what you say."

Hammond ignored him and looked at Connolly. "This your witness?"

"Yes. This is Raisa."

Hammond gave her half a smile.

"My name is Anthony Hammond. I'm a detective with the police department. Mike here says you can corroborate what his client has told us."

She glanced at Connolly. Connolly nodded. She turned back to Hammond.

"You won't arrest me?"

In the close quarters of the truck cab, Connolly found her accent more pronounced. Hammond seemed to notice it, too.

"No. I won't arrest you. Where are you from?"

The pickup slowed as they reached the next corner. Hollis moved his arm around Hammond's leg for the gear shifter.

"Hang on."

He downshifted. Everyone braced for the turn. The truck rounded the corner. The force of the curve pushed Raisa against Connolly. Her arm slipped around his knee. Her hair flipped past his nose. The smell of it tickled his nostrils.

The truck picked up speed. Hollis shifted gears. Raisa changed positions on the seat and glanced at Hammond.

"Bosnia. I am from Bosnia."

"How did you wind up here?"

"A man in Banja Luka."

"That's in Bosnia?"

"Yes. He told me he could get me a job. In entertainment. Modeling. Acting in motion pictures."

"Did he?"

She looked confused. Hammond asked again.

"Did he get you a job?"

"Yes. I went to work for him at a club in Mostar."

"That's also in Bosnia?"

"Yes."

"How did you get here, to America?"

"One night, a man came to the club. He liked the way I danced. He asked to go to a private room with me. After that, they told me I had to go to Italy."

"Do you know the man's name?"

"No."

"You went to Italy?"

"Yes. I didn't like it there. They were mean to us." Her voice dropped. "They beat us." She looked away. "They did other things to us."

"Why didn't you just leave?"

"They told me I owed them money."

"Why did you owe them money?"

"For transportation, food, lodging. They said I had to pay them for clothes. I had to pay for acting lessons in advance."

"Where were you in Italy?"

"They gave me a job at a club in Turin."

"In Turin?"

"Yes."

"How long were you there?"

She shrugged.

"I do not know. A year. Maybe more."

"What happened after that?"

"They said they were sending me to America."

"And that's when you came here?"

She nodded.

"First we went to Mexico."

"Where in Mexico?"

"Mexico City. We were there a few weeks, then they put us in a truck and drove us to Houston." She frowned. "I think that is in ... Texas."

Hammond nodded.

"How did you get across the border?"

She shrugged again.

"In the truck, I guess."

"You weren't stopped?"

She looked bewildered. Hammond tried again.

"You didn't see anyone at the border? An American, in a uniform?"
She shook her head. Hammond frowned.

"At a gate? Lots of people around? Americans? Asked you for a passport?"

She shook her head.

"I do not have a passport."

Hammond glanced away for an instant, then continued.

"What happened when you got to Houston?"

"They took us to a building. Gave us something to eat. We stayed there a day or two. Then someone came and drove us to New Orleans. That is where we met Mr. Rizutto."

"You work for Rizutto?"

"Yes. He said that he paid everyone we owed in Turin. So now, we owed him."

"Where did you work in New Orleans?"

"We didn't work there. Manny Fernandez brought us here."

Hammond shot Connolly a look, then continued.

"What do you do here? In Mobile?"

Raisa lowered her head.

"I am a prostitute."

Hammond nudged her with his elbow.

"Hey, you don't have to look away. Sounds like you've had a tough time just staying alive."

She lifted her head and managed a smile. Her eyes glistened. Hammond had a kind look on his face.

"Where do you work?"

"A tanning salon. Panama Tan. It's on ... I don't know the name of the street."

Hammond nodded.

"I know where it is." He gestured with his hand. "Mike says you live in that warehouse back there."

"Yes."

"How many of you are in there?"

"Ten ... now."

"There were more?"

"Yes. Sometimes more. Sometimes less."

"What happened to the others?"

"Some were sent to other places." She hesitated. Her voice dropped again. "Some have died."

Hammond frowned.

"How did they die?"

"Some of them tried to leave."

"They killed them for trying to leave?"

She nodded her head.

"That is what they said."

"When you came here—"

She interrupted him.

"One got sick. Mr. Rizutto's driver came and took her away because they didn't want to take care of her. Some of them were killed in the films."

"In the films?"

She nodded.

"They make us do things in films."

"What kind of things? What do they make you do?"

"We had—"

"Anthony." Connolly interrupted. "I don't think we need to get into details, do we?"

Hammond ignored him and focused on Raisa.

"You've personally been in these films?"

"Yes."

"And the other women, they were in them, too?"

"Not everyone. Some of them ... they don't think they would look good, so they don't use them."

"Where do you make these films? Here? In Mobile?"

"Yes. I don't know the name of the place."

Hammond glanced at Connolly.

"You know where she's talking about?"

Connolly nodded.

"Yeah."

Hammond turned to Raisa.

"All of you work at the tanning salon."

"Yes."

"And all of you have sex with people who pay you for it. Or pay Manny or somebody for it."

"Yes."

"Now, you mentioned Rizutto and Manny Fernandez. Is anyone else involved in this?"

"Mr. Rizutto owns us. Manny Fernandez works for him. He tells us what to do."

Hammond leaned against Hollis as he took several photographs from his pocket. He handed one to her.

"Do you recognize that man?"

"Yes. That is Mr. Rizutto."

He handed her a second.

"How about him?"

"Manny Fernandez."

She handed the photographs back to him. Hammond returned them to his pocket.

"Anyone else involved in this with Rizutto and Fernandez?"

"There is a man who comes with Mr. Rizutto. He drives the car for him." She glanced at Connolly. "And the man you showed me in the picture."

Connolly caught Hammond's eye.

"Perry Braxton."

"And there is another man," Raisa continued. "I don't know his name. He comes to the salon in the afternoon. And he comes to the building where we live sometimes with Manny Fernandez."

"He comes to the salon as a customer? For sex?"

"Yes. But he never pays."

"He comes to the warehouse for sex?"

"No. Well ... he asks about it, but mostly they talk about the building."

"The building?"

"Yes."

"What about the building?"

"The water leaks. The electricity doesn't work so good. It's hot. Sometimes there are rats." She grimaced. "Bugs. Big ones."

"So, he owns the building?"

"I don't know."

Hammond took a deep breath.

"What do you know about Perry Braxton?"

She looked confused.

"I do not know ..."

Connolly glanced at her.

"The man you told me about. From the photograph."

"Oh." She had a nervous smile. "I did not know his name. He comes to the salon almost every day."

"What about his wife? Did you ever see her?"

"I saw a—"

Connolly put his hand against her arm and gave Hammond a look.

"She's not talking about Braxton and Camille until we work out a deal."

Hammond looked upset.

"What do you mean? I thought that's what this meeting was all about."

"Henry wanted to know about Rizutto. She's told you about Rizutto, and a whole lot more."

Hammond gave a loud sigh.

"Anything I didn't ask her that you wanted her to tell me?"

"No."

Raisa turned to Hammond.

"When can we leave?"

Hammond was still aggravated. He stroked his cheek with the tips of his fingers.

"We'll have to work that out. I'll have to talk to the DA." He let his hand drop to his lap. "For now, you need to go back to the warehouse and keep doing whatever it is you've been doing. You have to act as if this conversation never took place. When we get everything arranged, Mike will come and get you. But it will take a while. Maybe a couple of weeks. Maybe longer."

Raisa gave a tired, heavy sigh. She propped her elbow on Connolly's knee and rested her chin in her hand.

Forty-three

*H*ollis brought the pickup to a stop at the curb on the street behind the warehouse. Connolly opened the door and stepped out. Raisa climbed out after him. They started across the vacant lot as the truck drove away. At the alley by the warehouse, Connolly moved the chain out of the way and pushed the gate open. They made their way past the loading dock to the door at the back of the building. She opened it, then paused.

"Will this take long?"

"A week or two. I'll let you know."

"He didn't look too happy. Is he mad?"

Connolly grinned.

"Don't worry about Hammond. He's always mad about something."

Raisa looked worried. Connolly put his hand on her shoulder.

"Really. It'll be all right."

She gave him a weak smile, then disappeared inside.

From the warehouse, Connolly retreated along the back of the building, through the gate, and across the vacant lot. He crouched in the bushes and waited. Minutes later, headlights from Hollis's pickup truck rounded the corner. He darted toward the road.

The truck slowed as it drew near. Connolly stepped into the street. The truck came to a stop. He opened the door and jumped inside. Hollis was alone.

"Where's Hammond?"

"Went home."

"I wanted to talk to him. He couldn't wait?"

"Said he needed to sleep."

Connolly sighed.

"Think he'll help us?"

Hollis shrugged.

"I don't know." He glanced at Connolly. A grin spread across his face. "Is this legal?"

"What do you mean?"

"What she said doesn't help your client. I mean, if you believe her, your client was involved in prostitution and pornography. And that stuff about those dead women. That doesn't help your guy sitting up there in jail, does it?"

"Doesn't help him prove his innocence." Connolly looked over at Hollis. "But he never was that innocent."

"Your guy did something bad, so you tell them something bad about someone else?"

"Something like that. Works better if the guy you tell them about is somebody they really want."

"You got somebody like that to tell on?"

"Yeah." Connolly gave Hollis a look. "Did you believe her?"

Hollis stared ahead through the windshield.

"Yeah." The grin vanished from his face. He shifted gears in the truck. "I believed her."

Connolly made it to the guesthouse before sunup. After a hot shower and a long nap, he arrived at the office early that afternoon. Mrs. Gordon was seated at her desk when he entered. She handed him the telephone messages without asking any questions. He took them to his office and sorted through them at his desk. A phone call from McNamara interrupted him.

"We need to talk."

"Did you talk to Hammond?"

"Yeah. Can you come over here?"

Connolly left the office and walked to the courthouse. He met with McNamara in the same interview room where they had spoken before. McNamara sat at the end of the table, his file open in front of him. Connolly sat with his back to the door.

"Hammond wants to talk to Braxton."

"Does he believe our witness?"

"Yes. I think the FBI might be interested in her, too."

"Braxton will talk, but we need a written agreement."

McNamara slipped a two-page document from his file. Connolly took the document and scanned over it.

"I'll go over it tonight and get him to sign it."

McNamara nodded.

"You understand, we aren't making a deal yet."

"I understand."

"What about the lady?"

"What about her?"

"Think she'll cooperate?"

"You mean testify?"

"Yes. Give a formal statement. Under oath. Testify if we need her."

"I think she'll talk if she and the other women can get out."

McNamara looked surprised.

"Get out? You mean, relocate?"

"Yes."

"We aren't really set up for that kind of thing."

Connolly felt frustrated.

"You keep saying that, Henry. You said that to Braxton." His voice grew loud. "Now, you're saying it again. You're asking these people to lay their lives on the line. This is the twenty-first century. Do you mean the district attorney's office can't arrange for someone to disappear?"

"We aren't the federal government. We can't change a Social Security number or erase a file or guarantee that no one will ever be able to find them."

"Come on, Henry. For a hundred dollars and a stroll down Dauphin Street, I can get a new Social Security card this afternoon. And a new driver's license to go with it." He looked away. Frustration began to boil into anger. He did his best to hold it in. "I can take care of getting them out. Can you handle the rest?"

"The rest?"

"No charges. No deportation."

"I don't know about the deportation."

Connolly banged his fist on the table. McNamara jumped.

"Henry!"

McNamara threw his hands in the air.

"Deportation is up to INS. I'm just a lowly assistant DA."

Connolly leaned forward.

"Then maybe you better get somebody else involved in this."

Henry bristled.

"This is my case. You'll have to deal with me."

"Then let's deal." Connolly propped his arms on the table and lowered his voice. "Look, I don't mind you making a reputation. It's all right with me if you want to work for the FBI. I just don't want it to be at my client's expense."

"Will he talk?"

Connolly was beside himself.

"He'll talk! He'll talk! I've been telling you that for a week." He paused and took a deep breath. "What about the women?"

"What about them?"

"Relocation." Connolly was shouting now. "Haven't you been listening?"

"I've been listening. And from what I've heard, they broke the law."

"They were forced into it! You aren't seriously considering charging them with something, are you?"

"I haven't heard anything about them being held at gunpoint and forced to enter our country illegally. I haven't heard anything about them being forced to have sex for money. From what I've heard, you've been in and out of the building two or three times. If you got in, they could get out. That tells me they're there because they want to be."

Anger boiled over. Connolly shouted.

"Are you out of your mind?"

"Me?! You give me information that busts a huge prostitution ring, and you want me to let the women who did the acts go free."

The door opened behind Connolly. He glanced over his shoulder. A young man stood in the doorway.

"Everything okay in here?"

McNamara nodded at him.

"Yeah. We're okay." He forced a smile. "Just a defense lawyer."

"Well, keep it down. They can hear you all the way out to the elevators."

The door closed. Connolly lowered his voice but picked up where he left off.

"Listen, I don't know what your childhood was like. I don't know who your parents are. But you are as naive as you look if you think these women are here because they want to be."

"Yeah, well, we'll see how it goes."

Connolly picked up the agreement from the table.

"No. We won't."

He crumpled the paper into a ball. McNamara frowned at him.

"What does that mean?"

"It means, if you're going to prosecute them, I won't let them talk."

"You can't keep them from it."

"Sure I can. I'll just tell them not to do it. You think they'll talk to you on their own?"

McNamara scowled at him.

"Aiding in the commission of a crime is the same as committing it yourself."

The agreement was now a tight ball in Connolly's fist.

"I'll buy them myself and become their pimp before I let you put them in jail."

With all his might, Connolly hurled the ball of paper across the table at McNamara and leaped from his chair. McNamara ducked. The paper ball sailed past his head. Connolly crossed the room and flung open the door. He let it bang against the wall as he stepped into the hall.

McNamara called to him from the interview room.

"Hey!"

Connolly turned to face him. McNamara stood on the opposite side of the table near the corner of the room. He picked up the wad of paper and tossed it out the door to Connolly.

"You'll need this."

Connolly caught it and walked up the hall.

Forty-four

*C*onnolly walked down the hall from McNamara's office to the elevator. Hot and angry, he jabbed the button with his finger, then hit it with his fist. When the elevator doors opened, he stepped inside and jabbed the button for the lobby.

A man standing in the corner chuckled.

"They make me mad, too."

Connolly glanced over his shoulder to see who spoke. He didn't recognize him.

"I get mad every time I go in there," the man continued.

Connolly shook his head. He was in no mood to talk. He stared ahead in silence as the elevator descended to the first floor.

When the doors opened, he walked across the lobby and stepped out to the sidewalk along Government Street. The air was hot and humid, but it felt good to be outside. He took a deep breath and let it slowly escape from his lungs, forcing his muscles to relax. A light breeze swept over him. It was cool against his damp skin.

Calmer now, he felt something in his hand. He glanced down at his side and saw he was still holding the wadded agreement McNamara had tossed to him as he walked out. He unrolled it, smoothed out the wrinkles as best he could, then folded it and stuck it in the pocket of his jacket.

From the courthouse, he crossed Government Street and walked up the alley to the office building. He entered through the service door, crossed the lobby, and exited the building through the main entrance on Dauphin Street. The Chrysler was parked out front. He opened the door, got in behind the steering wheel, and inserted the key in the ignition. The sound of the engine made him smile. He loved the way it started at the touch of the key. He lowered the window and steered the car away from the curb.

Two blocks up Dauphin, he came to the corner at Jackson Street. Tempting as it was to keep going, he turned right, crossed to St. Francis Street, and turned south toward the county jail.

❋ ❋ ❋

Braxton was seated at the table in the interview room on the eighth floor when Connolly arrived.

"They ready to deal?"

Connolly took out the agreement from McNamara and tossed it on the table. Braxton gestured with a nod toward the paper.

"What's that?"

"An agreement."

"For what?"

"For you to tell them what they want to know."

Connolly took a seat across from Braxton. He held the document with one hand and pointed to it with the other.

"First, they want you to agree to tell them the truth."

Braxton nodded.

"Not a problem. Why's the paper so wrinkled?"

"I wadded it up."

Braxton looked puzzled.

"Wadded it up? Why?"

"So I could throw it at Henry McNamara."

A grin stretched across Braxton's face.

"You threw it at him?"

"Yeah."

"Why?"

"Because he ... because he doesn't have half a brain." Connolly took a breath, then continued. "Whatever they ask, you have to tell them. They will attempt to verify what you say. If you lie to them, the agreement is off and you go to trial. Understand?"

Braxton nodded.

"I understand. What else?"

"If the agreement is canceled, they won't use anything you tell them against you. But they are free to use whatever evidence they've developed prior to the time you talk. And, if your case does go to trial, they can use evidence about the topics you talk about as long as they develop it from some other source, independent of what you tell them."

"What do I get?"

Connolly turned to the second page.

"If you cooperate, tell the truth, and testify against whomever they think you can help them with, they'll agree to let you plead guilty to manslaughter. They won't agree to any particular sentence. But they won't oppose your application for probation."

Braxton smiled.

"I can get probation?"

Connolly shook his head.

"That's not what they're saying. They're only agreeing to not oppose your application. They aren't agreeing to support your request for probation. They aren't agreeing to recommend you for probation. If you ask the court for probation, the court will ask them for their position. They won't oppose you."

Braxton still looked hopeful.

"So, I'll get it, right?"

"Not necessarily. It depends on the judge. They're probably willing to say all this because they're sure the judge will never grant you probation in the first place."

"What about relocation?"

"They still say they can't do that. They say they aren't the FBI and have no way to do it." He looked at Braxton. "You understand, they aren't agreeing to a sentence. They aren't saying you can go free if you testify."

"Okay."

"Your sentence will be up to the judge. He could give you a light sentence, or he could give you the maximum."

Braxton nodded.

"What do you think?"

"It's not much of a deal. It's not anything like what you wanted."

"What are my chances at trial? You think I'm going to lose?"

Connolly let the agreement slip from his hand to the table. He leaned away and folded his arms across his chest.

"To tell you the truth, I don't know."

Braxton frowned.

"You don't know?"

"No."

"Why not?"

Connolly threw his hands up in frustration.

"This case folds back on itself two or three times. They found Camille's blood in your Suburban. They found her shoe in there. But no one saw what happened, and there isn't enough evidence to say that's where she was killed." He ran his hand over his forehead. "There's a witness who saw you pick her up, but I'm not certain they know about him. There's another witness who saw Camille unconscious in your car, but if they put her on it'll destroy their case."

"So why don't we use her?"

"Because if she testifies, she'll say you were involved in prostitution and pornography, and she'll say other women were killed, and the jury will convict you in about ten minutes."

Braxton leaned away. Connolly sighed.

"That's the thing about this case. Everything that helps us hurts us." Connolly paused, then continued his litany of the evidence. "The body was found where you said you were fishing when she disappeared. But you were never there." He caught Braxton's eye. "On the other hand, you lied about where you were and gave the police a bogus receipt to back it up." Connolly shook his head. "I don't know. You might just beat the whole thing. Maybe wind up with a charge for lying to a police officer ... but this whole case could evaporate."

Braxton smiled.

"So, why should I want to plead guilty?"

Connolly shrugged again.

"I don't know. You don't have to. If you don't want to, don't do it. But if you go to trial, you'll have to testify to win, and if you testify, you'll have to tell the truth, and then you'll wind up telling them what really happened. And that will be enough to convict you of manslaughter."

Braxton gave him a smug look.

"Do I have to decide today?"

"No." Connolly spun around on the bench and stood to leave. "Think about it. I'll come back to see you tomorrow." He walked to the door. "They'll need an answer by then."

Braxton was still at the table.

"That's it?"

"That's it. You're the defendant. You get to decide whether to plead guilty or not." Connolly turned to bang on the door for the guard, then hesitated. He turned back to Braxton.

"The Trust owns the building where the salon is located. I assume it owns the warehouse, too?"

"Yeah."

"How did you get Defuniak to agree to that?"

"What?"

"How did you get Defuniak to agree to let you use the warehouse?"

Braxton stared at the tabletop. Connolly stepped back to the table.

"How did you get Defuniak to agree to let you use those buildings?"

Braxton looked at him.

"He likes women."

Connolly frowned.

"Likes women? You mean he likes sex."

Braxton shrugged and stood.

"What's the difference?"

He crossed the room and banged on the door. A guard came with a key and opened it.

* * *

Connolly left the jail and walked down the street to the Chrysler. As he opened the car door, he took his cell phone from his pocket and punched in Buie Hayford's number. Moments later, Hayford answered.

"You get anything on those oil leases?"

"Uhh ... not yet."

The tone in Hayford's voice made Connolly uneasy.

"What are you saying?"

"Well, I've been thinking. Maybe this isn't so good. For the Trust, you know."

Connolly listened in silence. Hayford continued.

"I mean, maybe you were right. Maybe there's just too much there to disturb. It's been a long time. I'm ... I'm just not sure I can get into all this now. You know. From the ethics of it and all."

Connolly scowled.

"The ethics of it?"

"Yeah. I have a duty to my clients. What you're talking about would open up a can of worms that wouldn't do any of them any good."

Connolly was growing more frustrated by the moment.

"What I'm talking about is the *truth*." His voice was loud. He paced back and forth alongside the car. "The truth about what happened to one of those clients you say you owe some kind of duty."

"Come on, Mike. You know what I'm talking about. It's not my job to find the truth. It's not yours either. Our duty is to represent our clients. To advise them of what the law is as it relates to their situation. We aren't inquisitors. We're counselors."

"Yeah, well. I'm not blind, either."

Connolly switched off the cell phone and tossed it on the front seat of the car. He got in and slammed the door closed.

Hayford was right. He didn't have a duty to uncover the truth. His only duty was to his client. Perry Braxton might be the worst person alive, but he was entitled to a defense. The state had to prove its case. That's what criminal justice was all about. It wasn't about the truth. Make the state prove its case and let the jury know when it failed. He started the car and steered it away from the curb.

But he couldn't put those women out of his mind, either. Raisa. The others. In that warehouse. The feel of her hand in his. Her dark eyes looking at him. What about them? Didn't they deserve the truth? Weren't they entitled to more than the lies that brought them here? The lies Rizutto and Fernandez gave them to keep them slaves?

The nagging, sinking feeling returned to his stomach. He swallowed hard. Tried to stuff it down, but it refused to go away. They were all manipulating him. First Braxton, now Hayford. He hit the steering wheel with his fist.

"Why won't anyone tell me the truth?!"

At St. Francis Street, he turned left, then took a right on Royal. Down the block on the left, Tidewater Bank Building rose into the downtown sky. Gleaming in the afternoon sun, its steel and glass exterior reflected the puffs of clouds as they moved through the bright blue sky. The sight of it set Connolly's teeth on edge. He snatched the steering wheel to the right and pointed the car toward an empty parking space. When the car came to a stop, he threw open the door and climbed out.

If Hayford won't help, I'll talk to Defuniak myself.

He glanced at his watch as he started across the street. It was four o'clock.

Connolly entered the lobby and checked the building directory. Defuniak's office was located on the twenty-first floor. He stepped into the elevator and pressed the button.

When the doors opened, he walked into the hallway and looked around. To the right was a suite of offices. A sign above the door identified it as the trust office. A secretary sat at a desk a few feet inside. Connolly started toward her. She smiled as he entered.

"Good afternoon, sir. May I help you?"

"I'd like to see Ford Defuniak."

"I'm sorry, sir. Mr. Defuniak isn't in the office today. Was he expecting you?"

"Apparently not."

She looked puzzled.

"Excuse me?"

"No." Connolly looked away. Coming there was a mistake. He backed away. "I didn't have an appointment."

"Could someone else help you?"

"No." He gave her a smile. "I guess not."

He started down the hall.

"Thank you, sir."

He tossed a wave over his shoulder as he walked to the elevator.

Forty-five

*C*onnolly spent a restless night at the guesthouse, wondering what Braxton would do. Wondering what would become of Raisa. Wondering what would become of him if he helped them. The following morning, he returned to the county jail. With little fanfare, Braxton signed the agreement. That afternoon, Connolly took it to the district attorney's office. He laid it on the table in front of McNamara.

"When do you want to talk to him?"

"I'll get with Hammond." McNamara sounded nonchalant. "We'll set something up next week."

"How do you plan to do this?"

McNamara gave him a blank look.

"Go up to the jail, I guess."

Connolly shook his head.

"Can't do that."

"Why not?"

"You talk to him there, everyone on the floor will know it. That's exactly what he wants to avoid."

"What do you suggest?"

"I suggest you come up with a better plan." Connolly stepped toward the door. "And make it soon. This thing isn't going to hold together forever."

Connolly spent the remainder of the week at his office, catching up on his other cases. Friday evening, he arrived at the guesthouse before seven for the first time in a long time. He took a hot bath and was asleep in bed before nine. When his eyes opened, it was ten the next morning.

After showering, he sat at the table near the kitchen and ate an English muffin with a cup of coffee while he read the Saturday morning paper. As he ate, he thought about Ford Defuniak and Hayford's refusal to delve into the oil leases. Frustration from the week before began to build once again. When he could stand it no more, he walked to the living room and picked up the telephone directory from the table by the sofa. He flipped it open and scanned down the page.

"Davis ... Deakle ... Dees." He mumbled to himself as he searched. "Ford De ... No. That's not his name. What is it?" He'd seen it on the building directory earlier in the week. He scanned down the listings. "Franklin. That's it. Franklin Crawford Defuniak III." He smiled. "That name fits him." He noted the address. "Forty-one sixty-two Rochester Road."

He gulped down the last of the coffee in his cup and walked down the hall to the bedroom. Minutes later, he stepped from the guesthouse dressed in slacks, a golf shirt, and cordovan loafers with no socks. The Chrysler sat a few feet away. He got in and started down the driveway.

Rochester Road ran from Airline Highway through a quiet neighborhood on the edge of Spring Hill not far from Mobile Country Club. Near Airline, most of the homes were single-story houses with large yards, a popular place for young couples with children who needed space to play. Farther down, the road wound around the back side of the country club and followed along the edge of the golf course. Houses on that end were larger.

Connolly turned off Airline and let the Chrysler roll quietly down the street as he watched for the address. Defuniak's house was located across from the tenth green. He turned the car into the driveway.

The house was a modest two-story brick federal to which someone had added rooms on either side of the first floor. The room on the far side was a sunporch. The room on the side closest to the driveway was a den. A door opened from the den to a stoop with three steps down to the drive. Connolly parked near the steps and got out.

A car sat in the driveway between the Chrysler and a garage at the end of the pavement. The garage was closed. Leaves from a pecan tree in the backyard were scattered across the top of the car. It appeared as though it had not been moved that day.

Connolly stepped to the door and knocked. From inside, he could hear the television blaring. When no one answered, he knocked again, harder. Still, there was no answer. He put his face to the window and looked inside.

A recliner sat across from the door. To the right, at the far end of the room, a television sat in an armoire that had been converted into an entertainment center. The lights were off in the room, but the television was on. A newspaper lay on the floor beside the recliner with a bag of potato chips and an open beer can. To the left, he could see through a doorway to the kitchen at the back of the house.

Connolly stepped away from the side door and walked around. He climbed the steps to the kitchen door and looked inside.

The back door opened to a small enclosed porch. A jacket hung on a row of pegs on the wall to the left. There was a window on the wall to the right. Below it was a bench with boots and shoes tucked neatly in place underneath. Ahead, he could see the kitchen. A cabinet to the left of the sink was open. A glass sat on the counter. Light from the window in the door reflected off the floor in the center of the kitchen. It looked like a picture from a magazine. Perfect.

Too perfect. Something wasn't right.

He let his gaze move around the room once more. The sink was a large farmhouse style made of white enamel with a single basin. It glistened in the light that bounced off the floor. The floor looked shiny and slick.

Shiny and slick.

He glanced up at the sink.

"The sink."

He twisted the doorknob and shoved. The door came open. He started across the floor in a hurry. Water splashed beneath his feet.

The faucet at the sink was on. Water from it had filled the sink and run over the edge, covering the floor in the kitchen and entryway. He splashed his way to the sink and turned off the water.

A plate and fork lay at the bottom of the sink over the drain. A sponge floated on top of the water. He tested the water with his hand, then reached inside and lifted the plate. The water in the sink flowed down the drain.

Connolly glanced around, then tiptoed across the room through the water to the hall. The hardwood floor was dry, but to the left, carpet in the dining room was soaked halfway across the room.

Down the hall he came to a staircase. A short hallway ran past it to the right and led to the front door. A doorway at the foot of the stairs opened to the living room.

He called out.

"Hello! Anybody home?"

No one answered.

He stood at the foot of the stairs and glanced up to the second floor. It was dark and quiet. He scanned across the living room. A doorway on the far side led into the sunporch. Both rooms appeared empty. He retreated to the center of the house and moved farther down the main hall.

To the left, he passed a bathroom. He looked inside. The room was empty. A few steps farther, he passed a bedroom on the right. He leaned inside and looked around. No one was there. Beyond the bedroom, the hall opened onto the back half of the sunporch. He stepped to the doorway.

A sofa sat to the right between the hall door and the door to the living room. Two chairs sat against the windows on the opposite side of the room. To the left was a second sofa.

And there on the sofa was Ford Defuniak, sprawled facedown across it. His left arm was stretched above his head, as if reaching for the phone that sat on a table a few inches away. Three bruises were visible on his arm, just below the bend of his elbow. Around them were four red marks. His right arm dangled toward the floor.

Connolly stepped toward him.

"Ford."

Connolly spoke in a low, hushed tone. There was no response. He touched Defuniak's hand. It was cold and lifeless. He moved back, took the cell phone from his pocket, and punched in the number for the police.

Fifteen minutes later, a patrol car arrived. Connolly met the officer in the driveway near the Chrysler.

"You the one who called?"

"Yeah."

"Where's the body?"

"In the house. Sunporch on the far end."

The officer stepped to the door at the den and jiggled the knob. Connolly moved to the corner of the house.

"Can't go in there." He pointed toward the back door. "Have to go in back here."

"You know him?"

"Yeah ... I've met him a time or two."

"What were you doing here?"

"I came to talk to him about something."

"How'd you get in?"

He led the officer toward the back door.

"Came around here. Looked in through the window. Water was running in the sink. It had run over on the floor. The door was unlocked. I went inside. Turned off the water. Found him on the sunporch."

The officer moved up the steps.

"Wait out here."

The officer disappeared inside the house. Connolly backed away and sauntered toward the driveway. As he reached the corner of the house, he heard a car door close. An unmarked car was parked behind the patrol car. A man in a suit moved around the Chrysler toward him. Connolly recognized him from court but couldn't remember his name. They shook hands.

"Mike Connolly."

"Yes, sir. Steve Sims. The officer inside?"

"Yes." Connolly pointed over his shoulder. "Through the back door."

Sims moved past Connolly and disappeared around the corner.

Before long a second police car came to a stop in front of the house. An officer got out and walked across the lawn toward the front door. Connolly leaned against the Chrysler and watched. In a few minutes, a paramedic crew arrived, accompanied by a fire truck.

Connolly took out his cell phone and punched in Buie Hayford's office number. He left a voice mail for him, then tried another number. He finally reached him at the golf course.

"Sorry to interrupt you."

"No problem. I'm not playing too well today. What's up?"

"I'm over at Defuniak's house."

"I thought I made it clear ..."

He sounded aggravated. Connolly cut him off.

"You ought to get over here."

"I told you I didn't want to get into this with him."

"He's dead."

"Dead?"

"Yeah."

He heard Hayford breathing heavy.

"I'll be over in a few minutes."

Connolly switched off the phone.

A TV news crew arrived a little later, followed by the coroner's hearse. Not long after that, Ted Morgan appeared. Sometime later, Sims came around the corner of the house.

"You want to come in here a minute?"

Connolly moved away from the car and followed him inside to the kitchen.

"What did you touch in here?"

Connolly glanced around.

"I touched the door when I came in. I touched the faucet. I turned it off." He leaned over the sink and pointed. "I touched that plate."

Sims looked over his shoulder.

"The plate?"

"Yeah. It was over the drain. Blocked it. I moved it to one side. The water ran out of the sink."

"Anything else?"

"Not that I know of."

Sims stepped away from the sink and moved toward the hall.

"Come on down here."

Connolly followed him. Sims glanced over his shoulder.

"Touch anything in here?"

"No. I don't think so."

They reached the staircase and the short hallway to the front door. Connolly turned aside.

"I walked up here." He glanced around. "I looked in the living room. I might have touched the door facing."

Sims stepped to his side.

"That it?"

"Yeah."

"Did you go through the living room?"

"No."

They continued down the main hall to the sunporch. Connolly glanced to the left. Defuniak's body lay across the sofa. A photographer snapped pictures. A video camera sat on a tripod in the corner. Ted Morgan stood to one side. Sims was next to Connolly.

"Is that the way you found him?"

Connolly nodded. For the first time he noticed Defuniak's hair was wet.

"Did you touch anything in here?"

"I touched his hand."

"Which one?"

"Right one. The one dangling off the sofa."

"Why did you touch him?"

"To see if he was alive. I spoke to him. He didn't respond. I tried to check for a pulse."

Ted Morgan glanced at him.

"Feel anything?"

Connolly shook his head.

"No."

Morgan wore rubber surgical gloves. He touched Defuniak's head.

"Was his hair wet when you saw him?"

"I don't know. I didn't notice it until just now, when I came into the room."

"You didn't notice it when you found him?"

"No." Connolly shrugged. "Sorry."

Morgan nodded. Sims nudged Connolly at the elbow.

"Okay. You can wait outside. We'll need to get a statement from you."

Connolly turned away and walked up the hall. When he stepped out the back door, he met Hayford coming up the steps.

"What happened?"

Connolly moved past him down the steps.

"I don't know."

"You found him?"

"Yeah."

"Was he shot?"

"No. I don't think so. I didn't see any blood."

A patrolman came around the corner of the house.

"They told me to come over here. Anybody know where Sims is?"

Hayford gestured to him with a nod.

"Come on. I'll show you."

Hayford stepped inside. The patrolman followed him. Connolly watched as they crossed the kitchen and disappeared up the hall.

With nothing else to do, Connolly wandered back to the driveway. He opened the car door and sat on the front seat of the Chrysler. An hour later, Ted Morgan came from the house. He paused as he passed the car. Connolly glanced up at him.

"Any idea what happened to him?"

"Looks like he killed himself."

Connolly frowned.

"Killed himself?"

"That's what the detective thinks."

"What do you think?"

"I don't know."

"What were those marks on his arm?"

"Needle tracks."

"Needle tracks?"

"Yeah. He was diabetic."

"Seems like a lot of shots to take. You think that's what killed him?"

"Could have. We'll have to wait for test results."

"How'd his hair get wet?"

"Good question."

"You don't seem too convinced about this."

Morgan smiled.

"Lots of unanswered questions."

Hayford came around the corner of the house. Morgan glanced in his direction, then stepped away. Hayford leaned through the open car door.

"You hungry?"

"Yeah."

"Meet me at the Blue Gill in half an hour."

Connolly nodded. Hayford moved down the driveway.

Forty-six

*T*he Blue Gill was a restaurant located on the causeway that ran across the northern end of Mobile Bay, linking Mobile with the eastern shore and trendy suburban life in Baldwin County. The restaurant catered to a crowd that enjoyed live music and local seafood. Housed in a rambling wood-frame structure, it sat at the edge of the water with an open deck in back that stretched over the marsh grass and tide pools.

Hayford was waiting for Connolly at a table inside. He caught Connolly's eye as he entered and waved him over.

"Sims give you a rough time?"

"Lots of questions," Connolly sighed. He pulled out a chair and took a seat. "Lots of questions."

"What were you doing at the house?"

"I went over there to talk about those oil leases."

"I figured as much."

A waitress appeared at their table. They ordered lunch. When she was gone, they resumed their conversation.

"What do you think happened to Defuniak?"

Connolly gave Hayford a matter-of-fact look.

"I think someone killed him."

Hayford nodded.

"Me, too."

Connolly glanced around.

"What did they tell you?"

"Sims thinks he killed himself. Morgan says that doesn't account for everything."

Connolly rolled his eyes.

"No kidding. They ran me out. Why'd they let you stay in there?"

"I told them I represented some of the businesses he managed and I wanted to stick around." He glanced away. "I also knew one of the patrolmen."

Connolly shook his head.

"There's no way he killed himself. What else did Morgan say?"

"He's particularly puzzled by the wet hair and the overflowing sink."

Connolly nodded.

"I think I know what happened there. What bothers me are the needle marks in his arm."

"I saw that."

"They were in his left arm."

"Yeah. I think he was diabetic."

"Maybe so, but the needle marks were in his left arm." He said it with emphasis this time. "Four of them."

Hayford looked unconcerned.

"So?"

"I don't think he would have given himself four injections."

"Unless he wanted to kill himself."

"But the marks were on his left arm."

"You've said that about four times. What's your point?"

"Defuniak was left-handed."

A frown wrinkled Hayford's brow.

"You sure about that?"

"Yeah. I talked to him a couple of weeks ago. At the country club. He mentioned he bought all his clubs at the pro shop there because they carried a lot of nice left-handed clubs."

Hayford looked away. He rolled his head to one side and stretched his neck.

"So, what about the wet hair?"

Connolly gestured back and forth with his hand and arm. Hayford looked puzzled.

"Dunked him," Connolly explained.

"Huh?"

"Filled the sink with water. Shoved his head in. Held him down."

Hayford's eyes were wide.

"You think so?"

"I'm sure of it. Look, when I got there the television was on. Loud. But the lights were out in the den."

The waitress returned to the table. She set a glass of water in front of Hayford. Connolly had iced tea. They waited for her to leave. Hayford took a sip of water and glanced at Connolly.

"So ..."

"I went around back. Saw the water running in the sink. It had been running a long time."

"Yeah."

"I figure they came in. Got him. Turned up the television to cover the noise ..."

Hayford interrupted him with a skeptical look. Connolly shrugged.

"Maybe they were paranoid. I don't know. This is just what I figure happened. They shoved his head in the sink. Held him under. Tried to make him talk."

"Tried to make him talk?"

"Yeah."

"About what?"

Connolly looked away.

"I ... I don't know."

Hayford gave him a look.

"What are you not telling me?"

Connolly avoided his gaze.

"Tell me about the oil leases."

"No." Hayford set the glass down. "Finish what you were telling me."

"Later. Tell me about the oil leases."

Hayford slipped his hand inside his jacket and took out a piece of paper. He handed it to Connolly.

"Defuniak signed those leases in the name of the Trust. Had the money sent to a bank in New Orleans. Bank account was in his name."

Connolly scanned the paper as they talked. It was a photocopy of the first page of an account statement from Acadian National Bank.

"Where'd the money go from there?"

"We're working on it."

Connolly looked up.

"But it went, right?"

"It didn't stay in that account very long."

Connolly glanced at the paper.

"How much money are we talking about?"

"Millions."

Connolly shook his head. Hayford took a sip of water.

"Finish what you were telling me."

"I can't."

"Why not?"

"It has to do with Braxton's case."

"This whole thing has to do with Braxton's case."

"I know. But this gets into some stuff I can't talk about."

Hayford looked aggravated. Connolly took a sip of tea.

"Tell me one more thing. Does the Trust own a warehouse on Morgan Street?"

"Why should I tell you, if you won't tell me?"

"I can't explain it right now. Does it?"

"Does it what?"

"Does the Trust own that warehouse?"

"It owns two or three. Which one are you talking about?"

"I'm talking about one at the corner of Morgan and Conception Street Road."

"Yeah. Used to be a mill of some kind."

"A mill?"

"That was a long time ago. They call it the Mill. I think the last time it was rented someone used it to store furniture. What's that got to do with anything we've been talking about?"

"I can't tell you right now."

Hayford scowled at him.

"What is there that—"

The waitress appeared again, this time with their lunch. Hayford managed a smile for her as she set plates of food in front of them. When she was gone, he turned back to Connolly.

"What is there that—"

Connolly held up his hand to stop him.

"I'll buy lunch. But I can't tell you about it now."

Hayford picked up his fork and began to eat.

Forty-seven

*C*onnolly left the Blue Gill and drove toward town. On the way, he took out his cell phone and called Hammond.

"This better be good," Hammond growled.

Connolly could hear the noise of a crowd in the background.

"Did you talk to McNamara about Braxton?"

"Yeah. Call me next week."

"We need to do it now."

"What?"

Hammond's voice sounded shrill. Connolly ignored his tone.

"We need to do it now."

"I can't do it now."

"Why not?"

"Well, for one thing, the game isn't over."

"What game?"

"My son's baseball game."

"How much longer will it go?"

"I don't know. We're in the third inning. We're up by four runs. If we blow them out, it'll be over after the fifth."

Connolly heard a noise on the phone that sounded like static.

"Are you there?"

He could hear Hammond's voice, but he wasn't talking into the phone.

"Get him. Get him. Yes!" Hammond's voice returned to the phone. "Threw him out at third."

"Your son?"

"No. My son's the pitcher."

"When can we meet?"

"I don't know. Call me Monday."

Hammond ended the call. Connolly grimaced and pressed the redial button.

"Not now," Hammond barked.

"They killed Ford Defuniak today."

The phone was silent.

"You still there?"

"Yeah."

Hammond's voice was different now. Serious. Connolly had his attention.

"You remember Ford Defuniak?"

"One of the men your lady mentioned the other night."

"Yeah."

"This thing is coming apart."

Connolly smiled to himself.

"Yep."

"We have to move fast, before they shut the whole thing down." Hammond's cadence was quicker. "They do that, we'll never find any of them."

"That's why I'm calling you."

"All right. Meet me at the jail in an hour."

Hammond ended the call. Connolly closed his phone and laid it on the seat.

An hour later, Connolly parked at the curb in front of the county jail. He passed through the security check at the lobby desk and made his way to the booking area. Hammond was waiting for him.

"Come on." Hammond stepped to the elevator. "They have him for us on the sixth floor."

"What's on six?"

"Infirmary."

The elevator opened. They stepped inside. Hammond pressed the button for the sixth floor.

"It's Saturday. Nobody up there except the nurse. We sent him on an errand that will keep him out of the building for an hour or two."

When they reached the floor, Connolly followed Hammond down the hall to an examination room. Like the interview room on the eighth floor, all the furniture was made of stainless steel. Most of it was bolted to the floor.

Hammond took a plastic card from his pocket and inserted it into a reader on the door facing. The lock clicked. Hammond pulled the door open. Behind them, the elevator bell rang. Connolly turned to see who was getting off. When the elevator opened, McNamara stepped out. Connolly moved inside the room. Hammond held the door open and waited for McNamara.

Braxton sat on an examination table in the center of the room. His feet dangled off the edge. He smiled at Connolly as he entered.

"What's this all about?"

"They want to talk to you. This was the best we could do, under the circumstances."

"What circumstances?"

"Defuniak is dead."

Braxton looked concerned.

"What happened to him?"

"Found him dead on the sunporch at his house. I think he was murdered. The detective who was there thinks he killed himself. The coroner doesn't know what he thinks yet."

"Who found him?"

"I did."

McNamara stepped into the room. He took a seat on a small stool near the foot of the table where Braxton sat. Hammond stepped inside and pulled the door closed.

"All right, Mr. Braxton. Your attorney has indicated you want to talk to us about matters related to your case. Are you ready to do that?"

"Yeah."

Hammond took a small tape recorder from his pocket. He switched it on and set it on a cabinet near Braxton. He stared at it as he spoke.

"We're here today with Perry Braxton. Mr. Braxton is represented by Mike Connolly, who is here with us. Henry McNamara from the district attorney's office is also present." Hammond glanced up at Braxton. "Mr. Braxton, you signed a written agreement with the district attorney that covers the terms of our arrangement regarding this meeting." He slipped the document from the pocket of his jacket, opened it to the second page, and showed it to Braxton. "I'm showing you the second page of that document. Is that your signature?"

"Yes."

"Did you read it before you signed it?"

"Yes."

"Did your attorney explain it to you?"

"Yes."

"Do you still want to talk to us?"

"Yes."

"You understand we can't guarantee you any particular sentence?"

"Right."

Hammond folded the document and returned it to his pocket, then continued.

"Okay. Tell us what happened to your wife."

Braxton shot a look at Connolly. Connolly nodded. Braxton took a deep breath, then began.

"I passed her on the street that morning. I don't remember the date. It was a Monday, I think. Her car had broken down. I stopped. Picked her up."

"Did she go with you willingly?"

"Yes ... she didn't like it, but she went with me. I mean, I didn't make her go. She just didn't like me and didn't like being around me."

"Why is that?"

"We were going through a divorce."

"Okay. You picked her up. What happened after that?"

Braxton frowned.

"I thought this was going to be about Rizutto."

"We'll get to him. What happened next?"

"We started up the street. We were going to the Chevron station on Old Shell Road. Her car's rather old. They work on it a lot. She started asking me about something. Made a couple of snide comments. I pulled over in the parking lot at the Presbyterian church. I shouted at her. She shouted back. I backhanded her. She hit her head on the window."

"Did it break the skin?"

"I don't know. I heard you found blood on the window. It could have."

"Did you knock her out?"

"Yeah."

"What were you arguing about?"

"She said she'd seen me with another woman."

"Who was that?"

Braxton dropped his gaze.

"One of the women at the tanning salon. Panama Tan."

"You were a customer?"

"Yeah."

"So, you knocked her out. What did you do?"

"I drove to the salon—"

"The salon?"

"Panama Tan."

"Why'd you go there?"

"I was scared. I didn't know what to do. That was the first thing I thought of. So, I did it."

"What happened?"

"When I got there, Manny Fernandez was bringing in the women. For some reason, Rizutto was there. I pulled up. Told them what happened. They saw her in the car."

"She was still unconscious?"

"She was starting to come around."

"What happened?"

"Rizutto laughed. Told his driver to take care of her."

"Did he?"

"Yeah."

"What did he do?"

"He got in my car. It's a Suburban, actually. He got in. Drove off with her. Came back in a little while. She was gone. The car was empty."

"What did you do?"

"Drove home. Took a shower. Went down to a job site on Dauphin Island."

"Tell us about the women."

"Not much to tell. I don't know any of their names. They all use names like Linda and Brenda, but that's not really their names. They're from someplace in Europe. Rizutto gets them through a connection he has."

"Who owns Panama Tan?"

"It's Rizutto's business. Manny Fernandez runs it."

"Does Rizutto own the building?"

"No."

"Who owns the building?"

"Tonsmeyer Family Trust."

"Defuniak set it up?"

Braxton nodded.

"We need a verbal response for the tape."

"Yes."

"What about the warehouse? Who owns it?"

"The Trust."

"This Tonsmeyer Trust you mentioned?"

"Yes."

"Are you a beneficiary of that trust?"

"No."

"Was your wife?"

"Yes."

"Did she know you were using these buildings?"

"She knew about Panama Tan. As far as I know, she didn't know anything about the warehouse."

"Did the business pay rent to the Trust?"

"I don't know. I doubt it."

"What sort of business did Panama Tan conduct?"

"The women are prostitutes."

"What else?"

"Rizutto used the women in porn films, but that wasn't really part of the same business. That was sort of a side thing he added."

"Did they take out-calls?"

"I don't know. What's an out-call?"

"Did they go to other places? Hotel rooms. Parties."

"I don't think so."

"Did your wife ever try to have the business ... Panama Tan ... did she ever try to have them evicted or thrown out of the building?"

"I don't know. I never heard her complaining to anyone."

Connolly hadn't thought of that. A sick feeling rose in his stomach. Hayford would have known they were there. He might not know about every piece of property. Might not keep tabs on it all. But he knew about this one.

Hammond pressed on.

"How many different women worked at Panama Tan?"

Braxton shook his head.

"I have no way of knowing."

"Are the same ones there now as in the beginning? Has there been any turnover?"

"There's been turnover."

"What sort of turnover? What happened to them?"

"I don't know exactly what happened to them."

"But you have an idea."

"Yeah."

"What do you think happened?"

"Some of them were killed."

"What makes you think that?"

"One of them got sick. Really sick. She didn't look too good. Nobody wanted to use her. Manny sent her down to give blood."

A frown wrinkled Hammond's forehead.

"To give blood?"

"Yeah. The blood bank downtown tests you before they let you give. They tested her. She was positive for HIV."

"She died of AIDS?"

"No. Rizutto's driver picked her up one night. Took her for a ride. She never came back."

"Anyone else?"

"There was one who died while they were filming."

"What happened to her?"

"From what I hear, it got kind of rough. Had her tied up. Hitting her. I guess it got a little too rough."

"Who hit her?"

"I don't know his name. They brought him in from somewhere. Good-looking guy. Big build."

"What happened to her body?"

"Same thing. Rizutto's driver hauled her off."

"Do you know his name? The driver?"

Braxton shook his head.

"No. And I don't recall anyone ever calling him by name, actually."

"Rizutto must have called him something. What did he say to him when he wanted him? 'Hey you'?"

"Most of the time, he just gave him a look and sort of nodded. Sometimes he'd just say, 'Take care of it,' like he wasn't talking to anyone in particular. This guy, the driver, would step up, take care of it. He knew what to do. Rizutto didn't really have to say anything."

For the next hour, Braxton told them details about how the women came to Mobile. How he got involved. Manny Fernandez's role. Their regular routine. Names of customers. Finally, McNamara glanced at his watch.

"We need to get him back upstairs."

Hammond clicked off the recorder.

"All right." He shoved the recorder in his pocket. "We'll have to talk some more."

Braxton nodded.

"All right."

Hammond turned away and opened the door. McNamara glanced at Connolly.

"You want to talk to him?"

"Not now. Just take him back to his cell." He turned to Braxton. "I'll talk to you later."

Braxton nodded. Hammond held the door open and motioned for him to move. Braxton slid off the table and stepped out of the room. McNamara followed. Connolly came out last.

Forty-eight

*H*ammond took Braxton upstairs to the eighth floor while Connolly rode with McNamara in the elevator to the first floor. They waited there for Hammond to catch up. He arrived a few minutes later. Connolly leaned against a desk, arms folded across his chest.

"All right. Where are we?"

Hammond stood a few feet away.

"I talked to Sims, the detective that's handling Defuniak's case. He's not convinced it's a murder."

McNamara glanced over at Hammond.

"We need to check out Braxton's story. Let them investigate Defuniak. Sort through this."

Connolly shook his head.

"This can't wait."

Hammond frowned at him.

"What do you mean?"

"They killed Defuniak."

"Who?"

"Rizutto."

"You know that for a fact?"

"I don't have to know it for a fact. Look, the guy was murdered. I was there. I saw the house."

"Sims doesn't think so."

"I don't care what Sims thinks. The guy was murdered, and it has something to do with this case."

"How?"

Connolly felt uneasy. He wasn't sure how much he should tell them.

"I can't tell you all the details yet."

McNamara gave him a mocking laugh. Connolly glared at him. Hammond continued.

"You think they killed him?"

"I think Defuniak was in this up to his neck. He started making some noise. They took him out because he was a liability. If I'm right, they think Braxton has talked, too."

"And the women will disappear."

"Yes. They'll be gone by Monday."

Hammond sighed. McNamara looked away.

"Well, there's not much else we can do about it."

The veins in Connolly's neck throbbed.

"You could get a warrant."

"For who?"

"For Fernandez. For Rizutto."

"On what charge?"

"Prostitution. Murder. Conspiracy."

McNamara gave him a smirk.

"Doesn't work like that."

"Why not?"

"We can't just 'get' a warrant. Somebody has to sign off on it. You think I'm going down to the magistrate based on this? Without anyone's okay?"

"You have two witnesses. What more do you want?"

Hammond shoved his hands in his pockets.

"Well, it isn't happening tonight. And it won't happen before next week."

Connolly glared at him in frustration. Hammond scowled in response.

"What?"

Connolly shook his head in disgust.

"Nothing."

He turned away and started toward the lobby.

By the time Connolly reached the Chrysler, he was sure he was right. Raisa and the others would be gone long before Hammond and McNamara decided their careers were safe enough to do something about the situation. Rizutto would disappear. Fernandez would be in New Orleans. All they would find was an abandoned building.

From the jail, he drove down St. Joseph Street. Night was approaching. The fading evening sky was growing dark in the east. To the west, shades of purple and red streaked up from the horizon as the sun disappeared in the distance. Connolly lifted his foot from the gas pedal as he approached Dauphin Street. In his mind, he sorted through the options.

If he took the women and Rizutto fled, Braxton could be stuck with going to trial. If he waited, they could be gone and he'd be stuck with no one to corroborate Braxton's story, in which case Braxton would be going to trial. Waiting was the safe thing to do. If he waited, at least he would be protected. The criminal case might fall apart, but Connolly wouldn't have to stick his neck out for anyone.

He smiled as he answered himself.

"Safety is for wimps."

He placed his foot against the gas pedal. The car picked up speed. He continued past Dauphin Street and crossed Government to Church Street. There, he turned right and brought the car to a stop in front of St. Pachomius Church. He took the cell phone from his pocket and punched in a number. Father Scott answered on the third ring.

"Catch you at a bad time?"

"No. Just finished supper."

"We need to talk."

"Okay. Come on by."

Father Scott lived in a house on Monterey Street in midtown. To get there, Connolly drove back to Government Street and turned left. At Broad Street, the traffic light caught him. While he waited, he placed a phone call to Hollis. The call rolled over to voice mail. Connolly pressed a button to end the call, then hit redial. Hollis answered.

"What do you want?"

"Where are you?"

"Fishing."

"I need your help."

"Doing what?"

"Can't get into it now. Meet me at the guesthouse."

"When?"

"How soon can you be there?"

"About an hour."

"That'll work."

The traffic light changed. Monterey Street was less than a block away. Connolly switched off the phone and made the turn to the right. A moment later, he brought the Chrysler to a stop at the curb in front of the house and walked across the lawn. Father Scott met him at the door.

"What's up?"

"Can we talk inside?"

"Sure."

Father Scott led him through the house to his study off the den and closed the door. Connolly didn't bother taking a seat. They stood facing each other in the center of the room.

"I need you to do something for me."

"Okay."

"I need you to get a message to someone."

Father Scott gave him an awkward look.

"All right."

Connolly shifted his weight from one leg to the other.

"Look, I know this sounds strange, but I really need you to do it."

Father Scott's face softened.

"What did you have in mind?"

"I need you to go to Panama Tan."

Father Scott gave him a pained look. Connolly continued.

"It's a tanning salon on Airline Highway. You know where it is?"

"I've seen the sign."

"I need you to go there tonight and tell—"

Father Scott looked alarmed.

"Tonight?"

"Yes. Tonight. A woman named Raisa works there. Petite." He gestured with his hand. "A little shorter than some. Brown hair ... they all have brown hair. Look, you'll know her. If you can't figure out who she is, just ask for her."

"Ask for her? What does she do there?"

Connolly folded his arms across his chest and tried not to smile.

"It's a front for a prostitution operation."

Father Scott took a step back.

"Prostitution? I can't—"

"You told me you'd help."

"I know, but tomorrow is ..."

"Look, you're always telling me I have access to people you never see. I'm giving you a chance to see some of them. I need you to do this."

"I wouldn't know what to do."

"It's easy. You show up like you're a priest who's going to this place and you don't want anyone to know about it."

"That'll be easy."

"You park in back. Go inside. Nobody will see you. They'll bring out the women who are available. They'll parade them out for you to choose."

A wisp of a smile moved across Father Scott's face.

"Sounds like you've been to these places before."

Connolly felt his cheeks blush. His lips stretched tight against his teeth in a nervous smile.

"Uhh ... never mind where I've been." He took a breath. "One of the ladies who comes out with them will do the talking. That woman will probably be Raisa. Choose her. She'll take you off to a room. When you're in there, she'll lock the door. After she does that, you get her close and give her the message."

"Get her close?"

"Yeah. You know. Like you want her to do whatever it is people do in there. They're used to sweaty, gross guys wallowing on them. She won't greet you with open arms, but you can get close to her."

"Why?"

"Because they probably have a camera in there so they can watch what goes on."

"Won't they know if nothing happens?"

"Yeah."

"So, how do we get around that?"

"Tell her to dance for you."

"Dance for me?"

"Yeah."

"What kind of dance?"

"She'll know what to do."

"Will she take off her clothes?"

"Yes."

Father Scott's mouth fell open.

"I can't sit there and watch her take off her clothes."

"Lower your head and close your eyes."

Father Scott sighed.

"What's the message?"

"Tell her I sent you and that we leave tonight."

"'We leave tonight.'"

"Right."

"She knows who I am?"

"No. Just tell her ..." Connolly hesitated. He was making up the plan as he went. "Tell ... tell her we'll pick them all up on the street behind the building where they live."

"This doesn't sound like much of a plan."

"It's not, but it's the best I could come up with on short notice. Just tell her I'll meet them there."

"You think she'll understand?"

"I don't know. But I don't have much choice."

Father Scott gave him a look.

"What's going on?"

"Things have changed. They have to get out. Now." He gave Father Scott a questioning look. "Will you do it?"

Father Scott took a deep breath. He looked away and ran his hands through his hair as if thinking it over. Finally, he turned back.

"Yeah. I'll do it."

He opened the door. Connolly followed him through the house. When they reached the front door, Father Scott called upstairs.

"I'm going out for a little while."

A woman appeared at the top of the steps.

"Okay. Everything all right?"

"Yeah." He smiled up at her. "Everything's fine. I'll be back in a little while."

Connolly opened the door and stepped outside. Father Scott followed him down the front steps.

"I assume I shouldn't tell anyone about this."

"I wouldn't. Just call me after you leave the salon. Let me know what happened."

"All right."

Father Scott disappeared around the corner of the house. Connolly crossed the yard to the Chrysler. He waited as Father Scott backed out of the drive, then turned the Chrysler in the opposite direction.

Forty-nine

The sun was gone by the time Connolly turned onto Tuttle Street. He steered the car into the driveway at the Pleiades and rolled quietly past the mansion. Lights on the first floor glowed through the front windows. Connected to a timer to create the illusion someone was home, they came on each evening at six. Connolly glanced at his watch. It was seven thirty. The day had been a long one. He felt tired.

At the end of the drive, he brought the Chrysler to a stop a few feet from the guesthouse. He climbed out of the car and walked inside.

In the refrigerator, he found a leftover piece of chicken and an overripe tomato. He stuck the chicken in his mouth and held it with his teeth while he set the tomato on the counter. A jar of mayonnaise sat behind a milk carton. He took out the milk, opened the carton, and sniffed. The odor wrinkled his nose. He set it in the sink, then took out the mayonnaise. He screwed off the lid and smelled it.

"Not too bad," he mumbled. "Not as bad as the milk."

He closed the refrigerator door and took a bite of the chicken he'd been holding in his mouth. As he ripped the bite from the bone, he knew it was no good. He spit the mouthful into the sink and threw the rest in the trash.

In a cabinet above the counter he found a loaf of sandwich bread. Plates were in the next cabinet. He took one out, set it on the countertop, and laid two pieces of bread on it. He spread some of the mayonnaise on the bread, added two slices of tomato, and folded it into a sandwich. He took a bite while standing at the counter, then carried the plate to the table to eat the rest.

Three bites later, the door opened. Hollis entered. Connolly glanced at him, then turned back to the sandwich.

"Catch any fish?"

"Not many."

Hollis walked to the kitchen sink and washed his hands.

"You got anything to eat?"

"Tomato sandwich."

Hollis took a slice of bread and slathered on some mayonnaise. Connolly heard the sound of the knife in the jar. Hollis leaned against the counter and talked while he ate.

"This bread is stale."

Connolly didn't bother to look.

"There's some Coke in the cabinet. Ice in the freezer."

Hollis opened the cabinet and took out a can of Coca-Cola.

"These chips any good?"

Connolly glanced toward the kitchen.

"I don't know. Can't remember when they were opened."

He heard the bag rustle as Hollis shoved his hand inside.

"Not too bad."

Hollis opened the refrigerator door. Connolly heard a clinking sound as he filled a glass with ice. The Coke fizzed as Hollis poured it over the ice.

"What did you want me to help you with?"

"We have to get those women out of that warehouse."

"Get them out? Where are we going to take them?"

"I'm not sure."

"You're not sure?"

"Depends on how many there are."

"I thought we counted twelve."

Connolly finished his sandwich. He rose from the table and carried the plate to the sink.

"We did. But they come and go."

"So what's the plan? We just wait around till morning and go get them?"

Connolly took a handful of chips from the bag.

"I sent a message to Raisa. Told her we were coming to get them tonight."

"Tonight?"

"Yeah."

"How'd you get her a message?"

"I got someone to go to the salon."

Hollis took another bite of his sandwich.

"That must not have been too hard. Did you offer to pay?"

Connolly felt his heart sink.

"Oh no!"

"What?"

"I forgot to tell him about paying."

"Forgot to tell who?"

"Father Scott."

"Who is Father Scott?"

"My priest."

"Your priest!" Hollis blurted. Bits of sandwich flew from his mouth. "You sent a priest to a whorehouse?"

Connolly grinned.

"It was the best I could do." His look turned sober. "But I forgot to tell him about paying."

Connolly's cell phone rang, interrupting them. He took it from his pocket and flipped it open. The call was from Father Scott.

"It's done."

"Have any trouble?"

"You didn't tell me about paying."

"How much was it?"

Hollis started to laugh, then choked on a bite of sandwich. He moved down the hallway, coughing and laughing. Father Scott seemed not to notice the commotion in the background.

"A hundred dollars."

Connolly did his best not to laugh.

"Did you close your eyes?"

"Yes."

"Are you sure?"

"Leave me alone. I'll have to take a bath in holy water after this."

"Did she say anything?"

"They'll be waiting for you."

"All right."

Connolly switched off the phone. Hollis returned to the kitchen.

"How much did it cost him?"

"A hundred dollars."

Hollis laughed.

"A priest in a whorehouse!"

Connolly leaned against the counter.

"Okay. He told them we're coming to get them. We have to decide how to do this. I can get four in the backseat and two up front."

Hollis shook his head.

"They're skinny. You can get five in the back."

"Maybe. What about your truck?"

"Three in the front seat. We can pile them all in the back."

Connolly shook his head.

"Somebody'll see them."

"Oh, like they aren't going to notice a middle-aged man in an antique Chrysler with prostitutes hanging out the window."

"They might. But the police will stop you if they see them in the back of your truck. They won't stop me."

"Seven in yours. Three with me. That's ten."

"If there's more than that, two can ride in the trunk."

Hollis nodded.

"Where are we taking them?"

Connolly sighed, thinking.

"We can take some of them to Mrs. Gordon's."

"You set this up with her?"

"Nope."

Hollis gave him a skeptical look. Connolly shrugged.

"It'll be all right. We can bring the rest here."

Hollis grinned.

"You're going to spend the night with a house full of—"

Connolly held up his hand to stop him. He gave him a stern look.

"They're not prostitutes."

"They sell their bodies for sex. They're—"

"Women. That's all. Women. Women caught in a desperate situation."

"Who would do anything for money."

"You've done some pretty tough things to survive, haven't you?"

Hollis didn't reply. Connolly moved to the living room. Hollis followed him.

"So, what are we doing?"

"We're waiting."

Connolly dropped onto the couch. He picked up the remote control for the television and switched it on. Hollis sat in a chair nearby and sipped from the glass of Coke.

Sometime later, Connolly awoke to find Hollis asleep in the chair, his feet propped on the coffee table. Connolly glanced at his watch. It was one in the morning. He rubbed his eyes and stood.

He walked to the kitchen and turned on the coffeemaker. Hollis moved his feet from the table and sat up straight.

"What time is it?"

"One."

Hollis ran his hands over his face and yawned.

"Want to go about three?"

"Two."

"Two? They'll just be getting there."

"I know, but I don't want them standing around out there waiting on us."

Hollis twisted his body around to one side of the chair. He laid his head on the armrest and closed his eyes.

"Wake me when the coffee's ready."

Connolly walked down the hall. He took a shower and changed clothes. When he returned, the coffee was ready. He poured a cup and carried it to the living room. He set it on the table and nudged Hollis.

"Sit up."

Hollis opened his eyes and stared at him. Connolly gave him a smile.

"Coffee's ready."

Hollis squirmed to a sitting position and took the coffee cup with both hands.

"You think this will work?"

He took a sip of coffee.

Connolly checked his watch.

"I don't know. But we're about to find out. Drink up."

Fifty

At one thirty, Connolly and Hollis walked out of the guesthouse. Hollis stepped to his pickup. Connolly opened the door to the Chrysler.

"Think we ought to go around and come in the other way?"

"You mean come down from Chickasaw?"

"Yeah."

"Nah." Hollis shook his head. "But we're leaving too early. Let's pull in behind the drive-in at Tidewater Bank and wait for them to go by."

Connolly gave him a puzzled look.

"Tidewater?"

"Yeah. Down at the foot of St. Michael Street."

Connolly nodded.

"All right."

He got in the Chrysler. Hollis started the pickup. Connolly led the way down the drive.

At Government Street, they turned right. The streets were empty and quiet. Ten minutes later they turned onto St. Michael and came to the intersection at Water Street. In front of them, warehouses lined the wharfs along the river across the street. Office buildings stood to the left. The Tidewater Bank drive-through sat on the corner to the right.

Connolly pulled into the shadows behind the building and switched off the lights. Hollis drove in behind him and stepped out of the truck. He came alongside the Chrysler and leaned against the driver's door. Connolly spoke to him through the open window.

"Think they'll see us?"

Hollis shook his head.

"Nah."

He took a package of chewing gum from his pocket and offered it to Connolly. Connolly shook his head. Hollis took a stick from the package and popped it in his mouth.

"Tell me something." He paused as he returned the chewing gum package to his pocket. "Suppose we get these women out of there. And suppose we find a place for them to sleep tonight. What are you going to do with them tomorrow?"

"I don't know."

"Think maybe you should have given that a little thought?"

"Yeah."

To the right, headlights washed over the row of warehouses across Water Street. Hollis crouched beside the Chrysler.

"Here comes a car."

The beam of light moved in their direction. Connolly slid low in the seat. They watched as a Chevrolet Suburban turned off Government onto Water Street and drove past. Behind it was a large black BMW.

"That's them," Connolly whispered.

When they were gone, Hollis stood. He stretched his arms over his head, then leaned against the car.

"Why did you choose the priest?"

"Only person I could think of they didn't already know."

Hollis chuckled.

"Priest in a whorehouse."

"You think they tape what goes on there?"

Hollis cut his eyes at him.

"What do you think?"

"Wonder what they do with them."

"I don't know. Great for blackmail."

"Blackmail?"

"Yeah. Catch somebody in there. Politician. A priest. Somebody like that. Get them on tape. Powerful stuff."

Before long, the Suburban returned. Connolly scanned the street behind it.

"Where's the BMW?"

"I don't know."

Connolly sat up in the seat.

"We better go."

"We better wait."

"No telling what they're doing over there."

Connolly reached for the ignition. Hollis grabbed his hand.

"You can't protect them right now."

Connolly strained to reach the ignition.

"We have to try."

Hollis had a firm grip on his wrist.

"Mike."

Connolly looked at him, desperate to go.

"We have to do something!"

"We will. But we can't do anything if we're dead."

They stared at each other. Hollis pulled Connolly's hand away from the ignition.

"Just wait."

Connolly relaxed. Hollis let go of his wrist. They waited in silence.

Ten minutes later, the BMW drove past. They watched as it disappeared around the corner on Government Street. Hollis ran his hands through his hair.

"Okay." He sighed. "Now we go."

Connolly led the way out of the parking lot onto Water Street. They turned left and wound through the warehouse district to Morgan Street. A few minutes later, they passed the corner at Conception Street Road. They continued to the next corner, then turned right onto the street that ran behind the warehouse. Connolly brought the car to a stop near the place where he and Raisa had met with Hammond in Hollis's pickup a few nights before. He scanned the darkness for any sign of the women. After a minute or two, he pressed the gas pedal and moved slowly forward. Hollis followed.

At the corner, they turned left and made the block. The second time by, he saw Raisa standing near the curb. In her hand she held a small leather bag. He brought the car to a stop beside her and waved her over.

"Come on. Get in."

She hurried to the car and opened the front door. Behind her, the other women emerged from the bushes. Connolly watched as they climbed in the backseat. Raisa slid next to him. Two others squeezed in beside her. Raisa was pressed against him. The smell of cheap perfume and stale cigarette smoke filled the car.

More women stood outside the car, unable to find a seat. Connolly pointed behind him to Hollis's truck.

"They can ride in the truck."

Raisa said something to them. The women hesitated. She said something else. Then they hurried to the truck. Someone closed the car door. Connolly turned to look at the backseat.

"One, two, three ..."

Five women were crammed in back. Three sat beside him in front. Each of them brought a single, small handbag. Connolly turned to face forward.

"How many are there?"

"Eleven."

"I thought there were twelve."

"They took Elsa."

"When?"

"Tonight."

Connolly felt his heart drop into his stomach.

"Where did they take her?"

"I do not know."

"Who took her?"

"Mr. Rizutto."

Connolly put his foot on the gas pedal, then hesitated. If Rizutto brought her back, he'd know the women were gone. He glanced at Raisa. She smiled at him. In his heart he knew he had no choice but to go. He pressed the gas pedal. The car started forward. Hollis followed.

In a few minutes, they reached the train station and turned left onto Water Street. At Government, they turned right and drove toward midtown. They made it to Mrs. Gordon's house on Houston Street without any trouble. Connolly parked at the curb and got out. Hollis brought the truck to a stop behind him.

The house was a two-bedroom 1920s bungalow with white clapboard siding and aluminum awnings. It had a large front porch and a tiny patch of grass for a yard. A tall cedar tree stood on one side, a narrow driveway ran along the other.

Connolly walked up the front steps to the porch and rang the doorbell. A few seconds later, he rang it again and pounded on the door. A light came on in the hall. Mrs. Gordon called from inside.

"Who is it?"

"It's me. Mike."

"Mike who?"

"Mike Connolly. Open up."

She peeked out from behind the curtain that covered the leaded glass window in the door. Their eyes met. She scowled at him and closed the curtain. The lock made a rattling sound as she opened the door.

"What are you doing here at this time of night?"

She wore a bulky housecoat that was tied at the waist and fell just below her knees. Underneath, she had on a pink nightgown that came to her ankles. On her feet she wore puffy pink slippers. Connolly found it difficult to suppress a grin.

"I need your help."

She was already looking past him.

"Who is that with you?"

"Hollis."

"Not him. Those women."

Connolly glanced over his shoulder. In the light of the porch the

Chrysler was an odd sight. Five women crammed into the back. Three sitting up front. All of them dressed for work. It looked like a rolling party.

"That's what I need help with."

Mrs. Gordon dug her hand in the pocket of her housecoat and took out a pair of glasses.

"If you expect me to bail you out with a bunch of women—"

Connolly cut her off.

"These aren't just any women."

She scowled at him.

"No kidding."

"They're ..."

"I can see what they are."

She adjusted the glasses on her nose. Connolly dropped his gaze to the floor.

"It's not what it looks like."

"That's what men always say."

Connolly smiled. Mrs. Gordon was awake now. She moved past him to the porch.

"This ought to be interesting."

Her voice had a dry, knowing tone. Connolly tried to explain.

"They've been shuttled around ..."

She turned to him again.

"So, what do you want me to do?"

"I need a place for them to stay. I can take two or three to the guesthouse. But I don't have anywhere for the rest."

"How many are there?"

"Eleven."

Mrs. Gordon did not respond immediately. She just stood there staring at them. Finally, she turned away and started in the house.

"Bring them inside."

"How many?"

She brushed past him as she moved through the doorway.

"All of them."

"All of them?"

"You can't keep them at your house. Hurry up. Before someone sees them out there."

Connolly moved down the steps to the car.

Fifty-one

The following morning, Connolly was awakened by the phone on the nightstand. He crawled across the bed to answer it. The call was from Mrs. Gordon.

"I fed them breakfast, but I need something for lunch."

He squinted at the clock.

"What time is it?"

"Nine."

He lay back against the pillow.

"What do you want me to get?"

"Anything, as long as it'll feed a dozen people."

"Everything else all right?"

"Yes. We're fine."

"Nobody suspicious coming around?"

"No. How long are they going to be here?"

"I don't know."

"You need to figure that out."

"Okay."

He rolled over and hung up the phone, then dragged himself to a sitting position on the edge of the bed. As he sat there, the reality of what he had done began to sink in. The women were safe. He and Hollis had rescued them from the warehouse; now he had to follow through.

Then he remembered Hammond.

A pang of guilt jabbed him in the stomach. Slowly, he leaned forward and stretched his arm toward the chair by the door where his pants lay. His shoulder was stiff and his muscles ached.

Staying out all night didn't used to be this rough.

He hooked a belt loop with his finger and pulled the pants to his lap. The cell phone was in a front pocket. He flipped it open and scrolled down the phone log to Hammond's number. Hammond answered on the third ring.

"Don't you have a life?"

Connolly ignored the tone in his voice.

"I took the women."

"What?"

Hammond's voice was so loud it hurt Connolly's ear.

"I took the women from the warehouse last night. If you want Rizutto and Fernandez, I suggest you get moving."

This time, he held the phone away from his ear as Hammond responded.

"I don't believe this!" His voice was even louder than before. "You have just destroyed the whole thing! You are unbelievable. You know that? Unbelievable!"

Connolly moved the phone toward his ear to respond, but Hammond continued to shout.

"Always think you know better than anyone else. Well, you don't. You don't!"

Connolly heard Hammond take a breath. He placed the phone to his ear.

"Fernandez will be at the warehouse by ten to pick them up."

He moved the phone away from his ear for Hammond's reply.

"Forget Fernandez. I've a good mind to come over there and throw your white—"

Connolly interrupted him.

"Anthony?"

"What?"

"I have eleven witnesses willing to testify against him on charges of prostitution ..."

"And I'll have you arrested for obstruction of justice."

Connolly continued.

"... sexual misconduct, rape, assault, battery, kidnapping, extortion. You want me to go on?"

Hammond sounded unconvinced, but he wasn't shouting anymore.

"What do you think you're doing?"

"When you get—"

"No! I want to know. What did you think you were doing?"

Connolly ignored the question.

"When you get Fernandez, you'll have the man who can give you Rizutto and his driver. The whole thing will come tumbling down."

"You're the one who's tumbling—"

Connolly forced himself to speak with an even, calm tone.

"You have Braxton. You have eleven witnesses. If you move now, you can have Fernandez for sure."

"This is—"

Connolly could stand it no more. He shouted into the phone.

"Anthony!"

"What?"

"You're wasting time. Get Fernandez."

Connolly switched off the phone. He tossed it on the bed and trudged down the hall to the shower. Thirty minutes later, he was dressed and headed out the door.

From the guesthouse, he drove out Government Street to the Winn-Dixie grocery store at Broad Street. He filled a shopping cart with everything he could think of and arrived at Mrs. Gordon's house a little after eleven. He parked the car in the driveway near the back door, gathered all the grocery sacks he could manage, and went inside.

Mrs. Gordon met him in the kitchen.

"What did you buy?"

"Stuff." He set the bags on the counter and started out the door. "There's more in the car."

The door banged closed behind him. It took four trips to the car to bring it all in the house. He set the last load on the kitchen table.

Mrs. Gordon looked through the sacks.

"So, what's for lunch?"

Connolly reached in a bag and pulled out a package of meat.

"Hamburgers." He reached in another bag. "Turkey sandwiches. The bread's in a sack on the counter." He grabbed another bag. "Chicken. Steaks in a sack somewhere. A roast. Two, actually." He turned to Mrs. Gordon. "If that doesn't work, we can order pizza."

She glanced around the kitchen.

"Looks like you bought enough for a day or two."

"My American Express card was screaming. Got enough bonus points for a free vacation."

Mrs. Gordon stepped to the end of the counter and found a sack full of produce. She took out two tomatoes and an onion.

"Hamburgers."

Connolly gave her a puzzled frown.

"Hamburgers?"

"We'll have hamburgers. The grill's outside. You're in charge. Did you get any potato chips?"

Connolly pointed to a sack on the table.

"Two bags. Right there."

"Get moving. Takes a while to get it ready."

Connolly pushed the sacks aside to make room on the counter and took out the hamburger meat. Mrs. Gordon pointed to the sink.

"Wash your hands first."

He washed his hands, opened the meat, and started pressing out hamburger patties.

Before he finished with the meat, the back door opened. Raisa stepped inside. In her hand she carried a shopping bag. She smiled at him as she passed through the kitchen. Behind her, Barbara came through the door. The smile on Connolly's face faded to a blank stare. Barbara grinned at him.

"Surprised?"

"Where have you two been?"

"Shopping."

Barbara moved to one side. Two more women from the warehouse came in behind her, each with a shopping bag. They disappeared down the hall beyond the kitchen. Connolly stared at Barbara. She shrugged.

"They had to have something to wear."

"Think it's safe for them to be out? I mean, what if somebody sees them?"

"I don't think the men they worked for will be where we're going."

She moved out of sight down the hall. Connolly heard her voice.

"Who's next?"

A moment later she appeared in the kitchen again, followed by three more women. She called to Mrs. Gordon as they moved toward the door.

"When were you planning to eat?"

Mrs. Gordon glanced at the clock on the stove.

"How about twelve thirty. Give you enough time?"

"Maybe. If we aren't back by then, save something for us."

Barbara smiled at Connolly as she disappeared out the back door.

Mrs. Gordon stood at the far end of the counter, slicing tomatoes and onions. She gave Connolly a look.

"Well, what was I supposed to do? They don't have clothes, other than those ... things they had on last night. They can't wear that any-where."

Connolly laid the patty in his hand on a platter with the others.

"I'm not complaining."

Mrs. Gordon finished with the tomatoes and onions. She rinsed her hands in the sink.

"Who else could I have called?"

"It's fine. It's fine." Connolly laid the last burger on the platter. "I just didn't expect to see her."

Mrs. Gordon dried her hands on a towel.

"Better get the grill ready."

Fifty-two

After lunch, Connolly wandered into Mrs. Gordon's living room. He took a seat in an armchair near the window and listened as the women talked among themselves. Raisa came from across the room. He stood as she approached.

"Would you like this chair?"

"No." She shook her head. "I will sit on the floor."

Connolly walked into the dining room and brought a chair. He pointed to the chair he'd been using.

"Sit."

Raisa took a seat. Connolly sat on the dining chair. She smiled at him.

"You were very brave to come and get us."

Connolly shrugged.

"It was nothing."

"What will happen to us now?"

"I'm not sure."

"Do you think they are looking for us?"

"I don't know."

From the kitchen, Connolly heard the back door open. He glanced down the hall to see Barbara enter with the women she'd taken shopping. They walked through the house to the living room. Her eyes darted from Connolly to Raisa, then away. She handed the bag in her hand to one of the women with her, then returned to the kitchen. Connolly excused himself and followed her.

"Get everything they need?"

"No. But we found enough for now."

Connolly opened the refrigerator and took out a container.

"Hungry?"

"Yes."

"Have a seat. I'll fix you a hamburger."

She took a seat at the kitchen table. He set the food on the counter and took a plate from the cabinet. He heard Barbara's shoes hit the floor as she kicked them off.

"Tired?"

"Not too bad." She paused a moment. "You know, she likes you."

Connolly gave her a look over his shoulder.

"Who?"

"The one you were talking to. What's her name?"

"Raisa."

"She likes you."

"I don't think so."

"Oh, I think so. Talked about you the whole time we were in the store." There was a playful, needling tone in her voice.

"Where'd you go?"

"Parisian's. I'm not kidding. She likes you."

"She's just a woman in a desperate situation."

"And you're her knight in shining armor."

He turned toward her.

"They were living in a warehouse. I couldn't leave them there. They'd been—"

Just then, his cell phone rang. Barbara grinned.

"Saved by the bell."

Connolly took the phone from his pocket. The call was from Hammond.

"All right, Mike Connolly. We arrested Manny Fernandez."

"Good."

"Rizutto and his driver got away."

"Not good."

"No. It's not. Fernandez is asking for you."

"Where is he?"

"He's with us right now. We're at the tanning salon. You can talk to him later. At the jail. Where are those women?"

"They're safe."

"I want to see them."

"Why?"

"I need to get a statement from them."

"You'll need an interpreter."

"Great." Hammond's voice had a sarcastic tone. "Know any?"

"I'll see what I can arrange."

"When can I see them?"

"Soon as I figure out a safe way to do it."

Connolly pressed a button on his phone and ended the call. Barbara caught his eye.

"Trouble?"

"Not yet."

When he finished putting the hamburger together, he placed it in the microwave. After a few seconds, he took it out and set it on the table in front of her. She smiled at him.

"You should have done this more often."

He took a pitcher of tea from the refrigerator and poured a glass for her.

"I have to go." He set the glass by her plate. "I'll be back after while."

"I'll be gone before you get back."

By then he was already to the hallway. He paused and turned toward her. Their eyes met.

"Thanks."

She smiled.

"You're welcome."

He moved through the living room to the front door and onto the porch. As he walked down the steps, a gray Lexus drove slowly past the house. The driver stared out the window. He had one hand on the steering wheel, the other held a piece of paper. The man glanced at the paper, then back to the house. Their eyes met. The man looked away. The car continued down the street.

Connolly walked around the corner of the house to the Chrysler and backed the car out of the driveway. The Lexus was stopped a little way down the street. Connolly turned the Chrysler in that direction.

As he got closer, the Lexus moved forward. In the next block, Connolly could see the tag on the car was a local number. A little farther, the car slowed and turned left into a driveway. A woman came from the house. She smiled and waved at the man in the Lexus. Connolly relaxed.

He continued down Houston to Dauphin Street, turned right, and drove toward the office.

As he drove, he thought of the women back at Mrs. Gordon's. What they really needed was a place to hang out for a while. A safe place to stay. Not an agency to resettle them. Not a detective to interview them. They just needed a safe place. Someplace close enough that he could get to them, but far enough away that no one would stumble across them.

By the time he crossed Broad Street, afternoon was fading into evening. The heat of the day had lifted. People were out for a stroll down the sidewalks. A couple sat on the grass in the park across from St. Alban Cathedral. The fountain was on, spraying water in the air. Music drifted into the street through the open door of a bar. He brought the Chrysler to a stop at the curb in front of the office building and stepped out.

Across the street, the shade in Bienville Square was already dark. A man sat alone on a bench, his hair shaggy and unkempt, his clothes wrinkled and dirty. He leaned against a black plastic garbage bag that sat beside him. Before long, the shadows around him would be swallowed by the night. The bench would become his bed.

Connolly turned away and started toward the building, but the sight of that man with the garbage bag sent his thoughts in another direction, to his brother and that day as young boys when they crammed what they could carry into a pillowcase and hitchhiked to their uncle's house in Bayou La Batre. Connolly went to law school. Rick became a doctor, a successful one at that. Big practice in Birmingham. A smile spread across Connolly's face. A lawyer and a doctor from nothing but trinkets in a pillowcase.

He crossed the sidewalk toward the lobby entrance. His mind rambled on from one thought to the next. Then, as he reached for the door, he froze.

Rick owned a house on the beach at Cape San Blas, a remote strip of Florida beach east of ... everything.

"It's perfect."

He took the cell phone from his pocket and punched in his brother's number.

"Hey."

"Mike. What's up?"

"You busy?"

"Not now. Just finished eighteen holes. Sitting here, relaxing in the clubhouse. What's going on?"

"Is anyone using your beach house?"

"No. Why?"

"I need it for a week or two."

"Yeah ... sure." There was a pause. "Everything all right?"

"Everything's fine."

"You know, I could take a few days off. Come down. We could go over to Bud and Allie's. Get some seafood."

"Actually, I have some people who need a place to stay."

"Oh ..."

"It's all right. They're okay. They just need a place to stay where no one will find them."

"Okay."

"No. Really. They won't tear the place up."

"Mike, I believe you. It's not a problem. I'll make sure no one bothers them."

"You sure?"

"Sure I'm sure. You can tell me all about it when it's over."

"Thanks."

Connolly switched off the phone and started back to the Chrysler.

At Monterey Street, Connolly turned left and drove to Father Scott's house. He parked out front and knocked on the door. Father Scott had a pleasant look on his face as he opened the door, but it vanished when he saw Connolly on the doorstep.

"I'm not sure I should let you in."

The tone of his voice indicated he was only half joking. Connolly gave him an awkward smile.

"I need another favor."

Father Scott stepped outside and closed the door behind him. They moved down the steps and stood near the driveway.

"What is it this time? Need me to visit someone in a massage parlor?"

Connolly ignored the question.

"I need to take those women from the tanning salon to my brother's beach house in—"

Father Scott was already waving his hands in protest.

"No. No. No. I did my part. It's somebody else's turn."

"There isn't anyone else."

"How are you going to haul all those women around?"

"Doesn't your church have a van?"

"Yes."

"I need you to drive them."

"Why me?"

"Because you're one of the few people I can trust."

Father Scott's face turned sober.

"Where is this beach house?"

"Cape San Blas."

"In Florida?"

"Yes."

"That's all the way on the other side of Panama City."

"It's a long way."

"Take all day to get there."

"More like all night."

Father Scott grimaced.

"All night?"

"We need to get them out of here now. Tonight."

"How many are there?"

"Eleven."

Father Scott dropped his head. He stared at the ground a moment.
"All right." He lifted his head and smiled. "When do we leave?"
Connolly glanced at his watch.
"It's five now. What about seven?"
"Okay. Seven."
"You want me to get someone to go with you?"
"You have someone in mind?"
"Yes."
Father Scott nodded.
"Might not be a bad idea."
Connolly shook Father Scott's hand and started across the lawn toward the Chrysler. Father Scott called to him.
"Hey, where will I meet you?"
"Get the van and gas it up. I'll call you with the address."

Fifty-three

onnolly turned the car around in front of Father Scott's house and drove down Monterey to Dauphin Street. While he waited at the corner for traffic to pass, he called Hollis.

"I need you."

"What for?"

"Can't say. Meet me at the guesthouse. You'll be gone overnight."

"Who said I'm going?"

"Meet me in half an hour."

Connolly switched off the phone. The traffic light changed. He tossed the phone on the seat and drove to Mrs. Gordon's.

Raisa was sitting in the living room as he entered the house. He motioned for her to follow him. She went with him to the kitchen. Mrs. Gordon stood at the sink. She glanced over her shoulder at him.

"Where have you been? We need to get started on supper. I'm not doing all of this by myself."

"I have a solution."

"To what?"

"To where they can stay for a while."

Mrs. Gordon dried her hands on a towel and turned to face him.

"And what might that be?"

"Rick has a house at Cape San Blas. They can stay there."

"Rick? Your brother, Rick?"

"Yes."

"When did you talk to him?"

"A little while ago. But they need to leave now."

"They haven't eaten supper."

"They can eat something on the way."

"How are you going to get them over there?"

"Father Scott will drive them."

"The priest from St. Pachomius?"

"Yes."

Mrs. Gordon laughed.

"This is going to look good."

Raisa interrupted them. She had a puzzled look on her face.

"We are going somewhere?"

"Yes. You're going to the beach."

She frowned. He grinned at her.

"Sun. Sand. Waves."

She smiled.

"The beach?"

"Yes. The beach. My brother owns a house on the beach in Florida. It's a few hours away from here, but you'll be safe there. Not many people go there."

The smile on her face grew wider.

"I have never been to the beach."

"You'll have fun."

"Will you be there?"

"No. But Hollis will go with you and help you get settled."

Her countenance changed.

"Hollis?"

"The man who was with me last night. The man in the pickup truck."

She nodded her head and stepped away.

"I will tell the others."

She disappeared down the hall toward the living room. Mrs. Gordon stepped past Connolly and moved across the kitchen.

"She likes you."

He gave her a smirk.

"Right."

Mrs. Gordon was almost to the back door.

"I can see it in her eyes."

"She's in a vulnerable position. What you see is fear."

"What I see is ..."

"Myrtice."

She jerked her head around at him, smiling.

"You've never called me that."

"Where are you going?"

"To the garage. I have an ice chest out there. We need to pack up all that food you bought so they can take it with them."

While Mrs. Gordon helped Raisa and the others get ready, Connolly drove to the guesthouse. Hollis was waiting by the pickup when he arrived.

"What's so urgent this time?"

"You and Father Scott are taking the women to my brother's beach house."

"Where's that?"

"Cape San Blas. You know where it is?"

"Other side of Port St. Joe. Over towards Apalachicola."

"Right. When you turn off Highway 98 to go out on the Cape, you're on Highway 30. Seems like you're going forever. Somewhere out there, you'll pass a café on the right called Simone's."

"Simone's?"

"Yeah."

"Like, Nina Simone?"

"I doubt Nina ever saw this place. But yeah. Simone. You'll know it when you see it. It's the first thing you come to." He paused for a moment. "It may be the only thing you come to. Anyway, about two miles past Simone's the road makes a right and runs along the Gulf. A mile past the turn you'll see a sign on the right that says 'On Call.'"

"On Call?"

"Yeah. That's the name of the house. Sits back from the road, sort of behind a sand berm. The Gulf is across the road in front of it." Connolly glanced at his watch. "We need to get over to Mrs. Gordon's. You need to get them on the road."

Hollis moved to the driver's door and climbed in the truck.

"Anybody there besides us?"

"Not supposed to be. If someone's there, tell them Rick said you could stay there and give me a call. The house has five or six bedrooms. They can figure it out. They can look around and find some swimsuits. They're usually hanging on the back porch."

"What will they eat?"

"You're taking it with you." Connolly took a handful of bills from his pocket. He gave them to Hollis. "Take this with you. Make sure they have everything they need before you leave to come back. They'll be stuck out there when you're gone."

Hollis took the money and shoved it in his pants pocket.

"All right. This ... Father Scott. He knows where we're going?"

Connolly closed the truck door. They spoke through the open window.

"He knows you're going to Cape San Blas. He doesn't know where the house is. I'll let you tell him." Connolly stepped back from the truck to leave, then hesitated. "That reminds me. I need to call him." He turned away. "Let's get over to Mrs. Gordon's."

Hollis started the truck. The sound of the engine reminded

Connolly of one more thing. He gestured with his hand for Hollis to wait.

"Leave the truck here. I'll give you a ride."

Hollis scowled at him as he switched off the engine and rolled up the window. Connolly walked to the Chrysler and opened the car door. He reached inside and took the cell phone from the seat. Leaning against the car, he punched in the number, then turned to Hollis.

"Sorry about that. I don't know what I was thinking. Let's leave your truck here instead of on the street over there."

Hollis shrugged. Father Scott answered the phone. Connolly turned away to talk to him.

"You ready?"

"Yeah."

"You're going to Houston Street. Turn off Government. It'll be the fourth house on the left."

Connolly switched off the phone and turned to Hollis.

"Get in. He's on his way."

By the time they reached Mrs. Gordon's, the women were ready. Father Scott arrived a few minutes later. Connolly and Hollis loaded the ice chest in the back, along with the bags of food Connolly brought to the house earlier that day and several more from Mrs. Gordon's pantry.

As the women walked down the steps toward the van, Connolly saw the lights go off inside the house. Mrs. Gordon appeared at the door with an overnight bag in her hand. She stepped onto the porch and closed the door behind her, then checked to make sure it was locked. Connolly moved to the bottom of the steps. He faced her as she turned from the door.

"What are you doing?"

"They don't need to be down there by themselves."

"You're going with them?"

"I'm not letting them go off with Hollis alone."

"Are you sure?"

"Of course I'm sure. I'll drive my car. It might come in handy if we need to find a store or something."

Mrs. Gordon moved down the steps. She nudged him aside and started toward the driveway.

"Send two over here. They can ride with me."

Connolly smiled and shook his head. He turned to the women on the first seat in the van.

"Want to ride with Mrs. Gordon?"

Raisa sat behind them.

"She is going with us?"

"Yes."

A smile broke across her face.

"Good."

She said something to the women in front of her. They nodded and moved toward the door. Connolly stepped back to let them pass. As they moved out of the van, Raisa caught his eye.

"Will I see you again?"

Connolly nodded.

"Yes. You will have to make a statement to the police. Probably the detective you talked to before. I'll set it up."

"We will come back here."

"Maybe. I'm not sure yet. I'd rather do it somewhere else. So no one can find out where you are."

She nodded.

"I will see you in a few days?"

"Yes. In a few days."

Connolly closed the door to the van. He leaned through the window in the passenger door and spoke to Hollis.

"Give Mrs. Gordon whatever's left of that money before you come back."

"Right."

He glanced over at Father Scott.

"Hollis will show you where the house is once you get there."

Father Scott nodded, put the van in gear, and drove away from the curb. Mrs. Gordon backed her car out of the driveway and followed them down the street.

Fifty-four

When everyone was gone, Connolly got in the Chrysler and drove to the guesthouse. He parked near the door and went inside. In the cabinet next to the sink, he found a can of Coca-Cola. He filled a glass with ice, poured in the Coke, and took a seat on the sofa. With his feet propped on the coffee table, he took a sip from the glass, then leaned his head back and closed his eyes.

Moments later, headlights washed across the room. He moved his feet from the coffee table and sat up. From the sofa, he could see out the large picture window on the front wall of the room. A car came up the driveway toward the guesthouse, moving slowly but steadily toward him. He watched as it came to a stop near the house.

When the driver's door opened, the dome light came on. Inside the car he could see Barbara sitting behind the steering wheel. She stepped from the car and disappeared around the corner of the house. He set the glass of Coke on the table and crossed the room to the door.

She smiled when she saw him.

"Hope I'm not interrupting anything."

He felt a grin spread across his face.

"No. Not at all."

He pushed the door open and stepped aside to let her pass. She glanced around as she entered.

"Nice place." She leaned around the doorway to look inside the kitchen. "Bigger than I thought it would be."

He closed the door.

"Yes. It has lots of room." He pointed toward the sofa. "Have a seat." He picked up the glass from the table. "I'm having a Coke. Want one?"

She shook her head.

"No, thank you."

She took a seat on the sofa. He sat beside her.

"You just in the neighborhood?"

She crossed her legs and folded her hands in her lap.

"I thought we could finish our conversation."

He gave her a puzzled look.

"Our conversation?"

"From earlier today."

"Oh."

He glanced away. Barbara uncrossed her legs and turned toward him.

"So, who is this Raisa?"

"She's a woman in a bad spot."

"I know that. Why is she at Mrs. Gordon's?"

"We took them from a warehouse last night."

"A warehouse?"

Connolly looked at her.

"They worked at Panama Tan. It's a tanning salon on Airline Highway."

Barbara raised an eyebrow.

"A tanning salon?"

Connolly grinned.

"Actually, it's ... a brothel."

She turned to look at him. He continued.

"Perry Braxton was tangled up with it. That's the reason ... part of the reason he and Camille were getting a divorce."

"I can imagine."

"They had them living in a warehouse. We figured out what was going on. Saw what they were doing. Decided to get them out."

"We?"

"Hollis and I."

She gave him a playful look.

"This was Hollis's idea?"

"No. It was my idea. At the time, it seemed like the thing to do."

"And now?"

His look turned serious.

"No one should have to live like that."

"What will happen to them?"

"Eventually, they'll give a statement to the police ... I guess. One or two of them will probably have to testify. Then, I suppose they'll either resettle here or go back to where they came from."

She looked at him.

"They can't go back."

"Probably not."

"If they go back, they'll just be right back in the same situation."

"Probably."

"So, what are you going to do? Are they going to stay at Mrs. Gordon's house while you sort everything out?"

Connolly shook his head.

"No. I found a place for them."

"Where?"

He looked away.

"Might be better if you don't know."

"Okay. Well—"

She slid forward on the seat to stand. He held out his hand to stop her.

"Listen. They're in some danger. I mean, the men they were working for are ... if they find them, they'll kill them."

She hesitated. He squeezed her hand.

"Please. Don't go."

She leaned back.

"Are you ... interested in her?"

Connolly smiled.

"No. I'm not interested in her. I mean, I'm interested enough to climb in a warehouse and haul them out. But no ... not like that."

She smiled.

"A knight, rescuing a damsel in distress."

"No." He grinned. "A knight rescuing eleven damsels in distress."

They burst into laughter. She looked at him.

"You ran off the other night. When we were talking on the steps."

Connolly stood and moved around the end of the sofa.

"You want something to eat?" He started toward the kitchen. "I haven't had dinner."

She continued to talk to him from her seat on the sofa in the living room.

"You never finished what you were going to say."

He walked into the kitchen.

"About what?"

She called to him.

"About what you'd say if you knew this was the last time you'd see me."

"You know what I'd say."

He opened the refrigerator door and glanced around inside, then closed it and opened the freezer. She came from the sofa and stood behind him. He felt her hand slide across his shoulders. Goose bumps stood up on his arms. She leaned close to his ear.

"I'm scared."

The warmth of her breath on his ear made the hair on the back of his neck stand up. He turned to face her.

"Scared?"

She nodded.

"Of what?"

"Alcohol. You."

A smile turned up one corner of his mouth.

"Me and alcohol. That's some powerful stuff."

He pushed the freezer door closed behind him. They were inches apart. He put his arms around her shoulders. She put her hands on his waist.

"Are you scared of it?"

"Not anymore."

She let her hands drop from his side and backed away. He moved his arms away and took her hand.

"Look, I know it was rough." He looked her in the eye. "It was worse than rough. And I would love to be able to promise you it would never happen again. But I can't."

Her eyes were full.

"I know."

"I can promise you this. I'm not going to drink tonight. And I won't drink tomorrow."

He pulled her toward him and took her other hand. They stood there in the kitchen, staring at each other, neither one saying a word. Finally, Connolly gave her a smile.

"Let's go out."

She looked puzzled.

"Go out?"

"To eat."

The corners of her mouth turned down. He gave her a puzzled look.

"What?"

A frown wrinkled her forehead.

"Not exactly what I was expecting."

She turned away. He pulled her back and kissed her.

"That more what you had in mind?"

She smiled.

"Close."

He kissed her again, slower this time, then guided her toward the door.

"Come on. Before we get ourselves in trouble."

Fifty-five

After dinner, Connolly and Barbara returned to the guesthouse. He walked her to her car and waited as she turned from the driveway and disappeared up the street. When she was gone, he went inside and made his way to the bedroom. He lay in bed and stared at the ceiling, thinking of her, remembering the life they'd had together, wondering what the future might hold. It was late when he drifted off to sleep.

The next morning, he was awakened by the telephone. The call was from Hollis.

"We're here. Finally."

"Long trip?"

"Yeah. Got in here about one this morning."

"Have any trouble?"

"No."

"Everything all right at the house?"

"Yeah. Looks pretty good. Everyone found a bed. They found some swimsuits on the back porch. They're all across the road at the beach. Even Mrs. Gordon."

"How's Father Scott?"

"He's all right, I guess. He's on his second cup of coffee. I think he's coming back in a little while."

"Don't forget to give Mrs. Gordon the money."

"I gave it to her already." Hollis hesitated. "Listen." His voice sounded tentative. "I ... uh ... think I'll stay over here with them a few days."

Connolly smiled to himself.

"Oh?"

"There's eleven. Twelve counting Mrs. Gordon. They don't need to be over here by themselves."

"Okay." Connolly grinned. "Whatever you think. Just keep the cell phone on."

"Yeah."

"You sure everything's okay?"

"Yeah. We're doing fine. I'll talk to you later."

Hollis ended the call. Connolly hung up the phone. He rolled on his side and checked the alarm clock. It was eight. He fell back on the pillow and rubbed his eyes. After a minute or two, he threw back the covers and plodded down the hall to the shower.

Connolly took his time that morning. He made a pot of coffee and toasted a bagel. He sat at the dining table while he ate and read the morning paper. When he finished, he checked the office voice mail. As he expected, there was a call from Braxton. Two from Manny Fernandez. Both men wanted to see him, but he wasn't ready to do that. Talking to them meant going to the jail, which meant there'd be a strong possibility he would run into Hammond or McNamara, or both, and neither of them would be glad to see him. Instead, he sat on the sofa, read more of the newspaper, and drank another cup of coffee.

It was noon when he parked the Chrysler on Dauphin Street. Upstairs, the office was dark and quiet. A red light blinked on Mrs. Gordon's phone indicating there were more messages waiting in the voice mail. Connolly ignored the light and moved down the hallway to his office.

At the door he hung his jacket on the coatrack, then took a seat in the chair behind his desk. He propped his feet on the desktop, folded his hands behind his head, and leaned against the wall. With his eyes closed, he expected to drift off to sleep. Instead, he thought of Raisa.

In his mind, he saw her eyes looking at him. They were like deep, dark pools that shimmered in the moonlight. He felt her again, her small, petite frame pressed against him as they slipped through the night to meet with Hammond and Hollis. She was vulnerable. He protected her. She was fragile. He lent her his strength. She was available, yet he would not exploit her. Only now, he fought to keep those thoughts from his mind.

He moved his feet from the desk and took out a file folder from another case. He opened it and tried to read. Moments later, he saw her again in his mind, standing in front of him. He felt her against him. That same musky, sweaty smell filled his nostrils. The scent he'd noticed in the car when he and Hollis took them to Mrs. Gordon's. She pressed closer. Her lips touched his, soft, warm, and wet.

He slammed the file closed against the desktop and stood to his feet. In two steps, he was around the desk to the coatrack. He grabbed his jacket and started up the hall.

From the third floor, he rode the elevator to the lobby and walked out to the street. The Chrysler was parked in the middle of the next block. He got in it and made his way to the county jail. A deputy met him as he entered the building.

"Anthony Hammond is looking for you."

"Is he here?"

"Not now. He left about ten minutes ago."

Connolly passed through the metal detector. The deputy banged on the door and shouted. In a few moments, the door swung open. Connolly stepped inside. As he passed through the booking area, a deputy stopped him.

"Anthony Hammond is looking for you."

"So I heard."

"He said if you came through here, not to let you leave before he gets back."

Connolly grinned at the deputy.

"And just how do you plan to do that?"

The deputy laughed and moved away.

Connolly stepped into the elevator and rode to the eighth floor. Fernandez was seated on the far side of the stainless steel table in the conference room when Connolly arrived.

"Before you say anything, let me tell you. I'm not representing you. I represent Perry Braxton. As a gesture solely and only as a courtesy, I suggest you say nothing to me about your case. If you talk to me, I will use whatever you say to protect Braxton's interests."

Fernandez smiled, revealing a missing tooth in front. The gap in his teeth caught Connolly's attention, then he noticed a dark bruise on Fernandez's cheek.

Fernandez lifted one hand in a weak wave.

"Good to see you, too." He gestured toward the bench on the opposite side of the table. "Have a seat."

Connolly was impassive.

"I prefer to stand."

Fernandez shrugged.

"Doesn't matter. This won't take long. Rizutto knows you took those women."

"How does he know that?"

"I told him."

"Why?"

Fernandez parted his lips and pointed to the gap. Connolly relaxed.

"You shouldn't have taken a beating on my account."

"I didn't exactly tell him you did it. When the girls went missing, he asked if I'd seen anybody hanging around out of the ordinary. I told him about seeing you that night at Shady Acres. He didn't like it that I hadn't told him before."

"Rizutto did this to you?"

Fernandez shook his head.

"Rizutto never hits anybody. Got Victor for that."

"Victor?"

"Victor Antonelli. His driver."

"You got a lawyer?"

"Yeah. Some kid."

"Appointed?"

Fernandez gave him a sarcastic look.

"You don't think I have the money to hire one, do you?"

"You better not say any more."

Fernandez waved him off.

"I'm not worried about him. He hasn't even been up here yet." He smiled at Connolly. "You sent a guy in there Saturday, didn't you?"

Connolly looked away.

"I knew it." Fernandez chuckled. "That guy looked like … like a priest or something. He'd never been with a woman like that in his life." A broad grin spread across his face. "I bet he hadn't even imagined something like that."

Connolly fought to keep a straight face. Fernandez glanced away.

"Look, Rizutto's not interested in the women." He pointed his finger at Connolly. "It's you he's worried about."

Connolly frowned.

"Me?"

"Yeah. He figures if it was up to the girls, they'd just disappear. Some of them might even come back on their own. But with you around, he figures you'll have them testifying against us. He's already convinced Braxton talked."

Connolly turned away and stepped to the door.

"Manny, I wish I could help you."

"Be like old times."

Connolly glanced over his shoulder as he banged on the door with his fist.

"Nothing is like the old times anymore."

The guard opened the door. Connolly stepped aside.

"I need to see Perry Braxton."

The guard nodded to Fernandez.

"Let's go."

Fernandez stood and moved around the table. He gave Connolly one last look.

"Watch your back."

Connolly responded with a nod. Fernandez stepped through the doorway. The guard escorted him out of sight down the corridor. In a few minutes, he returned with Braxton.

They sat at the table and talked. Braxton seemed combative and edgy.

"Why didn't you tell me they would ask all that stuff about Camille?"

"That's the way it works."

"I told them enough to get me convicted."

"Look, that's the way it works. There wasn't time to brief you on every single question."

"If you don't have time—"

Connolly's face went flush with anger.

"I had to get Hammond while I could. I didn't have time to hold your hand."

Braxton sighed. His countenance changed.

"It just caught me off guard."

"Defuniak was dead. Somebody killed him—"

Braxton interrupted him.

"That's not what I hear."

"No?"

"I hear he killed himself."

"You think he filled the sink with water, shoved his own head under, left the water running, wandered down the hall to the sunroom, injected himself four times in the arm with insulin, fell into an coma, and died ... all on his own?"

Braxton sighed.

Connolly continued.

"The situation was about to come unglued. So, I hustled them up a little."

"So, what happens now?"

"They've arrested Fernandez."

"I saw him."

"Did you talk to him?"

"No ..."

"Don't. It isn't going to help."

"Maybe."

"What did you talk about?"

"I wanted to know who moved Camille's body."

"What did he say?"

"Not much. Which tells me he knows a lot. I figure it was either him or Rizutto. Doesn't matter. They wanted me to take the fall. Now, that isn't happening. Did Hammond talk to those women?"

"He talked briefly to one of them. We'll arrange a formal statement from them."

"When are you going to do that?"

"As soon as Hammond has time to cool off."

"Cool off?"

"Yeah. After you talked to them, they started backing up. Talking about needing more time to investigate, that sort of thing."

"So?"

"So ..." A smile crept across Connolly's face. "I liberated those women from the warehouse."

Braxton's face turned red.

"You did what?!"

"I took the women out of the warehouse."

Braxton shouted at him.

"Are you out of your mind? If Rizutto finds out you did that, he'll kill you."

Connolly gestured for him to keep quiet.

"Not so loud. Hammond wasn't too pleased, either."

"What did he say?"

"He threatened to arrest me."

"Think he will?"

"He might have yesterday. I don't know about today."

Braxton sighed and shook his head. Connolly shrugged.

"Hey, I had no choice. If I waited, Rizutto would have moved the women. He and Fernandez would be gone. You'd be stuck in here with all this information that was of no value to anyone. And we'd be facing a trial on capital murder."

Braxton nodded, reluctantly.

"And now?"

"Now, the women are safe. They'll be available as long as they're needed."

"Rizutto will find them."

"I doubt it."

"You are crazy."

"Maybe so." Connolly grinned. "But I'm not afraid."

Fifty-six

he afternoon was almost gone by the time Connolly left the jail. Downtown, the streets were deserted. He walked to the Chrysler and got in behind the wheel. As he placed the key in the ignition, he glanced in the rearview mirror to check for traffic.

A man popped up from the backseat. Connolly recognized him immediately.

"Rizutto, get out of my car."

Rizutto smiled.

"Just drive like everything's normal."

Out of the corner of his eye, Connolly saw Rizutto's hand come up from behind the seat. He felt something nudge against the back of his head. In the mirror he could see it was the muzzle of a pistol.

Rizutto chuckled.

"You wouldn't want the day to end too soon, would you?" He lowered his arm and settled into the seat. "Let's go."

Connolly checked the mirror again. Rizutto sat in back against the door on the right side. His arms were folded in front of him. His face, stony and expressionless. Connolly steered the Chrysler away from the curb. Rizutto mumbled directions.

"Take a left at the next light."

Connolly turned left onto St. Michael Street.

"Make a left at Water Street. Get in the far lane."

Connolly turned left and moved to the right lane. When they reached the old train station, the traffic light was red. Connolly brought the car to a stop and waited. When the light turned green, Rizutto gave another order.

"Turn right."

Connolly made the turn. They wound through the warehouse district to Morgan Street. At Conception Street Road, they turned in front of the warehouse where the women had been living.

Rizutto chuckled again.

"You know this place, don't you?" He laughed as he answered his own question. "Yeah. You know this place. You and that nutcase Hollis what's-his-name."

Connolly glanced at him in the mirror. Rizutto grinned.

"I know all about your friend." He gestured toward the front of the car. "Watch where you're going."

Connolly looked forward again.

"Make the next left."

Connolly made the turn.

Around the corner, a tractor-trailer truck was parked in the street. The rear doors of the trailer were open. Ramps extended from the back of the truck to the pavement. A man stood beside the trailer. As they drew closer, Connolly recognized him. He was Rizutto's driver, Victor Antonelli.

Connolly slowed the car as they approached the truck. Victor waved them forward. Rizutto moved to the center of the backseat and leaned forward, his face next to Connolly's ear.

"Drive right up in the truck. Like a good little boy."

Connolly brought the car to a stop.

"You're out of your mind."

Rizutto shouted in Connolly's ear.

"I'll kill you right here!"

He jabbed the muzzle of the pistol hard against Connolly's head. Connolly moved to one side.

"All right. All right."

Rizutto leaned away. Connolly inched the car forward. Victor glanced nervously around, then scowled at Connolly and waved with his arm to hurry him along. The front tires bumped against the ramp. Connolly lifted his foot from the gas pedal. The car stopped.

Victor scowled and waved his arm more vigorously.

"Come on. Come on. We ain't got all day."

Connolly pressed his foot against the pedal. The Chrysler started up the ramp. The nose of the car rose into the air, rising higher and higher until the hood blocked the truck from view. The tailpipes scraped on the pavement.

When he was sure the rear wheels of the car were on the ramp, Connolly shoved his foot against the gas pedal. The tires squealed. The car shot up the ramp into the truck and sailed toward the end of the trailer. Connolly braced himself against the steering wheel. Rizutto shouted as he tumbled onto the backseat.

"What are you doing?!"

At the last second, Connolly jammed both feet on the brake pedal.

The tires squealed again. The car came to a sudden stop. Caught off guard, Rizutto was thrown forward. His head and shoulders came over the back of the front seat. Connolly threw his elbow out to meet him. He hit Rizutto squarely on the nose.

Rizutto screamed in pain. Connolly heard a thud as the pistol landed on the floor of the car. He shoved the gear shifter into park and reached over the backseat. Rizutto's face was covered in blood. He held his nose with one hand and tried to fend off Connolly with the other.

"Hey!" He shouted. "Hey! Victor!"

Connolly grabbed Rizutto's arm and came over the top with his right fist. As he pounded on Rizutto, the trailer doors banged shut. In the dark, Connolly hit him again and again. Finally, Rizutto slipped from his grasp and collapsed. Connolly went over the seat, hanging upside down as he frantically felt along the floor. Rizutto groaned. Connolly groped in the dark for the pistol.

Wham!

A fist came crashing down on Connolly's head. He struggled to keep from tumbling to the floor. Before Connolly could raise himself up, Rizutto had him in a choke hold. Connolly gasped for breath. Rizutto squeezed tighter. Connolly's face felt flush and hot. Air slipped from his lungs. He struggled to keep from fainting.

Then, he felt something.

His fingers slipped over the barrel of the pistol. He worked them down to the grip. Just when Connolly was about to pick it up, Rizutto jerked his arm tighter around his neck. His fingers slipped from the pistol. Connolly made a gurgling sound as his lungs fought for one last breath.

Desperate now, he stretched his arm as far as possible and kicked with his legs. His weight shifted over the seat. His head struck Rizutto's knee. On the floor, his hand slid across the pistol. This time, he wrapped his fingers around the grip. With all the energy he had left, he pointed the pistol in Rizutto's direction and squeezed the trigger.

A shot exploded from the pistol with a deafening roar inches from Connolly's face. For an instant, the muzzle flash lit the backseat of the car as bright as noon. Rizutto jumped. His arm let go of Connolly's neck.

Connolly gasped for breath. He pulled himself up from the backseat, pointed the gun toward where he thought Rizutto was sitting, and squeezed the trigger again. In the flash of fire from the barrel he saw Rizutto clutch his chest. Seconds later, Connolly felt him slump against the seat and slide onto the rear floor.

Connolly fell forward in the front seat and covered his ears. He gasped for air as he writhed in pain from the noise of the gunshots. With each breath, his mouth and throat burned. His eyes watered. He took another breath.

Exhaust!

The car was still running.

Frantically, he groped in the dark for the steering wheel. His head banged against the mirror, then his hand struck the dash. He felt his way to the ignition and turned the engine off, then leaned across the steering column for the light switch. The dome light above came on. He squinted against the glare.

Behind him, Rizutto lay on the rear floor. Blood oozed from his chest. His leg twitched.

Connolly turned off the light. He shoved the pistol in the waistband of his trousers and crawled across the front seat to the window on the driver's side of the car. Supporting himself against the trailer wall, he climbed on top of the car and crawled toward the back. There, he slid down the trunk lid to the floor of the truck. He leaned against the rear bumper and waited.

Five minutes later, the truck lurched to a stop. Connolly moved from the car to the back of the trailer and listened. The door on the cab opened, then slammed closed. The crunch of gravel beneath someone's feet moved down the side of the trailer. Connolly backed into the corner by the door. He was hot and sweaty. His heart pounded against his chest. He took a deep breath and forced his muscles to relax.

Then, the latch on the door rattled. Suddenly, light burst into the trailer as the door on the far side swung open. Victor leaned inside.

"Hey! You in there?"

With one quick move, Connolly stepped forward and swung his leg as hard as he could. The toe of his shoe struck Victor in the jaw. Victor staggered backward and grabbed his face. His eyes were wild with pain and anger. Connolly leaped from the truck. As he sailed through the air, he cocked his fist above his head. Victor ducked to avoid him and tripped over his own feet. Connolly crashed into him. His forearm smashed against the side of Victor's head. Both men tumbled to the ground.

Connolly scrambled to his feet and ran.

To the left was a tall crane. A large magnetic lifter dangled from a cable below it. Behind the crane tower was a car crusher. In front of it was a shredder. Flattened cars were stacked in a row twenty feet high that stretched from the shredder to a twelve-foot fence along the road. A sign on the fence identified the place as Stein's Salvage Yard.

Connolly ran from the truck toward a pile of chrome bumpers that lay between the truck and the flattened cars. As he ducked behind the pile, a gunshot rang out. A bullet bounced off a bumper next to his head. He crawled to the opposite side and took the pistol from his trousers. Across the way, Victor moved from the truck and worked his way to Connolly's right.

Another shot rang out.

Connolly turned in time to see Victor crouch behind a car near the crane. Connolly took a deep breath. If he waited there much longer, he would be dead. He held the pistol in front of him and charged from the bumper pile toward the stack of flattened cars. Victor poked his head out. Connolly fired off a shot and ran with all his might. Seconds later, a bullet whizzed past Connolly's ear. He pointed the gun in Victor's direction and fired a return shot as he ducked around the stack of cars.

Behind it was an open lane wide enough for two trucks to pass. On the other side of the lane was a mound of rusted scrap iron. Connolly paused long enough to catch his breath, then started down the back side of the stacks. Any moment, he expected to see Victor appear in front of him.

When he reached the far end, he glanced to the right. A narrow passage just wide enough for a truck to squeeze through led between the scrap iron and a large stack of neatly pressed squares from the shredder, squares that had once been automobiles. Behind the scrap iron was a pile of washing machines almost as high as the shredder.

Then, *bam!*

A shot hit the stack of flattened cars just above his head. Connolly glanced over his shoulder. Victor rounded the corner behind him.

Connolly ducked past the corner at the far end and worked his way along the opposite side of the stack. Between the cars, he saw Victor. Connolly raised the pistol and aimed it through an opening. As Victor came by, he squeezed off a shot.

Blood spewed into the air as the bullet tore through Victor's shoulder. He spun to one side. The pistol slipped from his hand and bounced off the ground at his feet. His mouth gaped open, his eyes wide with pain. Connolly watched as the twisting motion sent him spiraling to the ground. But he didn't watch for long.

He ran from the stack across the open yard toward the truck. As he ran, he shifted the pistol to his left hand and dug the cell phone from his pocket. When he reached the truck, he scrolled down the telephone numbers and pressed the button. Hammond answered.

"I'm not talking to you."

"Wait!"

Hammond switched off the phone.

Connolly pressed the redial button. The phone rang four times, then rolled over to Hammond's voice mail.

"Anthony." He was gasping, out of breath from running. "Pick up the phone. I've got Rizutto."

He switched off the call and moved around the bumper to the opposite side.

Across the yard behind the truck was an office shack. Through a window he could see the lights were off. The cab of the crane was empty, too. Above him, the magnetic lifter swung gently from side to side in the breeze. The cable squeaked as it moved against the pulley at the end of the boom.

Just then, the cell phone rang. It was Hammond.

"What are you talking about?"

"I'm at Stein's Salvage Yard. Get up here! Fast!"

"What are you doing there?"

A shot rang out. The bullet struck the corner of the truck. Connolly ducked. Hammond shouted into the phone.

"What was that?"

Connolly shouted back.

"He's shooting at me!"

Connolly moved down the cab to the drive wheels.

"Who's shooting at you?"

"Rizutto's driver."

Another shot hit the dirt beside Connolly. He peered around the rear wheels on the cab. Victor was stumbling across the yard toward him.

Connolly shouted into the phone once more.

"Get over here! Quick!"

He switched off the phone and ran to the far end of the trailer. He crouched beside the wheels and watched. Through the undercarriage he could see Victor's feet and legs as he moved around the truck. As Victor passed out of sight in front of the cab, Connolly moved around the end of the trailer to the opposite side, then ran back across the yard toward the stack of cars.

As he ducked around the stack, a shot rang out. Connolly looked out from between the cars. Victor staggered around the end of the trailer and moved across the yard toward him. His shirt was soaked with blood.

"He should be dead."

Connolly raised the pistol and pointed it at Victor once again. He watched and waited, hoping he wouldn't have to shoot. Victor kept coming.

In the distance, Connolly heard the sound of sirens.

"Come on, Anthony." He whispered. "Come on."

He steadied his hand against one of the flattened cars and followed Victor over the sight on the end of the pistol. With each step Victor took, Connolly grew more tense.

"Come on, Anthony." He murmured through clinched teeth. "I can't let him get to the corner."

Victor was only a few feet from the end of the stack when the first patrol car turned in at the gate. A second followed close behind. Victor spun around to face them.

Dust rolled up from the patrol cars as they came to a stop. Doors on either side flew open. Uniformed patrolmen leaped out, guns drawn, ready to fire.

"Drop your weapon!"

"Get your hands up!"

Victor raised the pistol. A patrolman to the left fired a single shot from a rifle. The shot struck Victor in the chest. The force of the shot lifted him off his feet and sent him sprawling backward to the ground. The pistol flew from his hand. His head bounced once as it hit the dirt. Then, he lay motionless and still.

Before Connolly could move, an unmarked car turned off the road through the gate. It came to a stop behind the patrol cars. The door opened. Anthony Hammond stepped out. He stared at Victor's body a moment, then glanced at the nearest policeman.

"What happened?"

"He had a pistol. We told him to drop it. He pointed it at us. Larry shot him."

Hammond sighed.

"Somebody write it up."

He scanned the yard, then cupped his hands around his mouth and shouted in a loud voice.

"Mike! Hey, Mike! You in here?"

Connolly stepped from behind the stack of cars.

"Right here!"

The pistol dangled from his hand at his side. A patrolman next to Hammond saw it and raised his pistol. Hammond gestured with his hand.

"Relax."

The patrolman lowered his pistol and slipped it into his holster. Hammond walked toward Connolly.

"You all right?"

Connolly gave him a weak smile.

"I guess."

Hammond stood in front of him.

"What happened?"

"When I left the jail this afternoon, Rizutto was in the backseat of the car. He brought me out here in that truck."

Hammond gave him a puzzled look.

"In the truck?"

"Yeah. Had it parked down there off Conception Street Road." He gestured to the yard around him. "I'd say they were going to put me in the crusher."

Hammond nodded.

"Where's Rizutto?"

"In the car. It's still in the truck."

Hammond looked alert.

"Is he alive?"

Connolly shook his head. Tears welled up in his eyes. His hand that held the pistol began to shake. Hammond's face softened. He leaned forward and took the pistol.

"It's all right." His voice was low and even. "You saved the taxpayers a lot of money."

Tears ran down Connolly's cheeks. He turned away. Hammond waved a patrolman over and handed him the pistol.

"Get a tag on this."

The patrolman took the pistol and stepped away. Connolly wiped his face with his hands.

"I think I know where they put Camille's body."

Hammond frowned.

"We already found her body. Remember? Found her floating in the water out at Horn Island." He took Connolly by the elbow. "Come on. You've had a tough day. Let me give you a ride out of here."

Connolly pulled away.

"No. Before that. I think I know where they put her before they dumped her in the water."

Hammond gave him an indulgent smile.

"Yeah? Where?"

"Come on. I'll show you."

Connolly led him past the stacks of cars and through the narrow passage behind the mound of scrap iron. Beyond the pile of washing machines was a mountain of discarded refrigerators and freezers. Hammond stared at the pile.

"You think she was in there?"

Connolly nodded and wiped his face again.

"Yeah."

Hammond stepped closer. Connolly moved past him and made his way around the far side of the pile. He opened a freezer. It was empty. He opened another. It was empty, too.

Hammond came up behind him.

"Find anything?"

"Not yet."

"Well, it was a good idea." Hammond backed away. "Come on. Let me get you home."

Connolly climbed over more junk and opened another freezer near the back of the pile. As he raised the lid, a swarm of flies rushed at his face. An awful stench engulfed him. Inside the freezer he saw a woman's body. Maggots swarmed over her face. It was more than he could stand. His stomach revolted. He turned away, hands on his knees, and vomited. The freezer lid banged closed. He vomited again.

Hammond stood a few feet away.

"You all right?"

Connolly took a handkerchief from his hip pocket and wiped his mouth. He pointed toward the freezer.

"In there."

He gagged again. Hammond moved past him.

"In where?"

Connolly held the handkerchief to his mouth and stepped to the freezer. He slapped the top with his hand.

"In here. But let me get out of the way."

He stumbled as he stepped aside. Hammond moved to the freezer and lifted the lid. Almost immediately, he let it go and turned away. Connolly watched at a distance.

"See it?"

Hammond nodded. He moved back from the freezer and took a cell phone from his pocket. He pressed a button on the phone.

"This is Hammond. We need the evidence techs at Stein's Salvage Yard. And call the coroner. We need a forensics team out here."

He closed the phone and turned to Connolly.

"You don't look so good."

"I don't feel so good, either."

Connolly took two steps, then everything turned black.

Fifty-seven

Sometime later Connolly became aware of hushed, soft tones floating through his mind. Gradually, the sounds became more distinct, finally separating into individual voices. He tried to open his eyes, but his eyelids wouldn't move. Footsteps came toward him. Someone knelt beside him. A hand touched his forehead.

"Mr. Connolly? Can you hear me?"

Connolly forced his eyes open, but his vision was blurred and out of focus. A wave of nausea washed over him. He closed his eyes and swallowed. A moment later, he opened them again.

A paramedic stared down at him.

"Are you with us, Mr. Connolly?"

Connolly groaned. The paramedic wiped a damp cloth across his forehead. He turned away and called to someone.

"He's starting to come around."

More footsteps approached. Hammond's face appeared above him.

"Mike, do you know where you are?"

Connolly managed a smile.

"Is this heaven?"

Hammond grinned.

"Not yet."

Connolly's voice was weak.

"They said we'd have white sandy beaches and ..."

Hammond reached down and took Connolly's hand to pull him up.

"He's all right." He pulled on Connolly's arm. "Sit up."

The paramedic stood.

"Not so fast. He'll just pass out again."

Connolly pulled his hand loose from Hammond's grasp. He propped himself on his elbows and took a breath, then pushed himself to a sitting position. The paramedic appeared with a can of Coca-Cola.

"Here." He opened the can. "My mother used to tell me this was the best thing to settle a sour stomach. Turns out she was right." He handed the can to Connolly. "But sip it slowly."

Connolly took a sip. Then another. After a moment, he glanced over at Hammond.

"How many bodies did you find?"

"I don't know yet. They're still looking."

Connolly took another sip from the Coca-Cola, then rolled to one side and stood. The paramedic held his arm to steady him.

"Are you okay?"

Connolly nodded.

"Yeah. I think so."

Hammond smiled at him.

"Why don't you go on home? I'll get one of the guys to give you a ride. We can take a statement from you tomorrow."

"Where's my car?"

"They took it out of the truck and got Rizutto's body out of it, but they aren't finished with it. They'll take good care of it."

Connolly nodded. Hammond turned away and whistled to get someone's attention. He waved a patrolman over.

"Take Mr. Connolly home. He can tell you where he lives."

The patrolman pointed to a car near the gate.

"Think you can make it to the car?"

Connolly turned to look. The world seemed to spin around him. He staggered backward. The paramedic caught him.

"Maybe we should get an ambulance."

Connolly smiled.

"I'm not that bad off." He took a step forward. "I'll be all right."

The patrolman escorted him across the yard past the truck. Behind it, the ramps had been placed against the end of the trailer. A few steps farther he saw the Chrysler sitting behind it. All four doors were open, and the backseat was out. An evidence technician was vacuuming the rear floor. Connolly stopped to watch.

The patrolman stood beside him.

"That your car?"

"Yeah."

"Man, what a land yacht." He smiled at Connolly. "They don't make them like that anymore."

"No. They don't."

Connolly moved toward the car. The evidence technician crawled from the backseat and turned to face them. He shouted over the noise of the machine.

"Don't come any closer." He switched off the vacuum cleaner. "Don't come any closer. We're still processing this area."

"This is my car."

"Don't come any closer."

A gray plastic tray sat on the ground beside the car. A stack of plastic Ziploc bags lay to one side. Next to them was a row of bags already filled with items collected from the scene. Each bag was labeled and sealed. Connolly squatted to look at them.

"This the stuff that came from the car?"

"Not all of it. Most of it came from that guy's pockets. The guy in the backseat."

Connolly flipped through the bags. The first one held a wallet. Behind it were a pen, a ring with three keys, and a half-eaten roll of Certs. The last bag held a dark blue bottle cap with white lettering on the top. Connolly took it from the tray and stood.

"Where'd you find this?"

He felt dizzy and leaned against the car. The technician pulled him away.

"Don't do that. We're not finished."

He took the bag from Connolly and looked at the label. He pointed to it as he read.

"'Decedent One.' That's the dead man in the backseat of the car. 'L Jacket Pocket.' That's the left pocket of his jacket."

The technician held the bag for Connolly to see. Connolly stared at the bottle cap.

"You found this in Rizutto's pocket?"

"Found it in the pocket of the man who was lying on the backseat of this car. Was that his name?"

Connolly nodded.

"Yeah. Pete Rizutto."

The bottle cap in the bag looked familiar. He was certain he'd seen one like it before, but he couldn't remember where. The evidence technician returned the bag to the tray.

"Don't mess with this stuff. You can look at whatever you need to see later. After we get through with it."

Connolly gave him a thin smile.

"Don't scratch my car."

"Yes, sir."

The technician turned on the vacuum and crawled back inside the Chrysler. Connolly started toward the patrol car.

It was after dark when he arrived at the guesthouse. The patrolman waited until Connolly was inside, then drove away. Connolly closed the door and started toward the bathroom. He undressed as he walked down the hall.

After a shower, he crawled in bed, pulled the covers over his head, and went to sleep. But it was a fitful sleep. Through the night he kept dreaming of Rizutto, of pounding him in the dark with his fist, of the fear that tried to grip him as Victor stalked him in the scrap yard.

When he awoke, brilliant morning sun shone across the bedroom. A headache pounded against his skull. He rolled over and covered his head with a pillow.

Noon arrived before he was ready to face the day. Two aspirins and another shower got him as far as the kitchen. There, he opened a cabinet next to the sink and took out a can of Coca-Cola. He took a glass from the next cabinet and shuffled toward the refrigerator. Ice clinked in the bottom of the glass. The sound rattled in his head where the pounding ache had only begun to subside. When the glass was full of ice, he returned to the counter and pushed the tab to open the can of Coke. It fizzed as he poured it over the ice. As the can emptied, he wondered what would happen to Braxton now.

Rizutto, Victor, and Defuniak were dead. Manny Fernandez was the only one left, and he was late to the case. Braxton had already agreed to cooperate. There wouldn't be much left for Fernandez to do except fill in the rest of the story. But somehow, knowing all that didn't satisfy Connolly's nagging sense that he'd missed something.

The last drops drained from the Coke can. He set it on the counter and took a sip from the glass. Turning around, he leaned his back against the counter near the sink and took another sip.

Rizutto and Fernandez were easy to understand. They were crooks. They preyed on whomever they could find. Victor was a hired gun. He did whatever Rizutto told him to do. They were involved in prostitution, the same business organized crime had been in since its beginning, even if this did have an international flair. And it wasn't difficult to see how Braxton had become involved with them. From what he'd heard, Braxton had been unfaithful to Camille since the night they became engaged. He'd lived on the edge a long time.

All of that was despicable, but Connolly understood how those pieces of the case fit together. What he didn't understand was why Hayford didn't want to delve into the oil leases. Nor did he understand why Braxton made up the alibi about being at Horn Island. And he still wondered what Defuniak was doing that got him killed.

He took another sip from the glass in his hand.

"Good stuff." He glanced down at the ice cubes swirling in the glass. "But I'd really like one of those ginger ales from Hayford's—"

And then he remembered the bottle cap from Rizutto's pocket.

Fifty-eight

*I*n less than five minutes, Connolly was dressed and ready. He came from the guesthouse expecting to see the Chrysler parked in its spot a few feet from the door. A wave of panic swept over him when he saw it wasn't there. Then he remembered the police had it at the impound yard. He glanced to the right. Hollis's truck sat a few feet away. He started toward it.

The door creaked as he pulled it open. Inside, the truck smelled like a mixture of swamp mud, dead fish, and used motor oil. Connolly lifted the floor mat and found a key. He climbed in and started the truck. The transmission made a grinding noise as he shoved the shifter into first gear. He rolled down the window and started toward the driveway.

At Government Street, he turned right, then cut across to Spring Hill Avenue. Minutes later, he turned into the drive at Hayford's office. Hayford was coming out the back door as Connolly stepped from the truck.

"Hey, Mike." His voice sounded cheerful, but in his eyes there was a look of surprise. "I was just leaving."

Connolly walked straight toward him. Rage and anger rose like a volcano with every step. Hayford gave him a puzzled look. When he was within arm's reach, Connolly swung his fist as hard as he could. It landed against Hayford's jaw. His legs buckled, sending him to the ground.

Connolly stood over him, shouting.

"It was you!"

Hayford rubbed his cheek.

"You hit me!"

Connolly shouted again.

"You set up that oil lease." He jabbed the air with his finger to punctuate each sentence. "You diverted the money from the Trust. And you were going to let Rizutto kill me!"

He punctuated the last sentence with a kick to Hayford's side.

Hayford rolled over and stood.

"You just bought yourself a lawsuit."

He wiped his hands together and turned toward his car.

"Great." Connolly followed him. "Sue me. I'd love to take your deposition."

Hayford gave him a sober look.

"You can't prove a thing."

"I'd have enough to stay in court."

Hayford gave him a smirk.

"If you knew what you think you know, I'd be worried."

Connolly ignored him.

"The other day, over at Defuniak's house. You and I were standing outside. You told that cop everyone was on the sunporch. How did you know that's where they were?"

Hayford did not respond. Connolly continued.

"How much did you give Braxton to keep quiet?"

Hayford smiled.

"Better watch out, counselor. You're about to reveal confidential information about your client."

Connolly frowned. Hayford grinned.

"Never thought about that, did you? Even if what you say is true, you can't do anything about it."

"I'm not—"

"You and your crusade for the truth just came to a screeching halt, pal. 'Cause anything you say about this case will be to your client's detriment. Everything you know about this case, everything you think you know, it's all covered under that wonderful umbrella called 'attorney-client privilege.'"

Connolly glared at him. Hayford grinned.

"You did a good job, Mike."

Just then, the back door of the office opened. Perry Braxton appeared at the top of the steps. Connolly's mouth fell open.

Hayford chuckled.

"Here he is now. He can tell you himself what he thinks about all this."

Braxton crossed the parking lot toward them. He smiled as he drew near.

"Let me guess what you two are talking about."

Deep inside, Connolly felt his stomach tie in a knot. He glared at Braxton.

"That's why you never would tell me everything."

Braxton gave him a questioning look.

"What are you talking about?"

"How much money did you get out of those oil leases?"

"What oil leases? I have no idea what you're talking about. But listen, I appreciate everything you did for me." He patted Connolly on the shoulder. "Especially the part about getting rid of Rizutto and Victor. I never really liked them."

Just then, a red Audi rounded the corner. On the front bumper was a baby blue Citadel tag. John Glover sat behind the steering wheel. The knot in Connolly's stomach rolled over. The car came to a stop a few feet away. Braxton walked to it and opened the passenger door.

"I'm sure you'll understand if I don't stick around for the rest of this conversation."

He opened the door and got in. Glover turned the car around and drove away. Hayford stepped to his car.

"Well, Mike. Seems like everything is done on this case. Hammond has Fernandez. No way to make a case for murder against Perry. Now that Rizutto's gone, they aren't interested in developing a case for manslaughter. So, McNamara cut him loose." He smiled. "You did a good job." He opened the door to his car. "Send your final bill to me. I'll take care of it. Perry's not going to be available for a while."

Hayford got in the car. Connolly watched as he backed away and disappeared around the far side of the building.

Connolly stood in the parking lot alone. A broad grin broke across his face. He whispered to himself.

"Only one problem with your theory, Buie." He took his cell phone from his pocket. "You aren't my client." With his thumb, he pressed a button on the phone.

"I can say anything I want to about you."

Seconds later, Hammond answered.

READERS' GUIDE

**For Personal Reflection
or Group Discussion**

Readers' Guide

A good story should leave you with a question. Could it happen that way? What made the writer think of this? Here are some questions I thought about as I wrote this book. These aren't *the* questions, and they aren't the only questions that arise from the text. But perhaps they will help you as you think about this book.

1. What does it mean to be enslaved? Were Raisa and the women who worked at Panama Tan slaves? Are women really bought and sold for use in the sex trade?

2. What is economic slavery? How prevalent is economic slavery in this country? In your community? Could this story take place in your community?

3. How does our lifestyle promote economic slavery in our own country? What types of conditions promote the kind of slavery that entrapped these women?

4. Symbolism is important in fiction. With a few exceptions, most of the good people in this story are called by their first name. Most of the bad, by only their last. The women in this story work at what Hollis calls an "electric beach." By the end, they are at a real beach. What other symbols can you find in this story?

5. Connolly wrestles with addiction to alcohol. Perhaps you don't have a problem with alcohol, but some kind of behavior grips you in a way that you can't control. What is it? How does that behavior affect your life? How does the struggle with it affect your life?

6. Connolly is asked to represent a man who is accused of a crime. From what Connolly discovers, his client may well have committed that crime. Does that matter?

7. Lawyers often say a criminal trial is not a quest to determine the truth but an attempt to determine if the state has shown sufficient cause to punish the defendant. Do you agree? Is there a difference?

8. Have you ever encountered a situation in which you were forced to break the law in order to do what was right?

9. Is there conduct that is wrong, regardless of what the law might allow?

10. Is there conduct that is correct or good, regardless of what the law prohibits?

11. Connolly wrestles with thoughts that both excite and disturb him. Thoughts about Raisa, Jessica Stabler, Barbara, and others. How did his thought life affect his conduct? What kind of thought life do you have? Does it affect your conduct?

www.joehilley.com

Read More
Mike Connolly
Mysteries!

Double Take
by Joe Hilley

Since we saw him last in *Sober Justice*, Mike Connolly has moved on from his live-in girlfriend and he's still sober, but his law practice remains on the skids—until he's asked to represent a former police officer suspected in the bombing death of a wealthy Southern heir. The case involves infidelity, drugs, money and espionage. Will Mike find new strength and new ways to solve this case or be dragged down by the characters he comes across? With a backdrop of shrimpers, strip clubs, and rowdy bars with men who fight dogs for entertainment, you won't want to miss this realistic, gritty mystery.

$12.99 • ISBN 1-58919-032-7 • Item #: 103814
320P • Paperback

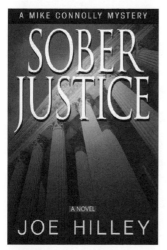

Sober Justice
by Joe Hilley

Mike Connolly, a divorced, alcoholic, fifty-something attorney, finds that his life takes an unpredictable turn when he is appointed to defend an indigent man accused of murdering a prominent plaintiffs' attorney. While defending his client, Connolly stumbles into a conspiracy and quickly finds himself in the midst of a complicated web of intrigue and deceit. The action builds to a dramatic and surprising conclusion as Connolly faces certain death and learns that sometimes even time and circumstance must yield to the purposes of God.

$12.99 • ISBN 1-58919-015-7
Item #: 103637 • 371P

To order, visit www.cookministries.com,
call 1-800-323-7543, or visit your favorite local bookstore.

Additional copies of *ELECTRIC BEACH* are available
wherever good books are sold.

❉ ❉ ❉

If you have enjoyed this book,
or if it has had an impact on your life,
we would like to hear from you.

Please contact us at:

RIVEROAK BOOKS
Cook Communications Ministries, Dept. 201
4050 Lee Vance View
Colorado Springs, CO 80918

Or visit our Web site:
www.cookministries.com